STAR WARS

THE ESSENTIAL GUIDE TO
WARFARE

STAR WARS®

THE ESSENTIAL GUIDE TO
WARFARE

JASON FRY WITH PAUL R. URQUHART

ILLUSTRATIONS BY DREW BAKER,
TOMMY LEE EDWARDS, IAN FULLWOOD, ANSEL HSIAO,
STEPHAN MARTINIERE, MODI, JASON PALMER,
CHRIS SCALF, DAVE SEELEY, DARREN TAN,
JOHN VANFLEET, BRUNO WERNECK,
AND PAUL YOULL

BALLANTINE BOOKS
NEW YORK

DEDICATION

JASON: This is for that kid who just got his first glimpse of the *Star Wars* saga today, and knows his or her life just changed. I hope books like this help you dream and have fun.

PAUL: To Mr. Henry B., in payment of an old debt of honor, which was not expected to involve Ewoks

Title page painting by Dave Seeley

"Armory and Sensor Profile" illustrations by:
Ansel Hsiao: Pages 7, 31 (middle), 46, 117, 135, 166, 167, 207, and 239 (top)
Ian Fullwood: Pages 19, 21, 29, 30, 31 (top), 34 (top), 52 (middle two), 57, 70, 79, 206, 218, 219, and 239 (middle and bottom)

"The Anaxes War College System" illustrations by Ansel Hsiao

Maps on pages 22, 26, 98, 112, 116, and 212 by Modi

A Del Rey Trade Paperback Original

Published in the United States by Del Rey, an imprint of The Random House Publishing Group, a division of Random House, Inc., New York.

DEL REY is a registered trademark and the Del Rey colophon is a trademark of Random House, Inc.

ISBN 978-0-345-47762-0

Printed in the United States of America

www.starwars.com
www.star-wars.suvudu.com

9 8 7 6 5 4 3 2

Interior design by Foltz Design

The *Lusankya* and the *Reaper* square off at Orinda (Darren Tan)

CONTENTS

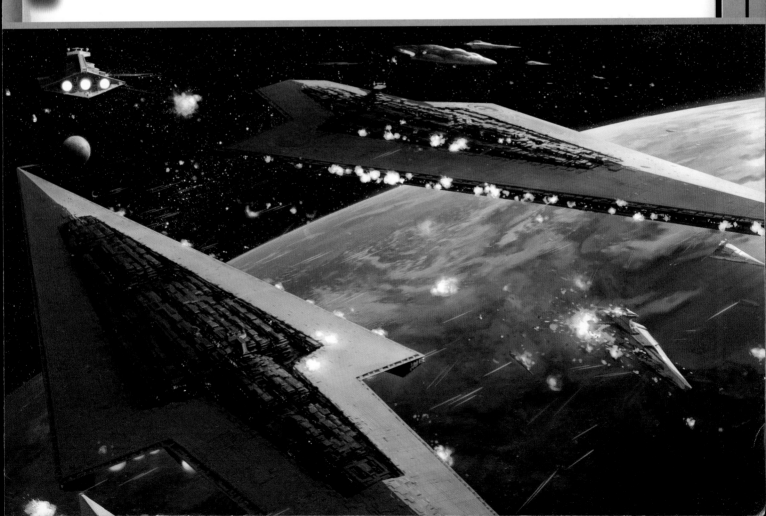

Osvald Teshik faces the Emperor's vengeance (Drew Baker)

At the Battle of Endor, Grand Admiral Osvald Teshik continued to fight after the rest of the Imperial task force retreated, engaging Alliance warships for four hours before his Star Destroyer was disabled and captured. He was tried and executed by the Alliance to Restore the Republic for atrocities committed against the citizens of the galaxy. The following is a transcript of his last statement:

I've been here before, you know. Four years ago, Emperor Palpatine sentenced me to death.

Why? Being Emperor is its own why. But he was angry that your privateers had been running wild in the Core, and that they'd kidnapped that swollen gasbag Adviser Veshiv from Esseles. Since I commanded that oversector, I had to sate his anger.

And to do that, I had to die.

So he sent me to Hapes aboard the Pursuit light cruiser Shepherd, *carrying two squadrons of TIE fighters and accompanied by eight gunships. My men thought we were a recon patrol and that our mission was to keep the Hapans honest. But I knew better—I knew we were going to a place from which we'd never return. When we came out of hyperspace I accessed my orders. They read* PROCEED AT SPEED TO ANDALIA AND ENGAGE ENEMY FORCES.

A good chunk of the Hapan war fleet was waiting there for us—five Battle Dragons and eight Nova battle cruisers. They'd been tipped off.

The crews expected us to run, and with reason. Against such odds, running was the only sane decision. I had to repeat myself when I told the deck officer to launch all fighters. I saw his face when he realized he was going to die. I saw he wanted to know why. We all do. We think it will matter, that knowing will grant us honor, that it will silence our futile bleating at the prospect of becoming nothing.

It doesn't. Nothing does. I knew what he wanted to know, but I didn't tell him.

The TIEs lasted two minutes. I watched the Battle Dragons' turbolasers lance out, brilliant green, searching in the darkness. I watched the Hapan gunners find the range, begin to turn TIEs into flowers of flame. I watched the fighters wheel around for another pass, their laser bolts sparking useless blue spirals and whorls off the Hapan shields. Then they were all dead, and it was our turn.

We were the last survivors. Six of the gunships were gone inside a minute, vaporized by the battle cruisers. The captains of the last two gunships panicked and turned into each other. They collided head-on. I watched the atmosphere boil out of their cracked hulls, condemning the men inside to bad deaths where they might have been blessed with merely pointless ones.

By then our shields were failing. I found myself wondering if the Emperor had a snoopship nearby, so he could see his sentence carried out, or if arranging it had been satisfaction enough, or if he even remembered.

Some of my officers were still barking orders—dead men clacking their jaws in a dumb show of honor. Others were begging me for new instructions. A few were sitting catatonic at their posts while the alarms screamed around them. Then the forward shields flashed and winked out of existence. The lead Battle Dragon launched torpedoes. I heard the deck officer yell "Incoming." He was still at his post.

The next thing I knew, I was floating in space in an evac suit. I don't know how I got there. I can only conclude that we were hit hard and my Academy training took over. I must have checked for escape pods, failed to find any, and got into a suit. I must have been in the rear of the bridge tower when the Hapans targeted my cruiser's main reactor. And I must have been close to a hull breach. So instead of being atomized with the Shepherd when the reactor blew, I was ejected from her.

It was scant reprieve. Something was wrong with my suit. It was torn, or a seal had melted. Either way I could hear the hissing and feel that my body was growing numb.

I hung there in space and watched the Hapan ships advance. The Transitory Mists were sheets of green and blue and red, and everywhere else there were stars—above and below, on all sides, because I wasn't looking up at the sky but floating in it. I'd never seen so many stars, not even as a boy on

Kallistas, lying on the roof of the threshing-house with insects humming in the summer dark. And I could see the band of the galaxy, a river of light bisecting the sky.

It was beautiful. It was the most beautiful thing I had ever seen.

Around me, it was different. I was surrounded by chunks of durasteel, bent and blackened. Everywhere there were lengths of wire and conduit, slowly wheeling end over end. There were drifts of transparisteel splintered into jagged shards, reflecting starlight. And there were men. A few were whole. Their bodies were bloated and blue and they looked surprised—mouths gaping, eyes staring. But mostly they were in pieces.

The Battle Dragon approached like an underwater leviathan. Your brain can't trust your eyes in vacuum—without an atmosphere to dull detail, everything is equally sharp. And when it's robbed of the ability to judge distance, the mind scrabbles for purchase. Is that chunk of durasteel a centimeter across and about to hit your faceplate, or a meter wide and the length of a landing field away? Watching the Battle Dragon coming, I tried to remember how large she was, tried to figure out how far away she was, tried to calculate if she would hit me.

She didn't—she passed right below me. She was far enough away that I didn't impact her particle shields, but close enough that I could count the rungs of the ladderwells on her sensor masts. They were crowned by running lights, which left spots on my vision when they flashed. She took forever to go by, while my feet kicked slowly above her. I fought down panic that she would suck me down after her or drag me into her wake. I reminded myself that there was neither air nor water between us, that what separated us was the absence of matter. Then she was gone, vanished into hyperspace with the rest of the task force, and I was alone with the stars and the dead.

And that was when it happened.

I didn't lose consciousness. I could still think and see. But I was no longer seeing what was around me or hearing the hiss of my ruined suit. I had a vision. I was shown everything at once—everything that had been and everything that will be.

I saw great beings made of light, who could be everywhere and nowhere at once. They were vaster than nebulae and tinier than cells, and they assembled solar systems like children with toys. I saw strange ships made of whirling, tumbling rods and cones, and heard them scream and moan as they shuddered by. I saw great chrome warships whose mirrored hulls turned sunlight into blinding sheets, and black battleships whose spines were crowned with terrible spiked cathedrals. I saw hammerheaded battle cruisers burning, and slab-sided Mandalorian constructs sparkling with rime. I saw Star Destroyers arrowing through the night, and blistered Mon Calamari cruisers schooling, and fighters of all shapes and sizes swarming. I saw ships that seemed built from clumps of multicolored wire, and ones that looked like organs torn from living things.

And I knew all these ships were filled with beings whose lives had been given to war. Hutt and Tionese, Republic and Sith, Loyalist and Separatist, Imperial and Rebel—I knew it didn't matter who had killed whom, or when or how or why. All at once I understood that those of us born to be sacrificed upon the pyre of war become one when we die—mingled smoke gone up to whatever gods you believe in. For they are the ones who created war. And they breathed it into our hearts when they created us.

War has always been with us, and always will be with us. I saw that too, as my flesh turned black and my brain froze in deep space. I saw beings by the billions undone in cruel and careless instants—by blasters and swords and teeth and fists. I saw fields and forests scoured into ash by orbital bombardments. I saw planetary cores cracked by flights of missiles. And I saw the battle station you destroyed, saw it hanging half complete above a green world.

Yes, I knew what has now come to pass—the Emperor's demise, the Death Star's ruin. Shall I tell you what else I saw—things that are yet to be? I think I will—because you won't believe me anyway. Nobody believes in their own end until it's upon them, until it can't be escaped. I saw ruined towers on Coruscant overtopped by curtains of spiked green and purple. I saw the forests of Kashyyyk burning, and the seas of Mon Calamari boiling, and planets ripped in two by the fiery lances of superlasers yet to be built. And other things I'll take with me, into the vanishing.

So why am I here? Because I was right. There was a snoopship there, sent to record my death for the Emperor's satisfaction. I must have activated my beacon—Academy training again—because the snoopship's crew found me and brought me aboard and handed me over to the medical droids. The only survivor of the Battle of Andalia was the man sent there to die.

Or a quarter of me survived, anyway—the rest was cut away and discarded, to be rebuilt as tubes and clockwork. After all that, the Emperor let me live. Why? Perhaps it was because he thought the lesson had been taught, and I still had value as a servant. Perhaps it was because he no longer cared. Or perhaps it was because he saw this day coming and desired a witness. As I told you, being Emperor is its own why.

Whatever the reason, I survived—and so now it falls to you to kill what's left. Go ahead, Rebel—let's get it over with. Turn Grand Admiral Teshik to smoke. But remember what I saw and take heed of what I said. You'll be smoke, too, soon enough. For each of our wars is just one little piece of a greater war, one endless and incalculably larger. And your Rebellion's part in that war didn't conclude with your victory at Endor. In fact, it's barely begun.

STAR WARS

THE ESSENTIAL GUIDE TO WARFARE

BEFORE THE
REPUBLIC

Very little is known about the galaxy's first civilizations, but the legends of the eldest spacefaring species tell an intriguingly similar story—about a terrible war waged with unimaginable weapons.

Pre-Republic specialists believe that the Columi, the Gree, the Kwa, and the Sharu all had contact with a species known as the Celestials, or the Architects, beings of astonishing power and malleable form. The Columi retreated from the stars after contact with the Celestials, and the Sharu sought refuge in primitivism. But the Gree, the Kwa, and the Killiks became their servants, helping build astonishing technological projects—projects some scientists believe included the assembly of star systems and the engineering of the hyperspace anomalies west of the Deep Core, if not the barrier surrounding our galaxy.

But another slave species revolted, wresting control of the Celestials' domain some thirty thousand years ago and waging war against the Gree, Kwa, and the Killiks. They were known as the Rakata, or the Builders, a species of bipeds with amphibian features whose technologies were powered by the Force.

Drawing on the Force made the Rakatan hyperdrive useless for traveling between points in realspace—instead, it homed in on the Force signature of planets brimming with life. Rakatan shields and energy weapons, meanwhile, used crystals to focus the Force.

The Force was fuel for the Rakata's Infinite Empire, and so they needed slaves—which they found on many worlds and trained to use their technologies. For millennia the Rakata ruled the galaxy, crossing space in their skipships, devastating planets with disruptor fields, and building armies of war droids. But then they too fell—cut off from the Force by a terrible plague. Their former slaves—humans, Duros, Herglic, Baragwin, Devaronians, Gossams, and others—rose up and hunted them down, leaving just a few bands of survivors in the Unknown Regions.

Those former slave species then reverse-engineered the Rakatan technologies, eliminating the role of focusing crystals and anything else that required the Force. A period of wild experimentation produced new technologies that became the basis of new territories—which then coalesced into the Republic.

A SOLDIER'S STORY: NOTRON IN FLAMES

The ancient history of Coruscant was shaped by war between the Battalions of Zhell—believed by some to be the ancestral human population—and the Taungs. During one skirmish, a volcanic eruption destroyed the city of Zhell. Taking this as a sign of divine favor, the Taungs christened themselves *Dha Werda Verda*, the Shadow Warriors, and celebrated their victory in the epic poem of the same name.

Dha Werda Verda encompasses more than seven hundred verses divided into eleven chapters. The best-known part is a fraction of the ninth chapter, presented here as translated by Baobab archivists:

> *And so upon his pyre burned the Doom of Ulmarah, and the warrior bands stood as ragged bandits, in zigzag lines of mourning. With the*

Rakatan warriors storm a Killik nest (Darren Tan)

dawn the flat-faced Zhell would come, cackling and howling, oozing mirth and tricks, and find the shade of the Doom departed and the Taungs unprotected.

And so with the dawn would our woe be revealed. Our once-bright armaments would become stacked grave goods, trophies for Zhell children. Our flesh would become smoke given to uncaring gods, and the sky would forget our names.

With death upon him Rexutu the Unconquerable prepared to be stripped of all by his enemy, but vowed that his honor would be last to be torn away. And so the Unconquerable gathered his kinsmen and his oath girdlings alike. They polished their fearsome helms, that they might flash even in the weak sun of Notron. They rewrapped the hilts of their weapons and pounded straight the shafts, that they might slake their thirst in Zhell ichor a final time.

Assembled they ascended, in taut Taung lines, to the high place where the Reaver had staked his standard before it was cast down into the mire. They gazed out over the gathering places and walking ways of Great Zhell where they scaled peak and cradled valley, the lines of lights ordering the night. They unfurled the Taung banner, reversed, a reckless thing snapping in the dark, awaiting Zhell eyes. And they performed ceremonies of leave-taking, for now they had died to the world and must be remade among the stars.

When the dawn came the Zhell awakened and saw the Taungs upon the high place and were afraid, for the morning light caught the glint of helms and weapons and created phantom warriors, made of dazzle and distance. But the cleverest of them were not deceived, and saw how few we were. And so they assembled without haste, merry in mockery, and prepared to march. And in the high place we awaited death.

But then came a shaking of the ground, and the sun's wan light was eclipsed by a bright and terrible fire that exploded from the rock. The patterns of Great Zhell shivered and broke. And after this came darkness, as the very air turned to black ash. The Zhell fell on their faces in terror, and from the high place we ran in haste to meet them, and we were cloaked in shadow.

The Maker had come to unmake, and the Taungs would be His instruments.

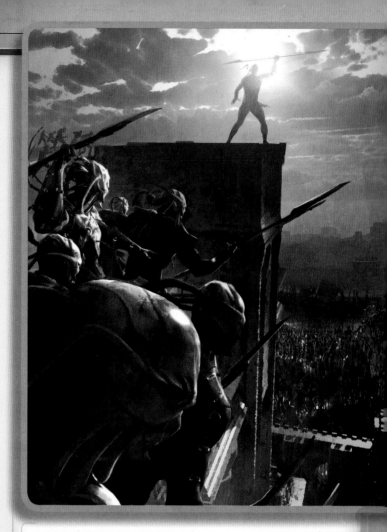

THE HUTTS AT WAR

Around fifteen thousand years before the Battle of Yavin (BBY), a terrible civil war—known as the Hutt Cataclysms—tore through Hutt Space, leaving several Hutt homeworlds barren wastelands. The surviving Hutts established a Council of Elders to prevent clan rivalries from exploding into open warfare, and instituted a new philosophy—*kajidic*—that rejected war and territorial conquest in favor of working from the shadows to manipulate others.

But before the Hutt Cataclysms, the Hutts conducted themselves very differently. They were warriors, leaving their homeworld of Varl to seek their destinies among the stars. When they encountered a species strong enough to resist them, that species was utterly destroyed. When they encountered a species too weak to be of use, it met the same fate. Only those species that were useful to Hutt ambitions but able to be mastered survived—and many of those were then worked to extinction.

The Hutts have always utilized a grab bag of technologies copied, borrowed, or stolen from others, and little is known about their own native technologies, if they ever existed.

Perhaps the best glimpse of the ancient Hutts comes from records kept by the Sakiyans, one of the few species of Hutt Space to maintain their independence and win the Hutts' respect. Sakiyan chronicles tell of Hutt cavaliers clad in iron shells, maneuvering via clattering metal limbs, treads, or wheels—perhaps ancient versions of the armored Shell Hutts who still dwell on Circumtore. Ancient Sakiyan tribute-counts also record payments for the Sakiyans' assistance in building Hutt *planechanga*—massive tubular railguns built to accelerate space rocks to planet-cracking velocities.

The victims of the Hutts' depredations are long gone and unable to bear witness to their oppressors' crimes, about which even the Sakiyans are silent. But the oldest legends of the Tion and the histories of long-established Rim worlds such as Delacrix and Rinn speak of the Hutts with fear and horror, recording that worlds caught between feuding clans or whose people somehow offended the Hutts were depopulated, poisoned, bombarded, or incinerated.

THE CONQUESTS OF XIM THE DESPOT

Galactic history has seen billions of admirals, generals, and warlords come and go. Most of their territorial gains have lasted decades at most; most of their names have been forgotten within a few centuries. But not all.

The Tionese empire of Xim began to fragment soon after his death, but the Despot's name has endured for twenty-five millennia, and still has the power to inspire and frighten. Depending whom you ask, Xim is a romantic swashbuckler, a sad symbol of lost power and prestige, the embodiment of human brutality, or an icon of madness and ruin. Scholars are similarly divided about this ancient son of the Tion Cluster, arguing about which of his deeds should properly be attributed to his father, Xer, and how many of the tales of the sprawling epic known as *The Despotica* are based in reality.

It's generally accepted that Xim was born on Argai, the son of the pirate-king Xer VIII. Xer and his pirates seized ships moving between hyperspace jump beacons through the nebula now known as the Indrexu Spiral, and the pirates' wealth and exploits attracted new raiders to Xer's banner. Battles at Panna, Duinarbulon, and Chandaar shattered the fleet of the Kingdom of Cron and made Xer its king. The teenage Xim made his first appearance soon after, becoming famous for his brutality during the slaughter of Cron's nobility known as the Cronese Sweeps.

Xer's forces stormed through the Tion, checked only by the well-armed, disciplined starfleet of the Livien League. After Xer retired to Raxus, Xim fulfilled his father's ambitions, smashing the league at Jhantoria. At Desevro, Xim met with Maslovar Tiatiov, the defeated planet's military ruler. Tiatiov showed the young Despot the Desevrar fighting academies and ministries, and explained how the Livien League had strengthened itself by turning its enemies' sons into janissaries and ministers.

Xim, impressed, spared Tiatiov's life. The Desevrar philosophy fueled Xim's Expansionist Period, a decade-long crusade that saw Tionese colonists advance in lockstep with Xim's forces. Worlds that opposed the Tionese were destroyed; those that accepted their rule became part of the ever-growing empire. By the end of the Expansionist Period, Xim ruled a vast domain—the Despot's territory extended from the Radama Void to Jabiim, including hundreds of thousands of worlds linked together by a network of jump beacons.

Adventurous Tionese scouts and merchants explored beyond this beacon network, hoping to win the Despot's favor by discovering rich new worlds. Some of those scouts returned to the Kiirium Reaches describing meetings with alien traders who served ruthless slug-like creatures.

The Hutts became the Despot's obsession. He burned to add Hutt trade worlds such as lush Ko Vari and fabled Sleheyron to his empire, and prepared for war, taking the

A warrior of the ancient Hutts (Chris Scalf)

old Rakatan title *Daritha*—ruler of worlds—for his own. He pushed his beacon network farther and farther to trailing, establishing a network of fortresses from which he might attack Hutt Space.

In the twenty-fifth year of Xim's rule, he assaulted Sleheyron and Ko Vari. Ko Vari was brutally sacked, while the drive to take Sleheyron failed, with the Despot's warships driven back to Xo's Eye (now known as Kessel) and lost in a tangle of black holes.

The lord of the Hutts, Kossak, was a wily foe. He lured Xim into ritual combat at Vontor, a world traditionally used for showdowns between Hutt clans. The *Daritha* would fight three battles at Vontor, all of which he would lose.

At the first, around 25,100 BBY, his warships were bested in space; at the second, a rematch sought by Xim, his Star Lancers and other ground forces were beaten by Jilruan flecheteers and Cyborrean heavy infantry, but Xim escaped with great stores of Vontorian kiirium. Offered a choice of ground or space combat at the Third Battle of Vontor, Xim chose ground and saw his janissaries and war droids overwhelmed by Nikto, Vodran, and Klatooinian berserkers led by Boonta the Hutt.

Xim had ignored his advisers and bled his empire dry creating warships and battle droids. At Vontor the depths of his folly were revealed: Fighting far from his own borders (and, it's whispered, betrayed by those close to him), Xim was not just defeated but captured, with his surviving orbital fortresses taken as Hutt trophies. The human who had dared oppose the Hutts was paraded in chains through Hutt Space. Xim's name would outlive many a civilization, but the former Despot spent his miserable final days as a Hutt slave.

DEBRIEFING: THE WAR ROBOTS OF XIM

Xim's war robots were technological marvels, likely derived from Rakatan designs—it was eons before war droids of comparable sophistication became common in the galaxy. While exalted in tales of the Despot, the war robots likely weren't run-of-the-mill infantry, but reserved for use as shock troops and ceremonial guards.

The war robots stood nearly three meters high. Their armor was made of an alloy of carbon, neutronium, and hadrium, later augmented with kiirium. They were armed with heatbeams, particle dischargers, and pulse-wave cannons. Some units utilized technologies that have defied technologists' reverse-

(CONTINUED ON PAGE 8)

ARMORY AND SENSOR PROFILE

TIONESE TECHNOLOGY

Like most pre-Republic galactic powers, the Tionese had been Rakatan slaves, and they inherited their oppressors' technology after the Infinite Empire fell. Under the canny administrators of the defeated Livien League, the Tionese created the galaxy's first great military-industrial complex. During Xim's time the Tion Cluster and the Thanium Worlds bustled with factories and shipyards that created warships, ground vehicles, war robots, and armaments for flesh-and-blood soldiers.

Particularly given their great age, Xim-era armaments are surprisingly common, allowing historians to reconstruct the Despot's technology with relative confidence. Xim's soldiers were divided into several castes. Most were janissaries from occupied worlds, trained as children for a lifetime of war. They wore armor and helmets of lightweight ceramic alloy and carried either slugthrowers or heatbeams, which fired jets of plasma. Heatbeamers wore tough, fireproof padded gloves and *kamas* as protection against their weapons' superheated exhaust.

Xim's elite soldiers, such as the Duinarbulon Star Lancers, known for their glossy black ceramic armor, carried beam tubes—ancestors of the blaster that required larger reserves of actuating gases to function. Beam tubes needed two hands to wield because of their large gas reservoirs, and backpack power cells that weighed more than thirty kilograms. Because beam tubes offered slow rates of fire and their power cells could only deliver one hundred shots, beam-tubers alternated fire by squad and carried large power generators on repulsorsleds.

The Despot's forces are popularly depicted as fighting on foot while supported by sleek warships, but this notion owes more to romance than reality. Xim's armies made use of tracked tanks, armored groundcars, and floaters that boasted beam-tube cannons, with elite vehicles armored in gleaming kiirium to reflect energy weapons.

XIM'S XOLOCHI
DREADNOUGHT

XIM'S THANIUM
STAR-GLAIVE

Less is known about Xim's warships. They were smaller than most Imperial-era craft, perhaps reflecting the Despot's pirate origins. The ancient Tionese saw starship construction as an art form, looking down on the mass production of ships. The bulk of Xim's warships would be classified as frigates or corvettes today, with Argaian hemiolia, Livien cutters, Thanium star-glaives, and Cronese battlebirds mixed and matched within squadrons.

Xim's airships primarily used torpedoes, concussion missiles, and pulse cannons that melted enemy hulls and disrupted circuitry with blasts of radiation. Xim's shipwrights armored the Despot's fleet with kiirium, a superconducting alloy that was a major breakthrough against energy weapons. Many an enemy turned his weapons onto the mirror-bright hulls of Xim's warships, only to see energy bolts coruscate harmlessly across the kiirium surface. Beneath those hulls, the ships' mytag crystalline vertices kept communications and sensors working under electromagnetic attack, and highly efficient Bordhell fuel slugs extended their range and speed.

Xim did have larger ships, believed to be cruiser-class: Cronese harpices, Brigian pentecenters, and Thanium polyremes were later joined by Yutuski rakehells and Xolochi dreadnoughts. And the legends speak of the treasure ship *Queen of Ranroon* and two flagships. The keel of the *Eibon Scimitar* was laid at the shipyards of Barancar, and later renderings of it inspired the Republic's long-lived *Invincible* class of heavy cruisers. The *Scimitar* was destroyed at the First Battle of Vontor and replaced by the *Deathknell*, which met a similar fate at the Third Battle of Vontor.

SHIELD TECHNOLOGY

Only armored hulls protected the first ships to explore the dark between the stars. But the many dangers of space travel quickly made it clear that better protection was desperately needed.

The first defenses were energy shields, originally designed to dissipate solar energy absorbed by hulls in deep space. Energy shields were soon refined into deflector shields, which could also defend against energy weapons. Deflector shields create layered force fields enveloping an object in a single field or series of intersecting fields, depending on the size of the object to be protected and the energy available to power the shield. Energy is diffused away from the point of contact and either absorbed by the shield or radiated away as waste heat.

Deflector shields, however, were a poor defense against impacts that couldn't be diffused, such as projectiles, micrometeorites, or asteroids. Particle shields offered an additional means of protection, absorbing the kinetic energy of a collision and diffusing it as deflector shields do. Particle shields also bind a ship's hull together at the molecular level.

For millennia, even small-sized starships have traveled with both kinds of shields. But the shield technology of the post-Imperial era little resembles that of the early Republic. Shields of all types require enormous amounts of power, and for eons only the largest starships could mount shield generators big enough to defend against energy weapons. Until the 7700s BBY, shields were primarily a defense against accidental impacts and radiation storms, not enemy ships. Armor was a starship's principal defense, with research focusing on alloys and coatings that could dissipate energy impacts.

Advances in power generation made shields practical for smaller ships and also let ships mount capable defenses against more powerful energy weapons. But even stronger shields could be penetrated. Directing energy against single points can overload the defensive field, allowing projectiles or energy blasts to pass through before the shield can regenerate, or burning out the generator powering that section of the shield. Particle shields must be lowered to allow ships to launch or projectile weapons to be fired, leaving vulnerable gaps. Finally, heat sinks, exhaust ports and other systems can't have particle shields, because heat, waste, and debris would be trapped inside—a problem that left the first Death Star vulnerable to Luke Skywalker's proton torpedo.

Planetary shields offer a defense against bombardment by capital ships, as well as sorties by starfighters and landing craft, but ground vehicles rarely have shields. Personal shields are largely a relic of history: They require large power packs if they are to function for a significant period of time, expose living beings to unhealthy radiation and magnetic forces, and sometimes fail in catastrophic fashion, flash-cooking those they seek to defend. Droids with properly shielded circuitry fear none of these things: During the Clone Wars droidekas were among the Confederacy of Independent Systems' most feared units. Fortunately for the Republic, the vast expense of producing and maintaining destroyer droids limited the number of units that could be deployed.

(CONTINUED FROM PAGE 6)

engineering efforts: Xim's Crimson Condottieri, for example, apparently used Force-sensitive Rakatan modules to enhance their limited behavioral circuitry matrices.

Though they were among the first combat automata ever produced, their toughness and effectiveness in battle have rarely been equaled. Shortly before the Battle of Yavin, a thousand war robots—Xim's fabled Guardian Corps—were activated on Dellalt and attacked a band of roughneck miners, fighting effectively and without the slightest hint that nearly twenty-five millennia had degraded their programming or physical systems.

Most of Xim's war robots were destroyed when the Despot was defeated at the Third Battle of Vontor, as berserk Hutt slaves overpowered them through sheer numbers. For ages, the Guardian Corps watched over the treasure off-loaded from the *Queen of Ranroon* on lonely Dellalt. Elsewhere, Tionese families handed down some units as bodyguards, while others guarded lost outposts of the Despot's empire, awaiting orders that would never come. Even in the final years of the Republic, scouts would occasionally discover a rogue planet or hidden asteroid base defended by an unimaginably ancient war robot.

The Hutts took hundreds of war robots from Vontor as trophies, and travelers in Hutt Space would sometimes stumble across them standing mutely in plazas and palaces. When the Yuuzhan Vong invaded Hutt Space in 26 ABY, the warriors received a shock: The war robots woke from their long sleep and killed thousands of the attackers before they were overcome and destroyed. Xim himself might have appreciated the irony.

WAR PORTRAIT: BOONTA THE HUTT

If not for the leadership of two great Hutts, Xim the Despot might have achieved his goal of making Sleheyron the Ninth Throne of his empire, avoided the fatal distractions of Vontor, and escaped his fate. And the history of the galaxy might be very different.

The first Hutt who stood in his way was Kossak Inijic Ar'durv. It was Kossak who persuaded the fractious Hutt clans that the Tionese were an existential threat; cajoled them into uniting against Xim (with Kossak himself as clan-general); exploited the Despot's pride and vanity to ensnare him in ritual combats; and lured the Vodrans, Niktos, and Klatooinians into Hutt service so their forces might tip the balance against Xim at the Third Battle of Vontor.

While Kossak was a political genius and a cunning

warrior, it took another Hutt to defeat Xim: Boonta Hestilic Shad'ruu, hailed as the architect of the Hutts' defenses and the assaults that destroyed the Despot's forces.

While the history of this period is hazy, most historians believe Boonta began his rise to power as a clan leader on Ko Vari, a rich trade world on what was then the Hutt frontier. Knowing he couldn't defend his world against the Tionese, Boonta determined that the invaders would pay dearly for it, sacrificing countless valuable slaves in suicidal attacks on the Despot's warships and ground forces. Xim responded by sacking the planet brutally, but Boonta had bought invaluable time for his fellow Hutts. Impressed, Kossak directed him to harass the Tionese worlds with slave-crewed privateers.

Boonta fought well at the First and Second Battles of Vontor. When Xim withdrew from the Moralan system in the hope of fomenting slave revolts against the Hutts, Boonta crushed the rebellious Moralan Parliament, sterilizing the planet as an object lesson for the Hutts' slave species. He then retook Ko Vari before leading the Hutt warships at the Third Battle of Vontor.

The Hutts say that on the night before the invasion of Moralan, Boonta gathered his kin, loyal retainers, and favored slaves and spoke of the Hutts and their rightful place in the galaxy. He swore he would rather die than live in a galaxy in which Hutts bowed down to bipeds, and in which the beneficence of their rule was replaced by the chaos of slave species scratching and crawling for brief dominance. Boonta's Eve is still celebrated as a Hutt holiday, a night in which slaves renew their vows of obeisance and are rewarded with a feast and trinkets.

Another tradition honors Boonta: popular Podraces on a number of Hutt-controlled worlds. The Hutts say such competitions date back to celebrations held by Boonta himself on reclaimed Ko Vari: Each year on Boonta's Eve, Tionese prisoners would be forced to run while the Hutts wagered on the results, with the stragglers in each heat put to death until the sole survivor was proclaimed winner.

The planet Ko Vari, meanwhile, is now called Boonta, in tribute to the Hutt who recaptured it from Xim.

THE ANCIENT REPUBLIC

"The goal of war is to take your enemy's possessions whole and intact.
A shattered country is not a prize but a burden."

—Sayings of Uueg Tching

CONTACT WITH THE TION

The ancient Republic was more a collection of civilizations than a common one, its worlds partially knit together by Rakatan-derived technologies. When they looked to the galactic Rim, young Core worlds such as Corellia, Duro, Alsakan, Axum, and Brentaal didn't think about common goals, but their own ambitions.

Galactic exploration proceeded rapidly, as brave hyperspace scouts pursued rumors of strange ships deeper into the galactic arms. At first it was traders, not warriors, who drove galactic expansion, bartering for navigational information and discovering that the stars were thick with new civilizations, as well as worlds ripe for colonization and exploitation. Colonization progressed slowly and steadily into what is now the Inner Rim, then rocketed along two narrow corridors defined by tangles of ancient trade routes. One corridor became known as the Corellian Run, because traders from that world were common sights along it. The other was dubbed the Perlemian Trade Route, because Perlemia's shipwrights built so many of its scoutships. At the end of the Corellian Run lay Kalarba, an entrepôt maintained by the master traders of Paqwepori Major, while the Perlemian led to the trade worlds Tirahnn, Nouane, and Roche.

Brave traders made fortunes on the Rim, and a network of depots and navigation buoys soon extended as far as Roche and Kalarba. While conflicts between different worlds' colonists and traders weren't unknown, shooting wars were rare and burned out quickly: The galaxy was too big to waste time on pointless conflicts.

But two powerful civilizations lay beyond the Rim. The Tion Cluster was much reduced from the splendor of Xim's rule, having fractured into a collection of squabbling states, but a common culture and Xim's "lighthouse network" of beacons linked its worlds, which hungered to reclaim their lost glories. And their old enemies, the Hutts, dwelled at the center of a web of lush planets, attended by slave species.

Both the Tionese and the Hutts saw the young, rich worlds of the Core as ripe for exploitation. Hutt raiders and slavers struck from the shadows to depopulate colonies and seize cargoes before retreating to their own domain. The Tion states, meanwhile, wanted the Core's superior hyperspace technology and wealth for their own—and the Perlemian was an ideal invasion corridor.

The Tionese War and its aftermath would change the Republic in two profound ways. The trade guilds and scout companies became military organizations, at first under the auspices of their homeworlds but eventually under more centralized control. And the worlds of the Rim sought Republic protection from the Hutts and the Tionese. Admitting such far-flung worlds made the Republic a galaxy-spanning civilization, and forced it to become a centralized military power.

First contact between the Republic and the Tionese (John VanFleet)

HYPERSPACE AND WARFARE

Statistically speaking, the universe is empty. But at faster-than-light speeds, it fills up very quickly.

—Admiral Pers Pradeux

Control space and you control any battlefield you can imagine. Unfortunately, you cannot control space.

—Admiral Firmus Nantz

Every object in realspace casts a mass shadow in hyperspace, and plotting a safe course between two points in realspace requires knowing the location of every large object between them. The reverse engineering of the Rakatan hyperdrive allowed civilization to reach galactic scale, ending the era of sleeper ships plying slow courses between distant stars. But galactic civilization only became a reality with the discovery of safe routes through hyperspace connecting those stars.

Routes are blazed by hyperspace scouts who make repeated microjumps and take careful surveys to record objects' positions. Those routes are then optimized and kept stable through constant tweaks to account for the ceaseless whirl of the stars, with new route and sensor data uploaded from starships when they reach spaceports. This constant flow of data allows well-traveled routes to remain stable, barring some catastrophic change along their lengths. Rarely used routes, on the other hand, can vanish within a few years.

As calculating a safe hyperspace route requires estimating the position of innumerable realspace objects, it demands immense computing power and memory. For much of galactic history, no starship had sufficient computing resources to calculate long jumps quickly or to keep more than a few courses in memory. Instead, massive supercomputers were constructed in deep space at the jumping-off points for common routes, and performed the calculations for starships. Space stations were built near or actually around these jump beacons, creating a series of way stations for travelers.

During the jump-beacon era, military forces could effectively pin ships at a given point by disabling its beacon. But by the 4100s BBY, that era was nearing its end: New navicomputers could store thousands of routes and calculate them with reasonable efficiency. Wary of rumblings beyond the Republic frontier, the Republic Navy conducted crash research to ensure that its ships could cross the galaxy quickly and safely without having to rely on beacons or spaceport data stacks. When war with the Sith and the Mandalorians reached Republic space, the navy destroyed many beacons in an effort to deny its enemies easy passage into the heart of the Republic.

After the jump-beacon era ended, any starship with a working navicomputer could traverse any known route in the galaxy. That made controlling hyperspace lanes far more challenging, as blockading one route merely pushed ships to one of many alternative ones.

Still, the way hyperspace travel had evolved made a seemingly impossible job somewhat easier. Many paths may connect points A and B, but only a few of them can be traveled quickly, and a military force that controls the fast routes can redeploy to intercept an adversary using the slow ones.

Commercial traffic on busy routes is managed through communications using hypercomms and navicomputers: Navicomputers send their starships' flight plans "ahead" via burst transmissions over hypercomms, with starports and navigation buoys replying via hypercomm with minute corrections to heading and speed that keep ships safely apart. Shut down this hypercomm network and ship traffic on busy routes slows to a crawl or halts—though the disastrous effects on commerce means such actions are extremely rare.

After the jump-beacon era, information and agility became the keys to a successful blockade. If you knew where your enemy was and could deduce where he was headed, you could dispatch nimble forces via faster routes to intercept him. (The bursts of Cronau radiation emitted by ships jumping to or emerging from hyperspace offer clues to a ship's course; those seeking to hide their origin or destination do so by making a succession of jumps, greatly expanding the tree of possibilities.)

A wild card for commanders is the possibility of secret routes. Spacers freely share navicomputer data about established routes for the common good—refusing to share data or falsifying it has been illegal for most of galactic history. But new routes are carefully kept secrets. Shipping companies, trade guilds, and individual species all have their own proprietary routes, which run the gamut from minor improvements to existing routes to secret connections between key worlds. Every star-spanning military maintains its own secret routes, of course, and its spies constantly seek to discover those of rivals and enemies.

In practice, secret routes rarely prove pivotal: They're hard to maintain and harder to keep secret. But they have proven vital to a number of military campaigns.

The blind jump made by the Daragon siblings between Koros Major and Korriban around 5000 BBY gave the Sith

Empire a route—the brief-lived Daragon Trail—that allowed it to strike at the heart of the Republic. During the Clone Wars, the Republic and the Separatists both negotiated with the Hutts for access to the great gastropods' smuggling routes through each other's blockades; the two sides fought for control of the secret Nexus Route connecting their core territories. General Grievous attacked Coruscant via a secret hyperspace route through the Deep Core, and the Separatists invaded Kashyyyk in the hope of seizing secret routes maintained by the Claatuvac Guild of Wookiee hyperspace scouts. The Claatuvac routes were long considered the stuff of legend, but they existed: Chewbacca used them profitably for smuggling, and passed them to Princess Leia after the Battle of Hoth, giving Alliance High Command a great asset in its struggle with the Empire. Later, Admiral Ackbar exploited the Yuuzhan Vong's ignorance of hyperspace routes by tempting them into a trap at Ebaq in the Deep Core, where their main war fleet was wrecked and Warmaster Tsavong Lah died.

WAR WITH THE TION

A surprise awaited Republic traders who pushed beyond the farthest trade stations on the Perlemian: They were not the first humans to come this way. In fact, a human civilization spanning a huge expanse of space awaited them.

The Tionese claimed that their cluster was the cradle of humanity, and took pride in Xim's accomplishments. But Xim had been dead for a thousand years, and Tionese history had not been glorious since his demise.

The Despot's empire had splintered into successor states soon after his death, with those states fragmenting into a brawling collection of kingdoms, satrapies, and petty holdings. Many of the Tionese rulers were little more than wealthy pirates who had tired of enforcing their will at the end of a heatbeam and tried to set up functioning states—which only signaled their vulnerability to younger, less wealthy pirates. Two things united Tionese culture: a love of wealth and a fear of external enemies. And the worst of those enemies were the Hutts.

Traders traveling under Hutt protection snapped up Tionese raw materials and finished goods at penurious prices. To refuse their terms was to get a visit from other Hutt servants in evil-looking warships of alien design, servants who enjoyed raiding Tionese worlds for goods and slaves. The Hutts themselves were never seen in the Tion—they remained safe in their distant realm, beyond all hope of retribution.

The Tionese greeted the arrival of Republic traders with a mixture of jealousy and wild hope. While Tionese technology had remained stagnant since Xim's era, Republic shipwrights had improved on the Corellian and Duro interpretations of Rakatan technology, incorporating advances from the Herglic, Devaronians, and Verpine. Republic ships were faster, more reliable, and could travel farther than anything in the Tion Cluster.

But at the same time, the Tionese saw an opportunity. No trip among the Tionese worlds was particularly safe, and Tionese ships bristled with plasma cannons and torpedo mounts. The Republic traders' sleek pinnaces and barquentines were lightly armed, and the new arrivals freely admitted that their central worlds had no great fleets of warships.

Emissaries from Desevro—once the mightiest world of the Livien League and the engine of Xim's expansionist empire—fanned out across the Tion, urging the Tionese to take advantage of the newcomers' naïveté. The pirate lords of the Indrexu Spiral agreed to a loose confederation, the loftily titled Honorable Union of Desevro and Tion. Next, the Desevrars forged an alliance with the Kingdom of Cron, now a patchwork state loosely controlled by Corlassi pirates. The potentates of the Jaminere Marches, surrounded by potential enemies, hastily joined the confederation, as did the Thanium Dominion. Under Desevrar leadership, the Tionese began reverse-engineering captured Republic technologies and building war fleets at Arcan, Jaminere, and Thanium.

War was coming, and no one in the Republic seemed to see it, despite warnings from another mysterious society living far from the Core. The Jedi Order had left its original home in the Deep Core centuries before, settling on a green world the Tionese called Idux but they themselves called Ossus. Except during their brief war with the Legions of Lettow, few in the Core had given much thought to the Jedi since their departure—and fewer had guessed that they were the young Republic's secret defenders, working quietly to check Hutt schemes and keep the Tionese divided.

Now strange warriors with glowing swords appeared in the Core, warning of war—but to little avail. Tionese war fleets stormed down the Perlemian, meeting little resistance. Abhean—the farthest major Republic world—fell to the raiders. Then Roche was lost, and Lantillies, and the trade world of Tirahnn, with the Tionese gaining new ships with every victory.

Belatedly aware of its peril, the Republic embarked on a crash program of warship production, with hulls taking shape above industrial worlds such as Axum, Foerost, and Perlemia. But it was too late: Convoys of Tionese raiders ranged up and down the Perlemian, backed by larger warships. Perlemia's fabled shipyards were all but destroyed by dreadful new weapons—pressure bombs, powerful airbursts whose heat storms and shock waves leveled cities—and Axum suffered the same fate. Pushing into the heart of the Republic, the Tionese rained pressure bombs down on Alsakan and Coruscant itself.

A desperate counterattack by ships drawn from numerous Core systems finally repulsed the Tionese. Away from the invasion route, shipyards at Corellia, Rendili, and Humbarine began turning out warships, and the Republic took the fight back up the Perlemian to the Tion, setting up a grinding series of offensives and counteroffensives that would range up and down the trade route for nearly a century. The Perlemian worlds became armed camps, and Core world inhabitants lived in fear of Tionese suicide ships. Elsewhere, Republic agents (many of whom were well-connected merchants) stirred up the Hutts against their ancient rivals, forcing the Tionese to guard their outlying possessions against raiders and pirates. Finally, following an agonizing internal debate, the Jedi entered the war as Republic commanders, concerned that the galaxy would sink into barbarism without their intervention.

The Tionese war effort had been doomed as soon as several key Republic worlds put their industrial might behind the military buildup. But decades of war had turned the struggle into a fanatical cause: Between the marauding Hutts and the technological superiority of the Republic, the leaders of the Tion felt their culture faced extinction. And so the Tionese fought on, subjecting Republic worlds and citizens to a steady drumbeat of sneak attacks, raids, and terrorist acts. That radicalized the Republic as well, and a strategy of total war was adopted. The Republic stormed up the Perlemian and through the Tion, with pressure bombs devastating Cadinth, Jaminere, Thanium, Chandaar, and Barseg. Desevro was the last to fall, absorbing a frightful punishment before finally offering its unconditional surrender.

It was refused: The Republic's military leaders had decided to sterilize Desevro as an object lesson to the rest of the Tionese.

That led the Jedi to break with the Republic. The Order had joined the war in order to prevent civilization from sinking into barbarism, but barbarism was winning the day anyway—and now the Jedi were a party to it. After tense meetings above blasted, exhausted Desevro, the Jedi agreed to serve as watchmen, ensuring the Republic's safety from an arc of fortress worlds around the Tion's Coreward borders.

The assault on the Republic turned out to be the Tion's last gasp as a galactic power: Within centuries it was part of the Republic, and no more troublesome than other regions with old quarrels against the wealthy systems of the Core.

Those systems soon regarded the centralized military as a danger, fearing a recurrence of the fanaticism that had been on display in the Tion. With the Tionese threat checked by both the Jedi and the Republic's economic might, the Core Worlds voted (over the objection of many Rimward systems) to disband the standing military, returning the majority of its units to the control of individual systems and sectors. The small Republic military would patrol the frontier and respond to crises, relying on sectorial and system interests to contribute forces in case of a larger conflict.

Finally, the Jedi's self-imposed exile from the Republic had come to an end. The tide of Republic expansion had reached Ossus, and the Jedi had chosen to play a formal role in the Republic's defense. Their decision would be the subject of debate on Ossus for centuries to come.

THE WAR OF THE JEDI AND THE LEGIONS OF LETTOW

According to ancient records, the Jedi Order began on Tython, where Force-users tapped energy they called the Ashla, rejecting the lures of dark energy they called the Bogan. The Force Wars pitted adherents of the two creeds against each other, with the Ashla victorious. But a new conflict later arose between the Jedi—then based on Ossus—and a splinter group that called itself the Legions of Lettow. Little was known conclusively of this conflict until the discovery of the warrior Arden Lyn, who had survived twenty-five thousand years in stasis before being awakened by Imperial agents in 4 BBY. Lyn killed Inquisitor Ameesa Darys and fought off Antinnis Tremayne, but was maimed and captured by Torbin, who filed these selections from her debriefing:

The Jedi? Those handmaidens of the Ashla, the weak side of the Force? For ten thousand years they sat on Tython, staring into the stars and debating the nature of the cosmos, like a sewing circle of widows on Peshara. They did nothing. They were nothing. And without us they might have remained nothing.

The Jedi called the Bogan the dark side, but it is the side of vitality, of purpose. For what does life

do? Whatever it must to survive. It thrums with the desire to compete, to overcome, to better itself. Is that selfish? Those who must fight to survive would laugh at the question. Striving, besting—these desires can lead to hate and to war, it is true. But they also drive love, passion, and creation itself. That is the Bogan—the power that drives all life, from one-celled organisms to the leviathans of deep space.

The crowning joke, Xendor liked to say, was that we created the Jedi. It was the followers of the Bogan who gave the Order something to define itself against. It was the followers of the Bogan who drove the Order to shape itself into something other than a band of useless mystics. The Bogan gave the Jedi focus. It gave them purpose. It made them strong.

The wars of Tython were ancient history in my time. The Ashla and the Bogan fought, and the followers of the Bogan were defeated, and so they fled Tython. They went in many directions, heeding the Bogan's commands. In some places they discovered others who had been awakened by the Bogan, and learned their traditions. In others they served as teachers of their own ways. But always the message was the same: Go forth, survive, multiply, succeed.

* * *

In my time neither the Jedi nor we Renunciates used lightsabers. As part of their initiation, Padawans would forge their own steel blades and imbue them with the Force. And we would do the same.

An initiate Legionnaire would select a bar of high-carbon steel and shape it into a blade in the academy furnaces. The work was physical—annealing, quenching, and tempering. But it was also mental—an initiate hammering at hot steel to bend it and temper it would also be directing the Force to flow into the blade, forming the atoms into a lattice. This lattice would harden the blade and focus its edge, and prepare the blade to receive the crystal. Once blade and lattice were forged, the initiate would place the crystal in the hilt and marry the lattices, submerging so deeply in the Force that blade and crystal and wielder became one. The wielder would channel the energies of the Force through the crystal and into the blade, making

it glow with a nimbus of energy. But sometimes the forging would fail. Sometimes blade or crystal would shatter.

So, sometimes, would the initiate.

* * *

The Jedi called it the Great Schism—as tends to happen, later events forced it to be renamed the First Great Schism.

We didn't call it anything.

The worlds of the Core had joined together to form the Republic. But there were dangers beyond the Rim—the old empire of Xim, the slave kingdoms of the Hutts, and all manner of satrapies and dominions that your historians have forgotten.

After my investment as a Steel Hand of Palawa, I journeyed to Pelgrin to learn my fortune from the Oracle. This was before the Jedi expunged all knowledge of the Oracle, as they expunged so much that threatened their own power and prestige. I listened to the clockwork of the Oracle, and it told me many things. It told me that I should go to Ossus, where I would meet a man fair of face and clever of mind, and make him my master.

Ossus was the headquarters of the Jedi Order, which had left Tython to distance itself from the machinations of the growing Republic. I was welcomed there, as were other Followers of Palawa—we were considered fellow students of the Force. But the Order was already changing, growing doctrinaire. Its masters had fallen prey to the whispering of the Snouts—the Caamasi, those ancient beguilers of humanity. And they had fallen prey to the whispering of their own ambition—the collective ambition that seeks to deny that of the individual, so that the strong can be weakened and ruled more easily. By the time I arrived it was too late—the Order had set itself upon the path it would follow. But that is never apparent at the time. Only later can we discern the point when change became an impossibility.

At Ossus I met Xendor, the man of my vision. He was a Kashi Mer exile, a master of the Breath, as his people called the Force. He was respected in the Order, but vocal in his disapproval of its increasingly exclusionary ways. He first came to me because he wished to learn more about the Palawan martial arts, but he warned me that we should converse quietly, away from the Jedi hierarchs. I don't know if he knew then that he would break with the Order and I would follow him. But I knew he would, just as I knew we would become friends and then lovers. The clockwork had already told me so.

At the beginning the break was peaceful. Xendor sought the hierarchs' permission to create an academy for the study of Force traditions—to tap the knowledge of the Chatos Academy and the Dai Bendu, the Palawa and the Kashi Mer, the Bogan and the Kel Dor sages, the Way of the Dark and the Protectorate of the Hidden. When they said no, as he'd known they would, he left the Order to found his own academy on Lettow. I accompanied him, and others followed—first by ones and twos, then in larger groups.

These newcomers took to calling themselves the Legions of Lettow, for they swore to defend us and our right to seek knowledge of the Force without the interference of the Jedi hierarchs and their pronouncements about what was correct and what was forbidden. The Jedi had sought to make the Force smaller, to cage it with rules and restrictions, but we knew that the Force was larger than any such mortal endeavors, and that it turned aside no one who was willing to learn its mysteries.

We had thought the Jedi would leave us alone, to seek our own path. But that was naïve. The mere suggestion that there was another way to know the Force—our mere existence—was a threat to them. And so they branded us dissenters and schismatics and pushed us toward open conflict.

* * *

They formed armies against us, and so we had to do the same. Xendor, to his dismay, became our general. I served as his right hand. To spare the galaxy bloodshed and pain, we tried to stop the war in its earliest stages, by bringing the fight to Ossus, away from the Republic worlds. We failed, and the Jedi pursued us into the Core. Xendor tried to alert the Republic to its peril, to make the people see that the Jedi would cloak themselves as protectors and guardians as they waged war and took the levers of power. But he failed, and it was war—war on Chandrila and Brentaal, then Coruscant and Metellos.

Xendor died at Columus, as the Jedi and the armies they'd beguiled closed in. I wasn't there, but I saw it as if I had been.

Awdrysta Pina, known as the Green Blade, was the leader of the Jedi forces. He was a good choice—a grim man and bloody-minded. He'd spent little time on Ossus, preferring to travel the ancient space lanes beyond the Rim in search of knowledge. I admired him, and so did Xendor—he was better suited to be a Renunciate than a Jedi. Except Pina had a fatal flaw—a child-like belief that order and structure were the pillars of civilization, and a refusal to see that they could become civilization's chains. What we understood as freedom, he could only see as chaos.

Pina's legions had one advantage over ours. They would use the Force to fight as a collective, subsuming their individuality to a battle-meld so that they moved and reacted as one. We could not match them in this. We would not match them in this. We would not fight like insects. At Columus, Pina's armies cut off Xendor and his vanguard from the bulk of his forces, and Pina's Jedi Knights advanced on my love as one. Beside him stood the mightiest of our warriors—the likes of Sethul Asaiage and Tun Bohoi—but one by one they fell to the Jedi hive. Until finally Pina struck down my love, and his spirit fled into the Dark, rather than be drunk by the Green Blade and destroyed.

* * *

Then they came to Lettow to kill the rest of us. I knew there was no hope of victory, only of escape. And so we held Pina's armies off just long enough to seek refuge beyond the Republic's borders.

I fled into the tangled stars beyond Kitel Phard, following secret ways Xendor had discovered. But the Green Blade followed, and I was cornered on Irkalla. I had the Kashi Mer talisman bequeathed to me by Xendor, the symbol of his sundered royal house, and when Pina battered the blade out of my hand I drew upon this talisman's powers, making it a lens for my rage and sorrow, for my love for Xendor and my despair over what had been taken from us. I exploded Pina's blade, driving its shards through his body. He was ruined, and I laughed out loud to see it.

But as I told you, Awdrysta was a bloody-minded man. He had learned to use the Force to bind and smother an opponent, to subdue one's life energies. Morichro, they called it. Even as his eyes grew dull, Pina did this to me. I felt my legs topple, my heart grow heavy and strain, my lungs flutter and struggle. I saw him die, but his spell could not be unmade. All went gray, and then black, and I knew no more.

Pina had not killed me, though many times I have wished he had. I do not know who constructed my tomb or set me within it. I awoke to your faces. I awoke to find that twenty-five thousand years had gone by—all I knew and all I loved curdled into history and then dismissed as myth. Not even dust remains of those who were dear to me. I have outlived planets, and the very constellations are scrambled and strange.

I am alone in a way none of you could possibly imagine.

* * *

Xendor told me he once journeyed to a dead world where the Force was worshipped as a triad of divine beings. The Daughter was the Light Side. The Son was the Dark Side. And the Father? The Father was the Force itself, perhaps. Xendor said he spoke with these beings, and I asked eagerly what he had discovered. He laughed at me, and dismissed the question.

"Even now, you refuse to understand," he told me. "There are as many truths to the Force as there are hearts within which the Force manifests itself. The existence of the triad has no more bearing on the reality of the Force than the Ashla and the Bogan, or anything I tell you, or anything you tell others. Any philosophy, creed, or religion that opens the heart to the Force proves itself to be true. My legions follow the dictates of such a creed. But that is only a demonstration of the application of power, Arden. It says nothing about the rightness of our beliefs, or the universality of our faith."

ARMORY AND SENSOR PROFILE

LIGHTSABER TECHNOLOGY

"This is the weapon of a Jedi Knight. Not as clumsy or random as a blaster. An elegant weapon for a more civilized age." —*Obi-Wan Kenobi*

The lightsaber has been the traditional weapon of the Jedi for millennia, symbolizing the Order's prowess in battle, as well as its wisdom. A lightsaber is a deadly weapon, but also a focus for a Jedi's meditation and sense of the Force—a well-trained Jedi feels as if he, his blade, and the Force are one single entity.

For much of the Jedi Order's history, building a lightsaber was a key step on a Padawan's path to Jedi Knighthood. In ideal circumstances, a Padawan would spend months building a weapon perfectly suited for his or her hand, selecting a focusing crystal or crystals, aligning the crystals within the hilt, and charging the weapon's power cell using the Force.

The components of a lightsaber aren't particularly rare or exotic—simple power cells, controls, conductors, and a reflector cup. While the best focusing crystals are rare and powerful gems, less exotic or synthetic crystals can serve a similar purpose. In extremis, Jedi have cobbled together lightsabers from commonly available parts. What *is* extraordinary is the precision with which the focusing crystals must be aligned, a process that demands both a supernaturally steady hand and mastery of the Force. No attempt to mass-produce lightsabers has ever succeeded.

The lightsaber draws energy from a power cell in the base of the hilt. This energy is fed into a chamber where it is focused by the crystals and shunted farther along the hilt, emerging as a blade-shaped energy field, thin and cylindrical and about a meter in length. The energy blade has no mass, but its gyroscopic effect creates the illusion of weight, and it is extremely difficult for an untutored user to control. The blade generates no heat, but can cut through most materials, with the exception of other lightsaber blades, force fields, and certain exotic metals and alloys.

The first Jedi weapons weren't lightsabers, but swords

FORCE-IMBUED SWORD

EARLY LIGHTSABER

MODERN LIGHTSABER

tempered, hardened, and sharpened by the Force. Some of these ancient Force blades had crystals set in the tangs of their blades; apprentice Jedi would use the Force to arrange the atoms in the crystals and the blade into complementary lattices, with the energies of the Force lending the blade a ghostly radiance.

The earliest true lightsabers joined focusing crystals with laser technology shared by visitors to the Jedi dawnworld of Tython. These first lightsabers were "frozen blaster" technology, used primarily as siege weapons for slicing through fortifications. Over time, the power packs required for them shrank until they could be attached to a Jedi's belt, with a flexible cable connecting the pack to the hilt of the lightsaber. It wasn't until after 5000 BBY that power units grew small enough to fit within lightsabers, giving the weapons their iconic form.

After the Battle of Ruusan the blades of most Jedi lightsabers were blue or green, but in earlier times blades of purple, gold, orange, yellow, and white were also common.

The Sith have traditionally used lightsabers that produce red blades, usually made with synthetic crystals. Jedi lore holds that red crystals are less stable than green and blue ones—but have an advantage that offsets this weakness. Whether natural or synthetic, red crystals glow in harmonic vibration when energized by the dark side of the Force, and sometimes produce spasms in the arced plasma of the blade that can disrupt another saber's blade. Thus, the very instability of red crystals requires the wielder of a Sith saber to remain attuned to the dark side during combat, both for possible advantage and to keep his or her weapon operating.

Lightsaber combat is an art form in its own right, one that has evolved along with the Jedi Order. Such combat is divided into seven distinct forms or fighting disciplines, known as Forms I through VII.

Form I, Shii-Cho, evolved during the long-ago transition from metal blades to lightsabers, and covers the basics of attack, parries, body target zones, and practice drills known as velocities.

Form II, Makashi, evolved during the wars between lightsaber-wielding Jedi and Dark Jedi, and covers the

various refinements of offense and defense between two opponents wielding lightsabers.

Form III, Soresu, developed as the Jedi faced enemies armed with blasters. Its efficient, compact maneuvers are designed to defend against ranged attacks, deflecting them while protecting the body.

Form IV, Ataru, is often seen as the pinnacle of Jedi abilities in combat. This wildly acrobatic style channels the Force to allow a Jedi to run, jump, and spin in ways no normal adversary can match.

Form V has two variations—Shien and Djem So—and evolved alongside Ataru. Both emphasize offense over defense. Djem So is an aggressive style for pressing the attack during saber duels, while Shien transforms a defense against ranged weapons into an offensive move by training the Jedi to deflect attacks back at his or her attackers.

Form VI, Niman, combines aspects of the other forms and seeks to moderate them, allowing a Jedi to counter any attack while maintaining his or her calm and remaining open to the will of the Force.

Form VII, Juyo, is the most difficult and demanding lightsaber form, involving bold and direct movements and drawing on a Jedi's focus and emotions. It demanded such intensity that the Jedi Masters of the Order's final years restricted its instruction, for fear that its demands left Jedi vulnerable to the lures of the dark side. A variant of Form VII, Vaapad, was invented by Mace Windu and sought to channel dark feelings—anger, fear, and the joy of battle—into skill in combat without allowing that darkness to infect the Jedi. Windu is believed to have shared his Vaapad techniques with only two other Jedi—Sora Bulq and Depa Billaba. Both were later lost to the dark side.

BLASTERS

No weapon has done more to shape the galaxy's history than the simple blaster. Countless companies manufacture blasters in all shapes and sizes, with optic scopes, triggers, and handgrips designed for any number of anatomies.

Blasters rely on two components: a gas chamber and a power cell. The chamber is filled with an energy-rich gas; when the blaster is fired, a set amount of this gas is forced

through a conversion enabler, where energy from the power cell excites the gas. The gas, now volatile, then passes through an actuating module, where it is converted to a particle beam, focused through a prismatic crystal or some other device, and emerges from the barrel's emitter nozzle as a bolt of glowing energy. The color of the bolt depends on the gas used and the crystal focusing device.

This basic technology has been adapted to many forms, from small sidearms, pistols, and rifles to artillery cannons and the giant turbolasers aboard warships. Blasters are simple to recharge and require relatively little maintenance to remain effective.

Other weapons are often lumped in with blasters despite having fairly different effects. Disruptors pack a huge amount of gas into each shot, doing far more damage to their targets. Most blasters have a stun setting, which feeds power through a secondary emitter, bypassing the gas chamber to shape an electromagnetic burst that disrupts targets' nervous systems, often leaving them unconscious. (Stun settings must be adjusted for a target's size and physiology: A stun bolt that would drop an Ewok will just annoy a Wookiee.) And ionization blasters are primarily for overloading droid circuitry.

BLASTECH DH-17 BLASTER

Though soldiers trapped in a shootout would swear otherwise, blaster bolts themselves carry no heat. But their displacement of matter produces kinetic energy that causes heat. The atmosphere is superheated by bolts' passage; materials struck by a bolt deform and fuse; and liquids inside physical bodies instantly change state into steam, expanding and doing terrible damage to surrounding tissue. In addition, the conversion enabler heats up as gas is energized by the power pack, and a small amount of ozone is emitted as a trace product of the bolt emerging from the emitter nozzle.

The first blasters were heavy artillery weapons that essentially combined large energy conductors with huge power generators. While capable of doing serious damage to their targets, they were difficult to move, tricky to control, and slow to recharge. As more efficient energy sources were found, blasters became smaller and more practical, finding uses as anti-infantry emplacements and then finally as hand weapons. The ancestors of handheld blasters were beam tubes, which gradually displaced heatbeams and plasma cannons (both of which used lasers to heat plasma) because they were safer to carry and wield and required less maintenance. Beam tubes were replaced by pulse-wave weapons, which were imprecise and lacked range; further improvements resulted in the mass production of weapons similar to modern blasters by 4000 BBY.

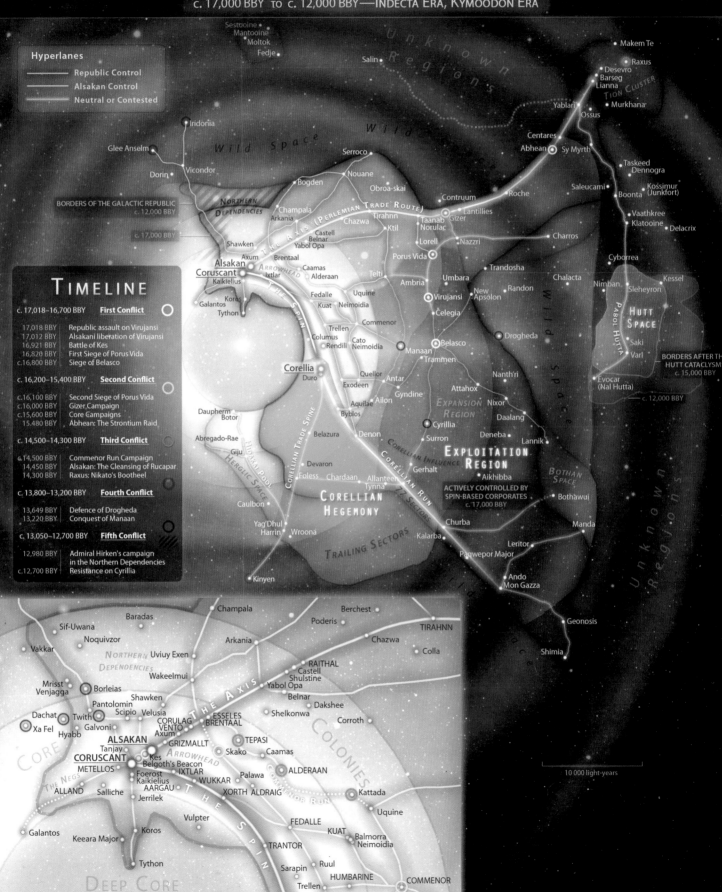

THE ALSAKAN CONFLICTS

The Alsakan Conflicts were a series of ancient clashes for leadership of the Republic between Coruscant and Alsakan, in which fleets of battleships attempted to decide the destiny of civilization. These ancient wars took place on a grand scale, with seventeen separate conflicts extending across 140 centuries. The first began in 17,000 BBY and the last campaigns ended in 3017 BBY.

Historians now generally agree that the Conflicts were an expression of socioeconomic tensions dictated by the geography of the growing Republic. Two major hyperlanes reach outward from Coruscant: the Perlemian Trade Route toward galactic east, and the Corellian Run toward the south. The open-bottomed triangle defined by these space lanes, known as the Slice, is the cradle of galactic civilization, and Coruscant owes its preeminence to its position as the common point from which the two great hyperlanes emerge.

Alsakan is Rimward of Coruscant on the Perlemian, a stopover between the capital and Axum. The sectors along the Perlemian were human-dominated, while the urban worlds of the Corellian Run were home to many species. Amid growing economic and political competition among the Core Worlds, Alsakan became the champion of those human-dominated sectors, which envied Coruscant's privileged position and influence over the worlds of the Run.

Additionally, the Corellian Run continues through Coruscant, becoming the Metellos Trade Route. Together they form a single hyperlane, originally known as the Spin and extending from Duros to Alland, with spurs to systems such as Salliche, Koros, and Kuat. This was the original spine of the early Republic, defining a civilization based on heavily urbanized and bureaucratic megaworlds, where a strong state was seen as the great protector against exploitation and inequality.

But the Perlemian Trade Route is not part of this political geography, and intersects with it only at Coruscant. Instead, the Perlemian's values were defined by those of Alsakan.

The Alsakani did not regard the Republic as the perfection of civilization; they had sought a limited economic and political union. Alsakan was aristocratic in its values, enthusiastic for open spaces and local independence, and cared little for bureaucracy or mass-produced goods except warships and blasters. The ancient Alsakani called the Perlemian the Axis, and their national epic, the *Archaiad,* describes that great route as "an arrow sent into the possible."

If the Axis was the arrow, Alsakan was the archer.

Thus was the young Republic divided between two very different civilizations, each born from a separate hyperlane. And in that uneasy juxtaposition lie the origins of the Alsakan Conflicts. Alsakani younger sons sought distance from authority and established small colonies in the Inner Rim, while the Spin's great trading conglomerates—the Grand Companies—pressed Rimward into the Slice in pursuit of raw materials. The settlement of the Inner Rim around the Perlemian was bolstered by refugees displaced by the Grand Companies' activities.

Around 17,000 BBY, Alsakan led the Axis worlds in moving south to block the Grand Companies, claiming resource-rich systems in the path of their expansion. The Grand Companies objected, and the burly armed freighters of Duros merchant barons clashed with armored Alsakani warships. The Republic backed the Spin merchants, turning a trade war into a shooting war. Eventually, a peace was forced by the Bureau of Ships and Services, which controlled the beacon system on which both sides depended, and threatened to withhold access to the hyperlanes if the war continued.

The Challat Compromise temporarily resolved questions of Senate representation, but Alsakan continued to sponsor settlement across the Slice toward the Run, seeking to seize control of raw materials. With another war seeming inevitable, Corellia—sympathetic to Alsakan but with deep ties to the Companies and the Run—inserted a clause in the Galactic Constitution known as *Contemplanys Hermi,* which gave it the right to recuse itself from the Republic if the two sides reopened hostilities.

The First Alsakan Conflict and its resolution set the pattern for fourteen thousand years of history: Alsakani nobles and Coruscant-backed megacorps competed for resources in the Expansion Region, while Corellia protected its own interests in the farther reaches of the Run but tried to avoid choosing sides, declaring neutrality when the first shots were fired. Each Conflict split the Republic into *three* de facto independent states, sometimes for centuries at a time. The early Conflicts saw repeated attempts to secure a decisive victory using battle fleets, but while both Coruscant and Alsakan were raided, neither system had the military resources to split its forces between attack and defense, and neither wished to leave itself defenseless. The only direct confrontation was the Battle of Kes, a tactical draw fought amid the hyperspace minefields between the two systems.

The clashes prompted a shift in tactics: Squadrons of great battleships became guardians of the Core, while swift cruisers launched raids and protected colonies in the Expansion Region. The cruisers proved their worth during Admiral Hirken's tenacious defense of Alsakani colonies in the Northern Dependencies, which decided the Fifth Conflict. The subsequent campaigns fell into a pattern: raids and ripostes in the colonies, cease-fires in the Core.

Eventually the Conflicts grew less brutal, the periods of peace stretched longer, and after 8000 BBY, new Alsakan Conflicts were considered minor, almost antiquarian diversions. The Seventeenth Conflict saw a final flaring-up of the old tensions, revived by continuing Axis militarism after the Sith Wars of the 3600s. The Republic Navy, under Supreme Chancellor Vedij, now had the superior industrial base to develop a fleet of *Invincible*-class fast battleships, designed to overwhelm Alsakan and Corulag's fleets in a direct assault. The Axis responded with mass-produced squadrons of sublight missile corvettes, which successfully defended the Perlemian systems from Republic raids, but the decisive role was played by the Corellians, who responded to saber-rattling on both sides by constructing a large fleet of long-range frigates.

These ships were originally designed as pickets for Corellia's own battleships, but technological breakthroughs during their construction enabled them to be fitted with fast engines, strong shields, and heavy turbolasers, rendering the massive battleships of both sides obsolete. In 3017 BBY, Corellian privateers inflicted dramatic defeats on squadrons at both Alsakan and Coruscant, leading the Republic to respond by declaring war on Corellia. Republic forces were rapidly outfought, and Prince-Admiral Jonash e Solo dictated a peace treaty at swordpoint on the floor of the Senate. The peace has held ever since.

ZENITH OF THE REPUBLIC

"Give me ground troops supported by airpower with supply lines guarded by the navy, and I'll promise you anything. Give me anything else and all I can do is my best."
—Alix Balan, general, Galactic Empire

THE REPUBLIC NAVY

The Republic was founded without a standing navy, for fear that the military would become a tool of powerful Core worlds and their interests. Originally, each Republic system maintained its own military and was expected to contribute warships and personnel to the common defense if a sufficiently dangerous enemy materialized.

A centralized navy was created to defeat the Tionese—according to navy lore, its headquarters was located on Foerost, the young Republic's greatest and best-defended shipyard. But this navy was largely disbanded after the Tionese War, and the Core Worlds' Senators resisted calls for its revival during the First Alsakan Conflict, reasoning that two powerful Core worlds fighting over colonies and commercial possessions was bad, but the prospect of civil war was worse.

As before, it was a threat from without that eroded the opposition to a centralized military. In the Duinuogwuin Contention of 15,550 BBY, Star Dragons assaulted Coruscant and feuding among Republic member worlds slowed the necessary military response. The Contention passed relatively quickly, but was followed by an era of dizzying expansion. The Republic's borders now abutted those of the powerful Herglic Trade Empire, with peaceful relations by no means assured. And beyond the frontier lurked raiders and slavers. The Mid Rim in the Slice proved particularly dangerous: Republic colonists were now perilously near Hutt territory, and many died at the hands of Hutt vassals or vanished into slavery.

Around 15,000 BBY the Senate finally heeded the pleas of outlying worlds, voting to restore the armed forces and place them under the control of the Senate and the Chancellor. The restoration of the navy was an immediate boon to shipyards and starship manufacturers across the Republic, sparking advances in hyperdrive and turbolaser technology. Some of the galaxy's best-known shipwrights originated in this era, and Anaxes, Byblos, Abhean, and Allanteen emerged as major naval hubs.

The new navy moved aggressively, defending colonies and commerce and taking the fight beyond the frontier—though few records have survived, naval songs still speak of brave deeds during conflicts at Esaga, Caulbon, and the Sundered Veil. The navy would become a tool of the Pius Dea theocrats after 12,000 BBY, then join with the Jedi in overthrowing Contispex XIX, helping restore some of the service's honor. As the Republic rebuilt, the navy became a pillar of its strength, and one of the galaxy's most respected institutions.

CONTISPEX'S CRUSADES

The man known to history as Contispex I was born on Coruscant and rose to prominence in the Coruscant Merchants' Guild, becoming legendary for his devotion to the Pius Dea faith, his opposition to corruption and vice, and his intolerance for any who didn't share his high standards. Such a man was deemed a natural for cleaning up the Senate; he was elected Chancellor after the impeachment and assassination of Chancellor Pers'lya of Bothawui in 11,987 BBY. Contispex would be chancellor for some forty years, and by the time he stepped down in favor of his son Contispex II, Pius Dea fanatics effectively controlled the Republic.

Admiral Hirken defends the Northern Dependencies during the Fifth Alsakan Conflict (Darren Tan)

CONTISPEX'S CRUSADES

c. 12,000 BBY to c. 11,000 BBY—PIUS DEA ERA

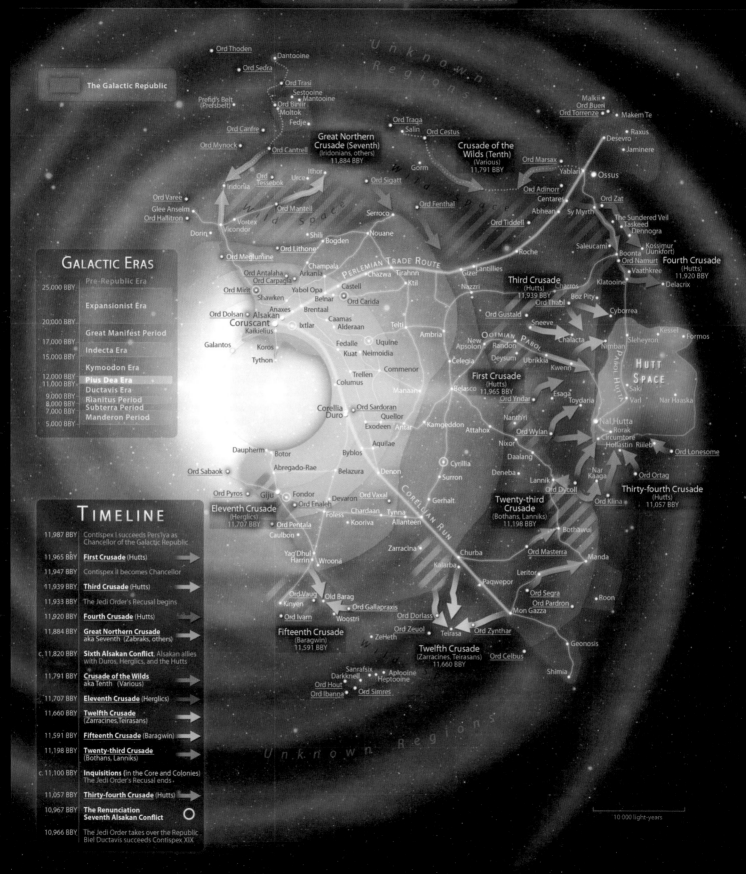

The Galactic Republic

GALACTIC ERAS

25,000 BBY	Pre-Republic Era
	Expansionist Era
20,000 BBY	
	Great Manifest Period
17,000 BBY	
15,000 BBY	Indecta Era
	Kymoodon Era
12,000 BBY	Pius Dea Era
11,000 BBY	Ductavis Era
9,000 BBY	Rianitus Period
8,000 BBY	Subterra Period
7,000 BBY	Manderon Period
5,000 BBY	

TIMELINE

11,987 BBY	Contispex I succeeds Pers'lya as Chancellor of the Galactic Republic
11,965 BBY	**First Crusade** (Hutts)
11,947 BBY	Contispex II becomes Chancellor
11,939 BBY	**Third Crusade** (Hutts)
11,933 BBY	The Jedi Order's Recusal begins
11,920 BBY	**Fourth Crusade** (Hutts)
11,884 BBY	**Great Northern Crusade** aka Seventh (Zabraks, others)
c. 11,820 BBY	**Sixth Alsakan Conflict**, Alsakan allies with Duros, Herglics, and the Hutts
11,791 BBY	**Crusade of the Wilds** aka Tenth (Various)
11,707 BBY	**Eleventh Crusade** (Herglics)
11,660 BBY	**Twelfth Crusade** (Zarracines, Teirasans)
11,591 BBY	**Fifteenth Crusade** (Baragwin)
11,198 BBY	**Twenty-third Crusade** (Bothans, Lanniks)
c. 11,100 BBY	**Inquisitions** (in the Core and Colonies) The Jedi Order's Recusal ends
11,057 BBY	**Thirty-fourth Crusade** (Hutts)
10,967 BBY	**The Renunciation** Seventh Alsakan Conflict
10,966 BBY	The Jedi Order takes over the Republic. Biel Ductavis succeeds Contispex XIX

Great Northern Crusade (Seventh) (Iridonians, others) 11,884 BBY

Crusade of the Wilds (Tenth) (Various) 11,791 BBY

Third Crusade (Hutts) 11,939 BBY

Fourth Crusade (Hutts) 11,920 BBY

First Crusade (Hutts) 11,965 BBY

Twenty-third Crusade (Bothans, Lanniks) 11,198 BBY

Thirty-fourth Crusade (Hutts) 11,057 BBY

Eleventh Crusade (Herglics) 11,707 BBY

Fifteenth Crusade (Baragwin) 11,591 BBY

Twelfth Crusade (Zarracines, Teirasans) 11,660 BBY

10 000 light-years

Pius Dea rose on Coruscant centuries before Contispex's time, and began with a call for communities to remain incorruptible by policing themselves. Under Contispex, the Pius Dea faith began teaching that fallen communities should be restored to purity by purging their unredeemable elements. Before a millennium of madness had ended, such purgings would take the form of endless wars, and numerous alien species would be judged unredeemable and exterminated.

Contispex I launched the first of his Crusades in 11,965 BBY —a preemptive strike against the Hutts beyond the Rim. Under his dynastic successors, dozens of crusades would follow, all launched with the Pius Dea rallying cry of "The Goddess Wills It!" While the Hutts were the first targets, other alien civilizations followed—until the paladins of Pius Dea turned against species whose loyalty to the Republic was unquestioned, and finally on human cultures accused of collaborating with hostile aliens.

Contispex I's overhaul of the Republic government gave fellow adherents the levers of economic and military power, and quickly purged all those who refused to convert to the ways of the Goddess. Within a generation, important government posts were reserved for members of the Pius Dea hierarchy; within two or three generations, many posts had become hereditary, with government duties becoming ritualized expressions of Pius Dea power. By the last centuries of the Pius Dea period, every new Chancellor took the name Contispex upon attaining office, whether he was a member of the bloodline or not.

Once the Pius Dea were secure at the top of the Republic ranks, they sought to purify the galaxy. Witch hunts exposed alien partisans in the Senate, and commissars were attached to military units to root out heretics and apostates. The Proscribed were exiled or imprisoned, their property confiscated for pontifical auction, and their families blacklisted from political or military life for three generations, breaking the power of many ancient Republic dynasties.

To Pius Dea adherents, chaos lurked beyond the Rim, and the will of the Goddess was that it be beaten back, with great treasures and secrets awaiting those who advanced Her cause. Pius Dea scouts pushed beyond the frontier, and many an intrepid star-sailor made a name and a fortune privateering for the Pius Dea.

Like most Republic institutions, the navy became a Pius Dea stronghold. Although the cult had originated with humans, as the struggle dragged on thousands of "Rimkin" planets were converted at blasterpoint and became servants of the Goddess. Defeated populations could retain autonomy through conversion, and individuals could move freely between worlds if they joined the military. While in theory people pledged allegiance to the Republic and its Chancellor, in practice they were beholden to their superiors in the Pius Dea hierarchy. By the 11,500s Pius Dea cathedral ships darkened the skies of millions of worlds, commanded by missionaries and crewed by descendants of their original naval crews. Though these great warships were destroyed or vanished into trackless space long ago, names such as *Illorbion's Hammer,* the *Shining Pathway,* and *Glory of Kamgeddon* still evoke dread on worlds they once imprisoned.

Pius Dea cathedrals were also centerpieces of the Republic's new Ordnance/Regional Depots along the frontier. O/RDs served as home bases from which naval units and missionaries alike pushed beyond the frontier into alien chaos, with the plunder of countless infidel worlds ferried back to Coruscant in the bellies of navy galleons. When existing worlds were revealed as impure, or new founts of chaos were found, the navy would advance and deploy troops by the millions. Those who emerged alive from the grinder of trench warfare had demonstrated their purity, winning great rewards for themselves and their families; those who died had their impurities washed away by sacrifice. Meanwhile, in the skies above, primitive bi-wing snubfighters fought intricate duels and armored men-o-war exchanged broadsides in deep space.

The Jedi Order struggled to find the right response to the madness of Pius Dea rule. In 11,933 BBY it declared itself no longer subject to Republic rule, retreating to Ossus and its academies. The Recusal set off centuries of recrimination and debate within the Order's ranks, and saw the birth of numerous splinter factions. Some Jedi became knights errant, carrying out unsanctioned missions against the cultists while the Order looked the other way. A misguided few became Pius Dea champions, and after the Crusades ended this splinter group would survive as the fanatical Order of the Terrible Glare. But most Jedi sat out the Crusades, despising the Pius Dea cause but unwilling to take up arms against the civilization they had safeguarded.

In the end, the Pius Dea order was thrown down by an unlikely alliance. The Alsakani and many of the worlds they controlled had seceded from the Republic in the 11,820s BBY, with vulnerable worlds near the Perlemian begging Alsakan for protection. (The Sixth Alsakan Conflict was a vicious war between Alsakan and the Pius Dea Republic.) In resisting the Republic, the Alsakani opened secret lines of communication with the Duros, the Herglics, and even the Hutts.

By the 11,100s BBY the Crusades' forward momentum

had finally stalled, and the Goddess's purifying gaze turned inward. Inquisitions tore through the Colonies and the Core itself, with the impure tried, condemned, and destroyed in mass trials. But at the same time, a desperate plan was taking shape. The Caamasi came to Ossus, pleading with the Jedi Order to abandon its centuries of Recusal. The Jedi agreed: To save the galaxy, they would remove the Chancellor, suspend the Senate, and take over the Republic. But they would need help. And so a secret faith began to spread among the Pius Dea adherents, a heresy masterminded by the Caamasi and stoked by Alsakani and Jedi agents.

In 10,967 BBY, the heretics declared themselves and the Pius Dea ranks were sundered by the Renunciation. Generational warships, O/RDs, and government offices witnessed terrible battles between the Faithful and the Renunciates. Alsakani battle cruisers attacked Pius Dea strongholds at Ixtlar, Fondor, and Cyrillia, backed by Jedi privateers and vessels commanded by Herglic, Duros, and Hutt slave species. The fight for the Republic had begun.

A year later, it was over. The Bureau of Ships and Services was one of the few galactic institutions that had not been taken over by the Pius Dea faith. The bureau's hierophants had also heard the Caamasi plea, and agreed to abandon their traditional neutrality. To purge the galaxy of the disease that was devouring it, the bureau secretly seeded Pius Dea warships with rogue navicomputer code. When BoSS sent out the signal, thousands upon thousands of Pius Dea warships leapt into hyperspace, never to be seen again.

The ships of the Pius Dea vanguard, however, emerged at Uquine, under the guns of a vast fleet of Renunciate battleships. Caught unawares, with their offensive and defensive systems inoperable, the helpless cathedral ships were methodically destroyed. The Jedi seized Contispex XIX on the bridge of the *Flame of Sinthara;* the last Pius Dea Chancellor was tried on Caamas and imprisoned there, denied all contact with his dwindling followers. Meanwhile, the Jedi did as they had promised, rebuilding the Senate and the Republic under the leadership of Biel Ductavis, who served simultaneously as the Supreme Chancellor and the Jedi Grand Master.

Within a few generations, the Pius Dea faith survived only on cathedral ships that had emerged in trackless space with their navicomputers wiped clean and their supralight engines and communications systems disabled. Aboard these doomed vessels, the Faithful were free to pursue their mad dreams of purity while crawling toward distant suns they would never reach.

ARMORY AND SENSOR PROFILE

PLANETARY DEFENSES

Every new starhopper is struck by the apparent fragility of a friendly world as seen from space—against the void, planets seem terribly small and vulnerable.

But planetary atmospheres are actually excellent insulators and defenses in their own right: For eons, no capital ship had weapons powerful enough to inflict sustained damage to targets on a planet's surface from space. That changed around 10,000 BBY, when the Kumauri Empire deployed planet-buster battleships with mass drivers that turned asteroids into missiles for bombarding worlds. (The Kumauri's advances in targeting are less remembered, but were arguably more important to this tactic's success.)

After the defeat of the Kumauri, planet-busting mass drivers became part of the Republic arsenal and a grim new tactic in the endless war between Coruscant and Alsakan, culminating in the Osara Mundicide during the Tenth Alsakan Conflict. The fear of bombardment, in turn, sparked rapid advances in defensive technologies and planet-based weapons that could keep capital ships at bay. Worlds that could do so deployed planetary shields beginning in the 9400s BBY. The first such shields were "encasing shields," so called because they formed solid walls of defensive energy, with no possibility of opening a gap through which ships could come and go or ground-based weapons could be fired. It wasn't until the Mandalorian Wars of the 3900s BBY that reliable "shutter shields" were deployed.

Of course, a primeval maxim of warfare is that the best defense is a good offense. While planetary defenses have a visceral appeal to galactic citizens, military leaders counsel that the best course of action is to keep hostile capital ships far away, where they can be dealt with by fleets. Failing that, planets with sufficient credits can buy ground-based weaponry that would give even a battleship's commander pause.

The first planet-based weapons were gigantic particle cannons derived from Kumauri and Alsakani designs, and predated the spread of planetary shields. These hypervelocity cannons were largely supplanted by turbolasers in the centuries after their initial development, but received a new lease on life after the introduction of effective defensive shielding for warships in the 7700s BBY, and have remained a common planetary defense ever since.

Planetary turbolasers, first commonly deployed in the 9200s BBY, fire immense bursts of energy through a planetary atmosphere into space, getting targeting information from orbiting satellites or warships. Because planetary turbolasers are essentially immobile and slow to select new targets and fire, worlds seeking effective protection must construct networks of these hugely expensive weapons. During the Imperial era, Kuat Drive Yards' w-165 turbolaser was the best known of these weapons.

KUAT DRIVE YARDS W-165 TURBOLASER

KUAT DRIVE YARDS V-150 PLANET DEFENDER

Another effective weapon is the ground-based ion cannon, which can disable the electrical systems of a warship in orbit.

As with planetary turbolasers, ground-based ion cannons are expensive, fixed-position emplacements that are difficult to target and slow to reload. During the Galactic Civil War, Hoth's Rebels defended Echo Base with a massive Kuat Drive Yards v-150 Planet Defender.

TRACTOR BEAMS

A tractor beam is simply a reversed repulsorlift drive. A repulsorlift drive generates an antigravity field, allowing a repulsorlift-equipped device to push off the ground and float in the air—a simple trick of hyperphysics demonstrated for schoolchildren on every reasonably advanced world. The tractor effect is similar in principle, but the field is used to grab and attract a smaller object. Tractor beams do everything from guiding starships into docking bays to snatching debris out of traffic lanes. And, of course, they're used to immobilize starships so they can be boarded—or destroyed.

Space tugs and docking bays use simple "point-and-pull" tractor systems, but a military tractor beam is meant to be used against moving targets that do not want to be captured. As such, military tractor beams require both the raw power to snare a fleeing spaceship and the precise aim to lock on to a small and agile target. Over the millennia, there has been a tug-of-war between tractor emplacements' sensors and beam strength and countermeasures taken by the small ships pursued.

Large starships typically house their tractor beam projectors in rotating turrets known as emitter towers. Imperial Star Destroyers, for instance, boasted ten Phylon Q7 projectors capable of arresting the motion of ships as large as Corellian corvettes. Because such emplacements require a large amount of space, ample power, and constant maintenance, capital ships are generally required for tractor interception operations.

Sometimes, of course, space and power are abundantly available. The first Death Star had more than seven hundred tractor beam projectors, enough to bring a dozen to bear on a target from any single point. Each of the Death Star's projectors was coupled to its main reactor at seven different locations to provide a steady flow of energy; when one of those links was severed, systems designed to prevent an overload spiral shut down the projector, allowing the *Millennium Falcon* to leave the station and race beyond the range of the tractor beam network.

An ancient tactic remains devastatingly effective against tractor beam emplace-ments: The target releases a decoy, ideally a proton torpedo or space mine, and then swerves sharply away. Unwary tractor beam operators will snare the bomb, and quickly find their emitters blasted into scrap.

XIM'S *EIBON SCIMITAR*

ALSAKAN'S *ATGEIR*-CLASS BATTLECRUISER

CAPITAL SHIPS

The galaxy has a dizzying number of ship-classification systems. Individual species, cultures, governments, and shipbuilders frequently follow their own contradictory classifications, and ship names are used and reused for vessels with very different capabilities and sizes. But whether the classification system is that of Kuat Drive Yards, the Lantillian Spacers' Brotherhood, or the Bureau of Ships and Services, all at least agree on this much: A capital ship is a military starship one hundred meters or more in length.

Every historical era has seen capital ships deployed, but ships larger than light cruisers have come in and out of favor over the millennia, with their perceived usefulness dependent on advances in the technology of interstellar warfare and changes in strategic philosophy.

The first great capital ship was the *Eibon Scimitar*, the legendary flagship of Xim the Despot, destroyed at Vontor. While popularly portrayed as a gargantuan ship, and an inspiration for capital ship designs for eons, military historians generally agree the *Scimitar* would be considered a heavy cruiser at best under the Anaxes War College system.

The galaxy's first capital ships used guided missiles, torpedo launchers and microwave lasers for offense. Such arsenals were countered by point-defense missiles, clouds of charged particles to diffuse energy weapons, and thin armor plating treated with reflective hull coatings such as kiirium. Ancient starships employed ray and particle shields for defense, but these early shields demanded so much power that they were impractical for all but the largest ships as a defense against offensive weapons. When early warship captains thought of defense, they thought of armor.

Alsakan's *Atgeir*-class battlecruisers were renowned for their supposedly impregnable shields, generated from crowns of dagger-like shield generators. But such ships were expensive to build and of little strategic use against fleets of cheaper, more nimble craft. In the early Alsakan Conflicts, Alsakan's great warships were chiefly used for home defense and triumphant but hollow tours of colonies; Coruscant rarely bothered with large capital ships during the Conflicts, with the *Gilagimar* a famous exception that proved the rule.

After the Duinuogwuin Contention, the Republic encountered few opponents with large warships, and so had little use for large capital ships— a better bet, strategically speaking, was to deploy speedy gunships that could escort merchant transports and colony ships. The next widespread use of large capital ships came around 10,000 BBY, when the Republic was briefly provoked by the rise of the Kumauri Empire.

The young conquerer Vall Kumauri had built a small fleet of massive battleships armed with mass drivers that used asteroids for bombarding planets. The Kumauri design was copied by the Republic, and planet-buster battleships cowed or destroyed several hostile civilizations encountered in the Republic's relentless expansion, as well as emerging as terror weapons in the Tenth Alsakan Conflict before advances in planetary shielding largely eliminated the threat of bombardment. But the Kumauri's most enduring contribution was the use of the alloy madilon to make smaller, more efficient hyperdrives; the production of synthetic madilon allowed starships to make longer jumps across the galaxy's network of jump beacons.

The Waymancy Storm of 7811 BBY led to the next major wave of technological innovation. First contact between the Republic and the warships of the Waymancy Hollow ended with the Republic ships torn apart by fusillades of laserfire: The Waymancy energy weapons were more powerful and had much faster rates of fire than anything the Republic could bring to bear, a product of the Sisters of the Machinesmith's extremely efficient power generators. After Waymancy's defeat, the Sif-Alulan process was reverse-engineered, with the Verpine master crafter Lyns Skutroo unveiling the squintpipe process in the 7700s.

The improvements in energy weapons fueled a brief period in which rapid-fire turbolasers outclassed all available defenses—even the ray shields of big capital ships collapsed under the combination of heavy impacts and rapid fire. That caused tacticians to reject capital ships in favor of swarms of gunships that could overwhelm opponents, and led to a search for stronger hull armor, with vacierite replacing kiirium. In the 7500s BBY, further refinements of the squintpipe process produced shields that were stronger and quicker to regenerate, and shield generators became small enough to generate protective fields around small starships. Reliable deflector shields were no longer just for battle wagons.

The squintpipe process sparked a golden age of warship construction, with shipwrights across the galaxy seeking to use improvements in shielding, armor, energy weapons, hyperdrive, and power generation to the best advantage. Capital ships reemerged as the mainstays of not only the

Republic military and its powerful sector fleets, but also militaries maintained by countless small dominions and pocket kingdoms beyond the Republic's borders. The wars between the Republic and the two-pronged threat of the Sith Empire and the Mandalorians were marked by titanic clashes between the largest warships yet seen in the galaxy.

The battleship era ended in the 2500s BBY amid economic strains, as tacticians came to prefer fleets of smaller cruisers. The Ruusan Reformations were a relief to a galaxy exhausted by centuries of war. The Republic Navy was disbanded in favor of a return to Planetary Security Forces, and capital-ship construction ebbed as peace settled over the Republic. For centuries after Ruusan, capital ships larger than light cruisers were rare and deemed extravagant.

That peace would last for nearly a thousand years, but by the end of this time the Republic was crumbling. The Hutts held economic dominion over a large chunk of the Slice, and much of the Outer Rim was effectively ungoverned. Unnerved by a resurgence of piracy, slavery, and lawlessness, worlds such as Kuat began building new capital ships for their sector fleets, as did mercantile powers like the Trade Federation and the Banking Clan. With more and more systems worried about defense and the Senate's Militarists pushing for the restoration of a centralized military, shipyards across the galaxy began turning out new warship designs, some of massive scale.

When the Clone Wars exploded, both the Republic and the Confederacy of Independent Systems deployed war fleets anchored by deadly new battleships. The Empire inherited not one but two military-industrial complexes, and ushered in an age in which capital ships grew more massive than ever before.

KUMAURI PLANET-BUSTER BATTLESHIP

OLD REPUBLIC—ERA SITH *HARROWER*-CLASS DREADNOUGHT

CLONE WARS—ERA TRADE FEDERATION CAPITAL SHIP *INVISIBLE HAND*

THE ANAXES WAR COLLEGE SYSTEM

During the Clone Wars, the reborn Republic Navy War College adopted—after sometimes fractious debate—a new classification system for capital ships, which became the standard used by naval officers in the Republic, Empire, New Republic, and Galactic Federation.

CORVETTE:
100-200 meters

FRIGATE:
200-400 meters

1 KILOMETER

CRUISER:
400-600 meters

HEAVY CRUISER:
600-1,000 meters

STAR DESTROYER:
1,000-2,000 meters

1 KILOMETER

BATTLECRUISER:
2,000-5,000 meters

DREADNOUGHT:
5,000 meters and above

1 KILOMETER

The Anaxes classifications superseded the system used by the Judicial Forces and Planetary Security Forces since the Ruusan Reformations. The largest class recognized by that system was the Cruiser, reflecting the Ruusan restrictions on warships larger than six hundred meters. By the time the Clone Wars erupted, many rich sectors had commissioned much larger warships for their defense, making Cruiser an increasingly meaningless class.

Ships smaller than one hundred meters were officially classified as Space Transports, and Starfighters were given their own class. Mindful of what had happened with the Cruiser class, the Anaxes architects extended their classification system to account for the possibility of truly gigantic warships.

The most controversial aspect of the new system was the inclusion of the Kuat Drive Yards designation Star Destroyer, which purists rejected as a corporate marque. But after heated argument, Star Destroyer was adopted, with analysts noting that commanders in the newly reconstituted navy had already fallen into the habit of referring to large new Republic and even Separatist warships by that name.

The system's architects also adopted a shorthand for use during engagements, one that lumped warships of different classes together based on their size and capability. Corvettes, space transports and starships acting as warships in-theater were designated as *gunships,* Frigates and lighter Cruisers—the workhorses of most military engagements—were ID'd as *cruisers,* and big ships of the line whose mere presence could change the course of a battle were referred to as *battleships.*

The Anaxes classifications were flexible, with warships sometimes moved up or down a class based on their armament or intended role. And veterans of other traditions sometimes persisted in using their own terminology, particularly during the heat of battle.

ION WEAPONS

Whether the weapon in question is a blaster designed to stop droids in their tracks or a cannon that can leave a Star Destroyer dead in space, ion weapons use the same principles: A burst of electromagnetic energy is amplified by ion accelerators to create a bolt that overloads electrical systems, tripping circuitry protectors and sometimes melting fuses and delicate connectors. Machinery hit by an ion blast must shut down to avoid permanent damage.

Ion and electromagnetic weapons have been part of galactic arsenals for millennia. Such weapons have mostly been used against vehicles and warships, though their usefulness is limited in ground combat because ion particles scatter, often causing collateral damage to friendly forces. Shipboard defenses against ion weapons include efforts to shield circuitry, pulse-modulated circuits, and cap drains designed to channel electromagnetic radiation away from vulnerable systems and dissipate

JAWA'S ION BLASTER

it harmlessly. Such weapons reached the apex of their development in the Clone Wars, when General Grievous's *Malevolence* boasted two powerful ion pulse cannons that could turn a good chunk of a Republic task force into scrap.

While shipboard and ground-based ion cannons are ancient, ion hand weapons first saw widespread use on the battlefield after the Great Droid Revolt of 4015 BBY.

Ion blasters proved useful during the Mandalorian Wars, disrupting the raiders' technology, and electromagnetic weapons were a mainstay of the Clone Wars, when clone troopers routinely carried "droid poppers," formally known as EMP grenades. The Battle of Malastare turned on the use of an experimental electro-proton bomb by Republic forces. Elsewhere, even pacifists such as Mandalore's Duchess Satine carried deactivator pistols that could short-circuit droids and disorient living enemies. And scavengers such as Tatooine's Jawas use jury-rigged ion blasters to immobilize droids that they can resell.

THE *MALEVOLENCE'S* ION PULSE CANNON

WARS WITH THE SITH

> "Never interrupt your opponent while he is making a mistake."
> —Firmus Nantz, admiral, New Republic

THE GREAT HYPERSPACE WAR

In 5000 BBY an armada of alien warships launched an unprovoked attack on the Koros system. This marked the end of two thousand years of peace—and introduced the galaxy to the Sith.

The reason for the attack was brutally simple: The supreme Sith Lord, Darth Naga Sadow, had discovered a secret hyperlane leading directly from his Outer Rim despotate into the peaceful systems of the Republic. The route had been revealed to him by a naïve exile from Koros whom Sadow now proclaimed as "liberator" of his home system—a liberator accompanied by a brutal Sith occupation force.

The Republic scouts Gav and Jori Daragon had blazed that hyperspace trail from the Core to Sith Space, discovering an empire in crisis. The distances separating the far-flung Sith baronies had eroded technological knowledge and choked off economic development. The old aristocracy had been replaced by brutal half-caste warriors, who emulated the ancient kings with self-destructive quests for absolute power. And the distant Republic was rumored to be plotting the overthrow of the Sith, to impose alien laws and the religious tenets of the Jedi Order.

Sadow, viceroy of Khar Shian—who was raised from birth to fight these threats—taught that only ruthlessness could save his civilization. He had rebuilt his military, reinforcing traditional missile frigates with battleships and starfighters. Massassi warriors now carried blaster rifles alongside their traditional bardiches, and blaster turrets crowned the backs of their elephantine cavalry. The lesser barons' levies were still dominated by tribal spearmen—but so were the armies of Republic outliers like Kirrek and Nazzri. Besides, throwing disks could skim through deflector shields, and war beasts could stride where armored vehicles could not.

When the Daragon twins arrived, Sadow kidnapped them, murdered his own Sith mentor to frame the Jedi for the crime, and created an invasion scare that secured his election as supreme viceroy of the Sith Empire. He then lured his rival Ludo Kressh into a trap, corrupted Gav Daragon with Sith training, and tricked Jori into returning to Koros aboard her scoutship—blazing a path for his armada to follow.

From their bridgehead at Koros, Sith raiding squadrons attacked Shawken, Metellos, and Basilisk, spreading panic and making defending fleets dance in response. But Sadow had reserved the most brutal attack for Coruscant itself.

An army of Massassi landed in Galactic City—barbaric, red-skinned alien slaves, bred for war and armed with spears and throwing disks. At their head rode Sadow's chief lieutenant, Shar Dakhon—a feudal lord in gilded armor, mounted on a mighty war beast. Their brutal attack on the Senate Building was made possible by battle meditation, a dark Force technique that gave the warriors suicidal strength, and conjured fearful fantasies in the minds of their opponents.

Eventually the Republic turned back the dark tide. Its fleets developed flanking maneuvers that proved effective against the Sith frigates, while on Kirrek and Thokos, Jedi leadership enabled the defenders to drive off Sith invasions. On Cinnagar, Gav Daragon was confronted by his twin sister—and, realizing the error of his ways, surrendered to

the Republic. The Sith had lost control of their bridgehead in the Core.

Facing defeat, Sadow pulled back most of his combat warships to Goluud, hoping to ambush the Republic there. But Gav Daragon martyred himself to give the Republic another key victory. Utterly defeated, Sadow retreated to his Outer Rim throneworld of Korriban. At that point, the Sith armada apparently broke into squabbling factions—for when the pursuing Republic fleets arrived, they found the wreckage left by a great space battle.

With their missile tubes empty, the battered survivors of the Sith armada lacked the firepower to resist the Republic's turbolasers. Sadow fled, leaving an overmatched remnant to fight a doomed battle in defense of Korriban. With the armada destroyed and Sadow deposed, Chancellor Pultimo authorized a full-scale invasion—and Sith Space was liberated from its tyrannical ruling caste.

WAR AND THE MANDALORIANS

Excerpted from "Industry, Honor, Savagery: Shaping the Mandalorian Soul," keynote address by Vilnau Teupt, 412th Proceedings of Galactic Anthropology and History, Brentaal Academy, 24 ABY:

After being driven from ancient Coruscant, the Taungs relocated to Roon and then wandered the Outer Rim, leaving hints of their passage in various species' chronicles and histories. But they attracted little notice until they conquered Mandalore around 7000 BBY.

At the time, Mandalore lay beyond the galactic frontier—but close to the Republic's outlying trade routes. Soon, rumors reached the Republic of worlds ruled by ferocious warriors. They served the god Kad Ha'rangir, whose tests and trials forced change and growth upon the clans he chose to be his people. In opposition to Kad Ha'rangir stood the sloth-god Arasuum, who sought to tempt the clans and drag them down into stagnation and idle consumption. By waging war in Kad Ha'rangir's name and according to strict religious laws, the Mandalorian Crusaders defied Arasuum and showed themselves worthy of favor.

The Crusaders fought the Mandallian Giants at Mandalore, but were so impressed with their prowess in battle that they agreed to coexist, and in time would admit them into their clans. They raided Fenel, a powerful, isolationist world known for its shipwrights and technologists, culminating with the Fenelar's extinction by the 6700s BBY. Armed with Fenelar technology, the Mandalorians then turned their attention to the Tlönians, a vicious arachnoid species known for their poison-sacs and habit of preying on ships foolish enough to stray beyond the frontier. Tlön was depopulated and incinerated by the 6100s BBY. Other worlds were spared: The Jakelians, for one, welcomed their new Mandalorian overlords, as did knots of worlds populated by humans centered on Concord Dawn and Gargon. Those worlds—along with the likes of Hrthging, Breshig, Shogun, and Ordo—became part of Mandalorian Space.

The Republic kept a wary eye on the Mandalorians, lest the Crusaders turn their attention Coreward to Nouane, the Obroa-skai region, and the wealthy trade worlds of the Great Tirahnn Loop. But while Crusaders did harry Republic settlements—sparking such skirmishes as the Pathandr Fury in 5451 BBY and the Nakat Incursions of the 5130s BBY—for the most part they remained beyond the frontier, pursuing their own mysterious missions.

The few Republic traders who knew Mandalorian Space had an unsettling message for the Republic: While the clans were given to jostling and quarreling, all heeded the commands of the clan leader, known as the Mandalore. And despite their nomadic ways, they were great tinkerers and canny technologists, improving Fenelar warships, Jakelian edged weapons, and even Republic rocket packs.

The final years of the fifth millennium BBY brought a Taung religious reformation. Instead of worshipping Kad Ha'rangir, the Taungs elevated war itself to the pinnacle of their cosmology—to make war was effectively to be divine. The reasons for this momentous change are imperfectly understood, but Mandalorian legend holds that the clan leader known as Mandalore the Indomitable had a vision while on the mysterious world of Shogun, returning to the clans with word of the revelation he'd received.

Soon after this reformation, the Crusaders

Sith and Republic warships clash above Coruscant (John VanFleet)

raided the galaxy's central systems. In 4024 BBY they attacked the planet Nevoota in the Colonies, exterminating its species during a three-year campaign. In 4017 BBY, Crusaders appeared in the Core Worlds, waging war against the inhabitants of Basilisk. Overrun, the Basiliskans seeded their own world with toxins to deny it to the Crusaders, who abandoned it but took numerous Lagartoz War Dragons, Basilisk warships, and war droids for their own use. Then, in 4002 BBY, the Crusaders ravaged the Deep Core world of Kuar, setting up camps there.

The Crusaders' next target was the carbonite-rich Empress Teta system—but fate had other plans. In 3996 BBY the fallen Jedi Knight Ulic Qel-Droma challenged Mandalore the Indomitable to single combat at Kuar. Qel-Droma defeated the clan leader, who agreed to serve him and his Sith master, Exar Kun.

No one will ever know what the Crusaders' plan was before Qel-Droma seized control of the Mandalorians' destiny, but the goal of Qel-Droma and Kun was simple: destroy the Republic and its Jedi. Serving the Sith, Crusaders riding Basilisk war droids stormed the Republic shipyards at Foerost, then invaded Coruscant in their stolen warships.

Mandalore the Indomitable was certainly true to his word: He helped rescue Qel-Droma from Coruscant after Aleema Keto betrayed him, then led his Crusaders to Onderon, where Basilisks and Onderonian beast-riders clashed in the skies. A Republic fleet raced to Onderon's rescue, forcing Mandalore the Indomitable into a risky retreat across an atmospheric bridge from Onderon to the moon Dxun.

The clan leader died in the attempt, but the Crusader who found his ceremonial mask (thus becoming the new Mandalore) was even more dangerous.

Mandalore the Ultimate had seen many battles and knew his fellow Mandalorian Crusaders were brave and skilled. But the new Taung clan leader wondered how much that mattered. His people remained a fractious society of restless adventure seekers, with little to show for their efforts but stolen technologies and a slice of space on the outskirts of the Republic.

There was a better way, and Mandalore the Ultimate was determined to find it. The defeated Crusaders returned to Mandalorian Space to learn that their leader had received a new vision on Shogun: From now on, non-Taungs who proved themselves in battle and upheld the Mandalorian warrior code were full members of the clans.

Moreover, the Crusaders would no longer simply pillage worlds and move on like some terrible storm. Now they would hold the territory they conquered, creating an industrial society based on warrior codes. Warriors would rule, supported by farmers, artisans, and manufacturers who accepted their place in the Mandalorian hierarchy, with slaves and those without honor below them.

Mandalore the Ultimate's decision swelled the clans' ranks with humans, Mandallians, Jakelians, and other Mandalorian vassals. Now the clan leader sent his Neo-Crusaders outward, conquering a swath of worlds between the Republic's borders, pockets of Republic colonial space, and the Tion. The Neo-Crusaders found rich worlds for Mandalore's growing empire, and billions of recruits: Hrakians, Elomin, Tiss'shar, Pho Ph'eahians, Togruta, Drackmarians, Thalassians, Nalroni, and Zygerrians.

The Sith War had left Republic authority largely theoretical beyond Centares; Mandalorian warships moved freely through the Tion, and began harassing the outlying worlds of the Hutts. Meanwhile, the Mandalorians were rapidly building warships at Breshig and Arda, utilizing vast caches of war matériel stolen during the Sith Wars from Foerost and Abhean.

In 3976 BBY a fleet of Neo-Crusader warships stormed Althir III, an industrialized world that gave Mandalore the Ultimate another productive planet for his war machine. Three years later the Mandalorians brutally subjugated Cathar, killing more than 90 percent of its population.

Alarmed, the Republic mobilized naval forces to guard Dxun, where clans of Mandalorians maintained a defiant stronghold, and to protect Taris and its neighbors along the Mandalorian Road. A motley if industrious city-world, Taris wasn't a member of the Republic, but possessed extensive trade ties with the worlds of the Northern Dependencies. (It would be admitted to the Republic in 3966 BBY.)

droids. Unprepared for such firepower, the Republic failed to hold the line. Serroco was scoured by nuclear fire, and Neo-Crusaders ravaged Nouane, whose elegant civilization and ancient mastery of statecraft epitomized all they despised.

All three offensives would fail, but it was a near thing. To galactic north, Republic forces counterattacked, aided by Zabrak military units, winning key victories at Iridonia and Ithor. That prevented the Mandalorians from executing a pincer movement against Coruscant, and allowed the Republic a corridor for reinforcing the Taris front. The Neo-Crusaders' central thrust did substantial damage in the Northern Dependencies, but stalled because of a lucky break on the icy planet of Jebble: the mysterious destruction of a massive army of Mandalorians and slaves that was preparing for an assault on Alderaan. To galactic south, the Neo-Crusaders left Eres in ruins, raided Azure and Contruum, and linked up with Mandalorian units at Dxun. The Neo-Crusaders smashed a Republic task force at Commenor and ravaged Duro in 3962 BBY—but that was as far as they would get.

A significant number of Jedi disagreed sharply with the Jedi Council's refusal to be drawn into the Mandalorian Wars, arguing that the Order was allowing misery and terror to spread unchecked. The leader of this movement is known to history as Revan, and his followers became known as the Revanchists. Together with the Jedi later known as Malak, Revan defied the Jedi Council, aiding targets of the Mandalorians' campaigns and seeking the truth of the Neo-Crusaders' conduct on worlds such as Althir and Cathar. Revan's discovery of the atrocities committed against the Cathar failed to sway the Council, but the Order did look the other way as the Revanchists and other Jedi were appointed generals in the Republic military.

That military had not been idle. The great shipwrights of the Core and the Trailing Sectors had sensed war was coming and stockpiled raw materials, allowing them to turn out warships such as Centurion battle cruisers and Hammerhead cruisers. (The latter would prove one of the most popular warships in Republic history, still used by

Spacers' tales told of massive Mandalorian war fleets lurking in the dark beyond the Rim, but for a decade the Republic did little but watch and wait, even as Neo-Crusader raids imperiled worlds from Corsin to Azure.

In 3965 BBY the Mandalorians began prodding the Republic forces arrayed against them along the Taris front, skirmishing at Flashpoint Station and Suurja even as other Neo-Crusaders stepped up their raids into the Northern Dependencies. But battle wasn't joined until 3963 BBY, when Mandalore the Ultimate's forces launched a three-pronged attack. Neo-Crusaders broke through the Republic lines and invaded Taris; skirted the Republic border to attack Ithor, Ord Mantell, and the Zabrak worlds around Iridonia; and blasted the border world of Eres III.

The warnings of traders and scouts now proved true: The Mandalorians had huge numbers of captured warships along with ones of their own making. The core of the Mandalorian fleets was Kyramud battleships and Kandosii dreadnoughts—Basiliskan and Fenelar designs, respectively—but to that the Neo-Crusaders added Althiri frigates and corvettes, along with gunboats of their own design and a slew of variations on Basilisk war

sector defense forces millennia later.) The Republic also benefited from a substantial technological breakthrough: a more efficient gravity-well projector that could be housed within the hull of a cruiser. The Republic's Interdictor-class cruisers proved essential in hampering Mandalorian warships' movements and trapping them in-system.

Revan and Malak helped prevent the Battle of Duro from becoming an even larger disaster, arriving with a fleet of Interdictors and preventing the Neo-Crusaders from escaping with massive stocks of matériel from Duro's orbital shipyards. Bowing to the feelings of Republic citizens and eager to register his displeasure with the Jedi Council, Supreme Chancellor Tol Cressa named Revan commander of the Republic's military forces.

Revan knew the Republic could win by following two tough courses of action: devoting its industrial might to defeating the Mandalorians, and being willing to pay a terrible price to do so. Often at immense cost, Revan pushed the

Neo-Crusaders steadily back, until he cornered Mandalore the Ultimate at Malachor V in 3960 BBY— an encounter infamous among the Mandalorians as Ani'la Akaan, the Great Last Battle. There, Revan activated a Zabrak superweapon known as a mass-shadow generator. This device, a massively scaled-up version of an Interdictor's gravity well, spawned a tremendous gravitational vortex that fractured Malachor V and destroyed much of the Mandalorian and Republic fleets assembled above that world. In the battle Revan killed Mandalore the Ultimate, ending the Mandalorian Wars at a stroke.

The Mandalorian warrior Canderous Ordo famously claimed that "as long as one Mandalorian lives, we will survive." But the disaster at Malachor V marked a turning point in the clans' history. After surrendering to the Republic, the disarmed clans retreated to their domain, rudderless without their leader. Some returned to their nomadic ways, but many others became mercenaries, dismissing the warrior codes that had failed to save them. Over

the course of a generation Mandalorian society had mutated from a loose agglomeration of Taung warrior clans into a powerful, industrial civilization led by warriors of many species, only to be shaken by the terrible defeat of Ani'la Akaan.

After Malachor V the warrior codes were followed rigidly only within Mandalorian Space. Outside those borders, Mandalorians became infamous as bounty hunters, assassins, and mercenaries—to say nothing of pirates and slavers. They were respected as warriors, but mostly despised for their amorality and hunger for credits. The Mandalorians' resentment of the Republic and the Jedi made them favored tools of the Sith, particularly in the Great War of 3681–3653 BBY, but they sometimes fought alongside the Jedi as well.

The century that began in 1100 BBY is remembered as one of the galaxy's darkest: The Republic all but ceased to exist beyond the Core and Colonies, and the Candorian plague ravaged world after world. Systems and sectors that could do so built fleets as bulwarks against the chaos that was devouring the galaxy; those that couldn't lived in terror of pirates and slavers—or floods of refugees from less fortunate worlds. The flame of galactic civilization was guttering and threatened to go out entirely.

Amid the horror, something unexpected happened. In 1058 BBY a mercenary named Aga Awaud returned to Mandalore to find that the Candorian plague had killed his family and most of his clan—and Mandalorian ships had to band together in caravans through Mandalorian Space, fearing raiders from the lawless surrounding sectors.

Awaud was appalled, and became the leader of the Return—a movement that urged Mandalorians to defend Mandalorian Space. In 1051 BBY he took the name Mandalore the Uniter. Under his leadership, Mandalorian Space not only survived the upheaval of the New Sith Wars but thrived, emerging as a regional industrial power and protector of neighboring systems and sectors. Mandalorian protection didn't come cheap, and often proved coercive, but it was far better than the alternative.

After the Ruusan Reformations of 1000 BBY, a resurgent Republic sought to knit itself back together, reestablishing its institutions in the Outer

Rim. The Mandalorians, at first seen as a welcome force for stability, increasingly seemed like a threat: They were taxing commerce along the Hydian Way and binding neighboring sectors with economic and defense pacts that were hard to refuse. And since Mandalorian Space wasn't part of the Republic, the Mandalorians refused to abide by the post-Ruusan restrictions on sector defense forces.

Some clan leaders warned that Mandalore the Ultimate's mistakes were being repeated: The Mandalorian way of life might endure so long as the clans wandered the space lanes, but as a people the Mandalorians had no hope of winning a fight with the Republic. They argued that Mandalore should join the Republic, immediately becoming one of its most powerful and influential sectors. But the peacemakers were shouted down: If Mandalorians weren't warriors, they weren't Mandalorians at all.

In 738 BBY the Republic created a task force made up of Judicial Forces and units drawn from Planetary Security Forces in the Expansion Region, with the Jedi Order coordinating the war effort. The Mandalorian Excision was brief but overwhelming: Key Mandalorian worlds such as Fenel, Ordo, Concord Dawn, and Mandalore itself were subjected to devastating bombardment, with swathes of those worlds still desolate in Imperial times. Mandalorian Space was occupied and disarmed, with a caretaker government created from elements of the failed peace movement.

The occupation would last for decades, and create a new schism in Mandalorian society. From the caretaker government emerged the so-called New Mandalorians, who bitterly resented the Republic but saw no hope in fighting it, and so renounced the warrior codes in favor of peace and neutrality. The New Mandalorians held most positions of power, and rebuilt Mandalore's industrial base over the next few centuries. Some unrepentant mercenaries and warriors were exiled to the moon Concordia, while others dispersed throughout the galaxy, resuming the Mandalorians' ancient trade as blasters-for-hire. The Mandalores of the post-Excision era were drawn from their ranks, though their authority was recognized by neither the New Mandalorians nor the sector government.

In the last century before the Battle of Yavin, two new Mandalorian movements arose. The mercenary Jaster Mereel, who became Mandalore in 60 BBY, sought to reinstitute the warrior codes. His True Mandalorians were opposed by mercenaries who argued that the way to restore the clans' honor was to topple the hated New Mandalorians and repay the Republic's savagery in kind. This group became known as the Death Watch.

Few Mandalorian clans were united on the subject: The New Mandalorians, True Mandalorians, and Death Watch could all claim Ordos, Vizslas, Kryzes, Fetts, Awauds, and Tenaus as supporters. The True Mandalorians were decimated at Galidraan in 44 BBY, while Death Watch allied itself with the Separatists during the Clone Wars, scheming to provoke a new Republic offensive that would eliminate their enemies. And as a final irony, Jango Fett—who claimed to be one of the last True Mandalorians—became the template for the Republic's clone army and supervised the clones' training. The Republic that had fought the Mandalorians so many times over the millennia now depended on an army of them for its defense.

THE ARMY OF LIGHT

The "Army of Light" is legendary as the last great Jedi host of the ancient Republic, mustered by Lord Hoth in the closing campaigns of the New Sith Wars. But the origins of this unique fighting force began to take shape several centuries before.

By the beginning of the New Sith Wars, the Republic had endured centuries of turmoil. Sith and Separatist forces had gained control of the Rim and pushed Coreward, while corrupt megacorps had shaken off all but the most self-interested ties to the government, and many civilized systems had simply closed their borders. Only Jedi Knights had the will and skill to defend the helpless.

These "Jedi Lords" began their careers as knights on quests to defend abandoned worlds from slavery and exploitation. Gradually they came to hold political authority over systems and entire sectors, and became hereditary barons and kings. The Jedi domains were islands of peace and justice, where honorable rulers fought to keep the Sith at bay, attracted other brave Jedi to their banners, and sired sons and daughters who followed their parents in the way of the Force. Eventually, even

the office of Supreme Chancellor and the rule of Coruscant itself were ceded to a line of Jedi Masters.

While post-Ruusan historians and Imperial propagandists emphasized the anarchy of these centuries, they also marked the last great age of the Jedi Knights, and many systems prospered under their rule. When Lord Hoth decided to take the offensive against the Sith in 1010 BBY, he gathered Jedi Lords and their bands of knights from across the galaxy, a movement that swelled until the last Grand Council of the Order declared all the Jedi baronies united as the Army of Light, commanded by Lord Hoth bearing the ancient title of Seneschal.

The core of this army consisted of seven legions led by the greatest Jedi Lords, who followed Hoth directly into battle, often piloting agile starfighters and speeder bikes. They were supported by Republic units that preferred Jedi leadership to the orders of the Admiralty, and by additional forces such as the private army of the half-Bothan Valenthyne Farfalla. Farfalla commanded one of the largest fighting companies of Force-wielders ever seen—a personal retinue of one hundred knights and esquires, and a feudal following of two hundred more. Farfalla's knights were equipped not with the usual starfighters, but with remarkable timber-framed space gunships, which had deflector shield skins backed by the strong and flexible wood of the wroshyr tree found on the Wookiee homeworld Kashyyyk.

Lord Hoth led his army to Ruusan in 1001 BBY, becoming enmeshed in a disaster. Casualties mounted, and orbital supply lines were blocked. Morale collapsed. Local levies, organized and armed with whatever was available, were thrown into battle, and for the final push every camp follower still able to stand was given a weapon and a place in the line. The final battle saw the Sith destroyed by the machinations of one of their own, Darth Bane, along with Lord Hoth and most of his knights. Victory was claimed by bureaucratic factions in the Jedi Order and the Republic—beings who opposed the entire concept of Jedi Lords, and had been appalled by the feudal ethos of the Grand Council.

Veterans of the Army of Light were ignored by the reformed Jedi Order, which was embarrassed both by their politics and by the tragedy of Ruusan. The few surviving Jedi Lords returned to their castles and took care of their men, calmly ignoring the orders of the Jedi on Coruscant, and maintained a wary detachment from the Republic for centuries. Even under the New Republic, the remaining Corellian Jedi and Teepo Paladins retained distinct identities, based on their descent from these ancient heroes.

WAR PORTRAIT: LORD HOTH

Lord Hoth never thought of himself as a general. In his youth he dreamed only of wielding a lightsaber; as he grew old, he saw himself as just a teacher and warrior. But he was the man on whose broad shoulders the responsibility of destroying the Sith came to rest.

Rohlan of Kaal was heir to a minor line of Jedi Lords from Yushan sector, but still in his teens when he left the citadel of his ancestors to win renown as the Knight of Hoth—the Jedi hero who freed the Corellian Trade Spine from Sith pirates. In his mid-twenties, after the Republic committed troops to consolidate his gains, he traveled to Coruscant and became Master Hoth, the respected battlemaster of the Jedi Temple—a warrior grown weary of battle, training a new generation of apprentices how to fight with a lightsaber.

Hoth's imposing physical presence and skill with a blade made him a hero for his trainees, but the tales of his exploits barely reached the marble corridors trod by the Temple's masters, and his simple loyalty to the Order clashed with the subtle theory and diplomacy that pervaded the senior ranks. The Jedi Council's great hope for the future was a slim, sophisticated young commoner from the capital named Skere Kaan, an expert in battle meditation, fleet command, and economic policy. Kaan had developed a radical theory about the anarchy that had shaken civilization for a thousand years: He blamed the Republic and the Jedi Order.

The Council, believing that they could moderate these daring arguments into a practical reform policy, rewarded Kaan with a Jedi Master's rank. But in 1010 BBY Kaan grew impatient with their interference and left the Order, leading a group of like-minded Jedi Knights in a dramatic schism. Calling themselves the Brotherhood, they announced their intention to conquer the fragmented Sith enclaves as a prelude to reforming the Republic—and within months Kaan had slain the worst of the Sith warlords and forced the rest to beg for peace. The Jedi Order sent its enthusiastic congratulations, but Kaan was busy remaking his conquests into a weapon to use against them. Within a year, he had assumed the throne of a new Sith Empire and declared war on the Republic.

Without waiting for the Jedi Council's next mistake, Hoth gathered his followers from the Temple and his veteran Jedi Knights from the Javin Marches. Adding allies from Corellia, Cularin, and Kamparas, he became Lord Hoth, the Seneschal of the Army of Light. For ten years he and his men methodically liberated Sith strongholds on the Outer Rim, while avoiding a direct confrontation with Kaan.

Rohlan of Kaal dueling Sith pirates on Hoth (John VanFleet)

Military historians now regard Hoth's war as an act of great generalship—a clear-minded campaign to weaken the enemy on the flanks while hardening and strengthening his own troops for a decisive blow against their isolated center. By the time of Ruusan, the Army of Light was larger and better trained than it had ever been, but Hoth's focus on the regional warlords also allowed Kaan to consolidate his hold on the Brotherhood and strike deep into the Core. It was Kaan's conquest of the Brentaal junction that forced Hoth to make his decisive move at Ruusan, where he led the Army of Light into a long, grim stalemate in the mud and gunfire of the Seven Battles. Darth Bane, in a plot to destroy his fellow Sith so he could establish his Rule of Two, convinced the Brotherhood to use a thought bomb against the Army of Light. The detonation of the bomb destroyed the Brotherhood of the Sith along with Lord Hoth and the majority of the Army of Light. Lord Berethon, one of only two Jedi Lords to survive the battle, said that the Army of Light had grown too big for Lord Hoth to lead: "From first to last, his instincts were those of a Knight, not a general." Hoth's best moments, like the Third Battle of Ruusan, were essentially small-unit tactics implemented on a grand scale, while his worst mistakes were either attempts to stand back and direct his forces on the map like an Academy-trained field marshal or harshly rational misjudgments, like the forced conscription of Jedi children to prevent their kidnapping by the Sith. Ultimately, Hoth's successes and his failures all suggest the same basic truth: One Jedi hero can do more good than an entire professional army.

ARMORY AND SENSOR PROFILE

INTERDICTOR TECHNOLOGY

A key to controlling space is the ability to force passing starships out of hyperspace. Every starship has fail-safes intended to force a reversion to realspace if a mass shadow is detected that's too large to be avoided with a small course correction. Since the earliest days of faster-than-light travel, pirates and military commanders have tried to exploit this for strategic purposes.

The Argaian pirates led by Xer, father of Xim the Despot, intercepted ships by towing ice asteroids into the narrow hyperspace lanes through the Indrexu Spiral, and similar tactics are still used today. Another tactic is to scatter bits of ice, dust, or metal chaff (popularly known as decant dust) across a hyperspace lane.

But such brute-force tactics are generally inefficient and pose navigational problems for those who use them, too. A better tactic is to simulate large mass shadows or dangerous hyperspace eddies. Mass mines—which project the signatures of much larger objects—are one alternative, though they are tedious to deploy and recover afterward. Another option is a quantum field generator, which disrupts the null field generator that keeps ships stable in their passage through hyperspace. But quantum field generators have immense power demands and can often damage a starfleet's own null field units.

During the Mandalorian Wars of the 3900s BBY, Zabrak engineers came up with a new tactic:

projecting a simulated gravity well into realspace, either to prevent starships from escaping into hyperspace or to drag them out of it. Starship-based interdictor fields proved an ideal solution: They were mobile, could be activated or deactivated as needed, and didn't leave space lanes needing to be cleaned up. After its introduction, interdictor technology sparked a technological spiral of advances and countermeasures. The relatively weak interdictors of the Mandalorian Wars were soon rendered ineffective by better hyperdrive sensor suites and multiphase null field units, and interdictor technology became a sidelight for millennia until the Clone Wars inspired aggressive new research.

The Empire built on the Republic's technological breakthroughs, and the bulbous gravity-well generators of Interdictor cruisers soon became familiar sights. These new projectors were powerful enough to catch almost any starship, but required the drive systems and spaceframe of a large capital ship. The protruding projectors also limited the available positions for weapons emplacements and launch bays, making interdictors underpowered as front-line warships. Only battleships were big enough to carry effective interdictor systems without serious penalties in cost or weaponry.

The arms race would continue: The Bakuran military introduced hyperwave inertial momentum sustainers, popularly known as HIMS generators, which produced hyperspace bubbles that could push interdictor fields aside. First introduced at the Battle of Centerpoint Station in 18 ABY, HIMS generators were used by the New Republic and the Galactic Alliance against the Yuuzhan Vong's dovin basals.

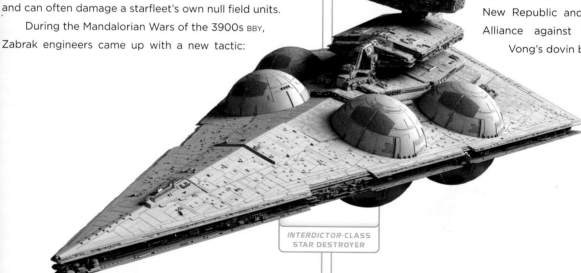

INTERDICTOR-CLASS
STAR DESTROYER

THE RUUSAN REFORMATIONS

In 1000 BBY, following the defeat of the Sith at Ruusan, Tarsus Valorum set out to heal a shattered galaxy and rebuild its institutions by making them more democratic and mutually supporting. The Ruusan Reformations were an unprecedented experiment: a voluntary dismantling of central authority over economic, political, and military power.

To make the Senate more governable, Valorum consolidated its millions of sectors into 1,024 regional sectors, each with its own Senator, though political necessity forced him to carve out exemptions for powerful worlds in the Core and Colonies, and to extend the right of representation to the galaxy's functional constituencies—ancient institutions with considerable economic power.

Though not formally bound by the Ruusan Reformations, the Jedi Order made fundamental changes as well. The Jedi gave up the bulk of their forces, from ground vehicles to warships and starfighters, and became part of the Judicial Department, reinforcing the fact that they answered to the Senate and were ideally counselors and advisers, not warriors. To decrease the chance that far-flung academies might stumble into dangerous explorations of the Force, Jedi training was consolidated in the Temple on Coruscant. And Jedi trainees would now be taken into the Order as infants, before they could be exposed to the temptations of the material world.

But for a war-weary galaxy, the most extraordinary measures of the Ruusan Reformations were the ones that abolished the Republic's armed forces.

The standing military was reorganized as the Judicial Forces, a relatively small assemblage of task forces and rapid-response fleets, intended to patrol the frontier and respond to crises. The Senate could authorize the Judicial Forces to requisition military units from systems and sectors, and the Supreme Chancellor could appoint Governor-Generals to coordinate military action with the Senator of a troubled sector. In the absence of a major crisis, the Planetary Security Forces—for fourteen millennia little more than an auxiliary of the Republic Navy—would be expected to keep the peace.

Determined to curb the Republic's regional rivalries and restrict sector fleets to defensive operations, Valorum ordered limits on fleet sizes and armament. Cruisers more than six hundred meters long were limited to Class Five hyperdrives by modern standards, and their navicomputers were restricted to local charts. Judicial Inspectors were given wide-ranging powers to enforce these regulations, and "bluecoats" with datapads became common sights aboard military vessels and in depots. Cruisers below the six-hundred-meter limit emerged as the workhorses of the sector fleets and the Judicial Forces alike, and remained the backbone of many military organizations long after the Yuuzhan Vong invasion.

The Reformations were less popular in the Rim world sectors. Decommissioned navy cruisers, frigates, and corvettes were assigned to these Sector Forces, and some wealthy sectors sold off capital ships in excess of their defense allowances to their poorer brethren. (Others, fearing a resumption of war, stripped their warships of weapons and key systems and mothballed them.) But the outlying sectors were last in line for the naval spoils. Exemptions to the Ruusan limits were allowed for frontier sectors and dangerous areas of the galaxy, but their Senators had to struggle with Judicial bureaucrats and Senate committees to win these allowances—and often couldn't afford to take advantage of them.

While Rim sectors struggled to police their worlds with creaky, undersized capital ships, wealthy industrial sectors built giant cruisers on a scale not seen for millennia, seeking to create impregnable defenses and impress their neighbors. Such sectors took advantage of loopholes in the Reformations: For example, systems and planets that had retained the right to direct Senate representation received additional military allowances. The new battleships were denied transgalactic capabilities and were hamstrung by armament limits, but they still made for formidable fleets—many of them concentrated in the regions of the galaxy that faced the fewest threats to law and order. Elsewhere, intergalactic organizations sought to flout the rules by building giant transports that could be quickly adapted into warships.

Yet another big loophole was an exemption granted to starship manufacturers allowing them to create prototype warships and experimental variants of existing models and classes. The exemption was intended to encourage sectors to establish their own shipyards and to ensure continued technological innovation. But it led to shipwrights creating "demonstration fleets" made up of variations on warship designs and leasing effective control of them to sectors that could afford them. In the Republic's final centuries, the shipwright exemption and armament limits encouraged modular warship manufacturing, allowing rapid alterations to ships' armament, capabilities, and functions. By then wealthy sectors were awash in warships, with their fleets' numbers swelled by "loans" from starship manufacturers.

DECLINE OF THE REPUBLIC

"Every profession penalizes those who employ inadequately trained personnel. Only in the military are those penalties so ruinous and final."
—Thull Yularen, instructor, Anaxes Citadel

TURMOIL ON THE RIM

The defeat of the Sith and the Ruusan Reformations brought centuries of peace and economic prosperity to the Republic, and the wise leadership of several extraordinary Chancellors rebuilt galactic society and fueled renewed exploration and colonization of the galaxy's northern and southern reaches.

But while the Republic withstood challenges such as the brief resurgence of the Mandalorians, its prosperity masked flaws and fault lines, particularly between the worlds of the Core, Colonies, and Inner Rim, and the planets farther out. The abolition of a central military may have curbed abuses of power, but it left outlying systems and sectors struggling to defend themselves against pirates, slavers, and the ambitions of small-time despots. Many worlds turned to megacorps and petty tyrants for protection, trading freedom and prosperity for security.

The rule of law was often taken for granted in the Core but theoretical on the Rim. Wealthy worlds colonized new planets in the Rim with scant regard for the rights of indigenous species, and the megacorps treated unexplored space as a private preserve for commercial exploitation. Sometimes such exploitation was so blatant that the Senate stirred itself to action: In 704 BBY it ended the disastrous experiment in corporate administration known as the Outer Expansion Zone after civil unrest gripped the Expansion Region north of Coruscant. But particularly in the Outer Rim, central authority was often weak to the point of being nonexistent, and abuses went unchecked.

In the centuries before the civil war that would spell the end of the Republic, swaths of the galaxy fell into economic stagnation and decay. The Senate made two significant moves in 124 BBY. First, it declared the entire Outer Rim and parts of the Mid Rim a free-trade zone in a bid to jump-start economic development and rebuild ties between the Rim and the Core. Second, it granted a number of megacorps the status of functional constituencies, granting them Senate representation.

These efforts did spur economic development, but the cost was a further diminution of central power, and even fewer protections for poor, remote worlds. The chief beneficiaries, meanwhile, were the Trade Federation and the other megacorps. Rimmers saw raw material taken away from their worlds and returned as goods they couldn't afford, while the Trade Federation cannily turned its economic might into political power, buying up blocs of votes in the Senate.

By the final decades of the Republic, it was clear that some kind of reckoning was at hand. Large portions of the Rim were abandoned to the growing might of the Hutts or exploited by wealthy, corrupt Senators, while in the Core the deal-making was more mannered but equally crooked. In many systems megacorps were the only law, and they were concerned with profits, not the rights of citizens, environmental protections, or economic development. As chaos spread, powerful sectors and megacorps first chafed at the limits placed on their military capabilities, then began to ignore these ancient laws the Republic could no longer enforce.

A movement of determined Senators, who took the name Reformists, sought to rekindle the spirit of Ruusan and check the megacorps' power. But many of their fellow Senators were either in the pocket of the megacorps, or too frightened to stand up to the commercial giants. The Senatorial faction known as the Militarists, meanwhile, sought to restore order by reviving a centralized military. But many Reformists were suspicious of their motives, and refused common cause with them.

The Republic began to fragment. A terrorist group known as the Nebula Front began attacking Trade Federation shipping, intensifying the cartel's calls that it be allowed greater freedom to defend itself. A manufactured bacta shortage led to a struggle among pirates, smugglers, and Republic paramilitaries known as the Stark Hyperspace War, with the Jedi and the Trade Federation caught in the middle. Uprisings blazed up on the edges of the galaxy, and elsewhere long-buried animosities began to smolder.

In the 30s BBY the Reformists sought to tax many Rim trade routes, undoing the tax advantages granted a century before to the likes of the Trade Federation, Corporate Alliance, and the InterGalactic Banking Clan. In return for accepting renewed taxation, the Reformists proposed allowing the Trade Federation to expand its defensive forces.

What the Reformists couldn't know was that when its profits were threatened, the Trade Federation would use its new military capabilities to blockade a Republic world. And no one knew that the galaxy's tensions were being stoked by a shadowy mastermind whose goal was to destroy the Republic itself.

THE PLANETARY SECURITY FORCES AND THE JUDICIALS

After the Republic military was disbanded, the Judicial Forces became the Republic's lone vehicle for waging war. The Judicial Forces were relatively small, designed to protect the galactic frontier and respond to short-term crises. If they faced a larger threat, the Judicials could call on the security forces of the star systems and the new regional sectors.

These Planetary Security Forces were smaller in number than their predecessors, and strict upper limits were imposed on the armament, speed, and mobility of their larger warships. But that was seen as a good thing in a galaxy bloodied by centuries of war. The Planetary Security Forces would use speedy, lightly armed patrol craft to keep the peace within their sectors, with a handful of larger warships defending key worlds and the Judicials prepared to respond to larger threats.

The Republic gave sectors a free hand in running their Planetary Security Forces, leading to divergent results, ranks,

and practices. Some Senators had a strong military tradition to draw upon, or represented the home sectors of Republic military academies not utilized by the Judicials; Planetary Security Forces such as the Garde d'Azure, Lantillian Planetary Security Forces, Greater Plooriod Wardens, Iseno Rangers, and Hertae Home Brigade became renowned. But other Senators saw their Planetary Security Forces as a source of credits for other needs, or packed their top ranks with cronies who'd never been on the bridge of a warship.

The Judicial Forces' first commander was Admiral Lune Banjeer, who'd served with distinction at Ruusan. Under Banjeer and his successors, the Judicials fought ably in the Unification Campaigns of the 900s BBY, achieving notable victories at Vondarc, D'rinba, and the Klina Marches, serving gallantly in the surface confrontation on Korvaii that ended the Melusi Uprising, and bringing the Belderone Contention to a fiery conclusion at the Battle of the Dandrian Ring. Later, the Judicials would play key roles in the Mandalorian Excision of 738 BBY, the Battles of the Black Delve in the 690s BBY, and the Utor Shock of 602 BBY. And many Judicial officers served with distinction as the galactic frontier pushed Rimward once again.

But a largely peaceful galaxy, the gradual weakening of central power, and periodic bribery scandals eroded the Judicials' funding and standing. Every Senator paid close attention to his, her, or its Planetary Security Forces, but few championed the Judicials, except to complain about their enforcement of defense limits. Exploration and colonization was increasingly the province of ambitious worlds and megacorps, and shipwrights found greater profits and prestige in contracts with Planetary Security Forces.

Moreover, these forces developed a strong tradition of their own. After the Mandalorian Excision, marshals and admirals from the Planetary Security Forces met at the Corsin Retreat to discuss best practices for coordinating action among PSFs. There, they decided to revive the moribund Republic Naval College on Anaxes.

The College of Planetary Security Forces—as the new institution was dubbed—revived naval traditions and pride, and Anaxes once again became the destination dreamed of by young men on countless worlds, while the Judicial Academy on Coruscant was mocked as a factory for court officers who got to fly. (The Judicials' army units were accorded more respect, or at least as much respect as naval loyalists could accord ground units.) As the Republic crumbled, the Militarists, Reformists, and Loyalists calling for the restoration of the navy looked to Anaxes for models, not Coruscant. And when the

Republic Navy was finally reborn, its leaders, traditions and even favored shipwrights were drawn not from the Judicials, but from the Planetary Security Forces.

During the Clone Wars, the Judicial Forces became part of the Republic Navy, with the Planetary Security Forces nationalized but left in place. The Empire weakened them further in favor of the Imperial Starfleet and gave control of them to the Moffs, few of whom were native to the sectors they controlled. The New Republic handed control of the Planetary Security Forces back to local authorities and strengthened them again, opting for a standing military much larger than the Judicials, but far smaller than the Imperial Starfleet.

ARMORY AND SENSOR PROFILE

STARFIGHTERS AND CARRIERS

Starfighter warfare emerged from technologies and tactics of air combat developed independently on millions of worlds, whether it was primitive planes, flying dragons, or advanced starfighters that were used in aerial combat.

Aerial units are essentially a form of cavalry, capable of reaching out beyond a main formation for scouting, skirmishing, or attack—missions known in modern parlance as "force projection." This capability naturally invites counterattack from enemy fighters, and most civilizations recognize a contrast between "snubfighters" capable of attacking ground targets and warships and "superiority fighters" designed to fight other fighters. While the basic repertoire of dogfighting maneuvers has been discovered by many different civilizations, the move to the open arena of space has rarely proved easy for snubfighters.

In atmospheric warfare, airfighters dominate the complex board game of the battlefield, as their speed and range can't be matched by ground vehicles or seagoing warships. These advantages are even more apparent in orbital defense operations, in which small flights of fighters operating from hidden ground bases can strike through cloud cover to launch torpedo runs against attacking capital ships and strafe incoming troop transports. Dedicated orbital defense fighters such as the Z-95 Headhunter Mark I and the T-36 Skyfighter remained popular until the Clone Wars.

To respond to these threats, attacking fleets must either reduce the armament of their combat warships to carry escort flights of starfighters, or else place larger fighter groups aboard dedicated carriers. Experience has shown that an effective fleet carrier—essentially a spacegoing airfield designed to support a battle line of warships—requires enclosed hangars and a hull at least the size of a heavy cruiser, but such carriers' huge launch bays and limited armament make them vulnerable targets.

If it is far more complex to attach fighters to a fleet than to operate them from the surface, it has always been natural to extend the range of ground-launched snubfighters beyond the gravity well. Although traditional doctrine holds that surface-based fighters' role in fleet combat is limited to orbital invasion scenarios, such fighters have proven capable of protecting civilian ships and outposts throughout a star system, attacking hostile asteroid bases, and driving off scout cruisers. Equipped with short-range hyperdrives, they can even slip into the atmosphere of worlds in nearby systems and strike ground targets—or jump into dogfights from improvised carriers located a safe distance away. Such carriers need neither the defensive systems nor the large fighter capacity of carriers designed to accompany battle fleets, and old cargo haulers can often be adapted for this role in relatively short order.

These qualities have long made deep-space snubfighters popular with military organizations whose resources and mission profile don't provide for capital ships. Deep-space snubfighters were common weapons for Republic militia and paramilitary groups, and became signature vehicles of the Jedi Knights—but the same capabilities also made them very attractive to pirates and mercenaries. This combination of utility and popularity established a low ceiling for snubfighter design and technology, with the typical pilot requiring little more than a cheap fighter with engines that could be repaired "in the bush." The scissor-winged Aurek tactical fighter remained the Republic's standard "hyperspace snub" for nearly four thousand years, while the Jedi favored an equally ancient lineage of Hoersch-Kessel designs, and pirates used whatever they could make fly. Until the closing generations of the Republic, snubfighter performance tweaks were achieved by Outer Rim engineers rather than shipyard design teams.

This changed with the intro-duction of new inertial compensators and astromech droids with greater capabilities, allowing older atmospheric defense fighters to be upgraded with better spaceflight capabilities. By the time of the Clone Wars, snubfighters such as the Koensayr Y-wing, the Naboo N-1, the Umbarans' advanced designs and the Z-95 had broken free from their forerunners' constraints, combining proven engine technology with enhanced maneuverability and marrying that to the combat punch of shields, missiles, and hyperdrives.

But starfighters remained under-valued in deep-space fleet combat. Many of the advantages of snubfighters disappear in the great distances between opposing battleship squadrons. Starfighters designed for fleet operations have traditionally been short-range superiority fighters intended for scouting ahead of assault fleets and countering attacking snubfighters. This view was shared by the Republic Navy and most other military organizations, with examples ranging from the Blade starfighters of the ancient Sith to the Trade Federation's swarms of vulture droids and the A-series interceptors of the Kuat Defense Force. Without requirements for long-range missions, hyperspace travel, atmospheric performance, or missile systems, the size, cost, and complexity of these fighters could be dramatically reduced while simultaneously enhancing their dogfighting performance—most were simply pairings of fast engines and blaster cannons arrayed around a cockpit. Such fighters could be carried in limited numbers

Z-95 HEADHUNTER

AUREK-CLASS TACTICAL STRIKEFIGHTER

NABOO N-1 ADVANCED STARFIGHTER

BTL-B Y-WING STARFIGHTER

aboard most combat warships, while multi-squadron groups were deployed aboard large command ships, often alongside ground assault troop transports.

When missile capacity was needed, naval commanders preferred specialist bombers—culminating in the Incom/Subpro ARC-170, adopted by the Republic shortly before the Clone Wars. These were large, complex, and expensive fighters, built around powerful sensor arrays and days-long mission profiles, designed to track down enemy fleets and launch surprise attacks. Supporters of these big fighters argued that this was the only scenario in which torpedo runs could effectively penetrate fighter screens and flak defenses, and it was only after the success of the N-1 and Y-wing at Naboo and Kaliida that hyper-snubs from an airfighter lineage were taken seriously as battleship-killers.

The *Venator*- and *Victory*-class cruisers of the Clone Wars were originally designed to operate NTB-30 torpedo bombers alongside short-range A-6 interceptors, but their capacity was largely given over to snubfighters by the end of the conflict, and designers such as Vors Voorhorian and Walex Blissex spent the war years developing a new generation of X-wings and Y-wings designed to dogfight on equal terms with any starfighter in space.

Faced with the growing threat from snubfighters, the supporters of traditional superiority fighters struck back. Even before Naboo, Raith Sienar had developed radical new fighter designs capable of outflying any snubfighter and deploying in large numbers from converted cargo bays aboard frigates and small cruisers. But the Trade Federation held patents on Sienar's engine technology, and the political repercussions that followed the Battle for Naboo led to the Republic releasing the designs to Kuat Systems Engineering. Kuat wanted to replace the underperforming CloakShape line, and used the Sienar concepts to build the Delta starfighters and Actis interceptors used by the Jedi Order.

These were expensive and fragile fighters, however, and after the Clone Wars the Kuat designs were superseded by Sienar's new TIE starfighter. Cheap, low-maintenance, and fast, the TIE instantly became the standard superiority fighter of the Imperial Navy. At the same time, the new *Imperial*-class Star Destroyer provided an effective platform for them: large enough to combine a carrier's launch facilities with the armament and armor of a battleship. As the Clone Wars ended, the long battle between short-range fighters and hyperdrive-capable snubfighters entered its next phase, with new generations of the TIE and X-wing set to become the standard combatants.

RANULPH TARKIN AND THE RISE OF THE MILITARISTS

The crumbling of order in the Outer Rim concentrated power in the region's most populous and prosperous systems, with stable worlds such as Christophsis, Columex, Lianna, Celanon, Botajef, and Entralla attracting investments and becoming regional power brokers. No world, however, reaped more benefits than Eriadu.

Located at the juncture of the Hydian Way, the Rimma Trade Route, and two important regional trade corridors, Eriadu became an industrial powerhouse under the leadership of the Quintad, five powerful families who'd emigrated to the Seswenna sector from Corulag around 900 BBY. The most powerful Quintad family was the Tarkins, who dominated the top spots in Seswenna companies, shipyards, and political parties.

Born in 97 BBY, Ranulph Tarkin made his mark early in both business and the military. He served in the Seswenna Defense Forces, leading a successful campaign against the Delmaasi pirates in 66 BBY, then became an executive at Quintad Orbital Manufacturing, where he struck deals with a number of Republic military manufacturers to lease space in QOM's network of shipyards and advanced factories.

By 57 BBY Tarkin was the most powerful man in the sector—but he was restless, alarmed by the breakdown of order across the Rim. He turned QOM over to a cousin and persuaded Seswenna's Senator, Ulm Brashere, to ask the Chancellor to appoint him Governor-General of the sector, responsible for its defense forces.

Given his wish, Tarkin began to strengthen Seswenna's military capabilities by building warships in its own facilities, but soon ran afoul of the Judicials, whose inspectors swarmed Seswenna's shipyards searching for regulatory violations. Frustrated, Tarkin turned to the shipwrights with which QOM had forged ties, striking lend-lease deals that placed dozens of corvettes, frigates, and cruisers under Eriadu's authority. These "demonstration fleets" were common in the Core, but this was the Rim, and Tarkin's ambitions alarmed the Judicials. His next moves worried them more: Tarkin struck mutual-defense pacts with adjacent sectors, trading economic assistance for agreements to combine forces in times of need; share navigational data among Planetary Security Forces; and treat their sectors as a single theater of operations. Tarkin then looked farther afield, seeking agreements with other sectors to exchange navigational data and allow safe passage by mutual consent.

At a stroke, Tarkin had turned a hodgepodge of Planetary Security Forces into a regional military power, dubbed the Outland Regions Security Force, and bred fears that he sought to establish a new empire. (His ambitions may have helped push Eriadu's rival Sullust and the Rimward sectors of the Rimma Trade Route into the Separatist camp a generation later.) Such talk outraged Tarkin, who sought to rebut it by becoming Seswenna's Senator, with his cousin Garvedon as Governor-General in his place. Break away from Coruscant? He would go there.

The new Senator arrived in 54 BBY and sounded the alarm about the Republic's lack of preparedness, noting Planetary Security Forces that were little more than security details for Senators and ones that had been disbanded entirely, enfeebled by regulations and hollowed by budget cuts. Should the Republic face a significant military threat, the Judicial Forces would find little strength to draw on.

Many Judicials agreed with Tarkin, and privately rooted for him to win his legal feud with their department. That feud turned vicious after Tarkin won appointments to several key committees and began hauling Judicial ministers before the holocams. All the while, he swore that nothing would delight him more than turning over control of the ORSF to those same ministers—provided they were part of a centralized Republic military.

Tarkin attracted many supporters, and became the head of a movement dubbed the Militarists by Senator Finis Valorum, their leading opponent and a man deeply suspicious of Tarkin's motives. (In an effort to outflank Valorum, Tarkin embraced the Militarist name.) Valorum wasn't his only opponent, though: His detractors noted that the ORSF was almost entirely made up of humans, which Tarkin insisted reflected not speciesism, but concern for unit morale and a desire to standardize systems and procedures. They also accused Tarkin of effectively buying the acquiescence of his impoverished neighbors, seeing sinister designs in the fact that the ORSF referred to its expanded theater of operations as the Greater Seswenna.

Tarkin was unmoved; he began to position the ORSF as the template for the restored armed forces, going so far as to call his regional force the Republic Navy. His plans attracted support from some of the Senate's Reformists, with whom he worked to make the Judicials more effective.

Tarkin had made his cause into a political movement, but he was stalemated. He needed a flashpoint that would expose the Republic's weaknesses—and in 46 BBY he got it. Iaco Stark, an entrepreneurial pirate who headed the Stark Combine, began raiding Trade Federation shipments of bacta, then at a premium because of a shortage. Tarkin was no friend to the Trade Federation, but he disliked Stark even more, and pushed the Judicials to hunt down Stark's raiders and destroy them. If the Judicials couldn't get the job done, Tarkin warned, the ORSF would.

When the Republic followed Valorum's advice instead, agreeing to a peace conference, Tarkin confronted the Trade Federation's Nute Gunray, vowing to expose the group's dirty dealings unless Gunray told him the site of the conference. A terrified Gunray revealed it would be held on the remote world of Troiken. That was on the other side of the galaxy from Eriadu, and sending the ORSF there would be a major violation of defense-fleet mobility regulations. But Tarkin knew a victory over Stark's forces would make him a hero, with cheers drowning out the bleating of bureaucrats.

Tarkin's fleet was led by fast and well-armed *Consular*-class attack ships and nimble A-6 interceptors, a mix reflecting the traditional military thinking that quick and maneuverable weapons platforms could outfight larger warships. Sympathetic Judicials lent him several full battalions of special-missions assault troops to provide a ground assault force. All Tarkin needed was a source of navigational data for his larger warships.

When he found that source, he was too eager to consider where it might have come from. The data included a concealed "Tionese program," and by the time the Militarist fleet mustered, every navicomputer was infected with a virus. When the fleet made the jump to lightspeed, two-thirds of the ships simply disappeared. The weakened remnant that arrived above Troiken was ambushed by the entire Combine fleet—the complete force of pirate ships and old military cruisers that Stark had assembled. The First Battle of Qotile was a humiliation for the Republic, with the heavy weapons of Stark's Kaloth warships and *Vainglorious*-class cruisers pounding the Militarists' smaller frigates and corvettes.

Once on the ground, though, the course of the campaign swung steadily in the Militarists' favor. The special-missions brigade rescued Senator Valorum and his Jedi escorts, and dug in beneath Mount Avos.

Official accounts claim that the battle was won by Jedi Knight Plo Koon, while Militarist memoirs describe Kel Dor as an alien interloper who pushed Tarkin aside. Regardless of which version one believes, the real heroes of the campaign were the dogged special-missions soldiers: When the Combine's mercenaries and enforcers attempted to storm the Republic positions on the slopes, they were driven back

by E-Web blasterfire and PLEX missiles. Soon thereafter, a small force of Jedi and Judicials escaped with Valorum.

On Coruscant, Mace Windu intimidated the Trade Federation's Viceroy Hask into mobilizing the Trade Defense Forces. Backed by Jedi starfighters, the TDF's heavy munitions cruisers broke through the Combine blockade and relieved the siege. Tarkin died battling the Combine's mercenaries beneath Mount Avos.

By doing so, he became a martyr—and did much to advance the Militarist cause. But others saw Troiken as a victory as well. Nute Gunray became the Trade Federation's Viceroy—and received an encrypted holocomm code from Stark, who urged him to contact the mysterious figure he described as his "shadow benefactor."

ARMORY AND SENSOR PROFILE

COMBAT DROIDS

War droids predate even the Republic—the Rakata, Xim, and the ancient Hutts all made use of automata in combat, and war droids (class four droids according to modern classifications) were developed shortly after labor droids—long before droids concerned with engineering and medicine, to say nothing of etiquette and protocol.

Combat seemed like a logical use for mechanicals: After all, droids' earliest duties were to perform tasks too dangerous for organics. But for all their effectiveness in combat, combat droids have never proven as effective as living beings at improvisation and dealing with the unexpected. Only when organics are unable or unwilling to go to war does the galaxy see widespread use of combat droids.

Philosophers have wrangled for eons over whether droids

are sentient, with those who say they are decrying the use of droids in war as little better than industrialized murder. For millennia, the trend in the galaxy was an increasing acceptance of droid rights—but that movement was interrupted by a series of shocks to civilization beginning in 4015 BBY.

That year saw the Great Droid Revolution, in which the Czerka assassin droid HK-01 seized power on Coruscant and thousands of other worlds. The Republic's Juggernaut war droids and the central computers of capital ships turned on their organic masters, as did countless mechanicals—from pint-sized industrial droids to artificial intelligences that had helped govern entire star systems.

Intervention by the Jedi brought the Great Droid Revolution to a halt after three months, after which droids were regarded with deep suspicion and subject to a web of regulations. War droids weren't seen in large numbers until the Sith War, the Mandalorian Wars, and the Jedi Civil War centuries later, and the Republic's use of war droids aroused widespread fear and revulsion among its citizens. Shortly after the Jedi Civil War ended, a cabal of droids seized control of the Gordian Reach, which had to be liberated by a war-weary Republic. These shocks brought about another wave of anti-droid fervor and new restrictions on their use.

In the last centuries of the Republic, the specter of droid armies reappeared. The galaxy's megacorps sought to automate the extraction, consumption, and transport of raw materials from the Rim to the Core, and from there it was a logical step to seeking droids to defend remote installations and shipping convoys. The Neimoidians in particular pursued droid research, as they disliked manual labor and mistrusted other organics as servants and laborers.

The Arkanian Revolution of 50 BBY saw rogue Arkanian scientists rebel against their world's government and assemble a cyborg army to fight them. Opposing them were cybernetic warriors serving the Arkanian Dominion and the Jedi Order, whose representatives included a strange band of Force-sensitive cyborgs in droid bodies known as the Iron Knights.

CZERKA ASSASSIN
DROID HK-01

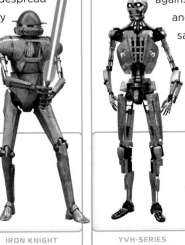

IRON KNIGHT

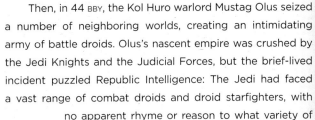

Then, in 44 BBY, the Kol Huro warlord Mustag Olus seized a number of neighboring worlds, creating an intimidating army of battle droids. Olus's nascent empire was crushed by the Jedi Knights and the Judicial Forces, but the brief-lived incident puzzled Republic Intelligence: The Jedi had faced a vast range of combat droids and droid starfighters, with no apparent rhyme or reason to what variety of mechanicals they might encounter at any one time. It was almost as if the entire war was a demented experiment in mechanized warfare. (Indeed, Olus's uprising would eventually be revealed as exactly that.)

In the 30s BBY, megacorps such as the Trade Federation, InterGalactic Banking Clan, and Commerce Guild began deploying combat droids to defend their interests, while secretly pursuing a massive military buildup in which manufacturers such as Baktoid Combat Automata, the Colicoids, and the Techno Union created a number of droid models designed to wage war against the Republic. B1 battle droids, droidekas, and starfighters known as vulture droids first saw action in the invasion of Naboo in 32 BBY; a decade later, the Clone Wars would see billions upon billions of droids battle the Republic's armies from one side of the galaxy to the other.

JUGGERNAUT
WAR DROID

YVH-SERIES
BATTLE DROID

While Republic propaganda emphasized the bravery and sacrifice of the living soldiers defending civilization against a metal horde, the Republic also sought mechanical soldiers—though with far less success. War droids such as TaggeCo's L8-L9 and Z-X3 models were failures, but the lessons learned were put to use in the Empire's secret Dark Trooper project, scuttled by the Rebel agent Kyle Katarn. During the Yuuzhan Vong invasion, the New Republic experimented with war droids known as Yuuzhan Vong Hunters. By then, the Yuuzhan Vong's bioengineered weapons terrified worlds far more than the thought of mechanical soldiers did.

RENDILI AND KUAT

Throughout galactic history, the planet Rendili has been synonymous with starship creation: A cradle of dry docks and orbital construction facilities surrounded the green world centuries before it became a founding member of the Republic.

During the time of the Empire, Rendili StarDrive was the latest incarnation of the planet's ancient shipbuilding tradition, long known for producing starships that could be easily scaled up or down based on clients' needs and adapted for a number of functions. Through the ages Rendili prided itself on efficiency and reliability, with little use for politics, design aesthetics, or pushing the envelope of research and development. Rather than worry about such things, its shipwrights reused designs from a grab bag of cultures and eras and acquired the rights to technologies once they became widespread in the galaxy.

For millennia before the Clone Wars, Rendili was the primary manufacturer of warships for the Republic Navy and star systems' home fleets, with some of its *Praetorian*-class frigates, *Hammerhead*-class cruisers, and *Thranta*-class cruisers seeing service for more than a millennium. After the Ruusan Reformations, Rendili built a far-flung network of shipyards by licensing its designs and production expertise to hundreds of Rim worlds. While supplying the Judicials with capital ships for rapid-response fleets, it devoted much of its industrial capacity to building patrol craft for the new regional sectors' Planetary Security Forces.

Rendili's wealth and stature seemed assured, but in the Republic's final centuries its dominance was challenged by new competitors with sharp elbows. The most determined was Kuat Drive Yards, which had a long history of building sector defense warships and escorts for mercantile fleets, but lacked Rendili's prestige. KDY poured trillions of credits into producing imposing battleships for the galaxy's home fleets, telling Senators and power brokers that such mighty capital ships were far more effective than undersized patrol craft.

Rendili scorned such ships as little more than trophy craft, noting that the Ruusan Reformations prevented them from being fully armed or operating beyond their sectors, and scoffing that no threat in the galaxy justified the creation of warships on a scale that barely fit within existing capital ship classifications. A century before the Empire's rise, Rendili unveiled the *Dreadnaught*-class heavy cruiser, intended as muscle for Judicial task forces and a flagship for Planetary Security Forces. By any measure, the Dreadnaught was a success—various models would see service under the

on KDY's shipyards, secret hyperspace routes, and specialist deepdocks designed for new classes of massive capital ships. And there was another Blissex employed by KDY: Walex's daughter Lira. Her gifts as a shipwright rivaled her father's, and she was eager to step out of his shadow.

The Republic feared—with good reason—that Count Dooku might prey on StarDrive's divided loyalties and persuade Rendili to defect. Hoping to retain Rendili's industrial capacity, the Republic asked it to work with KDY on the design and construction of the *Victory*-class Star Destroyer, a request the desperate company agreed to. But the friction with KDY only further exposed the fault lines in the Rendili ranks. Many of its licensee yards defected to the Separatists, and a Separatist coup in 20 BBY led to a showdown between Republic and Separatist warships in the system, with Rendili's Home Defense Fleet caught between the two sides.

The Republic won the day and kept Rendili in the fold, but StarDrive's fate was sealed. KDY would become the sole supplier of the Empire's Star Destroyers, with Rendili shifting the bulk of its work for the Empire to weapons platforms. Lira Blissex became the wife of a Grand Moff; her father defected to the infant Rebellion.

Republic, Empire, New Republic, and Galactic Federation. But the galaxy had changed—and KDY's new classes of larger, faster battleships won the day.

It was KDY, not Rendili, that was rewarded with the secret contract for the Grand Army of the Republic's warships and vehicles, and that emerged as the rearmed Republic's shipwright of choice, with the *Acclamator*-class transport and *Venator*-class Star Destroyer becoming Republic icons during the Clone Wars. Rendili fought back as best it could, with Arch-Provost Bengila Urlan ordering StarDrive spies and infochants to steal Kuati secrets and copy designs, touching off an intricate, sometimes murderous game of felinx-and-rodus between the two shipwrights.

The rivalry between Kuat and Rendili became part of a family struggle between the galaxy's most talented shipwrights. KDY's top shipwright was the legendary Walex Blissex, but he was alarmed by the galaxy's rush to war, and disturbed by the machinations of the Republic war ministers and their KDY ties. Arch-Provost Urlan thought he had crippled KDY when he lured away Blissex to make warships for StarDrive. But the Republic war effort already depended

D'HARHAN AND THE CYBORG WARRIORS

MARZOON SECTOR, MID RIM, 5 ABY

"You're mobile now, Balancesheet. So why always meet out here? Getting sentimental? In your profession that's unwise."

From its couch of spongy bladders the multilegged Assembler cocked its triangular head at its visitor, expressionless as always behind his mask of Mandalorian iron. Two arachnoid nodes, sensing their master was no longer focused on them, climbed up their strands of neural fiber to hide themselves among the vaults of dingy webbing that hid the durasteel walls, ceiling, and floor of the old XTS freighter's hold.

"Not sentiment, Fett. Security. For you and I to meet elsewhere would invite inquiries. *Why that meeting place? What significance could it have? What other information might it impart?* In this place, where my predecessor met its end, all is known and no inquiries are necessary."

Boba Fett let his eyes flicker across the Assembler's webbing, watching patterns of neural activity illuminate the strands, pulsing softly in accord with Balancesheet's thoughts and commands.

"Once you used this freighter's systems as your eyes and ears," Fett rasped. "Now nodes. And webbing. And a throne. And look how much you've grown, Balancesheet. You're the spitting image of Kud'ar Mub'at itself. What would it say, do you think?"

"You're not conversationalist enough for jibes, Fett. To business."

"Very well. Business."

"Four years ago. Circumtore. You, Bossk, Zuckuss, IG-88. And a fourth hunter. A cyborg."

"D'harhan."

"Yes. I wish to know about him. Where he came from. How he came to be what he was."

"Why?"

"Because I have a client who is interested, of course."

"Why?"

"Not your business."

"And in return?"

"I am asking very little. A brief reminiscence. A verification of certain facts already in my possession. I'd think you would do this small thing for me as a gesture of appreciation for our many transactions that have proved mutually advantageous."

"You'd be wrong."

"A trade, then. Your small bit of information for a similar bit of data in my possession."

"Regarding?"

"A bounty, of course."

Fett simply regarded Balancesheet. The hold was silent except for the thrum of the freighter's systems and the skittering of the nodes as they went about the business of the web.

"Tel Trevura," Balancesheet said finally.

Fett lifted his helmet slightly—for him, Balancesheet thought, that was a sign of considerable interest.

"Tel Trevura is dead," Fett said.

"Perhaps not."

"What are you offering?"

Balancesheet sent a pulse of its thought through the web and a node descended, a datacard held in two spindly legs. The node stopped, as directed, two meters out of Fett's reach.

"The coordinates of a crash site on a planetoid in Wild Space. The navicomputer was damaged and wiped, but the scouts who found the site reconstructed the transponder code. It matches that of the JumpMaster 5000 that Trevura took at blasterpoint on Svivren."

"Which means anyone who can read a BoSS registry will be all over the site," Fett said, unimpressed.

"No, it doesn't. In preparation for this day, my predecessor had the registry altered after Trevura stole his ship. No one looking in the registry will connect it with Trevura, or think it anything other than one of a hundred such crash sites cataloged every month."

"What's the trade?"

"The datacard, plus fifty percent of the bounty on Trevura. For answers to some questions about D'harhan."

"Thirty percent."

"Forty."

Fett dipped his gargoyle helmet in grudging assent.

"D'harhan, then. Where did he come from? I've heard it said he was an Arkanian Renegade."

"No," Fett said. "He came from somewhere much stranger. The Niorde system. Don't bother asking one of your nodes, it's uncharted. Deep in the Unknown Regions."

"You've been there?"

"A long time ago," Fett said. "During the Clone Wars."

"You couldn't have been more than a child."

The helmet dipped again.

"Who did you go with? The woman called Nashtah?"

"Not your business."

Balancesheet twitched a spiny leg in irritation. "Continue then. D'harhan."

Fett thought back, wondering what Balancesheet already knew, how much he should tell. It couldn't matter to D'harhan or anyone else on Niorde, unimaginably far away and utterly ruined.

"His world had been at war for centuries with a neighboring planet. Their rivals had hired mercenaries from the Leech Legions, and were preparing to unleash them on D'harhan's world. So a few dozen Niordi scouts decided to become living weapons. Artillery units that could move and think like organics."

"He was cybernetically altered?" Balancesheet asked, black eyes glittering like burned-out fuel crystals.

"Yes. In a secret laboratory on the fringes of the system. I was there."

He hesitated.

"Go on, Fett." Balancesheet edged closer.

Fett hadn't thought about those days in years; if Balancesheet hadn't been paying, he supposed he never would have. The whir of medical droids, the whine of saws,

the bright lights that never shut off, and the fitful movements of the Niordi under the surgical shrouds, as they were opened and changed.

"They removed his head, Fett," Balancesheet chittered. "Isn't that right? They removed your friend's head."

"He wasn't my friend. Yes, they removed his head. The brain was flash-frozen within seconds and transferred to a box within his breastplate. They threw the rest away. Most of the organs went, too—they kept the heart and the lungs, though those were relocated to make room for the tracking system and motors."

"They threw away his head and replaced it with a gun," Balancesheet said.

"Hardly a gun—a laser emplacement patterned after the ones on an Alsakan battle cruiser," Fett said. "Liquid-cooled, steam-vented, enough punch to penetrate the armor of a light cruiser. They enhanced his shoulders, arms, legs, and spine with durasteel, to take the weight of the thing. And they added a tail of articulated metal, to brace against the recoil."

"Was he different, afterward?"

Fett considered the Assembler.

"Was he different after he became a life-support system for a laser emplacement? I'd say so."

"Different how?" Balancesheet asked, either missing or ignoring the contempt in Fett's voice.

"He *was* his weapon. To look at something was to target it. To fire on an enemy was to live. Without it he was nothing."

"Did they win?"

"Win what?"

"D'harhan's people. Did they win their war with the Leech Legions?"

"No," Fett said. "There were complications. Half of the Niordi scouts died on the table. By the time the others were operational the Leech Legions had overrun Niorde. There was nothing left to defend. D'harhan and two dozen others attacked the enemy flagship. He was the only one to survive."

"So they had their vengeance, at least," Balancesheet said.

Fett shrugged.

"And what happened on Circumtore?"

"You already know that," Fett said, arms folded over his battered armor plates. "From Zuckuss. Maybe from others."

"D'harhan trusted you," Balancesheet said. "And you betrayed him."

"He trusted me to betray him."

"What does that mean?"

"He was tired of being what he was. And he couldn't be anything else."

"His last words to you. What were they?"

"I'm sure you already know them."

"I would like to hear them from you," Balancesheet said, its triangular face peering up at Fett.

"He said, 'I can stop now. But you still must go on.'"

"What did that mean?"

"I already told you that."

The web was quiet; even the nodes were still.

"It is a curious sentiment, desiring the cessation of one's own existence," Balancesheet said. "I cannot imagine it."

The Assembler cricked a foreleg and the little node reappeared with the datacard, which Fett took from its clawed grip.

"Do you ever feel that way, Fett?" Balancesheet asked.

"In my experience, being alive beats the alternative," Fett said.

And yet, Fett thought, Kud'ar Mub'at had felt differently in the end. The same Kud'ar Mub'at whose frozen, splintered neural fibers would float forever in the vacuum surrounding the freighter where they both stood. And if Kud'ar Mub'at had felt that way eventually, it stood to reason that Balancesheet would, too, one day. As, perhaps, Fett himself would.

But if that day were to come, Fett thought, it hadn't arrived yet.

And for now, that was enough.

Two Corellian Engineering Corp. YT-1300 freighters (John VanFleet)

MANUFACTURER: CORELLIAN ENGINEERING

The Corellian Engineering Corporation builds small, straightforward civilian freighters that customers transform into legends. CEC's most famous products are ships such as the *Millennium Falcon,* the *Wild Karrde,* and the CR90 Blockade Runners used by pirates and Rebels alike—hot-rod starships bristling with weapons.

Corellian stock hulls are designed as reliable cargo haulers with slow and simple engines, ships that independent pilots can afford to buy and fly. They are also adaptable platforms for tinkerers who seek engine upgrades and equipment modifications. Standard ships are regularly enhanced with official refit suites, or else rebuilt and up-weaponed by shadowport engineers and outlaw techs. These modified CEC ships are no longer "civilian" in any meaningful sense of the term: They're often the vessels of choice for pirates, smugglers, privateers, and slavers, as well as for reasonably honest starhoppers looking to stay one step ahead of trouble.

Official, militarized variants on a number of CEC hulls also exist, serving as long-range shuttles and gunships for galactic fleets and regional militias. Ranging from the venerable *Consular*-class light cruisers of the ancient Republic to the *Ranger*-class gunships that fought the Yuuzhan Vong under the Galactic Alliance, these hulls have extended CEC's dominance of the military market upward from the armed-freighter class to the ranks of small capital ships.

CEC also produces a small number of dedicated military designs, predominantly anti-pirate starfighters and gunships for the Corellian Sector Fleet. But CEC's largest yards can build dreadnoughts, and its reputation for solid spaceframes and excellent engines means it's often subcontracted to build large warships using other shipwrights' designs. Corellian-engineered Star Destroyers were considered the fastest ships in the Imperial Navy, at both sublight and hyperspace speeds.

CEC claims to be the galaxy's oldest starship manufacturer, with a direct lineage from the consortium that first developed the hyperdrive. In its modern form, it is a conglomerate uniting all the starship manufacturers based in the Corellian system, including the Keynne design bureau and the venerable Vanjervalis and Vaufthau shipyards. CEC's showcase facilities are located in massive orbital factories and dockyards above Corellia, but these are supported by a scattered, often secretive network of outstations, not to mention the aftermarket skills of every Corellian scoundrel with a hydrospanner.

FLASHPOINT: NABOO

"Preparing for war is science. Prosecuting it is chance."
—Mon Mothma, chief of state, Alliance to Restore the Republic

THE RISE OF THE TRADE FEDERATION

The Trade Federation began in 350 BBY as a Republic-chartered organization tasked with mediating disputes between the galaxy's merchants and its shippers—at the time, transportation megacorps such as Pulsar Supertanker, Quasar Cargo, Ororo Transportation, and Red Star Shipping were choking off commerce by shutting out competitors from Rim spaceports and refusing to share navigational information.

The Federation helped curb such abuses, and over its first century evolved into a shipping cartel in its own right, with members banding together to negotiate more favorable rates and policies and then contracting with Hoersch-Kessel to build a new fleet of Federation freighters. By 250 BBY the Trade Federation had left its original mission behind and become a powerful association working to advance trade interests in the Senate.

The Trade Federation wasn't just a lobbying group, however. It also worked to open up new regions of the galaxy for commerce, establishing a network of brokerage houses, retail outlets, depots, way stations, and landing fields in thousands of backwater systems. Such efforts culminated in the creation of the Trade Explorer Corps, which blazed many new routes into the Rim and beyond the frontier.

Inevitably, the defense of transports carrying raw materials and finished goods became part of its purview. Federation companies often found themselves relying on indifferent, corrupt, or nonexistent Planetary Security Forces for protection. The Federation contributed funds to improve sector fleets, but eventually its members decided to take matters into their own hands, voting to establish the Trade Defense Forces.

The Trade Federation of the late 200s BBY was hailed as an ideal Republic institution. It represented its members' interests capably and fairly on Coruscant, made investments that advanced commerce across the galaxy, augmented the power of Judicials and local forces with a well-regarded military arm, and was run by a diverse group of species and interests. But as the Trade Federation grew in power, it became the very thing it had been created to oppose: a cartel that dominated trade and ruthlessly eliminated competition. By the 150s BBY trade between the galaxy's central and outlying worlds was once again drying up. In an effort to jump-start commerce, the Senate wound up handing the Trade Federation even more influence.

The declaration of the Outer Rim as a free-trade zone in 124 BBY exempted the Federation from the growing snarl of taxes levied by system, sector, and regional governments. Much-reduced levies now flowed directly to the Republic, which promised to apportion them more equally. (Some Mid Rim sectors were exempted in 118 BBY.) Along with the establishment of the Free Trade Zone, the Senate extended its definition of functional constituencies eligible for Senate representation to include the galaxy's most powerful guilds and megacorps.

Granted a seat in the Senate, the Trade Federation soon became enormously powerful. The cartel moved swiftly and ruthlessly into the new Free Trade Zone, crafting agreements

Anakin Skywalker earns his wings above Naboo (John VanFleet)

with impoverished sectors that effectively handed over their representation and votes in the Senate. Other Rim sectors preserved their political independence but not their economic self-determination, becoming virtual thralls of the Federation. Within two generations, the Trade Federation controlled enough Senate votes to hamper competitors, influence courts, and stall legislation it opposed.

The Stark Hyperspace War of 46 BBY marked a turning point for both the Federation and its foes in the Senate. After the disruption of the bacta shortage and the war, the Federation began campaigning for the right to greater military capabilities, citing not only the danger posed by raiders such as Iaco Stark and the Nebula Front terrorists but also renewed factionalism in the Republic. Meanwhile, the Federation's opponents were pushing the Senate to take firmer control of galactic commerce and security in the outlying sectors.

And though few knew it, the Trade Federation had acquired a powerful new ally and patron: the mysterious Sith Lord Darth Sidious. Sidious—who first declared himself to high-ranking Neimoidians on the organization's seven-member directorate—held many levers of power in the Republic, able to manipulate the Senate, courts, and Republic bureaucracy. Under his influence, the Federation stepped up its secret military buildup, bought up more and more votes, and became far more aggressive in pursuing its policy goals.

In 33 BBY, with the Federation at the apex of its political might, Supreme Chancellor Valorum sought to bring the organization to heel. Prodded by Naboo's Senator Palpatine, Valorum pushed the Senate to do away with the Free Trade Zones while granting the Federation additional defense allowances. That drove the Federation into an alliance with the InterGalactic Banking Clan, Corporate Alliance, and Techno Union, which would also be hurt by renewed taxation. And in a direct strike at the Federation, four members of the directorate were killed at a summit on Eriadu organized by Valorum.

The attack on the directorate and Sidious's warnings convinced the directorate—now controlled by Neimoidians—to intensify the Federation's military buildup. Companies such as Baktoid and Haor Chall received gigantic contracts for the rapid creation of new warships and droid armies. War was coming.

Trade Defense Force crewers reunite with their families after a long cruise (Jason Palmer)

THE TRADE DEFENSE FORCE

Upon its establishment in 274 BBY, the Trade Defense Force's initial responsibilities were to escort convoys and maintain spaceport security, with dues paid by member firms funneled to regional sectors to beef up their Planetary Security Forces. Those Sector Forces didn't answer to the Trade Federation, but the TDF did—and over time its units became critical to ensuring security in poor Rim systems.

The bulk of the TDF's capital ship assets were corvettes, frigates, and gunships—fast attack craft intended to drive pirates away from slow-moving bulk freighters. The TDF acquired its warships from a number of shipbuilders, and later supplemented them with several new designs from Kuat Drive Yards: the *Auxilia*-class pursuit destroyer, *Lupus*-class missile frigate, *Munifex*-class light cruiser (known colloquially as the "Class 1000" after the TDF's initial order), and *Captor*-class heavy munitions cruiser. Meanwhile, TDF marines—trained on Balmorra according to that ancient world's proud traditions—defended freighters against boarders in space and bandits in port.

While the Federation's new fleet disturbed some in the Core, the TDF proved effective in a number of early engagements with pirates and raiders, and the Federation worked closely with the Judicials against bigger threats. Moreover, the TDF's assets were constantly spread across the galaxy's network of trade routes, arguing against the idea that they would be useful for direct military action. By the 200s BBY, the TDF had its own proud traditions, attracting talented naval officers who otherwise might have sought a career in the Planetary Security Forces or the Judicials.

But like its parent organization, the TDF changed. As the Trade Federation became more ruthless in exploiting outlying sectors, the TDF became an implement of the organization's will, with its turbolasers forcing concessions from backwater systems and driving non-Federation transports away from ports. And the Kuati and Balmorran traditions that had helped shape the TDF faded as first Gran and Sullustans and then Neimoidians took over key roles in the Federation. As the Federation pursued rapid militarization, the TDF's marines were largely replaced by battle droids, and converted Lucrehulk battleships increasingly enforced the Federation's policies.

THE GUNGAN GRAND ARMY

Naboo's Gungan Grand Army won renown for its exploits at the Battle of the Great Grass Plains, with military historians marveling at the chance to study a traditional land battle fought at close range between armies largely composed of infantry—the kind of confrontation rarely found in modern galactic society.

Amid such accolades, much is forgotten. For one thing, the battle was a diversionary tactic intended to give Naboo strike teams time to sneak into occupied Theed and capture the Trade Federation viceroy. For another, the Federation's own fears allowed the battle to unfold as it did: The Naboo blockade had been reduced to a single droid control ship, and the Neimoidians kept their droid starfighters in orbit because they feared the ground assault was a diversion for an attack on the blockade.

The Gungan Grand Army is a curious institution. The Gungans protect and police their territory by calling on militiagungs, able-bodied Gungans who provide their own uniforms and weapons. Each Gungan settlement is required to maintain combat readiness and conduct annual drills, ensuring that the Grand Army can be assembled in less than thirty-six hours.

The Grand Army draws its strength from two Gungan characteristics: their bond with Naboo's native animals and their curious technology.

Animals play key roles in the Grand Army. Giant fambaas carry its shield generators into battle, falumpasets drag catapults and battle wagons loaded with energy balls, and kaadu serve as rapid-response cavalry units. All Gungans respect and revere kaadus, but the bond between Gungan soldier and kaadu is particularly strong. When a Gungan becomes an officer, he or she receives a personal kaadu in a public ceremony, and will only ride another if the original kaadu should die or become too old for battle. Officers and their kaadus seem to share a telepathic bond, with the kaadu anticipating the officer's orders and alerting him or her to trouble that it spots.

The Gungan shield generators were originally used to keep giant swamp creatures and sea monsters away from settlements, but they are portable—provided something

as big as a fambaa is available to move one. In battle one fambaa carries on its back a shield generator, which fires an arc of plasma into a capacitor carried by another fambaa. The resulting plasma shield is 150 meters in diameter, and typically calibrated to repel small, fast-moving objects that generate heat, as well as big, slow-moving objects. At Great Grass Plains, it protected the Gungans against the Trade Federation's artillery and tanks, forcing individual battle droids to engage the Gungans. The two-part dynamos overheat quickly, and are typically among the first units targeted, giving the cockpit of the shield generator the grim nickname "suicide seat."

Gungan foot soldiers are organized into command units, each led by a general appointed for the battle. They wear armor of leather and metal and carry personal defense shields that protect against both blaster bolts and particle weapons—a technology that proved of great interest to the Republic in the aftermath of the Naboo invasion. (Republic scientists found the technology promising, but noted that the energy field generated considerable heat; the shield generator typically overloaded within fifteen minutes.)

Militiagungs typically carry cestas, atlatls, or arbalests, with some using electropoles. Typical Gungan ranged weapons are designed to fling energy balls—thin, super-charged organic membranes encasing unstable plasma energy. This "energy goo" is extracted from Naboo's core, either by deep-crust mining or by harvesting it from plasma-hungry plants known as locaps, and used to power many Gungan devices. Direct contact with this plasma stuns or electrocutes organic beings, and shorts out the circuitry of Droids and vehicles.

Battle droids attack Gungan forces at the Battle of the Great Grass Plains (Darren Tan)

ARMORY AND SENSOR PROFILE

B1 BATTLE DROIDS

Clone troopers dismissed B1 battle droids as clankers, blasting the spindly-legged mechanicals by the dozens in engagements from one side of the galaxy to the other. And from a military standpoint, B1s were worthy of their contempt: They were poor shots, they were thinly armored (particularly at the electromagnetic joints), they had lack-luster audiovisual sensors, and their cheap cognitive modules struggled to process any strategy handed down from central control computers that was more complicated than marching in one direction firing blasters.

But battle droids weren't made to be smart. They were made to be *cheap,* and they were. That allowed Separatist factories to produce them in staggering numbers—Republic citizens believed quintillions had been made. What B1s lacked in brains, they more than made up for in numbers, battering down planets' defenses.

The first B1s produced by Baktoid Combat Automata weren't meant for war, but for defending Trade Federation cargo haulers against pirates and bandits. At the Battle of Naboo, Anakin Skywalker's destruction of the orbiting Droid Control Ship eliminated the droid army's central control computer, forcing the army into hibernation mode. The sight of Gungans kicking motionless battle droids embarrassed the Trade Federation, which ordered many of its first-generation B1s retrofitted with cognitive modules that would allow for independent thought. That prevented remote shutdowns, but making B1s smart or truly combat-effective would have been prohibitively expensive. Instead, the Separatists built new generations of war droids with much-improved mechanical minds and muscle.

The B1s' squeaky, modulated voices may have seemed more comical than frightening, but many beings found their skeletal limbs and bleached coloration disturbing. Neimoidian crewers spread the rumor that the droids' elongated faces had been modeled after Neimoidian skulls. The truth was more mundane: The B1s were designed in imitation of their Geonosian builders.

B1 BATTLE DROID

DROIDEKA (DESTROYER DROID)

DESTROYER DROIDS

Nicknamed destroyer droids, death balls, or rollies, droidekas were among the deadliest infantry units deployed by the Separatists during the Clone Wars. The droids' double-barreled blaster cannons could take out light vehicles, while their deflector shields made them virtually immune to small-arms fire and were polarized to allow the droideka's own laser bolts to penetrate the shield. A droideka's shield was less powerful to the rear, but its tough bronzium armor offered substantial protection. Their keen sensor packages could detect enemies through sound, vibrations, or radiation, and they could curl into wheeled mode to pursue their quarries, snapping out of wheel mode onto their three pointed legs, powering up shields and opening fire before foes could react. Even Jedi Knights hesitated when faced with these powerful, ruthless killing machines.

Before the Clone Wars, the Trade Federation contracted the Colicoid Creation Nest to build initial allotments of droidekas; the delivery of fifty bargeloads of exotic flesh won the cartel a substantial discount on a license to build more units. To save credits and guard against Colicoid treachery, Nute Gunray insisted that the Colicoids ship droidekas without individual intelligence matrices, slaving them to guidance signals from a central control computer. This made the destroyers less effective in combat, a shortcoming remedied after the disaster at Naboo, when Separatist foundries began turning out self-directed units.

The Colicoids built droidekas (a name that combines the Basic word *droid* with *-eka,* Colicoid for "hireling" or "drone") in their own image. They built several other models of war droids as well. The Separatists used spindly, hook-armed infiltrators to cut through hulls and take over starships, while the Colicoids defended their homeworld with dreaded Scorpenek annihilator droids, encountered when the Republic stormed Colla IV late in the Clone Wars. Baktoid produced a droideka variant, the Mark II, in its Hypori foundries, but the Mark II's development came too late to be a factor in the Clone Wars.

AAT (ARMORED ASSAULT TANK)

The armored assault tank was the warhorse of the Trade Federation: a machine built for pitched battle, designed to break enemy formations with a shoulder-to-shoulder charge. As the invasion of Naboo showed, this tactic could prove decisive against both high-tech defense forces and primitive alien hordes.

The AAT's armored fuselage was narrow, with a crew cockpit at the front and an engine unit behind. The bow rested on a wide, shovel-shaped repulsorsled, while the main gun turret overhung the engine block at the rear, extending the total length to 9.75 meters. The vehicle was capable of speeds up to fifty-five kilometers per hour, and the turret gun provided long-range artillery fire against any ground target within visual range—normally enemy armor, light deflector shields, or large troop formations. To defeat scout vehicles and infantry, secondary weapons included twin repeating blasters flanking the hull, and two short-range blast cannons in front of the cockpit.

The repulsorsled also contained six missile launchers, normally armed with short-range energy flechettes to break up infantry formations. These launchers could also fire armor-piercing shells against enemy vehicles or heavy rounds to smash through reinforced emplacements, although these systems were hard to aim in battle.

The AAT was crewed by three pilot droids and one commander. They were simplistic drones who produced predictable tactics—but the vehicle's effectiveness wasn't diminished by their lack of initiative while part of a close-formation armored assault. When the Trade Federation was able to force a pitched battle, the AAT's only serious limitation was its inability to penetrate deflector shields—a drawback common to all repulsorlift vehicles.

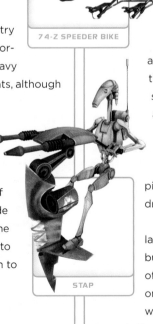

AAT (ARMORED ASSAULT TANK)

CK-6 SWOOP BIKE

74-Z SPEEDER BIKE

STAP

SPEEDER BIKES AND STAPS

Speeder bikes are single-seat repulsorcraft, usually consisting of an open-air pilot's seat astride an engine block, with steering vanes in front. They are also known as "swoop bikes," a name originally applied to lightweight racing models with an improved flight ceiling, but now used indiscriminately for any bike with sports pretensions. Panniers and postilion seats provide some models with the ability to carry minimal cargo and a single passenger; in military configurations, armament is usually restricted to a single light blaster.

Speeder bikes and swoops have been around for millennia, and entered military use through mercenary groups, acquiring a new popularity with regular light cavalry units under the "flying force" doctrine of the last decades of the Republic.

The Single Trooper Aerial Platform, or STAP, was the Trade Federation's version of the military speeder bike. It uses an unconventional configuration known as an airhook, consisting of a vertical repulsor keel with the pilot standing upright at the rear, feet placed wide apart to allow engine exhaust to discharge between the legs. This design originated with civilian speeder makers Longspur and Alloi, but when Baktoid acquired the license, they slashed the production cost, boosted the top speed to four hundred kilometers per hour, and armed the STAP with twin repeating blasters on the control yoke—an unusually heavy armament for a bike. Military STAPs are almost always operated by battle droid pilots—unlike organic pilots, their metal bodies were unaffected by the dramatic acceleration or the powerful exhaust jets.

STAP bikes were designed to be used in far larger numbers than most other military swoops, but their roles remained the same: scouting ahead of a campaign army, pursuing retreating enemies on the battlefield, and anti-insurgency patrol. They were among the most effective units of the droid army in the Naboo campaign.

LUCREHULK-CLASS BATTLESHIP

After the Trade Federation won the right to better defend its convoys, shipwrights licked their chops in the hope of huge new contracts. But the cartel's executive board never believed in spending a credit it didn't have to: It decided to refit a number of its *Lucrehulk*-class cargo freighters, made centuries before by Hoersch-Kessel, into warships. Besides saving credits, the conversion program allowed the Trade Federation to hide the extent of its military buildup—a course of action recommended by Darth Sidious.

Even as a cargo hauler, a Lucrehulk was an intimidating hulk more than three thousand meters in diameter. Now Baktoid Fleet Ordnance added new armor plating, beefed-up shields, and quad laser batteries that could rotate inward when not in use, concealing the battleship's offensive capabilities. Baktoid also reconfigured the hauler's innards to carry landing ships, AATs, multitroop transports (MTTs), and as many as fifteen hundred droid starfighters. While the laser cannons weren't terribly effective— their limited fields of fire betrayed the design's mercantile origins—Baktoid assured the Neimoidians that the clouds of vulture droids would make for a more than sufficient defense against any attacker.

The modular nature of the Lucrehulk allowed the Trade Federation considerable flexibility. The heart (and brain) of each Lucrehulk was its core ship or centersphere, which housed a huge central computer and power systems. Core ships could detach from the near-ring of cargo holds and engines, using their ion drives to descend to planetary surfaces and dock in repulsorlift cushions. Before the Federation's military buildup, it used core ships at the center of various freighter and tanker configurations; after the Battle of Naboo, the centerspheres became the heart of a number

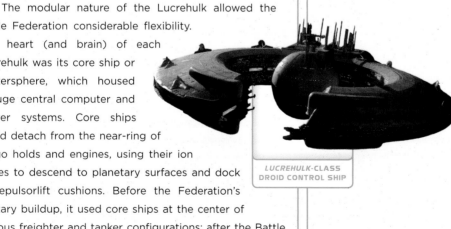

LUCREHULK-CLASS
BATTLESHIP

CORE SHIP

LUCREHULK-CLASS
DROID CONTROL SHIP

of different warships, including cruisers with improved weaponry and speedier destroyers.

At the urging of Sidious, the Federation responded to the Republic's decision to reinstitute taxes on Rim trade routes with a blockade of Naboo, the homeworld of Senator Palpatine. The Federation assembled a fleet of battleships led by the *Saak'ak* at its distribution center on Enarc, whose skies were often thick with Lucrehulks, and sent them to nearby Naboo.

While the battleships supplied the blockade's teeth, the most distinctive ship dispatched to Naboo was the Droid Control Ship *Vuutun Palaa,* a Lucrehulk variant bristling with antennas and signal receiver dishes. The droid control ship's massive central computer was programmed to command not just vulture droids, but the army of battle droids sent to take over the planet. When Anakin Skywalker fired a pair of proton torpedoes into one of the *Vuutun Palaa*'s reactors, the chain reaction destroyed the ship and the droids shut down.

The Empire nationalized the Federation after the Clone Wars and sold off the Lucrehulk fleet, including decommissioned battleships. Most were used by galactic shippers, but some wound up in the hands of Rebels or criminal organizations, and were turned back into warships. One converted Lucrehulk, the carrier *Fortressa,* was destroyed by the Death Star at Horuz in 0 BBY.

BEGIN, THE CLONE WAR DOES

"The sergeant is the army."
—Bric, instructor, Grand Army of the Republic

THE GRAND ARMY OF THE REPUBLIC

To the astonishment of the citizens it served, the Grand Army of the Republic emerged full-blown in a galaxy that found itself suddenly at war. Never before had a comparable military force been prepared in such secrecy—no sooner had Chancellor Palpatine authorized the creation of a centralized army than one materialized to intervene on Geonosis. And never before had a significant military force performed at such a high level in its very first engagements.

There was obviously a story behind the sudden appearance of an army of more than a million clone soldiers, outfitted with everything from assault ships and gunboats to speeder bikes and artillery. But amid the chaos of endless battles and the Republic's new emphasis on secrecy, that story wasn't understood until decades after the Clone Wars ended—and even then there were missing pieces and contradictions that nettled historians.

The Grand Army began as a vision of Sifo-Dyas, a Jedi Master from the Cassandran Worlds whose gift of precognition was tragically undercut by the fact that his peers rarely believed his visions to be true. Sifo-Dyas sensed that the Republic would soon face an existential threat—and so he sought an army that would allow it to survive, contracting with the Kaminoans to create it and supplying the initial funding.

But Sifo-Dyas never saw his army. He was murdered, and his secret project taken over by Darth Sidious. Sidious directed his apprentice, the fallen Jedi Count Dooku, to supply a prime clone to the Kaminoans, with the bounty hunter Jango Fett accepting the role in return for five million credits and an unaltered clone of himself, his "son" Boba. In his guise as Supreme Chancellor Palpatine, Sidious then funneled untold billions in credits from the Republic's budgets through a maze of intermediaries to the Kaminoans and to Kuat Drive Yards, whose Rothana Heavy Engineering subsidiary secretly created a slew of new warships and artillery weapons for the army. Obi-Wan Kenobi eventually discovered what was happening on Geonosis, but Sidious was untroubled: His plan had always relied on the Republic's arming itself. Sifo-Dyas had seen the future, but not the wheels driving what he saw, and had unwittingly helped bring about the very war that had alarmed him.

While specifications for the Grand Army's fighting vehicles and air support were developed by KDY amid great secrecy, Jango Fett took an active role in the outfitting of the clone troops and supervised their training. Fett trained the elite clones who became the Republic's Advanced Recon Commandos, recruiting one hundred training sergeants for the Grand Army, seventy-five of them Mandalorian mercenaries. This group—the *Cuy'val Dar*—played an integral role in preparing ARC troopers, clone commandos (who would eventually number ten thousand) and the army's ordinary clone troopers for the many varieties of warfare they would encounter in their desperate struggle with the Separatists.

The *Cuy'val Dar* also introduced Mandalorian traditions into the Grand Army—fitting considering Fett's Mandalorian heritage, but ironic given that the Mandalorians had been demolished as a fighting force by the Republic the clones would now serve. The Mandalorian warrior codes proved ideal for reinforcing the clones' genetically engineered inclination toward loyalty and unit cohesion: The Grand Army adapted the ancient Mandalorian

(later improved and deployed in numerous variations as Phase II armor) couldn't protect troopers from direct hits from blasters or projectile weapons, it was an excellent defense against glancing shots, impacts, poison gas, and heat.

But the single most valuable item in a clone trooper's kit was his helmet. Helmets bore a T-shaped visor derived from a traditional Mandalorian design, and an antenna in the helmet's fin linked each soldier to the rest of the fighting force. The helmet housed a sophisticated web of sensors and communications gear that let troopers send and receive audiovisual transmissions and sensor data, see in the dark and through smoke and fog, and interface with their weapons to display a targeting reticule on the helmet's heads-up display. Some troopers joked that they were just lever arms that let their helmets pull the trigger.

Standard-issue weapons for clone troopers were the DC-15 blaster and the DC-15 rifle. In addition, clones typically carried two thermal detonators, two concussion grenades, an electromagnetic pulse grenade (known colloquially as a droid popper), and a personal medpac containing synthflesh and bacta. While neither was a part of their standard-issue kit, clone troopers quickly learned the value of also carrying a multitool and sanitary wipes.

The Kaminoans were initially disturbed by the amount of individuality and personality displayed by the clones, but the Jedi and the Republic's non-clone officers encouraged the troopers to see themselves as individuals instead of as interchangeable parts of a collective whole. This was partially because it disturbed many non-clones to think of the clones as "living droids" differentiated only by identifying number, but also because clone troopers fought harder and better when they thought of their batchers as individuals.

Under the Jedi's direction, clones were encouraged to adopt nicknames for themselves, get tattoos, and customize their armor and even their hairstyles. But for most, the pull of the collective remained tremendously strong. When first allowed the chance for individual expression, many clones immediately fell to debating unit colors and insignias with their batchers, and many regarded their nicknames as nobody's business except for superior officers and their own batchers.

CLONE TROOPER RANK GUIDE

The rank structure of the Republic's new army was based on the tradition of the Judicial Forces. The company had its captain, every platoon had its lieutenant and sergeant-major, and each component squad was led by a sergeant and a corporal. In addition, the Kaminoans imposed an orderly system of color designation for the benefit of beings who lacked their ultraviolet vision: Captains wore red flashes on their white armor, lieutenants wore blue, and sergeants and sergeant-majors wore green. The role of corporal was traditionally awarded to the best soldier in the squad, but in an army of identical men, it was often rotated among the troopers, and carried no special insignia. The clone army was trained to be neat, disciplined, and obedient.

The higher ranks presented more of a problem for the cloners' tidy minds: They expected Jedi Knights to hold all command positions, but senior clone officers were needed during training and to maintain discipline and professionalism during campaigns. Experience also taught the Kaminoans that ordinary troopers' parade-ground obedience was a poor fit for senior leadership roles.

The solution: a special cadre of troopers created to hold the rank of commander. Identified by yellow striping on their armor, these clone commanders balanced creative initiative with the obedience prized by Kaminoans. They led small detachments and served as aides to Jedi Knights, and also occupied a hierarchy of leadership positions connected to larger units, culminating in the forty elite marshal commanders who liaised directly with the Jedi generals.

RANK	ARMOR FLASHES	HUD GLYPH	COMMAND ROLE
Marshal Commander		::::	Corps commander
Senior Commander		:::	Brigade/legion commander
Regimental Commander	Yellow	::	Regiment leader
Battalion Commander		:	Battalion leader
Major	Red	IIII	
Captain		III	Company (144 men)
Lieutenant	Blue	II	Platoon (36 men)
2nd Lieutenant		I	
Sergeant-Major	Green	/////	2-in-c of platoon
Sergeant		///	Squad (9 men)
Corporal	None	//	2-in-c of squad
Trooper		/	(none)

ARMORY AND SENSOR PROFILE

SUPER BATTLE DROIDS

After the debacle at Naboo, the Trade Federation sought to reinforce its military capabilities with a new, tougher infantry droid. Noting that Baktoid's E4 baron droid had performed well in limited duties on Naboo, the Trade Federation turned to Baktoid to refine the E4 for mass production as a heavy infantry unit.

Baktoid's answer—at two hundred times the price of a B1 battle droid—was the B2 super battle droid, heavily armored and sporting a rapid-fire laser cannon built into its forearm. B2s were designed to operate independently of a central control computer, but without central direction they weren't particularly smart. Supers would plod directly into a firefight, sometimes hurling other battle droids aside, without the slightest concern for tactics or self-preservation. And to the annoyance of the Neimoidians, B2s sometimes deleted enemies who moved out of visual range from their targeting modules.

Despite their limitations, B2s largely solved the Federation's problem, adding needed muscle to ranks of B1s. Super battle droids also proved adaptable to a number of combat roles, mounting missiles in place of their forearm cannons, swimming to reach their targets, or strapping on rocket packs and taking to the skies to intercept Republic gunships before they could land and off-load troops.

Baktoid experimented with B2 variants during the Clone Wars, though none was produced in large numbers.

Workers on Foundry engineered the four-meter-high B3 ultra battle droid, which not only dwarfed the B2 but bore an arsenal of built-in weapons. The B3 also sported an experimental density projector, which generated a powerful tractor field that allowed it to fix itself in place against any assault or smash through enemy ground units. The combination of the ultra's immense price and episodes in which its density projector froze and locked the droid in place conspired to make it a mere footnote in the history of the war.

B2 BATTLE DROID

B3 BATTLE DROID

C-B3 CORTOSIS
BATTLE DROID

The C-B3 cortosis battle droid was specifically designed to counter the Jedi generals. Having learned that cortosis ore could resist lightsabers' blades and even short out the weapons, Techno Union foreman Wat Tambor charged a factory on Metalorn with armoring B2s with cortosis plates. The C-B3s performed well in a daring raid on the Jedi Temple, but Anakin Skywalker destroyed the Metalorn facility and the design was effectively retired.

REPUBLIC ASSAULT SHIP

The Republic assault ship is designed for a demanding mission profile: race through hyperspace to contested systems, force a path through enemy warships, and land a small army directly on the battlefield.

The underside of this 752-meter heavy cruiser is dominated by an immense assault bay, capable of off-loading an entire legion of elite troops in short order. The hull is packed with barracks, vehicle hangars, and training facilities. The *Acclamator* has berths for sixteen thousand infantry, eighty fighters or shuttles—usually LAAT transports—and eighty-four armored ground craft.

Equally important is the massive hyperdrive fin, taking up the rearmost two hundred meters of the ship's length, and connected to power systems extending the length of the hull. Able to accelerate to a sustained cruising speed of point-six past lightspeed, this allows the *Acclamator* to rush in mere hours from secure Republic bases to distant battlefields.

A dozen quad turbolasers guard against attacking capital ships, and twenty-four anti-starfighter lasers adorn the hull, but the ship's main weapons are four missile tubes in the bows, capable of smashing through battleship blockades.

A fleet of twenty assault ships, constructed in secret at the Rothana shipyards, carried the first units of the Grand Army to the Battle of Geonosis. The Senate recognized their strength and quickly authorized the construction of a thousand more. With troops deployed in scattered campaigns, many acted as mobile depot ships and commando carriers, and new roles were constantly found. For the Battle of Muunilinst, the assault ship *Nevoota Bee* was adapted as a starfighter carrier, her vehicle decks crammed with 156 V-19 warplanes.

ACCLAMATOR-CLASS
ASSAULT SHIP

REPUBLIC GUNSHIP

The low-altitude assault transport is the iconic vehicle of the Grand Army. Its distinctive silhouette has become a signature of hope: Wings reach down on either side of a generous cargo bay, while tandem cockpits in the narrow forward fuselage provide commanding positions for the pilot and gunner.

At the center of the ship, where the wings meet the hull, sits an advanced repulsor drive coupled with two robust turbofan engines, capable of achieving speeds of Mach 0.5. Light shielding and detachable external drives enable the LAAT to orbit-drop from a spaceship, although sustained friction interaction reduces the effectiveness of this deflector in atmosphere to essentially nil, and the standard LAAT is unable to return to orbit from a surface launch.

The basic LAAT/i troop-carrier variant is 17.4 meters long, armed with three blaster cannons and top-mounted twin launchers for anti-vehicle missiles. Four additional laser pods and eight short-range anti-fighter rockets can also be fitted for heavy combat. The troop bay can hold up to thirty soldiers, but it normally carries two combat squads. Its main uses are for frontal assault and air-cavalry patrol missions.

Alternative variants on the LAAT are also numerous, including heavy-duty vehicle carriers, "Hutted-out" anti-armor gunships, and top-secret special-forces transports.

REPUBLIC
GUNSHIP

CLONE TROOPER FALLS IN A HOLE...

From Geonosian Debriefings, Vol. III (Subject: CT-1226):

They dropped my regiment near the bug arena, smack in the middle of all these Hardcell transports our guys had trashed. We broke left in a skirmish line, pushing across the plateau, toward where Intel said the Sep command center should be. Behind us came the AT-TEs, with two quartets of SPHA-Ts at the rear, arcing laser blasts ahead of us and protecting the Acclamators while deployment continued.

Pretty smooth, all things considered—the only thing that struck me compared with the live-fire exercises was the noise. Every time a SPHA-T fired up its cannon or a larty zoomed by overhead my comm system would overload and go staticky. I couldn't hear a thing the lieutenant was saying and I knew the squad couldn't hear me, but I could see everybody on the HUD, and we'd simmed this enough. So I didn't think we'd be okay, exactly, not with all that Seppie metal flying around out there. But I knew we could do our job.

Then the HUD lit up red everywhere. I cranked up my magnification and saw just about every kind of clanker on the Sep roster coming at us—a wall of Hailfires and spiders and supers and a bunch of red-armored B1s thrown in for kicks, all coming hot. On the one hand, that was good—the fact that they were putting up a hell of a fight suggested we were on the right vector. On the other, I sure hoped someone had called for air support, because we were about to get mauled.

The Hailfires were in missile range and I had warning indicators everywhere when it happened. One moment I'm running along and the next I'm on my back and looking back the way I came—upside down. I couldn't hear anything and my HUD was out.

So once my brain unscrambled I realized I was lying on the forward slope of a brand-new crater, with my feet higher than my head. At first I thought a Hailfire had shelled us, but it turned out it was a projectile from one of our own walkers—one whose guidance system was glitched. The impact had knocked me down and I'd slid back into the crater.

So I crawled up the slope and poked my head

Clone troopers prepare for insertion above Geonosis (John VanFleet)

up and immediately put it back down, because I'm looking straight at the photoreceptor of a Hailfire, coming toward me at full speed. I guess it didn't see me, because it rolled right overhead—one wheel on either side of the crater. The anti-personnel cannon couldn't have been more than a meter above me. I watched it head toward our lines and stop about fifty meters out to recalibrate its targeting. I raised my deece, then lowered it, because what could I do? It would have been like a pinprick against the thing even at close range.

I should've been looking the other way, though, because I turn around and there are two tinnies looking down into the crater pointing their E-5s at me. Worse, stomping up right behind them is a super—one of the artillery variants with a forearm missile launcher instead of the integrated cannons.

I don't know why the tinnies didn't just shoot me. I guess they were telling me to surrender and hadn't gotten the message that we were playing for keeps that day. I'm not sure because I still couldn't hear anything but the ringing in my head. I don't remember if I put my hands up or not—the next thing I know, the super's smashed them aside with its missile launcher. Knocked their heads clean off. So now I figure the super's going to take me out, but its terrain sensors pick up the crater and it pivots to go around the edge. The B1s were between it and the AT-TEs—it never even saw me.

Before the super could get too far away I lined up on the heat exchangers on its back—that's a vulnerable point, if you should find yourself behind one—and gave it everything I had with the deece. I knocked the super down hard just as it launched a missile at our lines, and it wound up with its launcher sticking into the dirt like a spear. Instead of going over the Hailfire's head, the missile hits it dead center and turns it into a huge fireball. I had to duck because pieces of the drive wheels are flying everywhere. I pick my head back up and the super's on its knees trying to get its launcher unstuck, its logic module trying to process what just happened. I knew how the thing felt. I also knew if it got back up it would be lights-out for me. So I hit it with a droid popper, ran over, stuck my deece in the heat exchanger, and gave it three or four shots. Scratch one super.

Taking out the Hailfire blew a hole in the Seps' defensive screen—a hole the AT-TEs marched right through. Five minutes later I get a hand up into the walker's crew cabin, where they had a new bucket with a working HUD waiting for me.

I got a commendation for that. I tried to refuse it, but the generals kept talking about quick thinking and resourcefulness. Quick thinking? Smartest thing I did was fall in a hole.

WORLD AT WAR: ROTHANA

The chilly, windswept world of Rothana was discovered around 800 BBY by hyperspace scouts in a poorly surveyed part of the Outer Rim and its location sold to Kuat Drive Yards. Astonished by Rothana's mineral wealth, KDY dispatched the brilliant engineer Quiberon Kuat to the system with thousands of workers and a fleet of ships. During his lifetime he turned Rothana into a self-sufficient web of mining operations, factories, and shipyards, which became the KDY subsidiary Rothana Heavy Engineering.

Rothana was a perfect place for pursuing secret projects—spying and espionage were routine in the Core Worlds, but Rothana was located in Wild Space and only accessible via hyperspace routes unknown to outsiders. Over the centuries Rothana became one of KDY's greatest assets.

It was also one of the shipbuilder's best-guarded secrets. Non-KDY starships weren't allowed to visit under any circumstances, and not even KDY ships were given Rothana's coordinates. Instead, they jumped to one of several points beyond Molavar, at the juncture of the Triellus Trade Route and the Manda Merchant Route, and downloaded encrypted hyperspace coordinates and a friend-or-foe signal from an RHE jump beacon. Broadcasting the friend-or-foe signal then temporarily deactivated the numerous gravity mines placed along the hyperlane to Rothana. (The Kuati Succession Crisis of 311 BBY was sparked by destruction of the star yacht carrying Ursela Kuat, KDY's principal director, along the Rothana Route. Only decades later did it come to light that Kuat had been killed by rivals on the KDY directorate.)

Starships that made their way safely to Rothana discovered a vast honeycomb of orbital shipyards and dry docks, guarded by a formidable Kuati corporate security fleet. Then there were the Rothanians themselves. Centuries of isolation had made them insular and strange even by Kuati standards, famed for elaborate etiquette far too complicated for outsiders to mimic.

A Y-wing patrols the Rothana factory perimeter (John VanFleet)

No RHE project was more veiled in secrecy than Project Icefang. In 31 BBY KDY principal director Onara Kuat received an astonishing order: KDY was to create a massive military force of new vehicles—gunships, drop ships, ground assault vehicles, heavy artillery units, and assault ships, enough to transport and equip millions of soldiers. KDY's only contact with its mysterious customer came when plans were approved on Kuat and credits changed hands—which they did, billions at a time, with perfect regularity.

To preserve secrecy, KDY was given billions more to create a hyperlane connecting Rothana and the extragalactic world of Kamino. The company scrambled to build new warships and adapt a few existing designs; over the next nine years, its new assault ships and vehicles traveled back and forth along the Quiberon Line for testing by the secret army taking shape near the Rishi Maze. (KDY conducted a handful of field tests elsewhere, but they were so few that sightings of AT-TEs and other new designs were dismissed as fantasies.)

During the Clone Wars, Rothana Heavy Engineering worked overtime to arm the Grand Army of the Republic, withstanding repeated Separatist plots to discover Rothana's location and destroy its capabilities. With the rise of the Empire, Rothana's veil of secrecy was finally lifted, as the area around it became the Quiberon Sector. But access to Rothana remained restricted, and the system was guarded by both KDY warships and Imperial patrols.

THE SEPARATIST WAR MACHINE

> "Courage is nothing but terror that holds its ground a minute longer."
> —Saens Sukko, chief sergeant, Republic Armed Forces

THE SEPARATISTS AT WAR

The Confederacy of Independent Systems was born in 24 BBY, when the Jedi renunciate Count Dooku commandeered a Republic communications station in the Tion Hegemony to broadcast a fiery speech blasting the Senate and the Jedi for allowing the Republic's ideals and morals to decline.

But while the Raxus Address shook the galaxy, setting off a wave of secessions by systems and sectors, throughout its brief history the Confederacy was more a movement than a formal, centralized government—a loose amalgamation of megacorps and worlds with a wide range of ambitions and political philosophies. Some of its members burned to destroy the Republic, but many others simply wanted to go their own way, and had little enthusiasm for replacing one central government with another.

The best-organized Separatist entities were its armed forces, and they, too, began as a loosely organized collective of military assets contributed by Separatist systems, sectors, and commercial factions. The Republic gave the Separatist war machine form and structure by deploying its newborn Grand Army and starfleets against Separatist worlds, forcing the Confederacy to centralize control of its military. That left advocates of peace in the Republic shaking their heads: Hadn't they warned that the threat of violence would transform Separatism from an incoherent protest movement into something much more dangerous?

The Separatists' initial military strength came from a hodgepodge of corporate and territorial assets. The Trade Federation, Techno Union, Commerce Guild, and IGBC had all invested heavily in warships and battle droids to defend their interests as security decayed in the galaxy, paying trillions of credits to military firms such as Baktoid Combat Automata, the Colicoid Creation Nest, Geonosian Industries, and Haor Chall Engineering.

These four corporate interests pledged their armies to the defense of the CIS, as did organizations such as the Retail Caucus, a conglomerate of commercial-goods makers that underwrote Separatist manufacturing plants in the early stages of the conflict.

But while popular accounts of the Clone Wars focused on the Separatists' legions of battle droids and corporate flotillas, the Confederacy relied heavily on the armies and defense fleets of sectors and individual star systems such as Umbara, Thustra, and Persavi that followed the lead of Antar, Ando, and Sy Myrth in breaking with the Republic. Many of the battles of the Clone Wars were fought between armies of organics, with nary a battle droid or clone trooper in sight. In some divided sectors, battles were fought by soldiers on both sides wearing identical uniforms and opposing fleets were made up of the same classes of warships and starfighters, with only new insignia and hastily applied coats of paint indicating the change of allegiance.

In the first few months of the war, the Separatists pursued a defensive strategy, seeking to blunt Republic drives into their patchwork territory. In these initial campaigns, the Separatist military forces worked together poorly at best. But the Republic was unable to take advantage of the Confederacy's disarray by mounting large-scale assaults on key fronts. Both sides faced a similar challenge: to build up

Count Dooku displays a Scorpenek droid to Separatist leaders (Tommy Lee Edwards)

the strength of their centralized militaries while coordinating the efforts of local forces.

The Confederacy's first offensive moves weren't bids for major territorial gains, but combinations of surgical strikes and terror operations intended to deny the Republic potential invasion corridors, undermine support for the war, and sever key fleets' supply lines. Only after a massive military buildup and the appointment of General Grievous to overall command was the Confederacy capable of a sustained strike deep into Republic space. Of course, by then the Republic had been able to devote its superior industrial capabilities to prosecuting the war.

At the outset of the war, each of the major Separatist forces—the droid armies of the Trade Federation and Techno Union; the Commerce Guild's Punitive Security Forces; the IGBC's Collections and Security Division; and the Corporate Alliance's Policy Administration directorate—had its own order of battle. Those orders of battle were reorganized by Grievous, who assembled task forces and armies from the various forces available to him. While each commercial faction had its own military leader, as did local forces pledging loyalty to the Confederacy, all reported to Grievous.

The command structure of the Trade Federation's droid army was arranged according to a very simple chain of command: Battle droids reported to droid officers, and droid officers reported to organic commanders.

- **Squad** (8 battle droids): A squad consists of eight battle droids. While organic squads were led by a sergeant, droid squads didn't need an officer, as the squad members were directed remotely or programmed before an engagement.
- **Platoon** (56 battle droids): A platoon consists of seven squads.
- **Company** (112 battle droids, plus support droids): A company consists of two platoons transported via either an MTT or a troop carrier, commanded by a battle droid officer.
- **Battalion** (784 battle droids, plus support droids): A battalion consists of seven troop-carrier companies and a squadron of twenty-four AATs, commanded by a battle droid officer.
- **Vanguard** (1,232 battle droids, plus support droids): Designed to break through heavy defenses, a vanguard

(CONTIUED ON PAGE 88)

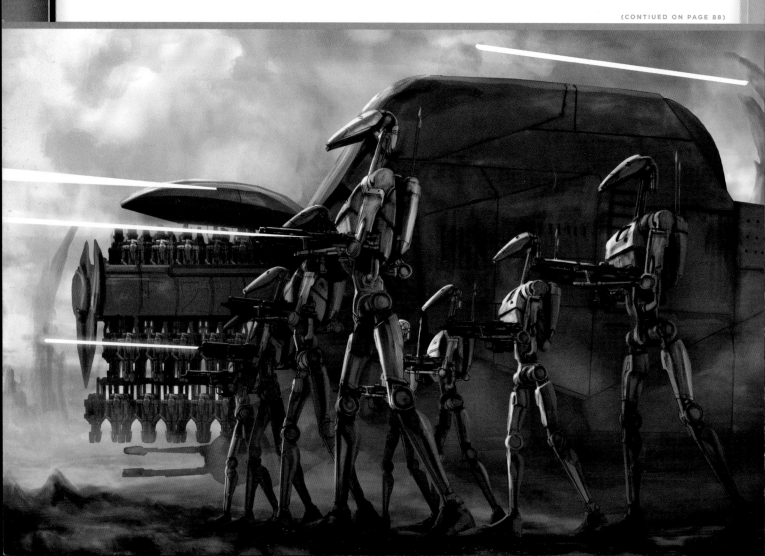

ARMORY AND SENSOR PROFILE

COMMERCE GUILD DESTROYER

When the Commerce Guild aligned itself with the Confederacy of Independent Systems, it brought no massive military infrastructure along with it—its Punitive Security Forces were relatively small, and the Planetary Security Forces it controlled were needed to protect the resource-rich worlds that were the source of its power. But what the guild did have was matériel— massive amounts of it. Guild Presidente Shu Mai directed guild workers to fill superfreighters with raw materials and transport them to Techno Union ship-yards, where work gangs began mass-producing capital ships for the Separatist cause.

The signature ship of the wartime guild was the *Recusant*-class destroyer, based on a Mon Calamari design stolen by the Quarren radicals who would supply some of the Separatists' greatest shipwrights. Commerce Guild destroyers were relatively cheap and quick to construct, pairing a light, angular superstructure with a heavy mix of turbolasers and smaller laser cannons.

Commerce Guild destroyers, first used as privateers to harry Republic shipping, were soon sent to the front lines. Their prow turbolasers gave them a significant punch at longer ranges, particularly when they were sent into battle in groups, while their lighter weapons and complements of droid starfighters (housed within the superstructure) provided an effective screen in close-range fighting. Tens of thousands of these ships supported the Separatists in countless battles across the galaxy, and Republic captains learned that even Star Destroyers were endangered by the forward-facing guns of multiple Recusants. Their vulnerabilities included very light armor, making them easy prey if their shields were taken down, and their droid brains' inflexibility in combat.

RECUSANT-CLASS LIGHT DESTROYER

MUNIFICENT-CLASS STAR FRIGATE

BANKING CLAN FRIGATE

The InterGalactic Banking Clan viewed the HoloNet as a tool of the Republic and refused to use it for financial transactions. Instead, it created its own separate communications network of subspace and hyperwave transceivers to ensure financial orders moved across secure channels.

The IGBC built a network of mobile transceivers, housed aboard heavily armed capital ships. These *Munificent*-class star frigates (technically heavy cruisers) ensured that the Banking Clan would have access to its network from hot spots, and allowed it to move massive stores of currencies, precious metals, and other assets around the galaxy in relative safety.

When the Banking Clan agreed to support the Confederacy of Independent Systems, Chairman San Hill committed thousands of Banking Clan frigates to the cause, as well as droid troops from his organization's feared Collections and Security Division.

The superior communications capabilities of Banking Clan frigates ensured that the Separatists enjoyed secure communications in battle and allowed the Hyper-Communications Cartel to broadcast a steady stream of propaganda to Republic worlds. But the frigates were also capable warships, ideal for protecting the biggest Separatist battleships against fighters and smaller cruisers, and capable of transporting droids and armor in reconfigured storage vaults. Most Banking Clan frigates were equipped with extensive jamming gear, originally intended to prevent espionage but ideal for disrupting the Republic warships' communications and sensors.

The Banking Clan owned a number of space stations outside of the galactic disk that housed secret vaults, communications facilities, and meeting spaces. In the run-up to the Clone Wars, many of those extragalactic stations were refitted as shipyards and staffed by workers toiling in lonely exile above the bright wheel of the galaxy. Those shipyards and others on IGBC-affiliated worlds such as Gwori turned out tens of thousands of Banking Clan frigates for Dooku's cause.

An MTT unloads its battle droids under heavy fire (Chris Scalf)

(CONTINUED FROM PAGE 86)

consists of eleven MTT companies and a squadron of eighteen AATs, commanded by a battle droid officer.

- **Regiment** (4,368 battle droids, plus support droids): A regiment consists of four battalions and a single vanguard, commanded by a battle droid officer. A regiment is the total force carried aboard one C-9979 landing craft.
- **Division** (21,840 battle droids, plus support droids): A division consists of five regiments, carried into battle via a section of five C-9979 landing craft.
- **Corps** (109,200 battle droids, plus support droids): A corps consists of five divisions, carried into battle via a squadron of twenty-five C-9979 landing craft.
- **Army** (218,400 battle droids, plus support droids): An army consists of two corps and represents the total surface force carried aboard a *Lucrehulk*-class battleship, commanded by the battleship's captain.

As with the droid army, the Confederacy's Navy was built up from hundreds of component fleets belonging to the commercial factions and Separatist systems and sectors, and combined under Grievous.

The command structure of the Separatist admiralty consisted of six levels.

- **Section** (2–4 vessels, plus maintenance and support crew): The smallest group in the Separatist admiralty is the section, commanded by a captain.
- **Flight** (4–16 vessels, plus maintenance and support crew): A flight consists of two to four sections, commanded by a commodore.
- **Squadron** (12–64 vessels, plus maintenance and support crew): A squadron consists of three to four flights, led by a commodore.
- **Task group** (36–640 vessels, plus maintenance and support crew): A task group consists of three to ten squadrons, led by a rear admiral.
- **Task force** (72–1,280 vessels, plus maintenance and support crew): A task force consists of two task groups, led by a vice admiral.
- **Fleet** (200–4,000 vessels, plus maintenance and support crew): A fleet consists of three task groups, led by an admiral.

WAR PORTRAIT: GENERAL GRIEVOUS

Long before he was Supreme Commander of the Confederacy of Independent Systems, General Grievous was a gifted Kaleesh warrior shaped by his species' long, bloody war against invading Yam'rii. Grievous was born Qymaen jai Sheelal, and became an expert sniper while still a youth. By the time he reached maturity, he had killed hundreds of Yam'rii and been hailed as a demigod.

After the death of his comrade-in-arms Ronderu lij Kummar, Sheelal took the fight against the Yam'rii to the invaders' worlds, where he massacred warriors and civilians alike. The Judicial Forces separated the warring parties, and the Republic imposed ruinous sanctions on Kalee. With few alternatives, Sheelal accepted an offer of employment from the IGBC chairman San Hill to serve as a collections agent in return for IGBC aid to his planet.

What happened next still divides historians.

Some say Sheelal took the name Grievous in memory of his friend Kummar, and voluntarily remade his body—and eventually his mind—to make himself the equal of the Jedi. (Some add that Sheelal had dreamed of being a Jedi and been rejected as a youth.) In seeking "improvements" to his natural flesh and bone, Grievous turned himself into a cyborg whose only remaining living parts were housed beneath his ceramic armorplast mask and duranium armor. Once Grievous opted for mechanical enhancements to his own senses and reaction times, even his mind was part machine, and his organic past faded into dim memory, crowded out by his need for vengeance against the Jedi and the Republic.

Others tell a tale in which Grievous is as much victim as villain. Citing thirdhand accounts obtained from the IGBC and Serenno, these scholars claim that Dooku and other Separatist leaders sabotaged Grievous's shuttle and recovered the badly wounded Kaleesh from the sea. What was left of his body was encased in armor, and his brain was altered by surgical droids, suppressing his memories and amplifying his aggression and rage. He awoke as a servant of the nascent Confederacy, engineered to lead its forces and destroy the Jedi. If this account of his origins is correct, Grievous apparently recalled little if any of his former life, with his memories destroyed or replaced by fictional constructs. But perhaps some echoes remained: He became enraged if mistaken for a droid.

Grievous's early history may never be definitively reconstructed, but his later deeds were chronicled in chilling detail. After the Battle of Geonosis, Republic Intelligence

General Grievous wades into battle (Bruno Werneck)

puzzled over sketchy reports of a strange droid that destroyed entire clone companies and several Jedi. At Hypori, the cyborg general declared himself, killing the Jedi Knights Daakman Barrek and Tarr Seirr. He would soon become the face of the Separatist military, waging war against the Republic with the same pitiless ferocity he had shown against the Yam'rii.

Scholars differ in assessing Grievous's abilities as a tactician. Some argue his attacks were brute-force affairs that succeeded only when he had an overwhelming advantage. But others note that Grievous had to mix and match very different Separatist assets in his campaigns, and did so ably. And they note that his constant aggression and willingness to absorb terrible losses without flinching served the Separatists well.

Grievous's greatest successes came during Operation Durge's Lance, the campaign into the Core that took Duro in a devastating assault, bombarded and depopulated the ancient world of Humbarine, and unleashed a terrible plague on Loedorvia. Soon afterward, Grievous would lead Separatist forces along secret routes through the Deep Core to Coruscant, where he captured Supreme Chancellor Palpatine in a daring raid. But his career was near its end: Obi-Wan Kenobi tracked Grievous to Utapau, cracked open his chest armor, and killed him with a blaster shot into his unprotected organs.

SUPERWEAPON: THE *MALEVOLENCE*

A massive warship boasting two tremendous ion pulse cannons, the *Malevolence* took shape at Quarren-controlled Pammant, one of the Separatists' most valuable shipyards. Its designer was the rogue Sullustan shipwright Ruggle Schmong, who had tried and failed to get SoroSuub to explore his design for a starship plant that recaptured waste heat and other by-products of propulsion. SoroSuub repeatedly brushed Schmong aside, pointing out that his plant would require a massive hull and his proposed storage batteries would need to vent recaptured energy on a regular basis, making it ill suited for anything except a gargantuan mining ship or warship—neither of which was practical.

The Separatists, however, saw a use for just such a warship. The plant would power two ion cannons, whose barely controlled eruptions of energy could lay waste to entire Republic task forces. The military value of such a warship might be questionable, but Dooku thought she would make a supremely effective terror weapon, one that would drive Republic worlds

to demand protection and so force Republic fleets to waste valuable time hunting the craft in the vastness of space.

Called a *Subjugator*-class heavy cruiser by her builders, the *Malevolence* was built within a gigantic dry dock that even the Republic's best operatives couldn't penetrate. And when the great ship lumbered out of dry dock, those spies were captured by Separatist agents who'd been watching them the entire time.

Grievous himself took command of the *Malevolence,* and reported to Dooku that the dreadnought had flaws: Schmong's plant had a bad habit of bleeding energy that would surge into her other systems, sometimes knocking shields, communications, or other systems offline. But the ion pulse cannons were as devastating as Dooku had hoped, and were complemented by a massive array of conventional turbolasers, tractor beams, and squadrons of vulture droids.

The *Malevolence* left a trail of destruction, wild rumors, and fear across the Republic, striking at systems including Phu, Abregado, Vanik, Ichtor, Vondarc, and Ryndellia before she was crippled by Y-wing bombers led by Anakin Skywalker, Plo Koon, and Ahsoka Tano at the Kaliida Nebula and destroyed near Antar. The *Devastation,* built with different capabilities on the same hull design, was destroyed by a Jedi strike team on her way to Coruscant.

WAR PORTRAIT: ADMIRAL TRENCH

Admiral Trench embodied the Harch species—long-lived, aggressive, and tough. Well into his second century by the time of the Clone Wars, this veteran of countless conflicts gave the Separatists much-needed experience in the war against the Republic.

Native to Secundus Ando, the Harch are distant cousins to the Aqualish species, with the relationship between them and the Ualaq subspecies the subject of much debate among geneticists. (The Harch consider such inquiries obscene.) The history of the Aqualish and the Andoan worlds—known among the Harch and some Ualaq as the Spiverelda—is long, bloody, and turbulent; at various points the Harch have served as the Spiverelda's despotic rulers, led the region from behind the scenes as wily advisers, and been cast down by their subjects. In the last century of the Republic, the Harch ruling nests were firmly allied with Ando in its struggle against the Andoan Free Colonies.

Trench made a name for himself during that struggle, defending Secundus Ando against raiders from the Free Colonies and leading counter-raids up the Horos Spine to Andosha. During the Andoan Wars of 57–39 BBY he emerged as Ando's greatest military leader, besting the Free Forces at Arbular, Horos, and finally the decisive Battle of Raquish in 39 BBY.

But Raquish quickly turned into a debacle. The Andoans had all but dismissed the prospect of Republic intervention, certain that Coruscant would confine itself to discussing Andoan demilitarization in committee. But the firepower on display at Raquish—and Trench's ruthless tactics—convinced the Republic to intervene. The two sides were separated, sparing the Free Colonies, and demilitarization of the sector was enforced by a sizable Judicial fleet.

Seeing victory become defeat radicalized the Andoan leadership and Trench. More than a decade later Ando would become one of the first worlds to secede from the Republic. Trench spent that decade serving the Corporate Alliance: He destroyed pirate bases at Ord Namurt and Engira, seized the Kurosti merchant fleet in a daring raid at Prospera Jang, and in 34 BBY masterminded the Corporate Alliance's assault on Malastare amid a disagreement about fuel allocations.

The Malastare crisis escalated after the Alliance hired Sikurdian pirates to seize Malastare's fuel tankers. Trench then gathered a fleet of Alliance *Fantail*-class destroyers and Sikurdian privateers and blockaded the Malastare Narrows, seeking to force a settlement on the Alliance's terms. After attempts to find a diplomatic solution failed, Malastare appealed to Supreme Chancellor Valorum to intervene.

Publicly, Valorum demurred. But he also feared that the Alliance might prevail in a shooting war, because the Dustig Sector Forces were weakened by corruption and neglect. Behind the scenes, he cajoled the neighboring Tyus and Var Hagen sectors to support Malastare, funneled credits to the Dugs to hire privateers, and dispatched military "observers" to the scene—including the Jedi Kep-She and a capable officer named Wullf Yularen, who'd fought Sikurd's pirates with the Kwymar Sector Forces. In the subsequent confrontation, Trench's flagship was destroyed and the Alliance forced to retreat, but many ships and lives were lost, and the ensuing scandal embarrassed the already embattled Valorum. (A year later the Trade Federation calibrated its own blockade of a Republic world with the lessons of Malastare firmly in mind.)

The Republic believed Trench was dead, but he managed to survive thanks to a pressure suit of Andoan mineral-fish armor and his own tough Harch hide. More than a decade later he reappeared, commanding the Separatist blockade of Christophsis from the *Invincible*. (Though technically classified as a Star Destroyer, the *Invincible* was billed as a dreadnought, one of the first of a line of scaled-up modifications of the *Providence*-class carrier/destroyer.) After recognizing Trench's insignia, Yularen studied everything Republic Intelligence had gathered about Trench's tactics. That knowledge helped him and Anakin Skywalker outwit the Harch admiral and break the blockade.

Trench was once again listed as killed in action. But Yularen had his doubts—after all, he'd seen the tough old spider survive the loss of a flagship before.

ARMORY AND SENSOR PROFILE

BIOWEAPONS

It is said that in the long history of warfare, infection and disease have killed more soldiers than actual combat. By the time of the Clone Wars that was no longer true—bacta, medical droids, and swift shuttling of injured beings to Republic Mobile Surgical Units and medical facilities had reduced the impact of such ancient battlefield woes. Moreover, the clone troopers' identical genetic blueprints made it possible to standardize their care: They shared a common blood type, and the Kaminoans' tinkering had eliminated the possibility of allergic reactions and tissue rejection.

But that shared blueprint made them vulnerable to the same illnesses, and gave Separatist researchers the ability to tailor viruses specifically for the clones. The Kaminoan traitor Kuma Nai released such a nanovirus on Kamino, killing the cloner Sayn Ta, but died before she was able to bring it to her Separatist paymasters. Later strains were spread by octuptarra droids: Veterans of battles such as Mikaster III and Uba IV would never forget the sight of octuptarras picking their way through the rubble, shrouded in veils of deadly, acidic vapor that ate through body gloves in minutes and left clone troopers convulsing and dying. Elsewhere, Separatist saboteurs volunteered to be infected and then infiltrated clones' staging areas and recovery wards.

Other Separatist bioweapons were less discriminate in their targets: Hive viruses could sicken and kill not just clone troopers, but other organics. The use of such weapons sharply divided the Separatist leadership. Dooku warned that such tactics fed Republic propaganda, painting the Confederacy as a mechanized army unleashed by a few wealthy organics, and Nute Gunray and Lott Dod saw bioweapons as insulting to Neimoidians, who were often reviled and feared as bearers of pathogens. But Grievous eagerly sought all such weapons. They were singularly useful in terrorizing civilian populations, which to Grievous was the essence of war.

TACTICAL DROIDS

Separatist leaders such as the Kerkoiden Whorm Loathsom and General Grievous himself took direct control of ground battles, fighting alongside the droid infantry. And many Separatist battlefields saw organic troops defend their homeworlds against the Republic. But there was considerable truth to Republic propaganda branding the Separatists as cowards hiding behind mechanical muscle: The Neimoidians, Skakoans, and Muuns thought of combat as a degrading task fit for lesser beings and mechanicals.

Tactical droids, formerly known as CDE-T units, were designed to lead the battle droid legions where organic leadership wasn't available. Baktoid Combat Automata designed them with advanced cognitive modules that could process vast quantities of data and feed them into superfast heuristic analytical processors. A tactical droid never left computing cycles idle; instead, it would constantly run simulations of imminent combat, calculating odds and changing its strategies on the fly.

In response to the entreaties of Baktoid designers, Separatist leaders allowed the CDE-T greater autonomy in making decisions, hoping that this would deliver superior results. And indeed, tactical droids proved far more capable than battle droid commanders in reacting to Republic tactics and changing situations. But that greater autonomy also led to a plague of behavioral anomalies.

Tactical droids were arrogant and pushy at best. They refused to accept roles subordinate to battle droid commanders and disdained organics as frail creatures ruled by emotions instead of the cool logic of mathematics. The complexities of organic relationships and hierarchies eluded them, and more than one Separatist officer discovered that his tactical droid had gone up the chain of command and recommended that he be replaced as unfit for a leadership role.

Occasionally, tactical droids refused to take no for an answer. The Third Battle of Aefao turned in the Republic's favor when the Chevin Major Hoom Garaf was executed by his tactical droid, sparking a chaotic firefight in the Separatist rear guard. On the other hand, before the First Battle of Plagen a tactical droid assassinated the Kerkoiden general Piar Nagelsa, discarded his battle plan, and led Separatist forces to victory.

T-SERIES TACTICAL DROID

CHATTY BATTLE DROIDS AND OTHER SEPARATIST TROUBLES

Following the Trade Federation's defeat on Naboo, it ordered many first-generation B1 battle droids retrofitted with cognitive modules that allowed independent thought. That prevented remote shutdowns and let the Separatists teach the droids new things by uploading new programming. With Separatist warships light on organic crew members, B1s were programmed to serve a number of roles, from pilots and gunners to emergency responders.

But the B1s were being pushed to the limits of their programming. Retrofits allowed them to perform more specialized tasks, but they weren't very good at them—and the Separatists needed their newer, more powerful cognitive modules for more capable war droids. Maintenance also became a problem: Diagnostics and memory defragmentation routines had a nasty habit of erasing the retrofitted B1s' specialty programming and heuristics, and so were frequently skipped.

Without proper maintenance, many early B1s' cognitive modules suffered data corruption and system errors, leading to shutdowns or behavioral anomalies. To the annoyance of Separatist commanders, retrofitted B1s often became "chatty," offering running commentaries on their situations as their modules struggled to process data overflows.

Such problems were of the Separatists' own making, the product of the Trade Federation's skinflint ways and the Techno Union's fetish for newer, better killing machines. But other problems were part of a shadowy war fought between Confederate and Republic saboteurs. A B1's malfunction might be the product of maintenance deferred too long, or evidence of a virus inserted into Confederate computer systems by Republic slicers. Such viruses could turn the course of battles: At Agomar, droidekas and super battle droids turned on each other with laser cannons blazing, vaporizing hapless B1s caught between them as clones watched and jeered.

Viruses could be repaired if discovered, but slicers had other ways of doing damage. One popular technique was to alter the code directing the Separatists' automated foundries and factories in small but devastating ways. Parts were made slightly too small or too large, targeting sensors were slightly miscalibrated, extra cycles were introduced into communications subroutines, and schematics were altered so that parts seized up, wore out, or burned up.

THE OUTER RIM SIEGES

"War is bloody mathematics seen through to the solution."
—Firmus Nantz, admiral, New Republic

THE JEDI GENERALS

Throughout its history, the Jedi Order oscillated between standing apart from the Republic's government and institutions and being tightly integrated with them. Beginning with their role as defenders against threats beyond the galactic frontier, the Jedi sought to protect civilization—and for all its imperfections, the Republic stood for millennia as the highest embodiment of civilization. From early in their history, the Jedi were wary of ruling others, fearing such power as an invitation to the dark side. They preferred to remain guardians and watchers, not military leaders, ministers, or kingmakers.

Yet over the millennia, the Republic occasionally fell into darkness, led astray by evil leaders who used the levers of democracy to amass power for themselves. And sometimes it faced terrible external threats—most notably that of the Sith, whose power would wax and wane over the eons. Each time civilization threatened to topple into ruin, the Jedi faced a momentous decision: Did the Republic's survival require the Order to intervene directly in its affairs?

At various points in galactic history, the Jedi reluctantly decided such intervention was necessary. They stepped in to prevent the young Republic from annihilating the Tionese, plotted in secret to overthrow the Pius Dea chancellory, and served as chancellors while directly ruling large swaths of Republic territory in the chaotic centuries before Ruusan. Each time, the Order surrendered the powers it had assumed, returning to its guardian role. But as the Republic decayed and the Separatists gained strength, the Jedi began to once again debate whether a more activist role was required.

By 22 BBY matters had reached a crisis point. This time it was the Supreme Chancellor himself who asked the Jedi to assume a new role: A powerful army awaited Republic command, but the Judicial Forces were ill prepared to lead them. Mindful that the Separatists were led by the Jedi apostate Count Dooku, the Jedi agreed to lead the Grand Army to Geonosis in an attempt to short-circuit the Separatist threat.

The Jedi—technically already members of the Judicial Department—were appointed officers in the Grand Army, as well as the Republic Navy, Starfighter Corps, and Special Operations Brigade. While the Jedi were officially part of the military hierarchy, their responsibilities and commands were fluid, with Jedi Knights such as Anakin and Obi-Wan leading troops into ground combat one day, commanding a naval task force the next, and accompanying commandos on a secret mission the day after that. For the sake of simplicity, Padawans considered suited for military duties were given the rank of commander, while Jedi Knights and Masters were referred to as generals.

This wartime bargain caused a rift in the Jedi Order. Some Jedi welcomed the chance to take action, but others saw leading troops as a betrayal of key Jedi precepts. Even Jedi who accepted their new responsibilities were badly strained. They grappled with the morality of leading clones who had been bred for war, and watched Padawans and younger Jedi Knights succumb to impatience and anger, burning for revenge on the Separatists and their leaders.

"In this war, a danger there is of losing who we are," Yoda admitted in one of his darker moments. But the Jedi Grand Master had no idea just how much truth his words held.

A group of Jedi and clone troopers study their latest objective (Tommy Lee Edwards)

ARMORY AND SENSOR PROFILE

JEDI CRUISER

The *Venator*-class Star Destroyer, popularly known as the Jedi cruiser because of its use as a flagship by the Republic's newly appointed Jedi generals, was designed to play any number of roles in the Republic Navy. It was fast enough to run down blockade runners and small enough to land on a planet, but big enough to lead independent missions against Separatist forces. Venators served capably as both warships and starfighter carriers, with dorsal flight decks and launch bays that allowed hundreds of fighters to launch in short order. The Venator's dual bridge reflected its two missions: The port bridge was used for starfighter command, with the starboard bridge the standard helm. Emblazoned in Republic red, the Venator would emerge as an emblem of the Clone Wars.

The Venator was joined by other ships in the new Star Destroyer class. Walex Blissex had left KDY for Rendili StarDrive, and his *Victory*-class Star Destroyer emerged from a collaboration with KDY ordered by the Supreme Chancellor and known as the Victor Initiative Project. The Victory was smaller but more heavily armed than the Venator, with a much smaller starfighter complement. The Victors were pressed into early service after the Separatist Admiral Dua Ningo broke out of Foerost with his Bulwark Fleet, chasing Ningo across the Core Worlds and finally destroying him at the Battle of Anaxes. Late in the Clone Wars, the Venators were themselves supplanted by two new classes of KDY Star Destroyers: the hangarless Tector and the Imperator. While the Tector would see relatively limited use, the Imperator class would be renamed the Imperial, and become the signature warship of the Empire.

VENATOR-CLASS STAR DESTROYER

JEDI STARFIGHTERS

Shortly before the Battle of Geonosis, Saesee Tiin supervised the creation of a corps of Jedi starfighter pilots, and worked with Kuat Systems Engineering on a replacement for the Jedi Order's small, aging fleet of Delta-6 starfighters.

The new starfighter, the Delta-7 Aethersprite light interceptor, was a significant advance on earlier models in the Delta line, boasting a state-of-the-art targeting system, an advanced shielding system that directed protection as needed, and the capability to hardwire an astromech droid into the fighter. As with earlier Delta models, it was designed by Walex Blissex, who drew upon the design of the Aurek strikefighter used by the ancient Republic. (That same design would inspire the A-wing series Blissex created for the Alliance.)

The Delta-7 was designed as a medium-range reconnaissance vehicle and lacked the ability to calculate hyperspace jumps. For faster-than-light travel, Jedi mated their Delta-7s with Syliure-31 hyperdrive rings made by TransGalMeg. Obi-Wan Kenobi flew a Jedi Order Delta-7 across the galaxy on the trail of Jango Fett.

Blissex adopted a number of the Jedi modifications in the Delta-7B, which also added a standard astromech port forward of the cockpit. But his next Jedi starfighter was a bold new direction: a fast, agile craft designed as an extension of a Jedi pilot's abilities and reliant on her Force-enhanced senses. The Eta-2 Actis interceptor lacked shields, and its armor, sensors, and systems were radically stripped down, allowing a Jedi behind the stick to fly almost as fast as she could think.

Kuat Drive Yards became a dominant military manufacturer for the Empire, but its specialty was warships, not starfighters; most Imperial starfighter contracts went to Sienar Fleet Systems. But the Eta-2 wasn't forgotten: Sienar borrowed some elements of the last Jedi starfighter for its TIE fighter, such as the twin ion engines, the radiator panels,

DELTA-7B STARFIGHTER

ETA-2 ACTIS-CLASS STARFIGHTER

and the design of the viewport. Moreover, the TIE was an extension of the minimalist philosophy behind the Eta-2: a fast, nimble fighter for a daring, skilled pilot. Unfortunately, very few TIE pilots were the equals of Jedi.

AT-TE

The All Terrain Tactical Enforcer Assault Walker, or AT-TE, emerged from a Rothana Heavy Engineering industrial security vehicle used to defend mining facilities in the wilds beyond the Rim, with its six-legged stance borrowed from Rothana's arctic horny whelmer.

When Kuat Drive Yards won the contract to outfit the Republic's clone army, it beefed up the AT-TE into a formidable ground vehicle, one that could handle everything from transporting troops to supporting them and assaulting hard targets. The AT-TE's principal weapon was a heavy mass-drive projectile cannon, backed up with six anti-personnel laser cannons. The AT-TE's feet had clawed magnetic grapples, allowing it to climb steep slopes and even cliffs, and its natural grounding made it immune to ion weapons and able to pass through particle shields, unlike repulsorlift vehicles. The Battle of Bothawui demonstrated the vehicles' versatility, as Anakin Skywalker deployed them on asteroids as a screen against Grievous's task force.

The AT-TE was a mainstay of Republic forces in countless battles of the Clone Wars, and performed well, though it proved vulnerable to mines and its stubby legs limited gunners' field of fire. KDY would attempt to address such shortcomings with long-legged walkers such as the AT-HE, a forerunner of the mighty AT-AT.

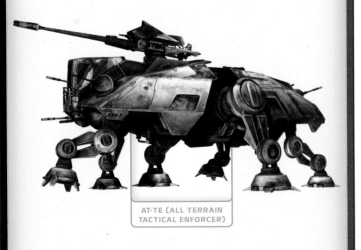

AT-TE (ALL TERRAIN TACTICAL ENFORCER)

THE SECTOR ARMIES

The Ruusan Reformations decentralized the bulk of the Republic's military power, establishing the Judicial Forces as a rapid-response force and giving responsibility for defending the new regional sectors to the Planetary Security Forces.

This system proved all but useless against the growing Separatist threat. In search of greater coordination and control, Supreme Chancellor Palpatine invoked ancient Republic law, appointing Governor-Generals to coordinate military action in each sector in consultation with its Senator, while answering to the Chancellor. In the final days of the Republic, this system would give rise to a permanent class of regional governors, who assumed direct control of the regional sectors when the Senate was disbanded.

The Governor-Generals greatly improved the effectiveness of the Planetary Security Forces in supporting the war effort, but they weren't an answer to coordinating the overall strategy of the war. The Republic armed forces were divided into twenty Sector Armies, each charged with military control of a different kind of sector—known as an oversector or priority sector. (Contrary to what one might have gathered from the HoloNet, the Republic's armies contained both clone troopers and non-clone units—some epic battles of the Clone Wars were fought without a single clone in the Republic ranks. While clone and non-clone units sometimes served side by side, coordinating the two proved difficult; with the exception of officers, most non-clone troops served in the Planetary Security Forces, which were largely used in defensive deployments, or with the Judicials.)

In the first weeks of the war, the GAR numbered the equivalent of just two Corps, but soon 3 million troops were ready, and each standard Sector Army numbered nearly 150,000 clone troopers, a number that grew dramatically as more clones were grown and entered the war.

Each Sector Army was divided into four subordinate corps, paired with four navy assault lines, each containing two *Acclamator*-class transports and two frigates. This formation was designed around the so-called 1/4/16/64 Plan, in which one corps acted as a mobile armored reserve while the others were divided into progressively smaller components for more local missions. In practice, one corps in each Sector Army remained largely intact as an assault division, but the others were divided into hundreds of fast-moving raiding companies, with only a dozen or so formations operating at battalion or brigade level—most of them usually drawn from the reserve corps itself.

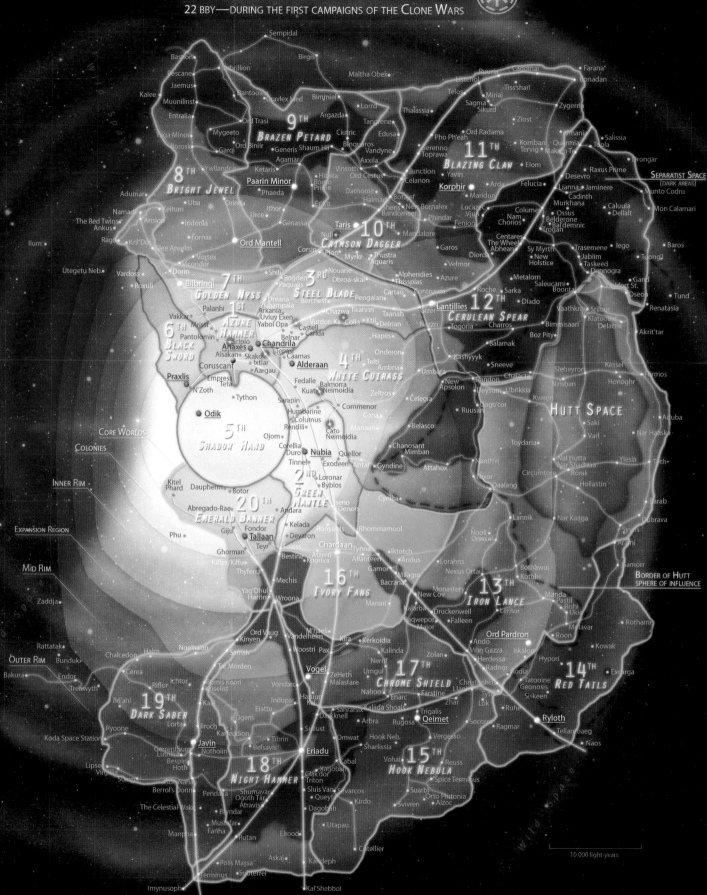

SECTOR ARMIES

22 BBY—DURING THE FIRST CAMPAIGNS OF THE CLONE WARS

Sernpidal

Bastion
Bescane
Jaemus
Kalee
Muunilinst
Entralla
Vaga Minor
Borosk

Dubrillion
Birgis
Maltha Obex
Bimmiel
Dantooine
Gravlex Med
Lorrd
Argazda
Edusa
Thalassia

Putrri
Cacomal
Listehol
Telos
Farana
Bonadan
Mirial
Sagma
Zygerrin
Sikurd
Ziost

Pho Ph'eah
Ord Radama
Korriban
Tervig
Quermia
Makem Te
Urmana
Salissia
Toola
Drongar

Mygeeto
Ord Trasi
Ord Binir
Generis
Agamar
Ciutric
Shaum Hii
Vandyne
Axxila

Serenno
Toprawa
Gizer
Arda
Elom
Felucia
Desevro
Lianna
Cadinth
Murkhana
Jaminere
Munto Codru

9TH BRAZEN PETARD

11TH BLAZING CLAN

SEPARATIST SPACE
(DARK AREAS)

Garqi
Ketaris
Vinsoth
Hitoka
Borgo
Prime
Ord Cestus

Korphir
Maridun
Lucazec
Vjun
Columex
Ossus
Belderone
Baldemnic
Trogan
Caluula
Dellalt
Mon Calamari

8TH BRIGHT JEWEL

Paarin Minor
Phaeda
Urce

Dathomir
Halmad
heris
New Bornalex
Phindar
Nam
Chorios
Sy Myrth
New
Holstice
Trasemene
Iego
Tasheed
Baros
T+oong

Adumar
Uba
Orinda
Ithor
Genassa
Taris
Garos
Diorda
Velmor
Centares
The Wheel
Abhean
Jabiim
Dennogra
Gand

Namadii
Keitum
Null
Mandalore
Azure
Metalorn
Saleucami
Roche
Sarka
Vaathkree
Sriluur
Klatooine
Delacrix
Oseon
Tund

The Red Twins
Ankus
Ansion
Iridonia
Fornax
Corsin
Ploo
Myrkr
Thustra
Aquaris
Alpheridies
Thisspias
Contruum
Diado
Bimmisaari
Boz Pity
Akrit'tar
Renatasia

Ilum
Rago
Elee Anselm
Vicondor
Vortex
Shili
Bogden
Paqualis
Nouane
Obroa-skai
Cartao
Nazzri
Togoria
Charros
Balamak

7TH GOLDEN NYSS

3RD STEEL BLADE

12TH CERULEAN SPEAR

Ütegetu Neb.
Vardoss
Roxuli
Dorin
Bilbringi
Drearia
Champala
Berchest
Tirahnn
Taanab
Lantillies

Vakkar
Palanhi
Arkania
Uviuy Exen
Yabol Opa
Vurdon Ka
Colla
K'til
Delrian
Kashyyyk
Sneeve
Kessel
Permos

1ST AZURE HAMMER

6TH BLACK SWORD

Mrisst
Pantolomin
Scipio
Alsakan
Skako
Castell
Carida
Belnar
Chazwa
Hapes
Onderon
Telti
Ambria
Umbara
Pandon
Qiogo'cor
Ubrikkia
Kwenn
Sleheyron
Honoghr
Nimban

Anaxes
Ixtlar
Chandrila
Tepasi
Caamas

Alderaan
Zeltros

4TH WHITE CUIRASS

New
Apsolon
Ruusan
HUTT SPACE
Aduba

Praxlis
Coruscant
Aargau
Fedalle
Balmorra
Celegia
Belasco
Saki
Varl
Nar Haaska

Empress
Teta
N'Zoth
Kuat
Neimoidia
Commenor
Cona
Manaan
Chanosant
Mimban
Toydaria
Nal Hutta
Nar Shaddaa
Rorak
Ylesia
Teth

Tython
Sarapin
Humbarine
Columus
Rendili
Cato
Neimoidia
Nanth'ri
Circumtore
Hollastin
Tarab

5TH SHADOW HAND

Odik
Ojom
Corellia
Duro
Nubia
Quellor
Nixor
Daalang
Lannik
Nar Kaaga
Dubrava

Syvris
Arami

CORE WORLDS

Tinnel
Exodeen
Antar
Gyndine
Attahox

COLONIES

Kitel
Phard
Dauphern
Botor

2ND GREEN MANTLE
Loronar
Byblos
Iseno
Denon
Cyrilia

INNER RIM

Abregado-Rae
Giju
Fondor
Andara
Kelada
Devaron
Ronyards
Rhommamool

Samorr

20TH EMERALD BANNER

Phu
Ghorman
Tallaan
Teyr
Foless
Bestine
Atzerri
Koonva

13TH IRON LANCE

BORDER OF HUTT
SPHERE OF INFLUENCE

EXPANSION REGION

Kiffex/Kiffu
Thyferra
Mechis
Yag'Dhul
Harrin
Wroona
Chardaan
Tynna
Iktotch
Allanteen
Gamor
Aridus
Lorahns
Nexus Ortai
Monastery
New Cov
Bothawui
Kothlis
Manda
Pastil
Rishi
Ukio
Rothana

MID RIM

Zaddja
Milagro
Bacrana

16TH IVORY FANG

Manari
Kalarba
Druckenwell
Falleen
Leritor
Molavar
Roon
Kowak

Ord Vaug
Kinyen
Vandelhelm
Kira
Kerkoidia
Kalinda
Zolan
Paqwepor
Major

Ord Pardron
Ando
Mon Gazza
Herdessa
Radnor
Iskalon
Hypori
Excarga

OUTER RIM

Rattatak
Bunduki
Chalcedon
Halm
Noe'ha'on
Sarrish
Tar Morden
Woostri
Pax
Nerrif
Umgul
Zhar
Christophsis
Rodia
Tatooine
Geonosis
Siskeen

Bakura
Endor
Cerea
Ichtor
Vogel
ZeHeth
Malastare
Farstine
Llanic
Tyne's
Horn
Ruhe

17TH CHROME SHIELD

14TH RED TAILS

Trenwyth
Riflor
Bomis Koori
Kuiselist
Vondarc
Indupar
Kalida Shoals
Enarc
Trigalis
Lok
Socorro
Ragmar

19TH DARK SABER

Bri'ahl
Kaal
Eiattu
Ogem
Kashyyyk
Sanrafsix
Arbra
Qeimet

Ryloth

Ryoone
Jiroch
Karfeddion
Darkknell
Rugosa
Vohai
Vergesso
Tellanroaeg
Naos

Koda Space Station
Javin
Nothoiin
Tibrin
Belsavis
Omwat
Hook Neb.
Kabal
Reuss

18TH NIGHT HAMMER

15TH HOOK NEBULA

Lipse
Virgillia
Sumitra
Bespin
Hoth
Eriadu
Xagobah
Triton
Sluis Van
Queyta
Sevarcos
Kirdo
Sharlissia
Suarbi
Orto Plutonia
Alzoc
Spice Terminus

The Celestial Wake
Berrol's Donn
Pendara
Shumavar
Ogoth Tilr
Atravis
Clak'dor
Dagobah
Svivren
Utapau

Isis Naha
Blyndar
Mustafar
Fanha
Rutan
Elrood
Cotellier

Manpha
Askaj
Kandeph
Stobrerrel

Polis Massa
Terminus

Imynusoph
Kal'Shebbol

10 000 light-years

Wild Space

As the war unfolded, commanding Jedi generals often led reinforcements to relieve other Sector Armies, and advances and retreats muddled territorial boundaries, leading to overlapping oversectors and commands. By the end of the war, the effective numbers of troops in some oversectors had increased many times over, while others had diminished to little more than bookkeeping formations. The major fleets also became operationally separate from the armies. The twenty army commands remained, however, and in the first days of the Empire they became power bases for a new class of regional governors—the Grand Moffs.

What follows is a snapshot of the twenty Sector Armies:

"RESERVE" SECTORS

With their headquarters in the Core Worlds, these six commands were designated as reserves, but their roles varied.

The First and Second armies were defensive commands for the heart of the Republic, but also provided a reserve of troops for campaigns across the galaxy. The Third and Fourth armies were designed as rapid-response commands for Mid Rim and Outer Rim campaigns, with bases inside Sector 1.

Sector 5 and Sector 6 were garrison commands in areas believed to be secure, used to provide training and support.

FIRST ARMY, CORUSCANT SECTOR (AZURE HAMMER COMMAND)—HQ ANAXES—MOFF TRACHTA

The First Army was the main defensive command around Coruscant, and took the Anaxes fleet base—the defender of the Core since the Azure Imperium joined the Republic—as its headquarters.

SECOND ARMY, CORELLIAN SECTOR (GREEN MANTLE COMMAND)—HQ NUBIA—MOFF VORRU

The Second Army defended the Denon and Duro hyperlane junctions, and blockaded the Neimoidian Purse Worlds.

THIRD MID RIM ARMY (STEEL BLADE COMMAND)—HQ CHANDRILA—MOFF SEERDON

The Third Army was intended as a reserve command for Mid Rim operations, and also given responsibility for patrol along the Perlemian. Its forces fought extensively alongside those of the Twelfth Army in the Clone Wars.

Aayla Secura and Commander Bly on Saleucami (Chris Scalf)

FOURTH OUTER RIM ARMY (WHITE CUIRASS COMMAND)—HQ ALDERAAN—MOFF PRAJI

The Fourth Army was a reserve force to support Mid and Outer Rim campaigns, and extensively reinforced the Thirteenth Army, essentially becoming an Outer Rim command as the war intensified. Sector 4 troops did see action within their own theater late in the war, blockading and then invading Neimoidia.

FIFTH DEEP CORE ARMY (SHADOW HAND COMMAND)—HQ ODIK—MOFF GANN

The Fifth Army was a reserve army garrisoning the Deep Core, and many of its assets were shifted to busier theaters in relatively short order, leaving skeleton forces behind.

SIXTH NEGATIVE REGIONS (BLACK SWORD COMMAND)—HQ PRAXLIS—MOFF WEBLIN

The Sixth Army was a reserve command dominated by repair yards and training camps. Its territory continued the half circle of Azure Hammer in the western quadrant, with an extended theater of operations intended to guard against threats from the Unknown Regions. As with the Fifth Army, many Sixth Army forces were shifted to areas of greater need, leaving the oversector thinly defended.

NORTHERN CAMPAIGN SECTORS

Systems Armies Delta, Epsilon, and Zeta divided the northern quadrant beyond the Core perimeter.

SEVENTH ARMY, IMMALIA SECTOR (GOLDEN NYSS COMMAND)—HQ BILBRINGI—MOFF WESSEL

The Seventh Army was primarily a defensive command, charged with patrolling the Namadii Corridor as far as Ansion and the broad sweep of space between Dorin and Bogden; the Seventh also stood ready to support the Fifth Army against threats from the Unknown Regions, and its forces conducted secret scouting missions beyond the frontier.

EIGHTH ARMY, ORD MANTELL SECTOR (BRIGHT JEWEL COMMAND)—HQ ORD MANTELL—MOFF VANKO

The Eighth Army focused its operations against Muunilinst and Mygeeto, and saw some of the heaviest fighting of any Sector Army. It was repeatedly reinforced by units from reserve commands.

NINTH ARMY, RELGIM SECTOR (BRAZEN PETARD COMMAND)—HQ PAARIN MINOR—MOFF WESSEX

The Ninth Army saw extensive fighting early in the war, as the Republic tried to break the Separatist lines connecting Muunilinst and the Outer Hydian.

TENTH ARMY, QUELII SECTOR (CRIMSON DAGGER COMMAND)—HQ TARIS—MOFF TANNIEL

The Tenth Army's primary role was to defend the Outer Hydian, standing ready to reinforce the Ninth and Tenth armies while guarding against the possibility of the Separatists wooing neutral systems in the region led by Mandalore's Duchess Satine.

ELEVENTH ARMY, GORDIAN REACH SECTOR (BLAZING CLAW COMMAND)—HQ KORPHIR—MOFF RENAU

The Eleventh Army was a military salient to prevent the Separatist enclaves on the Hydian and Perlemian from joining forces.

TWELFTH ARMY, MALDROOD SECTOR (CERULEAN SPEAR)—HQ LANTILLES—MOFF THERBON

The Twelfth Army was charged with invading and controlling the Separatist enclave on the Outer Perlemian, which included many of the Confederacy's most productive and best-defended industrial worlds. The Twelfth advanced early from its secure rear base at Lantilles to Centares, with forces from Sector 3 reinforcing its Coreward positions. Twelfth Army forces played a major role during the Outer Rim Sieges.

SOUTHERN CAMPAIGN SECTORS

THIRTEENTH ARMY, TRANS-NEBULAR SECTOR (IRON LANCE COMMAND)—HQ ORD PARDRON—MOFF BYLUIR

The Thirteenth Army was given a sprawling theater of operations because its responsibilities included the core territories of the Hutts, where few Republic forces were deployed with the exception of the Toydaria base. The Thirteenth defended Kamino against repeated Separatist attacks, and held the line against the Separatist attempt to cut off the Republic's Rimward forces at Christophsis. Sector 13 was extensively reinforced by the Fourth Army.

FOURTEENTH ARMY, TOLONDA SECTOR (RED TAILS COMMAND)—HQ RYLOTH—MOFF RAVIK

The Fourteenth Army deployed on the Outer Corellian Run and was primarily a defensive command intended to protect Rothana, Excarga, and the Rimward approach to Kamino. It reinforced the Thirteenth Army repeatedly, and repelled a Separatist attack in its own theater of operations at Ryloth.

FIFTEENTH ARMY, SARIN SECTOR (HOOK NEBULA COMMAND)—HQ QEIMET—MOFF KINTARO

The Fifteenth Army was envisioned as primarily a reserve force able to reinforce troops seeing combat on the Corellian Run, Hydian Way, and Rimma Trade Route.

SIXTEENTH ARMY, PALLIS SECTOR (IVORY FANG COMMAND)—HQ CHARDAAN—MOFF COY

The Sixteenth Army was an important but largely defensive command, ready to move Coreward to reinforce Corellia or Rimward up the Corellian Run, and protecting the Coreward Hydian Way and the Shipwrights' Trace.

SEVENTEENTH ARMY, DUSTIG SECTOR (CHROME SHIELD COMMAND)—HQ VOGEL—MOFF HAUSER

The Seventeenth Army defended a salient around Malastare, and reinforced the Eighteenth Army in a number of campaigns.

EIGHTEENTH ARMY, SESWENNA SECTOR (NIGHT HAMMER COMMAND)—HQ ERIADU—MOFF TARKIN

The Eighteenth Army defended the besieged salient around Eriadu, where propaganda made Tarkin and his mix of clone army and Outland Regions Security Force troops into heroes, and saw extensive action along the Hydian and Rimma.

NINETEENTH ARMY, JAVIN SECTOR (DARK SABER COMMAND)—HQ JAVIN—MOFF SULAMAR

The Nineteenth Army was charged with defending the outer Trade Spine, and fought a number of battles as the Separatists advanced from Kinyen to Bomis Koori, retaining control of the Kriselist junction in a hard-fought campaign.

TWENTIETH ARMY, TAPANI SECTOR (EMERALD BANNER COMMAND)—HQ TALLAAN—MOFF GRANT

The Twentieth Army fought a skillful back-and-forth war on the Rimma and Trade Spine around Thyferra and Bestine, where Separatist forces maintained significant strength until Grievous stripped the region of assets for his raid on Coruscant.

ARMORY AND SENSOR PROFILE

ARC-170 FIGHTER

Built by Incom and Subpro, the Aggressive ReConnaissance-170 starfighter was designed as a rugged, durable fighter suitable for long-range missions and able to stand on its own without support from carriers and warships.

The ARC-170's split transverse wings unfolded to expose heat sinks and radiators, aiding the fighter's shielding and helping it shed excess heat. Its nose was packed with sensors, scanners, and jammers. Armament was provided by two forward-facing laser cannons, two aft cannons, and a sextet of proton torpedoes.

The ARC-170 was a critical part of the Republic Starfighter Corps during the Outer Rim Sieges, battering Separatist warships and ground targets while Jedi Eta-2s and lighter V-wings gave it cover. The ARC-170 proved particularly valuable as a part of the Open Circle Fleet, with the ranks of clone pilots supplemented by non-clone volunteers who'd proved themselves in the Planetary Security Forces and Judicial service. The Empire selected some of those pilots as the progenitors of new clone lines.

The ARC-170 began as a heavier version of Incom/Subpro's Z-95 Headhunter, beloved by pilots across the galaxy as a reliable, easily modified fighter. During the Clone Wars, the ARC-170s would be modified to produce a pair of heavier bombers, the PTB-625 and the NTB-630. In later years the ARC-170 would be succeeded by the T-65 X-wing, which sacrificed some of the ARC-170's firepower in favor of regaining the Z-95's agility.

ARC-170 FIGHTER

LETTER FROM CHRISTOPHSIS

The following letter, from Padawan Ahsoka Tano to her friend Tallisibeth Enwandung-Esterhazy, represents a rare firsthand account of this important battle; how it came to be among the papers of the Yularen family is unknown.

Hey Scout,

Well, here I am. I just helped kick the Separatists off a planet called Christophsis in Savareen sector, and I have a new Jedi Master called...wait for it...SKYWALKER! Yeah, that one! Turns out he's only four or five years older than me. Might be cute if he didn't have that weight-of-the-galaxy thing on him all the time. (I know, Jedi Code and all. A girl still notices!)

Anyway! The battle started without me, so this first bit is just what I heard from the clones. The Separatists invaded Christophsis to cut off our forces in the Outer Rim, and to prepare for a strike at Kamino and Rothana, which would be pretty much a huge disaster. They put a droid army down on the surface, so General Kenobi sent in Skywalker and three Jedi cruisers—but when they got there, they found one of the big Separatist fleets in orbit, lots of battleships under a Seppie called Admiral Trench.

Skyguy (that's what I call him—I think he kinda likes it) decided to attack the blockade anyway, which didn't really work, so General Kenobi wasn't all that happy when he showed up with the flagship to find the other Jedi cruisers all beat up. Thankfully, he brought along a new ship that could sneak through the blockade (the clones wouldn't tell me more than that), and Skyguy insisted on flying it down with supplies for the refugees. Then, halfway down, he decided to divert into the blockade and attack Trench's cruiser . . . which was a bit crazy, but also sort of the right thing to do.

So, Skyguy's broken the blockade, but there's still this droid army in Crystal City, commanded by a big alien with a weird accent. I think his name was Loathsom, and apparently he had his own tank regiment there as well. So Kenobi deploys the clone troopers to kick them out while Yularen stays topside with the Jedi cruisers to keep the rest of the Separatist fleet off their backs. But the clones keep getting ambushed when they try to set up a forward base, and someone manages to set off a bomb inside the main base that takes out all the AT-TEs. So we just lost our way of watching what the bad guys are doing, and our main ability to fight back. Not good!

Pretty quickly, General Kenobi realizes that this means the droids are about to attack, so he gets the clones to set up a defensive perimeter, just in time to stop a big attack by the battle droid army, which turns out to be way bigger than we thought—lots of infantry, tank regiments, and these huge tri-droids. I saw the wreckage later.

Anyway, I got there just after the artillery bit. It felt different, being in the middle of a battlefield. Kenobi and Skyguy and the clone commanders are all really military, and professional—and tall—but I think they like me. And you have no idea what it's like to see a front-line fleet in orbit, all the big ships up close in the starry blackness. Really cool.

Of course, as soon as I get down and introduce myself to Skyguy, the droid cruisers come back and kick our fleet out of orbit. So we've got droids overhead, and droids a few blocks away, and just my shuttle for transport for the entire assault force . . . and to make matters worse, Loathsom has set up a deflector shield over his position that blocks our guns, and he's sending all kinds of droid tanks back to squish us, under the cover of the shield dome so our guns can't stop them.

So Skyguy decides we have to take down the shield—and we means him and me. So, my first day on the job, and I'm sneaking into a Separatist base under the shield perimeter . . . and then these sentinel droids show up and start shooting, so Skyguy holds them off while I try and blow the shield generator. Yeah, I've been on Christophsis about an hour, and I have to pull a wall down on some droids to save my master's behind. He wasn't exactly grateful, but I think he just doesn't like it when he feels like he has to rely on other people.

While I'm off doing this crazy stuff, General Kenobi had been negotiating our surrender with General Loathsom, which I think was just to buy us time. Once the shield goes down (and did I mention that was me!) we can start shooting droid tanks again. And just when we've won, Master Yoda shows up with a big fleet from Coruscant. So maybe I didn't need to spend my lunch break dodging blasterfire. Still, I hope Skyguy noticed my moves, and the whole saving-his-life thing.

Anyway, that was Christophsis—terrifying and exciting and exhausting. Now Skyguy and me and a bunch of clones are off on a secret mission, which of course means I can't tell you anything else, sorry. I'll write again soon, because I miss the Temple, and I miss you. At least I do when I get time to breathe!

Your friend,

AHSOKA

THE OUTER RIM SIEGES

By the third year of the Clone Wars, the citizens of the Republic were weary of war, and terrified of deadly Separatist incursions such as Grievous's strike against the Core and Dua Ningo's breakout from Foerost. The war seemed like it would drag on forever.

But the reality was different: The Republic was winning.

The Republic had finally directed a substantial proportion of its industrial might to the war effort, and its production now vastly outstripped Separatist capabilities. New laws and amendments had tamed the Republic's tangle of competing priorities, jurisdictions, and commands, giving the Supreme Chancellor and his key ministers the ability to direct wartime production and military assets quickly and efficiently. The economic powers that had underwritten the Separatist movement were under a terrible strain, and the citizens of the Confederacy of Independent Systems no longer believed the Republic would sue for peace.

The Separatists had never controlled substantial swaths of territory outright, but for much of the war, this hadn't mattered: The understaffed Republic military had needed to extinguish the fires of Separatism in system after system and hunt down Separatist task forces and fleets charged with launching hit-and-fade attacks throughout Republic space. The Separatists had a loose network of far-flung factory worlds, a vast fleet of warships, and millions of targets to choose from. They could be everywhere and nowhere at the same time, placing the Republic in a grim trap. It could defend its worlds against Separatist terror and incursions, giving the core Separatist territories time to crank out new warships and droid armies, or it could try to reclaim those territories while leaving Republic worlds vulnerable in the public perception.

This puzzle was never solved; instead, the Republic outgrew it, with its massive military buildup and coordination of existing forces finally allowing it to pursue both goals and begin to grind down the Separatist war machine.

By the third year of the war, the Separatists had been ejected from their bases in the Core and the Colonies and driven back to the Mid Rim and Outer Rim in the Slice. Steady pressure had cleaved Separatist-controlled regions in the New Territories into two pieces. The Separatist enclave on the Corellian Run Coreward of Ando had been reclaimed, with Confederate forces falling back to the Outer Rim in disarray. And much of the Rimma had been retaken as well, with the Separatists clinging to holdings around Xagobah and Yag'Dhul.

The main thrusts of the Outer Rim Sieges came in six theaters—dubbed Mygeeto, Serenno, Felucia, Siskeen, Yag'Dhul, and Praesitlyn after key Separatist worlds in those theaters. In what would prove to be the final weeks of the Clone Wars, Republic forces were making progress in all six campaigns and cleaning up remaining Separatist resistance elsewhere, such as within Neimoidian space.

In the New Territories, Plo Koon broke the Separatist

Ki-Adi-Mundi and his troops in action on Mygeeto (Drew Baker)

defenses at Ywllandr, clearing the way for Ki-Adi-Mundi's forces to assault the key InterGalactic Banking Clan world of Mygeeto. Jedi-led fleets assaulted New Bornalex and Ord Radama, attempting to clear the way to the key world of Celanon and Dooku's homeworld of Serenno. The fiercest fighting came in the Felucian theater—home to many of the Confederacy's key factory worlds—with pivotal battles at Kashyyyk, Boz Pity, Saleucami, and Felucia. Forces from Rothana and Excarga sought to clear the outer Corellian Run of Separatist units. And the Praesitlyn theater saw troops from Eriadu besiege worlds such as Xagobah and Sluis Van—with the Separatist leadership evacuated from Utapau to Mustafar.

Fighting was different in the Yag'Dhul theater, which the Separatists abruptly all but abandoned to supply warships for General Grievous's daring strike at Coruscant via a secret route through the blazing heart of the galaxy. At first the strike exceeded even Grievous's hopes: He spirited Supreme Chancellor Palpatine off the planet to captivity aboard his flagship, the *Invisible Hand*. This was the moment of Grievous's greatest triumph, and the cyborg warlord waited to see Palpatine humiliated in a HoloNet broadcast and carted off to captivity and torment. But the Separatists' ultimate master, Darth Sidious, ordered no such transmission, and bade the *Invisible Hand* to hold its position. Within hours Count Dooku was dead, the fleet had been shredded above Coruscant, Grievous himself had fled in an escape pod, and Anakin Skywalker had somehow landed half of a Separatist flagship intact, saving Palpatine and perhaps also the Republic.

The raid was the Separatists' last gasp. Grievous himself would soon die on Utapau, and Anakin Skywalker, now Darth Vader, would slaughter the Separatist leaders on Mustafar. With its droid armies deactivated, the Confederacy of Independent Systems would effectively cease to exist. But all had proceeded according to Sidious's plan: By the time the Outer Rim Sieges ended, the Separatist cause was dead. So, too, was the Jedi Order, and the Republic it had served.

ORDER 66: THE ROAD TO EMPIRE

From the Journals of Kol Skywalker, 123 ABY:

> Nearly a century and a half after Darth Sidious's triumph, I am struck by how few within the Galactic Alliance and the Jedi Order truly grasp the complexity of the plot he wove to destroy the Jedi and the Republic.
>
> Consider everything that Sidious needed to restore Sith rule. He needed a centralized military state created where none existed. He needed the galaxy's powerful corporations and guilds brought to heel. He needed the idealistic, charismatic members of the Senate killed or marginalized. And he needed the Jedi Order destroyed. Even for a Sith

as powerful as he, it must have seemed like a mad dream. But over decades of careful planning and manipulation, he made it a reality.

To understand how, begin with his guise as Palpatine, Senator from Naboo. As his political career blossomed, Palpatine became a trusted ally of Chancellor Valorum—and helped push the galaxy into war. Palpatine encouraged Valorum to adopt measures that radicalized the Trade Federation—an organization that Sidious controlled, and had encouraged to invade Naboo as a protest against Valorum's policies. In the chaos that followed the invasion, Palpatine manipulated Naboo's Queen Amidala into a no-confidence vote in Valorum, then rode a wave of sympathy for the Naboo to his own election as Chancellor.

Palpatine was now the highest-ranking elected leader of the Republic—but the Republic was so weak and rotten that he had no effective control of it. To gain that control, Palpatine needed an existential threat to the Republic. He needed an enemy, and a war. Working as Sidious, he created both. One by one he drew other megacorps and economic powers into the same web that had ensnared the Trade Federation, creating the Separatist movement. He seduced Dooku into abandoning the Jedi Order to become the Separatists' public face and his own secret apprentice. Through Dooku and his other pawns, he ensured the creation of a terrifying Separatist war machine. As Palpatine, he manipulated the Jedi Sifo-Dyas into secretly ordering the creation of a clone army. As Sidious, he arranged for Sifo-Dyas's murder, and the existence of the army was kept secret.

During Palpatine's second term as Chancellor—the final one he could serve under the Galactic Constitution—the Separatist crisis he had engineered exploded, and the galaxy began a steady march to war. Working behind the scenes as Supreme Chancellor, Palpatine ensured the passage of the first of many Republic laws and amendments that would steadily erode the power of the Senate, delivering control of the Republic into his hands.

There were literally hundreds of acts, amendments, decrees, and directives that chipped away at the Republic's laws and the rights of its citizens and gave more power to the Supreme Chancellor, not to mention the appropriations bills and deregulation measures whose Senate passage Palpatine engineered. Every act was approved by

Palpatine with a show of reluctance and a promise that it would be set aside as quickly as possible. But six measures above all ensured that when Palpatine moved to eliminate his enemies and declare himself Emperor, no one was able to stop him.

The first was the Emergency Powers Act, which eliminated term limits for the duration of the Separatist crisis, keeping Palpatine as Supreme Chancellor and giving him widespread latitude in taking measures to end that crisis.

Next came the Military Creation Act, which reestablished a centralized Republic military, allowing Palpatine to order the Kaminoans' secret clone armies into battle.

After that came the Enhanced Security Enforcement Act, which abrogated or suspended many of the rights of Republic citizens for the duration of the Separatist crisis. Widespread surveillance, search and seizures, detention without trial, secret trials without due process—all of these tools were wielded in the name of security to create a police state under the Supreme Chancellor's control.

Next came the Reflex Amendment, which allowed Palpatine to bypass the Senate and the bureaucracy in directing the war effort. Palpatine used this power to begin to build a quasi-military government structure in parallel to the Senate, appointing Governor-Generals to coordinate the Republic's sector defense forces and industrial production.

On the heels of the Battle of Coruscant, the Senate approved two Security Act amendments—the Supreme Command Amendment and the Judicial Command Amendment. The two measures formally named the Chancellor Supreme Commander of the Republic armed forces and the Jedi Order for the duration of the war, creating an explicit chain of command every clone trooper understood.

Finally, there was the Sector Governance Decree, which appointed regional and planetary governors for each sector and system. This decree made the military system of Governor-Generals ubiquitous and permanent, creating a new power structure that would lead to the Senate being sidelined and ultimately disbanded.

The Sector Governance Decree came in the final days of the Clone Wars, which fulfilled the rest of Sidious's mission. The Republic was reorganized as a centralized military power answering only to the Supreme Chancellor. The Jedi were kept off balance

and distracted, and their ranks thinned by battle after battle. The galaxy's economic institutions either swore loyalty to the Republic and became part of its military-industrial complex, or declared loyalty to the Separatists and set the stage for their own disenfrachisement. And Sidious offered just enough clues to draw out his enemies in the Senate and the Jedi Order, manipulating them into conspiring against his rule and leaving themselves vulnerable with gestures such as the Petition of 2,000.

In its final days, the Jedi unwittingly gave Sidious exactly what he wanted. They pushed Anakin Skywalker, my ancestor, into a close association with Palpatine, hoping to discover the identity of the Sith Lord they knew stood close to the pinnacle of Republic power. They never dreamed the Sith Lord was the Chancellor himself. And the Jedi really did move to forcibly remove Palpatine from office, and make plans to take control of the Senate until its corrupt members could be purged. In his first address as Emperor, Palpatine said the Jedi had plotted against him and the Republic and attempted to assassinate him—and all of that was true, from a certain point of view.

Imagine the reaction of Mace Windu when he discovered Palpatine was the Sith Lord the Jedi had hunted so desperately. All at once he must have grasped the enormity of what Sidious had done—and realized that the future of the Jedi Order hung by a thread. But Windu didn't understand everything. He didn't know that Sidious had all but completed his seduction of Anakin, playing on his terror of losing the woman he secretly loved. And he didn't know that Sidious had an army of executioners at the Jedi's backs.

Order 66 came with the greatest of the Jedi Masters far from Coruscant, mired in the deadly distraction that was the Outer Rim Sieges. Most of the Jedi were alone, their senses dulled by war and the dark side, and surrounded by troops they had grown to trust. Order 66 was one of more than a hundred contingency orders every clone had memorized, covering emergency situations that might occur during the war. Only in retrospect does its drab military-speak strike us as sinister: "In the event of Jedi officers acting against the interests of the Republic, and after receiving specific orders verified as coming directly from the Supreme Commander, GAR commanders will remove those officers by lethal force, and command of the GAR will revert to the Supreme Commander until a new command structure is established."

That Supreme Commander was Palpatine. The very genes of his clone army had been altered to ensure loyalty and obedience, and the clones had been conditioned since birth to follow orders efficiently and without question or debate. When the clones received Order 66, the vast majority of them simply followed it, turning their guns on their Jedi Generals. Because they did so with neither malice nor hatred, few Jedi sensed anything amiss until the first blaster bolts ripped through them.

Within a few hours, the Jedi had been reduced to a handful of hunted outlaws. Within a few days, Palpatine was Emperor. The megacorps and guilds were dissolved, nationalized, or broken. His political enemies were dead, in detention, or living in fear. And a vast military machine answered to his orders and his alone.

His triumph was complete.

THE RISE OF THE EMPIRE

> "Give me a good plan I can execute today over
> a perfect plan I can execute next week."
> —Airen Cracken, supreme commander, New Republic Intelligence

THE IMPERIALIZATION OF THE GALAXY

Having established the foundations of the Empire during the Clone Wars, Emperor Palpatine moved quickly and ruthlessly to build on those foundations after the Declaration of the New Order.

Palpatine's wartime Governor-Generals were now a permanent class of regional governors, charged with keeping the peace, coordinating the Empire's vast military resources, and upholding the tenets of the New Order. Palpatine struck a conciliatory tone in his first meetings with Senate leaders, promising that he would not disband the ancient legislative body and would seek its counsel in enacting new laws. But he also warned that his judgments would now be final: Imperial decrees would be issued without debates, court proceedings, Senatorial overrides, or chatter about constitutional precedent. Those inclined to protest undoubtedly paused to consider the fate of sixty-three Senators (all signatories of the Petition of 2,000) who had been arrested on charges of conspiracy and treason.

While the Senate would continue to exist for years, Senators no longer had control over their sectors' military forces, or any legislative ability to shape Imperial policy. Once the Sector Governance Decree was enacted, a frustrated Mon Mothma of Chandrila noted, as a practical matter the Senate no longer existed.

Indeed, the Sector Armies organized to fight the Clone Wars remained, and responsibility for supporting them fell not to the Senate, but to twenty of the most powerful new regional governors. The oversector boundaries of the Clone Wars would be realigned with navy commands and morph as the Empire's priorities changed, with some growing and others disappearing entirely. And Wilhuff Tarkin, the Moff of Greater Seswenna, suggested a reorganization of the oversector system that included the concept of flexible priority sectors in which the Empire was pursuing active military campaigns or special projects. When Tarkin's plan was accepted, oversectors became a permanent part of the Empire, and the Moffs who controlled them—including Tarkin—were given the new rank of Grand Moff.

Most of the megacorps and guilds that had supported the Separatists vanished, as the Empire either nationalized them or forced them into treaties that distributed their holdings to Loyalist corporations such as Kuat Drive Yards, Sienar Fleet Systems, and TaggeCo. At the suggestion of the ambitious Baron Orman Tagge, Separatist-aligned corporations were stripped of their holdings in the Corporate Sector, with an expanded Corporate Sector Authority created to reward Loyalist firms. The Loyalist megacorps found themselves substantially wealthier, but the fate of entities that had backed the Separatists provided an object lesson in the perils of opposing Palpatine.

Other changes were afoot. Republic Intelligence became Imperial Intelligence, known as the Ubiqtorate. Most of the old Republic ministries reported to the Emperor and his top advisers through the Commission for the Preservation of the New Order, or COMPNOR, whose purview included not just the bureaucratic functions of government but also control of the arts and youth education. Access to the HoloNet was restricted. And Coruscant itself became known as Imperial Center.

THE RECONQUEST OF THE RIM

In the decades before the Clone Wars, most of the Outer Rim barely acknowledged the crumbling Republic's authority, and worlds as far Coreward as Gyndine were controlled by the Hutts. The war against the Separatists changed this state of affairs: Republic forces marched up the Hydian Way and the Perlemian Trade Route to the Corporate Sector and the Tion Hegemony; the front lines in the New Territories were pushed as far as Mygeeto; and the Republic created substantial power bases around Eriadu and Rothana. But a military occupation wasn't the same as a stable system of laws. And while the Hutts had seen their sphere of influence shrink drastically, many Rim worlds remained lawless, paying the newborn Empire as little mind as they had the Republic.

Things were about to change. The Clone Wars were over, but Kuat Drive Yards and Sienar Fleet Systems kept producing warships and ground vehicles at a rapid pace, while new clones continued to emerge from a number of facilities. The reason for this continuing mobilization was simple: Palpatine was determined to extend Imperial rule throughout the civilized galaxy.

Less than a year after the Declaration of the New Order and the Jedi Purge, Imperial forces divided troublesome areas of the Mid Rim and Outer Rim into a number of oversectors, taking aim at Separatist holdouts as well as pirates, slavers, and criminal gangs. During the Galactic Civil War, the Empire's defenders often recalled this period fondly, nostalgic for the years in which the starfleets and soldiers of the Empire ruthlessly rooted out Separatists and criminals and restored the rule of law in the outlying systems.

The bulk of the Imperial fleet still consisted of *Victory*- and *Venator*-class Star Destroyers, but as the pacification of the Rim continued, *Imperial*-class Star Destroyers joined more and more task forces, and squadrons of TIE fighters flew alongside older V-wings and ARC-170s.

In 19 BBY Imperial forces pushed into the Rim on three fronts. The Ciutric theater had become a rallying point for Separatist forces that had abandoned Muunilinst and Mygeeto, crossed the Void of Chopani, and joined forces with pirates and Thalassian slavers, attracting funding from shadowy interests on Celanon and Serenno. Destroying these forces fell to Crimson Dagger Command, which mobilized from Axxila. Admiral Terrinald Screed's starfleet engaged

the holdouts, with ground operations falling to General Hurst Romodi. Screed triumphed at the Battle of Vinsoth and pursued the Empire's enemies to Binquaros, where the Muun leadership dug in for a siege. Leaving Romodi to move in with ground forces, Screed pursued the holdouts' task force of Banking Clan frigates, Commerce Guild destroyers, and Thalassian privateers to Bimmiel, where he annihilated them.

But disaster struck while Screed was engaged: Other Imperial units had driven pirates and Mandalorians from the Salin Corridor, winning engagements at Fenion, Phindar, and Sheris. But the fleeing pirate fleet bested Screed's rear guard at Botajef, and broke Romodi's siege at Binquaros with the help of mercenaries hired on Serenno. The freed Separatists fled for the Unknown Regions, but a pirate captain betrayed them and they were intercepted at Vardoss, where Screed and Romodi put an end to them.

The sectors of the outlying Mid Rim beyond Kashyyyk and Lantillies had seen some of the fiercest fighting of the Clone Wars, as the Confederacy of Independent Systems sought to protect its industrial worlds. Costly Republic victories at Jabiim, Saleucami, Felucia, and Boz Pity had eaten away at the so-called Foundry of the Confederacy during the Outer Rim Sieges, and the area had seemingly fallen when the droid armies were shut down via a signal from Mustafar. But the Sy

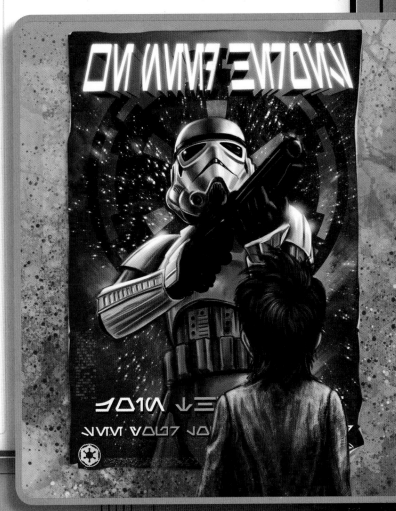

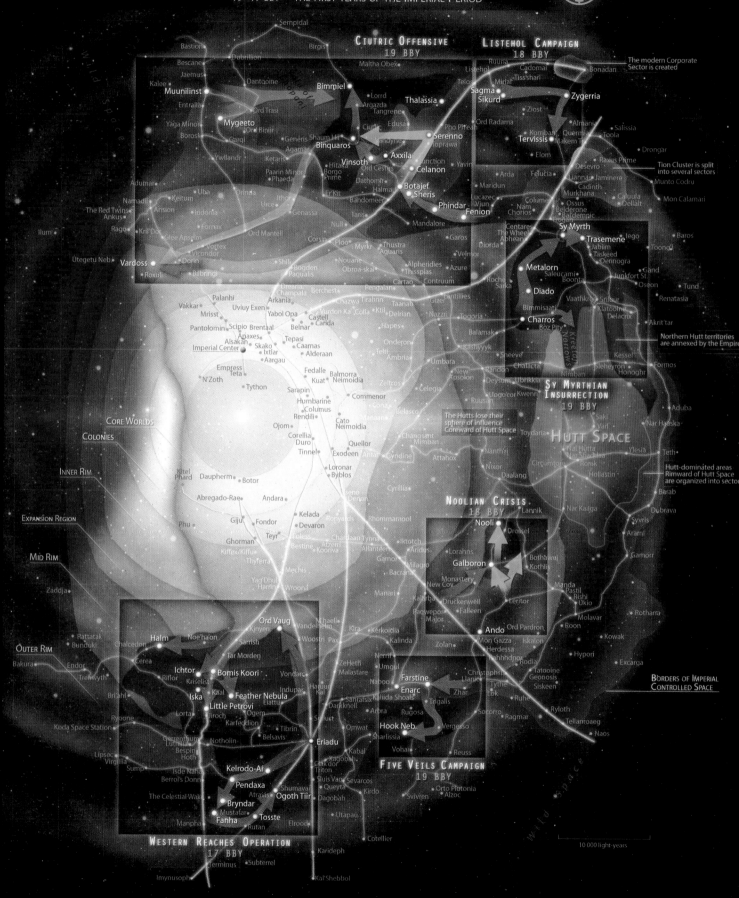

RECONQUEST OF THE RIM

19–17 BBY—THE FIRST YEARS OF THE IMPERIAL PERIOD

CIUTRIC OFFENSIVE
19 BBY

LISTEHOL CAMPAIGN
18 BBY

The modern Corporate Sector is created

Tion Cluster is split into several sectors

SY MYRTHIAN INSURRECTION
19 BBY

Northern Hutt territories are annexed by the Empire

The Hutts lose their sphere of influence Coreward of Hutt Space

HUTT SPACE

Hutt-dominated areas Rimward of Hutt Space are organized into sectors

NOOLIAN CRISIS
18 BBY

CORE WORLDS

COLONIES

INNER RIM

EXPANSION REGION

MID RIM

OUTER RIM

BORDERS OF IMPERIAL CONTROLLED SPACE

WESTERN REACHES OPERATION
17 BBY

FIVE VEILS CAMPAIGN
19 BBY

10 000 light-years

Myrthian leader Toonbuck Toora was determined to fight on, and managed to reactivate significant numbers of ground forces, naval units, and factory worlds.

The Twelfth Sector Army, relocated to Charros, ground down Toora's forces over several months of fighting, with Admiral Adar Tallon and General Jan Dodonna prevailing at Diado and Metalorn, besieging Sy Myrth under Dodonna's expert direction, then chasing down Toora's flagship *Defiance's Banner* with a task force led by the *Praetor*-class battlecruiser *Battalion*. Toora's fleet was cornered at Trasemene and ripped apart by the *Battalion*'s batteries, ending the Sy Myrthian Insurrection. (A few dead-enders would continue to harry the Republic from the lawless Kreetan Narrows in Hutt Space, ultimately leading to the area's seizure by the Empire.)

The third confrontation of 19 BBY pitted Imperial forces against remnants of the Trade Federation. The Federation had ceased to exist when Acting Viceroy Sentepeth Findos signed a treaty giving the Empire control of its resources. But Marath Vooro, the cartel's customs vizier, refused to acknowledge that treaty—and retained control of Trade Defense Fleet units and droids at Enarc. Vooro's defiance cheered Separatist sympathizers, but he had no effective commanders to back up his words, and a starfleet under Octavian Grant smashed his forces at Farstine, then pursued them down the Five Veils Run, capturing Vooro in the fringes of the Hook Nebula.

The exploits of Romodi, Screed, Tallon, Dodonna, and Grant were celebrated in the Core, but the next year brought two new campaigns. Forces under Admiral Wullf Yularen faced off against an ominous union of Sikurdian pirates, Zygerrian slavers, and Tervig slavers. Their gangs had turned the Listehol Run and the Shaltin Tunnels into perilous trade routes for shipping, and were raiding the newly reorganized Corporate Sector. Given command of a fleet of *Invincible*-class heavy cruisers earmarked for the CSA, Yularen and a young captain named Bannidge Holt complemented the ancient battle wagons with squadrons of TIE fighters launched from a small complement of *Venator*-class Star Destroyers. Their fleet withstood a Sikurdian swarm at the Battle of Sagma, interdicted Zygerria (which negotiated peace with an Imperial adviser who arrived backed by stormtroopers), and served as a base of operations for raids on Tervissis. Tervissis would prove intractable and eventually be invaded in 13 BBY.

The second campaign of 18 BBY, the Noolian Crisis, came in the Mid Rim. After the fall of Ando, Aqualish and Harch raiders harried Imperial forces in the southern Slice, launching hit-and-fade attacks on medical facilities and the supply chain. Funded and armed by secretive enemies of the Empire, the Aqualish seized Nooli, Galboron, and several outlying worlds in Bothan space before being defeated in the Battle of Galboron by a task force led by Captain Par Lankin.

But no campaign captured Imperial citizens' imagination like the Western Reaches Operation of 17 BBY. In the final days of the Clone Wars, the remnants of General Grievous's forces had fled Rimward of Bomis Koori, seeking shelter amid the area's pirate bases and slaver nests.

Palpatine was determined to pacify the Western Reaches, and handed responsibility for the operation to Wilhuff Tarkin, based at Eriadu. Mindful of the number of Separatist dead-enders and pirate bands in the region and the lack of reliable Planetary Security Forces, Tarkin appealed for substantial military resources. He got everything he asked for and more: The newly minted war heroes Screed and Holt were given command of naval operations, with Romodi appointed to lead the ground war.

Their exploits were adapted into breathless holodramas such as *The Charge at Feather Nebula* and *The Guns of Kelrodo-Ai,* which also featured a canny starfighter pilot named Shea Hublin. The battles of Ord Vaug, Halm, Pendaxa, and Ichtor soon became famous, and Imperial citizens of a

Suspected Separatists confront Imperial justice (John VanFleet)

certain age would always remember where they were when they heard that Holt had been killed and Romodi badly injured by an Iska pirate ambush at Bryndar.

Screed and Hublin smashed the Iska pirates at Fanha, with the pirate lord Guun Cutlax escaping into the lawless Atravis Sector, where he linked up with Separatist holdouts led by the rogue Aqualish general Kendu Ultho. Hublin's squadrons shredded Cutlax's privateers at Tosste, and the endgame came at Ogoth Tiir, where Ultho was killed and his remaining forces captured.

WAR PORTRAIT: ADMIRAL SCREED

Terrinald Screed rose to prominence as one of the heroes of the Clone Wars and the Empire's Rim campaigns, but fell out of favor and died a victim of a squabble between post-Imperial warlords.

After studying at Prefsbelt and Carida, Screed became a member of the Republic's Judicial Forces, and was decorated for leading the fleet action that broke the Biskaran Pirates' siege of Niele in 35 BBY, losing an eye to a Biskaran vibro-ax. The scarred young officer with the cybernetic eye then became an outspoken Militarist and one of Senator Palpatine's earliest allies, campaigning publicly for the Military Creation Act.

Screed was granted a captain's rank in the Republic Navy, and he and his fellow captain Jan Dodonna won distinction battling Dua Ningo's Bulwark Fleet. Screed and Dodonna checked Ningo's forces at Ixtlar, Alsakan, and Basilisk before a decisive confrontation at Anaxes, where Dodonna engaged Ningo's warships long enough for Screed to ambush the Separatists, emerging from hyperspace in perfect position to fire a fusillade that ripped through Ningo's battle cruiser *Unrepentant*. Screed launched his attack at point-blank range, and the bridge of his own flagship, the Victory Star Destroyer *Arlionne,* was torn open by the explosion of the *Unrepentant*. He suffered near-mortal injuries, but laboriously traversed the Azure Walk on Anaxes to receive the Holt Cross just three weeks later, agreeing only to be supported by his fellow honoree Dodonna, since "I have leaned on Jan in far more dangerous instances than these."

Screed took over command of the Coruscant Home Fleet, an important posting that also allowed him to recover from his injuries. Made an admiral in the New Order, he served with valor at Vinsoth, Bimmiel, Vardoss, and in the Western Reaches.

It was an impressive list of accolades, but also the pinnacle of Screed's career. Within a decade the admiral had become a slave owner and mastermind of dodgy economic schemes in the Outer Rim, seeking worlds that the Empire might exploit and thereby keep his own coffers overflowing. No year went by without the scarred old officer being trotted out for some fete in the Core Worlds, but the man who had been one of the most articulate Militarists now rarely spoke, and was soon back aboard his *Gladiator*-class Star Destroyer *Demolisher* searching for new sources of plunder. After the Battle of Endor, he sought to attract forces to his banner, but was captured and killed by Zsinj.

After his defection to the Rebel Alliance, Dodonna was once asked what had become of his old friend. "No man becomes what he despises all at once," he replied. "It happens little by little, through the smallest betrayals and abandonments. I think Terrinald knew on some level that the New Order he had done so much to support was hollow and built on lies, as I discovered. But his conclusion was different from mine—Terrinald concluded *everything* was built on lies. And in a galaxy like that, a man may as well become a liar himself."

SECTOR GROUPS AND THE IMPERIAL NAVY

The forces commanded through various oversectors became collectively known as the Imperial Starfleet, and took their orders from the Admiralty on Imperial Center. But the Empire's Moffs objected that the starfleet often robbed them of resources without sufficient consideration for their local needs. After some Moffs sought to raise local militias, the Empire stepped in and created Sector Groups directly controlled by the Moffs, though their decisions were carefully scrutinized by Imperial advisers.

These Sector Groups were largely drawn from the Planetary Security Forces, which had been nationalized in the final days of the Republic. Their combat and defense missions were split between separate fleet components, known as "superiority" and "escort." Superiority fleets were built around the new *Imperial*-class Star Destroyers. Officially, each was assigned a battle squadron of eighteen smaller ships, but in practice Star Destroyers were normally accompanied by just two or three escorts, if any—an Imperial

Star Destroyer was designed to operate without support, and was too fast for any escorts except the speediest light cruisers. While superiority forces were officially assigned to fleet combat, they were normally used as mobile reserves, projecting Imperial power in response to local threats.

Escort forces, on the other hand, were designated for combat against pirate gangs and Rebel raiders, which in practice meant they were the Empire's first line of defense, protecting civilian freighters, attacking corsairs' hideouts, and serving as guardships at remote outposts.

The Empire's early escort squadrons leaned heavily on old Trade Defense frigates and Corellian corvettes, but Kuat Drive Yards soon introduced cheap new designs. The EF76 was an ungainly combination of weapons, sensors, and TIE racks that became the most effective light warship of recent centuries, while the escort carrier was basically a vast hangar bay with engines at the back, designed to counter Rebel attacks with a swarm of TIE fighters.

Despite the Imperial Star Destroyer's fearsome reputation, the most common warship in the navy was the Sienar IPV-1, a corvette-sized patrol craft with a small flight crew, impressive performance, and heavy armament—but no hyperdrive and

(CONTINUED ON PAGE 118)

Captains Screed and Dodonna receive the Holt Cross on Anaxes (Chris Scalf)

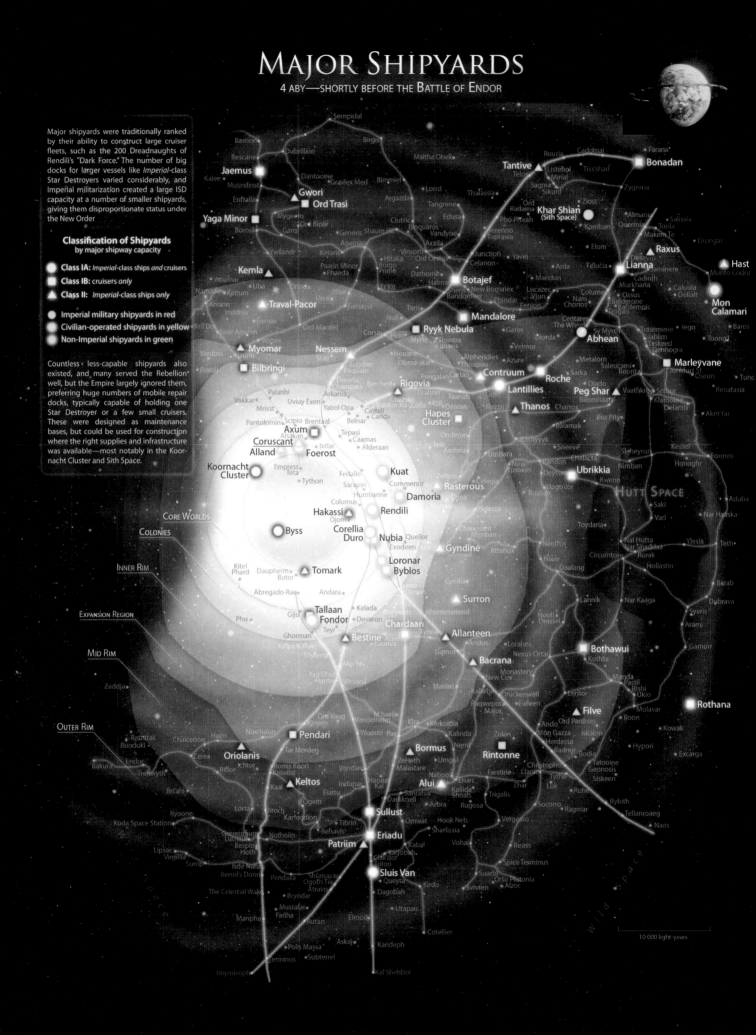

MAJOR SHIPYARDS
4 ABY—SHORTLY BEFORE THE BATTLE OF ENDOR

Major shipyards were traditionally ranked by their ability to construct large cruiser fleets, such as the 200 Dreadnaughts of Rendili's "Dark Force." The number of big docks for larger vessels like *Imperial*-class Star Destroyers varied considerably, and Imperial militarization created a large ISD capacity at a number of smaller shipyards, giving them disproportionate status under the New Order

Classification of Shipyards
by major shipway capacity

- **Class IA:** *Imperial*-class ships *and* cruisers
- **Class IB:** cruisers *only*
- **Class II:** *Imperial*-class ships *only*

- Imperial military shipyards in red
- Civilian-operated shipyards in yellow
- Non-Imperial shipyards in green

Countless less-capable shipyards also existed, and many served the Rebellion well, but the Empire largely ignored them, preferring huge numbers of mobile repair docks, typically capable of holding one Star Destroyer or a few small cruisers. These were designed as maintenance bases, but could be used for construction where the right supplies and infrastructure was available—most notably in the Koornacht Cluster and Sith Space.

CORE WORLDS
COLONIES
INNER RIM
EXPANSION REGION
MID RIM
OUTER RIM

HUTT SPACE

10 000 light-years

ARMORY AND SENSOR PROFILE

IMPERIAL STAR DESTROYER

Embodying Emperor Palpatine's power and ruthlessness, the *Imperial*-class Star Destroyer came to symbolize the Empire during the Galactic Civil War. Other capital ships of its time were larger and more powerful, but the Imperial Star Destroyer was the backbone of the Imperial fleet. The appearance of an Imperial Star Destroyer's dagger-shaped hull above a rebellious world meant that its citizens had attracted the Emperor's baleful eye.

Bristling with turbolasers and ion cannons, a Star Destroyer could fulfill a number of combat roles. Its powerful weaponry—improved in the Imperial II model—allowed it to assault other ships of the line or planets, while its speed and suite of tractor beams proved capable of apprehending small, nimble craft. Its complement of soldiers, AT-ATs, and even a prefabricated garrison base made it an effective transport for ground assaults. And its complement of seventy-two TIE fighters made it a reasonably effective carrier.

The Imperial Star Destroyer emerged from designs pursued by Kuat Drive Yards and Rendili StarDrive during the Clone Wars, with the *Acclamator*-class transport and *Venator*- and *Victory*-class Star Destroyers serving as predecessors for a new, sixteen-hundred-meter warship designed by KDY's Lira Wessex and originally known as the *Imperator* class. The first ship of the new class was the *Executrix*, with the *Exactor*—the first of Darth Vader's many

Imperial flagships—second to glide away from KDY's docks. (A related design, the *Tector* class, was produced in much smaller numbers.)

The combination of KDY's history of warship customization and the Empire's insistence on using interchangeable components led to many variations on the basic *Imperial*-class model, as well as much smaller and larger hulls built along the Star Destroyer's wedge-shaped lines.

Smaller members of the KDY Star Destroyer "family" included the four-hundred-meter *Imperial II*-class frigate and the five-hundred-meter *Pursuit*-class light cruiser, while a trio of six-hundred-meter cruisers—the *Enforcer*, *Interdictor*, and *Vindicator* classes—were common sights on the galaxy's star lanes. Far larger warships also followed the famous Star Destroyer design, among them the eight-thousand-meter *Mandator*-class dreadnaught, a successor to KDY's *Procurator*-class warship. And then, of course, there was the nineteen-thousand-meter *Executor*-class Star Dreadnought. These titanic battleships, the largest built by the Empire, served as sector command ships and mobile headquarters, but their true purpose was to terrorize the Emperor's enemies and convince them that resistance was impossible against a military that could construct such monstrous craft.

Imperial-class Star Destroyers and other ships of this extended family remained common sights in the fleets of the New Republic, Imperial Remnant, and Galactic Alliance, with new models such as the *Republic*-class Star Destroyer and the *Galactic*-class battle carrier serving alongside them.

IMPERIAL STAR
DESTROYER

(CONTINUED FROM PAGE 115)

only light shielding. Deployed in sufficient numbers, IPV-1s were capable of defending systems against almost any opposition, and skirmish lines of up to twenty-four ships were found everywhere the Empire wished to retain a military presence.

The reorganization of the navy into Sector Groups brought command complications, requiring large numbers of new flag officers. While senior captains remained in charge of battle lines, new brevet ranks were introduced at the squadron and task-force level—although in practice these were sometimes consolidated into a single level of command. Command of a Sector Group belonged to a High Admiral, but this was often a ceremonial post occupied by a Moff. Where this was the case, or where there were separate superiority and escort fleets in a sector, senior officers were appointed as Fleet Admirals, devaluing the former rank of regional commanders.

Separate fleet commands were also created to organize army assault ships and repair docks, but the most important non-combat battlegroups were the Support Fleets, charged with securing the logistics of the entire Empire. This burden fell in equal part on Corellian corvettes and massive FSCV transports.

THE ACADEMY SYSTEM

The Republic had had no centralized military between the Ruusan Reformations and the Clone Wars, but the Imperial military inherited a long-established system of schools and officer-training academies that had served the Republic's Judicial Forces, Planetary Security Forces, and the galaxy's mercantile fleets and hyperspace scouts. These schools had kept the culture and traditions of the army and navy alive, and the Empire built upon their efforts to create an academy system that ensured a steady flow of capable officers.

Young men and women without wealth or connections who sought a military career had to begin their journey at a military school, pilot institute, or training academy maintained by an individual planetary or system government. The quality of these institutions varied hugely; some degrees were considered impressive, while others were bemoaned as a waste of a good piece of flimsiplast. Cadets who did well in such schools or began with family connections attended regional sector service academies, where they went through basic training, learned military history and theory, and were subjected to tests and evaluations aimed at determining what military career might suit them best. Under the Empire, some general-service sector academies remained, but many were accredited as Sector Naval Academies or Army Officer Training Academies, feeding the two main branches of the military.

Cadets with top scores were invited to take entrance examinations for the main service academies, at which the Empire groomed its most promising officer candidates. (Occasionally youths with exceptional abilities or political connections received direct appointments.) There were two main service academies, supported by a number of schools for specialists, cross-commission training, research and development, and investigations into strategic analysis and theory.

Cadets rarely applied to a specific service academy; instead, upon acceptance they were scrutinized by intake officers, who assigned them to a specific academy and recommended the duration and nature of their initial training program. The reasons for intake officers' decisions were endlessly debated by cadets; the process was sometimes political, but more often reflected a genuine desire to get the most out of the Empire's considerable investment in a cadet. Once assigned to a service academy, some cadets were graduated, commissioned, and posted to active duty after a minimum term, while others might be transferred repeatedly among academies and assigned different courses of study.

The Imperial Army Academy was on Raithal, in the Colonies. Most of its cadets endured a grueling one-year training program that included simulations and live-fire drills in drop camps on a variety of worlds, as well as rigorous psychological examinations and indoctrination in the precepts of the New Order. Raithal trained ground troops for the Planetary Security Forces and Judicials, and was initially reserved for non-clones preparing for careers in the Imperial Army, as opposed to the all-clone Stormtrooper Corps. But as non-clones entered the stormtrooper ranks, Raithal cadets began to be tapped for stormtrooper training on Carida. Particularly promising cadets or those seeking specialized army careers might also go on to Carida, though most were assigned to Corulag.

The location of the Imperial Naval Academy was officially classified, but any youth dreaming of a starfleet career knew it was located on Prefsbelt—as with Raithal, Judicial and Planetary Security Force cadets had trained there for generations. At Prefsbelt midshipmen began with academic study and tactical simulations, before moving on to leadership courses and active service rotations as ensigns. Most entered naval service after three years at Prefsbelt, but some did shorter stints, shifting to a flight school or continuing their studies at Carida, Corulag, or Anaxes.

(Two other main service academies attracted cadets,

Flight-school cadets learning advanced dogfighting techniques (Chris Scalf)

though they were far less prestigious than Raithal and Prefsbelt. The Imperial Exploration Academy, which turned out scouts for the Imperial Survey Corps, had its headquarters on the Inner Rim world of Vanik, while the Imperial Merchant Galactic Academy was located on Rhinnal. The Merchant Galactic, a civilian auxiliary of the navy, specialized in military transportation and logistics, with many of its graduates serving aboard commercial freighters after fulfilling their obligation to the Imperial Supply Fleet.)

Graduates of Raithal or Prefsbelt might go on to one of the Empire's three specialized military schools, all of which had deep roots in the Republic military. Corulag trained navy midshipmen, army cadets, flight school pilots, and specialists from all services, with an emphasis on active training. The embodiment of naval tradition, Anaxes offered active training and combat simulations, served as a think tank for promising cadets and active-duty officers, and tested new warships and equipment via training cruises.

Carida's Republic Defense Academy had been created to train PSF and Judicial ground forces, and during the Clone Wars it specialized in training non-clones to lead clone divisions, a mission it continued with the Stormtrooper Corps.

Over time Carida became a training center for clones bred for greater independence and leadership, the equivalent of the Republic's ARC troopers, with live training supplementing lessons learned through flash instruction.

Once the Empire opened the stormtrooper ranks to non-clones, Carida drew the best and bravest army cadets, with its two-year stormtrooper training program legendary for its brutality. Carida turned out more than just stormtroopers, though—numerous army, navy, and flight school cadets spent semesters there, and the planet was the headquarters of the Imperial Engineering Academy.

Lastly, there was the Empire's flight school system, reserved for top graduates of the Sector Naval Academies and Prefsbelt. Few flight schools had fixed locations; most were based on capital ships, including Imperial Star Destroyers, Venators, and a handful of captured Lucrehulks. The most prestigious was the Vensenor Flight Academy, housed on the *Venator*-class Star Destroyer of the same name.

IMPERIAL NAVY RANK GUIDE

CODE CYLINDERS	POSITION	PLACK	LINE RANK	SPECIALIST RANK	SPECIALIST PLACK
	Warlord		Grand Admiral	Promoted into Line	
IIII	High Admiral	▟▟▟▟▟	Admiral		
III	Fleet Admiral	▟▟▟▟	Vice-Admiral		
II	Admiral or Commodore or Commander	▟▟▟	Rear Admiral	General	▟▟▟▟ I
	Captain	▟▟	Senior Captain	Colonel	I ▟▟▟ I
I			Senior Cmdr.	Major	▟▟▟ I
			Junior Cmdr.	Commander	I ▟▟ I
	Lieutenant	▟	Senior Lt.	Captain	▟▟
			Junior Lt.	Lieutenant	I ▟ I
	Midshipman	▮	Ensign	Officer	▟

Horizontal lines that do not align in the "plack" section indicate where the relationship between position and rank can vary.

In theory, the plack is associated with line rank, but officers with the position of fleet admiral and ship's captain always wear the insignia of a full admiral and a senior captain (or captain of the line), respectively.

Code cylinders are encrypted devices designed to regulate computer use aboard Imperial Navy ships, also used as rank identifiers. The additional override cylinders of flag officers relate to their fleet responsibilities. Typically, new code cylinders are issued with every new assignment, and officers not on active duty do not normally wear them. They are worn in small pockets near the shoulders of the uniform tunic, with the first one always placed on the left-hand pocket beside the rank plack. Specialist code cylinders are worn in the same positions, but serve purely as insignia.

Position is an officer's current assignment to a specific ship or unit, as opposed to permanent rank. The positions of *Warlord* and *High Admiral* are essentially honorary, normally held by Grand Admirals and Moffs.

A *Fleet Admiral* commands a fleet, and is usually the senior officer in a sector. The main practical sub-unit of the fleet is the *squadron*, and its flag officer is usually called the *commander*, although he is officially appointed as its *admiral*.

Between the fleet and the squadron there is an extra level, the *Systems Force*, the overall commander of which is styled a *systems admiral* or *commodore*. In practice, however, most Systems Forces contain just one squadron, and the systems admiral and squadron commander are the same officer.

Below the squadron level, small groups of escorts or light cruisers are commanded by senior captains, while the commanding officer of a ship is always the *captain*, and officers serving in a ship's crew are known generally as *lieutenants* regardless of rank, although ensigns can be addressed as *midshipman*.

Line rank is held by line officers, the men who command the bridge crew, captain ships, and hoist their flag over fleets. There are very few officers with permanent line ranks above senior captain (formally known as captain of the line).

Specialist rank is for personnel of the Flight, Support, and Engineering branches. These ranks are similar to the Imperial Army. The few specialist officers raised above the rank of general are promoted into the line at the rank of vice admiral, though they retain the honorific branch titles of *air marshal*, *war commissar*, and *master engineer*.

The junior ranks of specialist officers, captain and below, are prefixed by *flight*, *support*, or *engineering* according to branch. Flight Branch pilots also have their own positional titles: *squadron leader*, *wing commander*, and *group captain*.

Some specialist officers use additional code keys not shown in the table. Generals with large base or project commands will receive the code cylinders of a squadron or fleet commander. TIE squadron leaders, normally flight captains, use the insignia of a ship's captain, as a fighter unit is considered the equivalent of a small-ship command.

The Imperial Naval Academy on Prefsbelt (Chris Scalf)

WORLD AT WAR: PREFSBELT

Prefsbelt began as a secret—a green world far beyond the galactic frontier, colonized by Republic citizens fleeing the tyranny of the Pius Dea cultists in the 11,600s BBY. The name is a corruption of Prefid's Belt, a constellation in the skies of Fedje that includes Prefsbelt's sun.

In the 10,970s BBY, the Renunciate Admiral Pers Pradeux discovered Prefsbelt's location and made the world a retreat for Renunciate naval officers plotting the overthrow of the Faithful. After the Renunciates' victory at Uquine in 10,966 BBY, Pradeux and his fellow officers reorganized and rebuilt the Republic Navy during a series of meetings at Prefsbelt, forging the traditions that continued to underpin the service millennia later.

Prefsbelt's significance made it the logical site for the Republic Naval Academy, but for more than a millennium its location remained a closely guarded secret. While the secrecy didn't last, the Academy's presence on Prefsbelt remains officially need-to-know, and no well-bred midshipman or officer would refer to the two in conjunction.

Anaxes may be the pinnacle of naval pomp and circumstance, but Prefsbelt is richer in tradition. It's a pleasant world, with the Academy sprawling across the hills around Castle Pradeux, whose ancient stones are dwarfed by soaring buildings and towers as well as by the 12 Mounts, named for great naval battles. A kilometers-long passage from Castle Pradeux leads into the heart of the range, and the night before graduation awed midshipmen walk the pitch-black passage in silence, emerging in the dimly lit Naval Crypt, where the Father of the Navy himself is entombed. There, each midshipman dedicates himself or herself to the service.

After graduation the midshipmen recess down the Incline, dotted with monuments and historical artifacts, and are conveyed by hovertrain to the bustle of Prefsbelt Green. There they ascend the skyhook to Prefsbelt Black, where they receive their orders and are assigned to warships. Few will ever see the Academy again; most will remember it fondly throughout their days.

WAR PORTRAIT: WULLF YULAREN

Wullf Yularen grew up on Anaxes, the son of the legendary Thull Yularen, who followed his lengthy service in the Republic's Judicial Forces by becoming an instructor at Anaxes. At the Yularen estate in the Sirpar Hills, young Wullf diagrammed famous naval battles with tabletop toys, quizzing his father about how Darsius deployed his cruiser line at Brightday and learning tales of naval traditions dating back to the Pius Dea Renunciates.

Yularen's surname could have won him an easy Judicial posting, but the son didn't need to be told that wasn't proper: After graduating from Prefsbelt, Wullf immediately opted for the Planetary Security Forces and sought a dangerous posting in the wild and woolly Kwymar sector. There he routed slavers on the Listehol Run and destroyed a number of Sikurdian pirate nests in Wild Space.

Yularen resigned his rank for a position in the Senate Intelligence Bureau, where he spent a decade pursuing an anti-corruption agenda with the same discipline he'd brought to naval service. Unfortunately, he did his job too well, making powerful enemies in both the bureau and the Senate. Yularen found himself blocked and sidelined—at which point he acquired a powerful patron in Supreme Chancellor Palpatine, who tapped him for a special unit investigating corruption and Separatism.

The Senate saw Palpatine's special unit as a threat to its power and prerogatives, and managed to starve the new service of credits and reduce it to a shell. Forced into early retirement, Yularen stewed on Anaxes, but Palpatine soon called upon him once again. He persuaded him to accept a place in the new Republic Navy, promoted him to admiral, and assigned him to Anakin Skywalker's Jedi cruiser.

Yularen admired Skywalker's abilities and his unshakable faith in himself, but he was horrified by the Jedi's routine flouting of orders and casual attitude toward security. As the Clone Wars ground on, Yularen came to wonder if the Jedi weren't an impediment to an efficient, secure war effort—they followed a separate chain of command, one not always responsive to orders from Coruscant.

After the Declaration of the New Order, Yularen saw the chance to revive his anti-corruption efforts. The Republic's crooked ministers and bureaucrats had blocked the efforts of Supreme Chancellor Palpatine, but they wouldn't dare resist the orders of *Emperor* Palpatine. Yularen became an agent in the new Imperial Security Bureau and worked with quiet efficiency to purge the Imperial military and ministerial ranks of all those with ties to the underworld or Separatist leanings. By the time of the Battle of Yavin, he had become a colonel in the ISB, and won a coveted assignment to the Death Star battle station.

Wullf Yularen is briefed by Obi-Wan Kenobi in the field (Bruno Werneck)

EMPIRE TRIUMPHANT

> "Soldiers win battles. Generals take credit."
> —Kal Skirata, instructor, Grand Army of the Republic

FROM CLONE TROOPERS TO STORMTROOPERS

The Empire's first stormtroopers were the clones it inherited from the Republic, still clad in Phase II armor they had customized with unit colors and markings. But everything about the Empire's shock troops—their armor, weapons and even their genetic makeup—would soon change.

In the final weeks of the Clone Wars, the Grand Army's ranks swelled with new clones produced on Centax 2 using Arkanian cloning techniques. The newborn Empire continued to create clone stormtroopers via Kaminoan and Arkanian techniques, using the Fett line as well as new lines created from other prime clones.

A refinement of the Arkanian technique created the GeNode clone lines, producing tough, unswervingly obedient stormtroopers whose minds were manipulated to prevent them from understanding they were clones or discussing cloning with other GeNode clones. The GeNode conditioning fell out of favor because its failures tended to be spectacular, with GeNodes awakening to find themselves surrounded by identical faces and seeking to destroy these impostors in rage and terror.

Clones remained an integral part of the Stormtrooper Corps and other services throughout the Empire's existence, but became less and less important to the Imperial war machine over time. Kaminoan methods were slow and expensive, while Arkanian processes produced subpar soldiers. Meanwhile, the Empire had no shortage of humans who could be recruited or conscripted for military service. In the decade before the Battle of Yavin, the percentage of clones shrank to perhaps a third of the overall Stormtrooper Corps.

Even before introducing stormtrooper armor, the Empire decreed an end to the Republic tradition of unit markings and individualizing soldiers' kits. Clone trooper armor was returned to a blank white, to emphasize the troops' uniformity and obedience to the New Order, and officers addressed clones by unit number, not nicknames. The clone trooper's BlasTech DC-15 blaster was replaced by the stormtrooper's BlasTech E-11, whose extendable stock allowed for greater accuracy in long-range combat.

DEBRIEFING: STORMTROOPERS

The Stormtrooper Corps supported both the Imperial Army and Navy, while belonging to neither. Stormtroopers emerged from unique training regimens, had their own command structure, and generally relied on their own infrastructure for support. Whether serving as elite shock troops advancing ahead of army units or ensuring the loyalty of crews in the navy, their sole loyalty was to the Emperor, and they existed to enforce his will on the military ranks and the galactic populace alike.

The Order of Battle for the Stormtrooper Corps mirrored that of the army at lower tiers, with its command structure topping out at the legion. In addition, stormtrooper units didn't include support personnel.

- **Squad** (8 troopers): A stormtrooper squad includes a sergeant and a corporal.

- **Platoon** (32 troopers): A platoon consists of four squads, commanded by a lieutenant and a sergeant-major.

- **Company** (128 troopers): A company consists of four platoons, led by a captain.

- **Battalion** (512 troopers): A battalion consists of four companies, led by a major.

- **Regiment** (2,048 troopers): A regiment consists of four battalions, led by a lieutenant colonel.

- **Legion** (8,192 troopers): A legion consists of four regiments, led by a high colonel.

Stormtrooper training included not just grueling physical tests but also extensive indoctrination, which produced unswerving loyalty to the Empire. Very few attempts to bribe, blackmail, or seduce a stormtrooper succeeded.

A stormtrooper's standard armor and black body glove served as sophisticated survival gear, allowing troopers to withstand heat and cold, poisonous or corrosive atmospheres, and even brief exposure to vacuum. Stormtroopers undertaking more specialized missions wore different equipment and armor. Snowtroopers wore insulated gear and warmers over the lower parts of their helmets, sandtrooper armor included cooling units and a helmet with a sand filter, radtroopers wore shielded armor to protect against radiation that would kill an exposed being in minutes, and jump troopers were trained and equipped for aerial assaults, following the tradition of the Republic's jet troopers and rocket-jumpers. Other variant roles and kits included scout troopers, swamptroopers, seatroopers, magma troopers, and spacetroopers.

While stormtrooper armor was typically unadorned white, some elite or experimental units stood out for their unit markings or colored armor. The shadow stormtroopers that served Blackhole and Carnor Jax wore black armor made of stygium-triprismatic polymers, elite units known as novatroopers wore black-and-gold armor, and rumors persisted that the Imperial Royal Guard sometimes took the field in crimson armor.

Under the Empire, stormtroopers were exclusively human except for a handful of experimental units whose existence was classified. That changed in the decades after the Battle of Endor, when nonhuman stormtroopers appeared in the service of the Imperial Remnant, the Empire of the Hand, and Roan Fel's revived Empire.

THE IMPERIAL ARMY

Stormtroopers were the best-known Imperial soldiers, but they were relatively rare sights in the galaxy: The garrisons of military bases and occupied worlds were made up of army troopers, who substantially outnumbered their counterparts in the Stormtrooper Corps. Army troopers piloted most of the Empire's ground assault vehicles, and sometimes served aboard warships as marines. In battle they wore partial body armor and helmets over gray jumpsuits.

The Imperial Army evolved from the non-clone Republic Army, created by nationalizing and amalgamating ground units of the Planetary Security Forces and Judicials. With the exception of pilots, clones were rare sights in the army's ranks.

The Order of Battle for the army included larger divisions than those of stormtroopers. The following complements don't include command elements and support personnel attached to a given unit:

- **Squad** (8 troopers): An army squad includes eight troopers plus a sergeant, with one of the eight troopers serving as a corporal.

- **Platoon** (32 troopers): A platoon consists of four squads, commanded by a lieutenant and a sergeant-major.

- **Company** (128 troopers): A company consists of four platoons, led by a captain.

- **Battalion** (512 troopers): A battalion consists of four companies, led by a major. The battalion was the minimum deployment for an army ground operation unless stormtroopers were included in the deployment.

- **Regiment** (2,048 troopers): A regiment consists of four battalions, led by a lieutenant colonel.

- **Battlegroup** (8,192 troopers): A battlegroup—the standard deployment for major Imperial Army offensives—consists of four regiments, led by a high colonel. The battlegroup was an Imperial designation that replaced the Republic designation of division. The equivalent in the Stormtrooper Corps is a legion.

- **Corps** (32,768 troopers): A corps consists of four battlegroups, commanded by a major general. A corps was deployed as a unit for major planetary operations.

- **Army** (131,072 troopers): An army consists of four corps, commanded by a general.

- **Systems Army** (as many as 393,216 troopers): A Systems Army consists of between one and three armies operating in the same system, and is largely a bookkeeping designation, not an operational unit.

- **Sector Army** (as many as 1,572,864 troopers): A Sector Army consists of between two and four Systems Armies, and is commanded by a marshal—generally an honorary title held by a Moff.

Army pilots drove AT-STs and AT-ATs, as well as the Empire's less celebrated but more common ground vehicles: juggernauts, compact assault vehicles, hoverscouts, mobile command bases, command speeders, and floating fortresses. Some army pilots specialized in tracked, wheeled, repulsorlift, or walker-type vehicles.

A FEMALE STORMTROOPER REMEMBERS

From the memoirs of Isila Drutch, 291st Legion, 33 ABY:

I was born on Parshoone, in the Perinn sector— New Territories, back of beyond. My father fought with the Republic Navy at Venestria and Ord Trasi, and was aboard one of the old Tectors—the Archer, she was called—when the Separatists shut down their clankers and the war stopped. He always talked about his navy days, but I was a born ground-pounder. Tooka dolls? Please. I was drawing up fortifications and organizing skirmish lines.

There isn't a lot of sitting around on Parshoone— if you're able, you work. I was never big, but I was tough—and I never, ever quit. When I was seventeen I applied to the Parshoone Sector Service Academy and chose an army concentration. First year, I was top of my class and the commandant said he'd sponsor me for Raithal. My reaction: "Why not Cliffside?"

matriarchy back before Ruusan. Nearly as big as a Houk and twice as mean. TD-1123 was small like me, a crack shot. She got killed by an abo in a firefight at Jiroch-Reslia. I never knew where she was from. I know the navy had hang-ups about women in the service, but that's because so many of them were from the Core, with fancy Core notions. That kind of poodoo didn't fly in the white-hats—we didn't even have separate barracks. Didn't need them.

So why are people surprised to hear about a female stormie?

Well, it's true there aren't many of us. No female clone lines, or at least I never heard of any. The physical regimen is brutal, yes, and human females are going to wash out more. But that's physiology, not prejudice—if you can pass white-hat training, you're a white-hat.

A lot of it is just ignorance: When my squad was shelled up in our whites, you couldn't tell I was a woman. The only thing you could see was that I was a little short. A lot of civvies have probably stood a meter from a female stormtrooper and never known it.

But it's also that people don't know just what stormie training does to your mind. It was four years during which they broke us down to nothing and built us back up into pillars of the New Order. After that, we fought and moved and spoke and thought like stormtroopers—male and female had been taken out of the equation along with everything else.

I do remember being on leave in some wrong-end-of-the-bantha cantina and there was one of those pinups of a girl in femtrooper gear. Some of the barves in my squad pointed it out to me, I think maybe one of them asked why I was wearing the wrong kit.

I looked at it and had to laugh.

First off, I don't care if you're built like an Askajian—nobody needs a chest plate that looks like it has its own gravity-well projectors, particularly not while they're wearing a body glove made for vacuum. As for going into combat with a bare midriff, I wouldn't recommend it. Though I could've told you that on Parshoone—I didn't need two years on Carida to figure that one out.

Carida sent a major out to get a look at me—he arrived in blackcap, gave me the coldest look I'd ever seen, and took me through three days of hard physical training. One canteen, no rations, not a wink of sleep. Running and hand-to-hand drills, and at the end his uniform still looked perfect, right down to the gig line. He gave me a nod and said, "See you at Cliffside." I didn't know I'd made it until then.

Carida was hard—but not because I was a female. Sure, I got looks from barves who'd come from worlds where girls only got to play dress-up. But only at first. Within a couple of weeks I was just Drutch. Anybody who was going to give me any problems was too tired to do it—plus they'd seen I was as good as any of them. Maybe I couldn't lift as much or run as fast, but I could shoot straighter and last longer and put up with more.

Four years later I walked the edge and earned my white hat—now I wasn't Drutch anymore but TD-4388, 291st Legion Dalisor. I was the only female in my company, but the legion had two other females. TD-5144 was from Pargaux, which was a

DEBRIEFING: THE 501ST

The Empire's 501st Legion—nicknamed "Vader's Fist"—was the New Order's best stormtrooper unit, fighting with discipline, bravery, and unquestioning loyalty in numerous campaigns. Battle-hardened Rebel irregulars dismissed many stormtroopers as "plastic soldiers" who relied on armor and numbers. But the 501st was different: News that the legion was entering the battlefield reduced Rebel forces to a grim silence.

The 501st began as a brigade within the Grand Army of the Republic, seeing its first action at Kamino, and units within that brigade were assigned to Anakin Skywalker after he took command of the Kaminoan clones. Skywalker and his Padawan Ahsoka Tano generally operated with the 501st's Torrent Company, led by Captain Rex.

Supreme Chancellor Palpatine took note of the 501st's successes, approving of Skywalker's unorthodox methods and the way they were adopted by Rex and his troopers. At Palpatine's direction, the 501st changed from a conventional unit into something quite different: an amalgamation of units whose troopers were given secret training and transferred to battlefields and units as the demands of the Clone Wars dictated. Skywalker led 501st units at Christophsis, Teth, Bothawui, JanFathal, Quell, and Kothlis, not to mention in the Second Battle of Geonosis. All the while, the members of the 501st were carefully watched and tracked so the best could be selected for special assignments.

Legion units played a front-line role in the Outer Rim Sieges, fighting at Mygeeto, Felucia, Kashyyyk, and Utapau. In the Battle of Coruscant they defended the capital against General Grievous's daring raid and fought gallantly, though in vain, to prevent Palpatine's kidnapping. After the Jedi Rebellion, they responded to Darth Vader's call, taking heavy casualties in overcoming resistance at the Jedi Temple.

After the Republic's reorganization as the Empire, 501st units helped reconquer the Rim and neutralized some of the gravest threats to Imperial power, suppressing Naboo's opposition to Imperial policy and a clone uprising on Kamino. While many of its missions were classified and hidden even from the Senate, the 501st fought on worlds such as Kessel, Gon Tiek, New Plympto, Murkhana, Maun Digitalis, Honoghr, and Mustafar, often alongside Darth Vader. The legion's association with Vader led to missions tracking down the Death Star plans, storming the Rebel base on Hoth, and defending the second Death Star at Endor.

With Emperor Palpatine dead, the 501st was one of many proud Imperial traditions degraded as warlords squabbled over the Empire's leadership. Because the legion had only rarely operated as a whole, it fragmented into individual units under the control of various leaders, and soon effectively ceased to exist.

But the 501st was remembered, and Grand Admiral Thrawn reconstituted it as part of his Empire of the Hand. This was a new 501st, open to soldiers from any number of backgrounds, including nonhumans. In 130 ABY the 501st remained a name to be reckoned with, serving as Emperor Roan Fel's guard; under General Oron Jaeger, the legion remained loyal to Fel, rejecting the authority of Darth Krayt.

WAR PORTRAIT: GENERAL ROMODI

Born on the nondescript trade world of Matacorn, Hurst Romodi distinguished himself fighting Aqualish rebels in Lambda sector's Planetary Security Forces, and became one of the first non-clones to command clone troopers in the Clone Wars. Colonel Romodi was decorated for his efforts at Peldon Minor, Tulatharri Junction, and Mygeeto, and commissioned as a general in the Imperial Army.

Romodi and Admiral Terrinald Screed worked together in the Ciutric Offensive of 19 BBY, hammering Separatist remnants in the Kanz, Tragan Cluster, Ciutric, Nijune, Sprizen, and Quelii sectors. The army and navy weren't exactly known for smooth cooperation, but Romodi and Screed trusted each other; Romodi remarked that his forces always knew they had guardians above the blue sky, while Screed noted that Romodi had an instinctive sense for which operations demanded a more delicate touch than a warship's turbolasers were capable of. The two won much-celebrated victories at Vinsoth and Vardoss and returned to Imperial Center as examples of what the New Order could accomplish.

Two years later, Romodi was back in the field, leading the ground operations for the Western Reaches Operation, directed from Eriadu by Wilhuff Tarkin. Battles such as Kelrodo-Ai and Ord Vaug were recorded by HoloNet news crews, and Romodi became famous for his habit of directing offensives from the open top hatch of a floating fortress, heedless of artillery shells bursting around him. Warned that such impacts would leave him deaf even with his helmet's noise-cancellation fittings, an irritated Romodi summoned a medical droid and ordered his eardrums replaced by cybernetic implants.

(CONTINUED ON PAGE 131)

ARMORY AND SENSOR PROFILE

AT-AT AND WALKER TECHNOLOGY

The idea of mounting armored units on motorized legs can be traced back to ancient droids such as the war robots of Xim the Despot and the hulking combat mechs of the ancient Hutts. Usually standing less than three meters tall, these walking war machines were created not as armored vehicles, but as infantry support units capable of hefting heavy blaster cannons and marching into places ground vehicles could not reach.

By the Empire's time, however, large "walkers" dominated ground combat—above all. Standing 22.5 meters high, the long-striding All Terrain Armored Transport—known as the AT-AT or simply the Imperial walker—loomed over the battlefields of the Galactic Civil War like a huge armored version of ancient pachyderm cavalry. The machines' resemblance to giant animals or insects often unsettled organic foes, who felt as if they were facing malevolent beasts.

The long-legged AT-AT built on Kuat Drive Yards' success with the AT-TE, and first saw service during the Clone Wars. Hundreds were built in facilities on industrial worlds such as Kuat, Carida, and Belderone. Walkers served a dual combat role: Their chin-mounted heavy laser cannons and cheek-mounted repeating blaster cannons made them formidable ground vehicles, and their thick armor made them effective transports for speeder bikes, scout walkers, and ground troops, which deployed from a rear assault ramp while the walker kneeled, or used boom racks and drop lines to descend from the body. Imperial Star Destroyers and other large warships carried complements of walkers, ferried from orbit by drop ships and barges.

AT-ATs weren't perfect weapons—their fields of fire were limited and their giant legs demanded constant maintenance. And contrary to their reputation, they weren't invulnerable: The flexible "neck" connecting the command section and the body section was a weak point, as was the walker's belly. But few enemies found themselves able to stand and fight when they felt the ground shake beneath an AT-AT's armored feet and saw the giant, eerily organic-looking machine closing on their positions.

Besides psychological effects, walkers have some advantages over other ground vehicles. Tracked or wheeled vehicles need a low-riding chassis, impeding their line-of-sight weapons and limiting their ability to travel over obstacles, while their complex traction systems are vulnerable to close-range rockets or grenades. Repulsorcraft can rise up above obstacles to give their guns a better aim, but their drive units are easy targets for anti-repulsor missiles and mines, and they cannot pass through deflector shield perimeters. The placing of an armored chassis on tall legs solves all these problems, and also protects the crew from mines.

The primary mission of walkers is frontal assaults against enemy fortresses, the form of attack at the centerpiece of modern ground warfare. Deployed just beyond range of the enemy's weapons, an AT-AT can stride over defending trenches and armor traps, push easily through a shield perimeter, and use its superior height to attack targets far beyond the normal horizon of a ground vehicle. The same qualities also make walkers useful in a secondary role on patrol in rough terrain. As a result, heavy striders such as the AT-AT and scout walkers such as the AT-RT and the AT-ST are used in elite assault divisions as well as for mobile warfare and garrison duty in remote systems. Their repulsorlift rivals are better suited for "mid-intensity" combat, such as urban warfare and fast-moving campaigns in grassy or forested terrain.

AT-ST

AT-AT

(CONTINUED FROM PAGE 129)

At Bryndar, Romodi and Admiral Holt were ambushed by Iska pirates posing as local officials; shrapnel from a fragmentation grenade ripped through his face, arms, and chest. Despite being blinded and badly injured, Romodi refused to leave the front, directing the campaign's endgame from a bacta tank while aides described the course of ground operations to him.

Romodi became the Senator of his native Lambda sector, and his terrible scars and unblinking cybernetic eyes made him a fearsome presence in the Senate Rotunda. He became one of Palpatine's staunchest allies and a fierce advocate for military intervention, but it soon became apparent that his injuries had been worse than anyone on Bryndar had suspected. He spoke of recurrent nightmares and lamented that he had trouble focusing.

As an Imperial Senator, Romodi had access to the best medical care in the galaxy. But neither flash-therapy nor nano-surgery could help him; all available medical miracles had been used up simply saving his life. He retired after a single Senate term, was offered a position as Tarkin's adjutant,

and later served a largely decorative role as the Death Star's battle station operations chief. During those years, observers would occasionally ask why Tarkin tolerated the presence of an aide who was only fitfully lucid. Those foolish enough to do so within earshot of the Grand Moff received an icy lecture about sacrifice and loyalty.

DARK TROOPERS AND DROID STORMTROOPERS

The Dark Trooper Project dated back to an alliance between an obsessive Imperial Army officer and a noble industrialist. As relations between the Republic and the Separatists worsened, Baron Orman Tagge prepared a prototype combat droid, the L8-L9, designed to fight in conditions too hazardous for clone troopers. The L8-L9's arms ended in a combination of flamethrower/plasma weapons and spinning claws that could saw through durasteel. But Tagge's dreams of selling war droids to the Republic collapsed when his prototype unit was dispatched by Asajj Ventress in a gladiatorial arena on Rattatak.

Tagge tried again after the Clone Wars ended, enlisting the help of Rom Mohc, a Grand Army veteran who believed single combat was the only honorable form of warfare. As with the L8-L9, their Z-X3 war droid was proposed as a backup for clone soldiers, engineered to fight in dangerous radiation or vacuum. Tagge and Mohc's Droid Trooper Project produced an initial batch of seventy-odd Z-X3 units for the Empire to experiment with. The Z-X3s proved deadly and adaptable, but the Imperial military viewed the use of mechanical troops with distaste, and the project was rejected. (A few Z-X3s did serve in Imperial garrisons, but most found their way into private hands—during the Galactic Civil War, Luke Skywalker and his droid counterparts clashed with one aboard the space station known as Kligson's Moon.)

Refusing to admit defeat, Mohc kept pushing his ideas and won support from the Imperial Department of Military Research. A secret project—which Mohc gave the ominous code name Dark Trooper Phase Zero—took aging clone soldiers and replaced their limbs and organs with cybernetic parts. These cyborg stormtroopers proved effective in combat, but many rebelled at finding themselves more machine than man, and killed themselves rather than become what they had fought on the battlefields of the Clone Wars.

Mohc contended that the project had been a success, undone only by the weakness of its organic components, and shortly before the Battle of Yavin he won lavish funding for his Dark Trooper Project, which took shape aboard a KDY-designed dreadnought known as the *Arc Hammer*.

There were three stages of Dark Troopers, as well as a scattering of prototypes. Phase I Dark Troopers were metal skeletons armed with a cutting blade and shield cast from lightsaber-resistant phrik. Phase II Dark Troopers— the project's basic combat units—were clad in phrik body shells, armed with assault cannons, and equipped with repulsorlift engines, making them devastating opponents in aerial assaults. The Phase III Dark Trooper was clad in thick armor, sported a cluster of missile tubes, and could operate independently or be used as an exosuit by a single operator. It's believed that only one Phase III Dark Trooper was constructed, and it was destroyed—along with the *Arc Hammer*—by the Rebel operative Kyle Katarn. An infuriated Palpatine then canceled the project.

IN THE EMPIRE'S SERVICE

Few sounds evoked greater fear in the Empire's enemies than the howl of a TIE fighter overhead. But not all of the Empire's military strategists held starfighters in high regard. This dispute was the continuation of an argument that had raged since the Republic's rapid rearmament during the Clone Wars.

The hordes of starfighters bankrolled by the Separatist guilds were intended to overwhelm the relatively small warships of the Republic's Planetary Security Forces. The first big capital ship of the wartime Republic, the *Venator*-class Star Destroyer, carried a substantial fighter complement whose primary mission was to neutralize the threat of Separatist fighters. The standard Venator design featured a long dorsal flight deck that allowed hundreds of starfighters to launch in short order, as well as a bridge dedicated to fighter operations.

The Venator proved its worth as both a fighting ship and a carrier, but many Republic strategists thought it would have been more effective if designed for a single role. Commanders, meanwhile, knew the Venator's bow doors opened and closed slowly, leaving the ship vulnerable even with beefed-up, power-hungry deflector shields.

Subsequent Star Destroyer designs scrapped the dorsal flight deck, making do with a smaller, ventral hangar and a reduced starfighter complement. Bigger capital ships were built around more powerful reactors, allowing them to be more heavily armored and carry tougher shields and more powerful weapons—all of which made Separatist starfighters less effective.

The *Imperator*-class Star Destroyer became the *Imperial* class under the New Order, and the backbone of the Imperial Starfleet. TIE fighters were seen as a complement to Star Destroyers, serving as escorts, scouts, hit-and-fade raiders, and bombers supporting ground troops. As such, they lacked hyperdrives, deflector shields, and even life-support systems, and their lack of fuel limited them to short-range operations.

While not designed as a carrier, the Star Destroyer's sheer size allowed it to carry a full wing of TIEs. That was more than enough to handle most threats considering that no galactic power existed with the financial or military muscle to take on the Empire, and so the idea of large carriers won little support within the navy.

Some naval strategists disagreed, championing the value of more robust starfighters and carriers. Kuat Drive Yards' escort carrier, which could ferry a full wing of TIEs, was developed after the Empire's defeat at the Battle of Ton-Falk, but soon largely relegated to protecting convoys. After the Battle of Yavin, Admiral Ilon Drez persuaded the navy to authorize the construction of KDY's *Lancer*-class frigate to protect against starfighters, but it wasn't until Grand Admiral Thrawn's time that Lancers became an important part of Imperial tactics.

The Star Destroyer's role in the starfleet went largely unchallenged until the Rebel Alliance emerged as a credible threat. The Alliance's military doctrine was based around starfighters that were capable of long-range, independent operations, fast enough to counter TIEs, and powerful enough to punch a hole in the shields of big capital ships, leaving their key systems vulnerable to subsequent attack runs.

The three Dark Trooper phases (Bruno Werneck)

ARMORY AND SENSOR PROFILE

TIE FIGHTERS

The TIE fighter was built around amazingly efficient twin ion engines that emerged from experiments conducted in the 30s BBY by Raith Sienar in an effort to resurrect an ancient Sith design. Sienar's prototype Sith Infiltrator, designed for Darth Maul, boasted engine technologies Sienar would perfect with his SIE-TIE system, unveiled in 22 BBY.

Like all ion engines, Sienar's design used microparticle accelerators to excite ionized gas until it was moving at a substantial fraction of the speed of light, then blast it out of painstakingly calibrated rear vents. But the SIE-TIE was the most precisely manufactured propulsion system in galactic history: efficient, lightweight, and containing neither moving parts nor high-temperature components.

The rollout of the T.I.E. starfighter—the first model in the TIE line—coincided with the Empire's rise. The T.I.E.'s distinctive ball cockpit sat suspended between solar panels that doubled as vertical wings, a design that shared elements with Kuat Drive Yards' Eta-2 Actis Jedi interceptor and V-wing fighter. Early Imperial conclaves frequently devolved into arguments between Sienar and KDY representatives about who had stolen what from whom.

Sienar Fleet Systems won the bulk of Imperial starfighter contracts, and the basic TIE fighter (the TIE/LN model) became the mainstay of the Starfighter Corps. TIEs were incredibly maneuverable in dogfights due to their lightweight engines and the fact that they were stripped of all components deemed nonessential.

TIE FIGHTER

TIE INTERCEPTOR

Sienar experimented with many TIE variations, prototypes, and limited-production starfighters, adapting the TIE's systems and unmistakable look for everything from shuttles and landing craft to tanks and submersibles. But three prototypes were critical in the evolution of the line.

Defending the Death Star, Darth Vader had piloted a prototype code-named the TIE Advanced x1, a bat-winged TIE with experimental deflector shields, heavier armor, and a hyperdrive. Vader's TIE could take more punishment than a standard TIE, but its armor and inefficient shield generators made it only slightly faster than standard TIEs, and x1 prototypes saw limited duty.

Two subsequent designs—the TIE Advanced x2 and the Advanced x3— emerged as the best candidates for incorporating the Advanced x1 technologies into a new TIE model that would become the Empire's primary starfighter.

The Advanced x2 scrapped much of the Advanced x1's heavy armor, but kept the deflector shields and hyperdrive and added a warhead launcher. Dubbed the TIE avenger, or TIE/AD, it married the basic TIE's speed and maneuverability with the superior systems of Vader's craft. But it was also very expensive, and aroused fears among navy traditionalists that the starfleet would be reduced to carriers and swarms of snubfighters—tactics last seen pursued by the mechanized battle groups of the Separatists.

The Empire opted instead for the Advanced x3, which became the TIE interceptor, or TIE/IN. Faster than the original TIE, it traded the original's chin-mounted laser cannons for a quartet of cannons set on the tips of its bat wings. By the Battle of Endor, TIE interceptors accounted for about 20 percent of the Empire's starfighter corps.

The success of the avenger and other robust models such as the TIE defender wasn't forgotten, though. After the Emperor's death, warlords such as Grand Admiral Thrawn saw their starfighter pilots as too valuable to leave poorly protected. They increasingly opted for more durable TIE models and retrofitted TIE interceptors with shields, saving poorly armored TIEs for droid brains to fly.

WAR PORTRAIT: BARON FEL

In this excerpt from Voren Na'al's *Oral History of the New Republic*, recorded shortly before the Liberation of Coruscant, Wedge Antilles remembers Soontir Fel, then thought to be dead. In reality, Fel had joined Thrawn's Empire of the Hand:

Fel? I knew of him long before I knew him, and I met him ship-to-ship before I ever met him face-to-face. That was in a New Republic detention cell, and I never would have gotten to shake his hand if Horton Salm hadn't been able to coax a crippled Y-wing into making a quarter turn. Because I would have been dead.

Fel was born on Corellia like me, but way out in the boonies—the Astrilde Bottomlands. That's farm country—his father was a transport pilot for an agro-combine. Ag pilots' kids have rocket fuel in their veins; Fel told me he was flying skyhoppers before he was ten, and quietly took over his father's piloting duties after the old man was poisoned by fumes from a leaking fertilizer boom.

When Fel was eighteen, he stopped a group of teenagers from assaulting a family friend. To avoid a messy trial, the combine's director hushed up the incident. Fel was given a Senatorial appointment to the Imperial Naval Academy—one that would unfortunately prevent him from testifying. His family would be taken care of by the combine, without any problems related to, say, fathers allowing their underaged sons to use combine equipment. On Corellia we call that an offer you can't refuse. Fel took it.

Han Solo was a classmate of Fel's at Carida—he said he'd never seen a pilot as good, but that Fel's rigidity prevented him from being even better. But then Han's rough-and-tumble city Corellian, and Fel's country Corellian, and the two have never really understood each other. Fel graduated and was assigned to the Thirty-seventh Imperial Fighter Wing, based out of Kriselist. It was busy out there, and soon got busier: He flew sorties against the Lortan Fanatics, turning the Thirty-seventh's Sixth Squadron into one of the Empire's best over two tours of duty. I've often wondered what would have happened to him if he hadn't begun his Imperial service flying against such obvious evil. If he'd witnessed some of the things that turned other pilots into defectors, maybe we'd be having this conversation on Coruscant already.

Anyway, the Empire takes notice of any TIE pilot who lives longer than expected—make it more than a year or so and they decide you're too valuable to keep trying to kill. They gave Fel command of a Dreadnaught heavy cruiser, Pride of the Senate, and reassigned him to Baxel sector to chase pirates and smugglers. He hated it, of course; Fel would rather spend a month in a cockpit than an hour on a bridge. And Baxel was absolutely the wrong place for him—the Moff out there was snuggled up to the Hutts like a bantha-tick. Fel fought at Nar Shaddaa, where he defied Admiral Greelanx by delaying his retreat so he could recover his TIE fighters. He told me later he didn't know Greelanx was supposed to lose, or that the battle was all for show. He tried to win—and he nearly did.

Someone in the Empire didn't like that—the next thing Fel knew he was assigned to Prefsbelt as a flight instructor. There he taught a lot of ours—including Tycho and Biggs and Hobbie. Yeah, Hobbie and Fel—I have trouble believing it, too. Tycho says Fel was intimidating but fair—though he was old-line Imperial through and through, always talking about justice and order and incapable of admitting the Empire he served only believed in the latter.

When Hobbie and Biggs defected aboard the Rand Ecliptic, Fel paid the price. They transferred him to the 181st, known as the One-Eighty-Worst—a dumping ground in the Albarrio sector for those who had disgraced themselves or made the wrong enemies. That was where I first heard about him—he was the man who'd remade a One-Eighty-Worst squadron into a feared unit.

After Ord Biniir, everybody had heard of him. Ord Biniir was out in the New Territories; a Rebel cell had taken it, and Fel led the attack that took it back. Men who were there said the Imps swarmed them with an entire wing and were relentless, their tactics so perfect that they could barely get a fighter off the ground. It was a horrible defeat—except for the fact that it was the same day as the Battle of Yavin.

The Empire needed a victory to peddle to the masses, and Fel had given them one—he was made a major. I wonder what he must have thought: Some

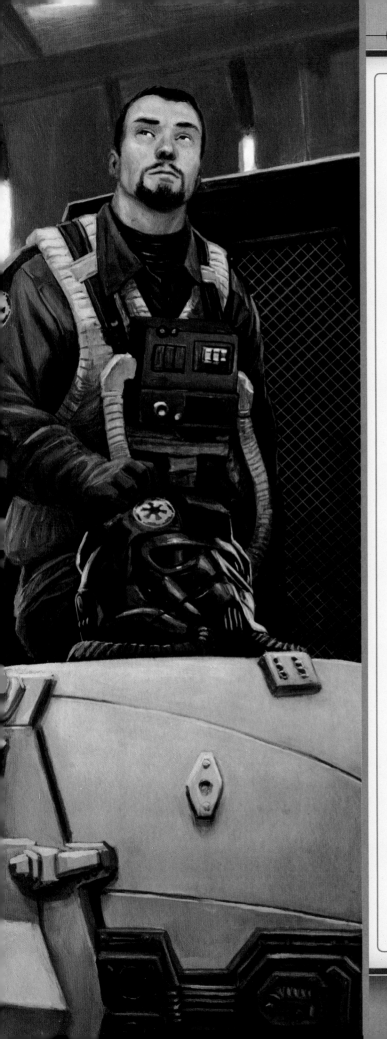

of the same men who had exiled him to the Outer Rim were now saluting him at parades on Imperial Center. That was also where he met my sister. I remembered her as Syal, though I hadn't seen her since I was a boy; the galaxy knew her as Wynssa Starflare, the holostar.

The next big furball Fel took part in was another disaster for us: Derra IV, where Commander Narra died and the Imps punched a huge hole in our supply lines. For that he was made a colonel, and given a barony to boot. But Fel told me Derra IV was where he and the Empire began to part ways. The Derra ambush had been drawn up by Grand Admiral Thrawn, but while Fel and the rest of the 181st were celebrated, Thrawn was ignored. Fel told me he went into indoctrination on Carida having barely met a nonhuman, so it was no surprise that he took all that poodoo about High Human Culture seriously. Thrawn made him reconsider—his tactics at Derra IV had been perfect, worthy of study at every flight school in the galaxy. If they were the product of an alien brain, what did that say about High Human Culture? And why would the Empire hide the architect of such an ingenious strategy?

Fel and the 181st fought at Endor, protecting the Empire's communications ships—the battlecruiser Pride of Tarlandia and the Impstars Chimaera and Avenger. We knew we were in trouble when we saw the red stripes on the interceptors' wings and were told the call signs were for Saber Squadron. Fel went through Green and Blue squadrons like a scythe, but there were too many of us, and too many contradictory orders for him. We took down the Tarlandia, and then the second Death Star, and Fel retreated to Annaj.

I saw him nine months later, of course, at Brentaal. Ysanne Isard had him defending Brentaal, but she wanted the planet to fall so her rival Sate Pestage would be weakened. She stuck Fel under the thumb of Admiral Isoto, a sad old glitbiter who hadn't walked a bridge in years. For Fel, it was Nar Shaddaa all over again: a sham battle arranged by politicians who didn't care that their schemes got men killed.

He fought anyway—because he knew Rogue Squadron was coming, and we were the point of the New Republic spear. He figured if he could destroy us, he could save the Empire—not for Pestage or Isard, but for the competent, honorable leader he was convinced was out there somewhere. And once again, he nearly won: His squadron shredded Aggressor Wing, Fel crippled Colonel Salm, and then he latched on to me after a head-to-head pass. I was juking and weaving, but I knew he was getting closer and closer to the kill shot.

I would have been space dust, except Fel forgot about Salm. Horton somehow got his wrecked Y-wing around and hit Fel's squint with his shocker. I remember looking at his TIE, sitting there dead in space, and thinking of the best pilot in the galaxy stuck in there in his easy chair, and how mad he must have been.

So we tractored him and he answered the Intel boys' questions and then he said he wanted to talk to me. That was when I first heard his story—and learned he was my brother-in-law. And that was when he offered me a deal: Help him find Syal, and he'd defect.

I agreed—how could I not add the best pilot in the galaxy to my squadron, particularly with Coruscant awaiting us? But first I stuck him in the simulator and made the rest of the Rogues fly with him over and over again. Holy sabercats was he ever insulted—he told me he'd flown grain barges when he still had baby teeth, and there was nothing a slicer-stick could teach him. I said I understood that, but he'd killed a lot of my pilots, and if they were going to take a shot at him, I wanted it to be in sim, not in space. That silenced him. Until that moment, I don't think he'd imagined that his sense of duty might strike others as blind faith, or cold-blooded murder.

So once I was convinced no one would put a torp up his tailpipe, he became Rogue Ten. And he was as good as advertised. It wasn't just his perfect sense of his fighter, the way it was an extension of his body. It was his SA—his ability to somehow keep the entire theater in his head even as he dived in and out of furballs. It was like some part of his brain had programmed the whole battle and watched it unfold even as the rest of him was busy somewhere else. If you showed him the initial situation, he just knew where everybody would be and when and what they would be doing. It was uncanny.

His defection was too grievous a blow to the Empire for Isard to let stand: His family was safely out of her reach, but he wasn't—and eventually one of her teams got him. Sorry, Voren, but the details are classified. Intel says he's dead, and if it was at Isard's hand, I guarantee he told old Iceheart exactly what he thought of her, and the Empire she'd helped turn into something he could no longer serve.

I can't say I liked him. I can't even say I really knew him. I don't know if anybody did. But I respected him. He was an honorable man with a fatal flaw—he assumed other people were honorable, too. If I had to guess, that was why he kept serving an Empire that was unworthy of him for so long.

HAN SOLO'S MILITARY SERVICE

From: Voren Na'al
To: Arhul Hextraphon
Subject: Re: General Solo's Military Career

Dear Arhul,

In preparation for my interview with General Solo, I've been poring over the Academy records NRI captured in its infiltration of the Ompersan data vault, and thought I'd share the outlines of General Solo's Academy career and service in the Imperial Navy.

It's oversimplifying matters only slightly to say the Empire couldn't figure out what to do with Cadet Solo. On the one hand, his instructors acknowledged his gifts as a pilot and his instinctive grasp of strategy; on the other, they had deep reservations about his judgment, conduct, and suitability for the rigors of military service. Honestly, I know more than a few members of High Command who might agree with that assessment.

Despite his humble origins, Solo received a direct referral from Renn Tharen, a Corellian shipping magnate, to the Imperial Naval Academy, qualifying him for entrance examinations without a sector-academy credential. Solo took the entrance exams on Coruscant, doing poorly on the cultural portions and the advanced mathematics, but acing the technical portions and receiving top-of-the-line marks in the piloting tests. Though there's an odd note there—apparently he flew through the Arch of Triumph instead of taking the parade route above it. I'd like to have seen the face of whatever flight instructor he had along for the ride.

Instead of a three-year posting to Prefsbelt, Solo was assigned to a two-year program on Carida. There his record is about what you'd expect from his entrance

Imperial Captain Han Solo loses a career and gains a Wookiee (Chris Scalf)

exams: His piloting marks were practically off the charts, his academic record was mixed, and he racked up a fair number of demerits and conduct reports.

Flight Instructor Badure clearly liked him: He filed a glowing report about one of his first training missions, noting that he'd managed to land a malfunctioning U-33 orbital loadlifter by executing a number of difficult flight maneuvers, saving the lives of numerous cadets and Commandant Wyrmyr. And Student Adviser Cal-Meg notes his innate intelligence and that he worked hard to bring up his grades.

But Solo also ran with a crowd the Academy dons didn't approve of. Besides the demerits you'd expect a young Corellian to accrue, in his second year a tribunal investigated his role in a prank that blew up Carida's Mascot Moon. Dean Wyrmr himself initiated expulsion proceedings, but the testimony of a cadet named Tedris Bjalin (later an Alliance defector) cleared Solo of any involvement. Solo graduated with honors, largely because of his phenomenal flight marks, but rather than being commissioned immediately, he was recommended for Officer Candidate School at Prefsbelt, with a suggestion that he be dual-tracked for fleet operations and starfighters.

At Prefsbelt Solo's course clearly bent toward flight school—NRI's documents include a scathing report about his deportment from Captain Meis, who reported that he was argumentative and insubordinate on capital ship training cruises. But even Meis acknowledged his abilities as a starfighter pilot, and Flight Instructor Habadon called him "perhaps the best instinctive pilot I've ever taught, possessing an innate understanding of both piloting and battlefield tactics that's vanishingly rare in the service." Habadon noted that his fellow midshipmen were in awe of Solo's ability at Fornax Toss and Whip the Dart, a rare official acknowledgment of the unofficial, intoxicant-fueled dormitory games played by budding pilots.

At Prefsbelt it seems that the Empire finally decided what to do with Han—he was commissioned as a junior lieutenant and transferred to the highly regarded Austringer Flight School, whose focus was prepping ace pilots to be wing commanders. At last he graduated, apparently without a single demerit, and was finally deemed ready for active duty. He was promoted to lieutenant, and posted to the Imperial Star Destroyer Flanchard, patrolling the Suolriep sector.

It's amazing to think of it, Arhul, but that one choice undid the Empire's considerable investment in Han Solo. The captain of the Flanchard was Pter Nyklas, and he was about as bad as it got—a believer in High Human Culture who saw the bridge of an Impstar as a license to kill. Worse for the Empire, the Flanchard frequently handled slaving details, a duty most Imperial captains loathed but Nyklas seemed to love.

According to Solo's own testimony at his court-martial, seven months after his posting his TIE squadron engaged a slave ship near Komnor. Solo's TIEs disabled the slave ship and found that the slavers aboard had been killed by a single Wookiee, whom Solo discovered wounded in the cockpit. While the squadron was engaged, the other Wookiees fled in another ship. Nyklas was outraged; according to Solo's testimony, he ordered him to kill and skin the survivor, an order that Solo refused and then formally protested to the fleet admiral. I know I don't need to tell you the name of the Wookiee.

Solo was grounded and formally reprimanded, and I wonder why the Empire didn't transfer him to another sector group, or at least to another fleet. Instead they left him with Nyklas, who tried to break him: On a duty rotation on Imperial Center, he forced Solo to supervise Chewbacca and a gang of Wookiee slaves on a construction project, and whipped Chewbacca repeatedly. When the Wookiee finally lost his temper, Nyklas drew his blaster—but Solo stunned him before he could shoot. The two fled, but were trapped on the planet. According to Solo's testimony, he was contacted by Captain Habadon, who persuaded him to turn himself in and testify about the extenuating circumstances.

It still surprises me that Solo wasn't executed—either Habadon pulled some pretty big strings, the Empire had substantial reservations about Nyklas, or both. As it was, it was still pretty bad for Solo. He was dishonorably discharged at the conclusion of a formal hearing, with all the naval ceremonies: They stripped his dress uniform of rank insignia and broke his saber over a knee. He wasn't shot, but he was left literally in rags, and with a black mark like that no reputable shipper or flight service would employ him.

The Empire thought they'd ruined Han Solo—and in a sense they had, for he was never the same again. The galaxy should be profoundly grateful for that.

Your friend,
Voren

FIGHTER PILOT SLANG

3-9 line: A line across a fighter's wings, based on an imaginary clock in which 12 is ahead of a fighter and 6 is behind. The goal of dogfighting is to keep bandits in front of one's 3-9 line.

ACM: Aerial combat maneuvering, better known as dogfighting.

Bandit: A hostile fighter or starship.

Big L: Lightspeed.

Bingo: Having enough fuel for a safe return.

Bluelined: Disabled by an ion cannon blast.

Blue milk run: An easy hop.

Bogey: An unidentified fighter or starship.

Bright: A TIE/Advanced fighter.

Bumping: Engaging in ACM.

Centurion: A pilot with one hundred landings on a carrier or fighter base.

Check your 6: "Be careful, watch out behind you."

Clear skies: "Be well," a traditional spacer's farewell.

Clutch: A squadron of TIE fighters.

Cold nose: Operating with sensors down.

Dirt flier: An atmospheric fighter pilot.

Dirtside: On a planet's surface.

Dragship: An Interdictor cruiser.

Drift factor: A measure of a pilot's flakiness or inability to follow orders.

Dupe: A TIE bomber.

Easy chair: The pilot's seat in a fighter.

Edge: An A-wing fighter.

Eyeball: A basic TIE fighter.

Fangs out: Eager for a dogfight.

Flat-hatting: Showing off or engaging in dangerous maneuvers.

Flying the same vector: Thinking along the same lines.

Full DSW: Having enough power for drive, shields, and weapons.

Furball: A hectic dogfight.

Gain angles: Maneuver for a better shot in a dogfight.

Get lines: Disengage and jump to hyperspace.

Go black: Head from a planet's atmosphere into space.

Go blue: Head from space into a planet's atmosphere.

Goes away: What an enemy fighter does when you hit it.

Goo: A planet's atmosphere.

Gripe: A mechanical problem. An up gripe is a problem that allows continuing operations; a down gripe does not.

Hangar queen: A fighter that's often unable to fly because it needs repairs, and thus is raided for parts.

Hawk circle: A formation of fighters waiting to land.

Hop: A mission.

HUD: Heads-up display.

Impstar: An Imperial Star Destroyer.

Judy: Comm call indicating you are intercepting a bandit.

Klick: Kilometer.

KM: "Kriffing magic," a pilot's all-purpose explanation for how technology works.

Latch: Get into position to destroy an enemy fighter.

Loud handle: The lever that triggers a fighter's ejection seat.

LTS: "Likely to survive," indicating approval of a pilot's skills.

No décor: "Speak freely," without worrying about rank.

Painted: Scanned by sensors.

Peeper: A TIE fighter used for reconnaissance.

Pointer: An X-wing fighter.

Roof: A carrier's flight deck.

SA: Situational awareness.

SD Vic: A *Victory*-class Star Destroyer.

Senth Herf: An admiring assessment of another pilot's abilities.

Shock: To hit a bandit with a blast from an ion cannon.

Shocker: An ion cannon.

The Show: ACM; dogfighting.

Skull: A Z-95 Headhunter.

Spinner: A B-wing fighter, also known as a cross.

Splash: Shoot down.

Squint: A TIE interceptor.

Suicide sled: A starfighter, particularly one with weak shields.

Vapebait: A poorly skilled fighter pilot.

Wishbone: A Y-wing fighter.

Zero angle: The position behind the stern of a bandit.

WAR PORTRAIT: SHEA HUBLIN

One of the young Empire's war heroes, Shea Hublin grew up in the cityscape of Talcene, racing swoop bikes as a boy and making a good living as a teenage courier for the planet's notoriously competitive industrial guilds. He joined the Republic Navy at sixteen and had finished five months of flight school when he got the news he dreaded most: The Separatists had surrendered.

But Hublin's chance at glory hadn't passed him by. He

was assigned to the Imperial Star Destroyer *Destrier* and rapidly made a name for himself as an ace V-wing pilot in the Seventy-seventh Wing, fighting pirates, smugglers, and Separatist holdouts on the Great Gran Run.

In 17 BBY the *Destrier* was attached to the Western Reaches Superiority Force commanded by Admirals Bannidge Holt and Terrinald Screed and directed by Moff Tarkin. At Kelrodo-Ai, Hublin's pilots flew into the teeth of the Citadel of Axes, taking terrible losses but ultimately bringing down Kelrodo-Ai's planetary shields in preparation for a successful ground assault. Those exploits made him the talk of the HoloNet, and the young pilot's aristocratic features and widow's peak soon adorned recruitment posters across the galaxy. Hublin won further glory at Halm, Little Petrovi, Ichtor, Fanha, and Tosste, and trainee pilots across the Empire begin celebrating their kills with the waggle of wings they'd seen on holo-reels.

After the Western Reaches Operation ended, Hublin was named air marshal of the Greater Seswenna and given a marquisate on Eriadu, where he married Eris Harro, heiress of one of the Quintad Houses. But he continued to fly for Tarkin, leading anti-pirate operations across Oversector Outer.

Hublin's squadron was ambushed by Rebels at Vale in 13 BBY, and he lost a leg and half of his right arm. When his wife demanded he retire from the Starfighter Corps, he switched to a line command, leading a squadron from the bridge of the Imperial Star Destroyer *Kabalian Cross* and earning the sobriquet "the Rebel Destroyer." But he fell out of favor for urging the naval hierarchy to replace the TIE fighter with a shielded, hyperspace-capable fighter.

Hublin didn't care; he had made a home on Eriadu, and was content to serve the interests of the Seswenna sector. As the years passed, he continued to wage war on the sector's Rebels and criminals, occasionally putting on his many medals for a gathering of Western Reaches veterans or some other military assembly. When Grand Moff Ardus Kaine transferred his Oversector Outer flag from Eriadu to Bastion, he asked Hublin to accompany him, but the legendary pilot indignantly declined; Eriadu was his post.

Instead, he cast his lot with Superior General Delvardus and his Eriadu Authority, climbing back into a TIE interceptor to defend his homeworld. His skills seemed undiminished at first, as he led a squadron against Nagai raiders at Chelleya in 4 ABY, driving them away from Eriadu. He turned his back on Delvardus when the Superior General announced plans to invade the Core Worlds, but reluctantly came to the warlord's aid a year later, when Delvardus was mauled by Sien Sovv at Sullust. At Sanrafsix, his squadron was shredded by flights of X-wings, until only Hublin remained. As laserfire arced toward his TIE from multiple angles, he switched his comm to an open channel. "Eriadu endures," he said quietly, and died.

THE ORIGINS OF REBELLION

> "What matters isn't the size of the nek in the fight but the size of the fight in the nek."
> —Cyborrean proverb

A LIGHT IN DARK TIMES

Padmé Amidala called Supreme Chancellor Palpatine's Declaration of the New Order the death of liberty, accompanied by thunderous applause. But on many war-weary worlds, the applause was sincere. The Separatists were defeated, their relentless metal armies finally still and silent. Having steered a corrupt, disintegrating government through the horrors of war, Emperor Palpatine now promised to restore order to a civilization that had feared it might never return.

Palpatine's military moved against slavers, pirates, despots, and Separatist holdouts, forcing lawless sectors to once again abide by the rule of Coruscant. And citizens who had felt disconnected from out-of-touch Senators found a new voice through groups such as the Commission for the Preservation of the New Order, or COMPNOR.

But ominous whisperings reached the ears of those who cared to listen. They told of swift and arbitrary Imperial justice and of military force used indiscriminately against civilians. Dissenters and protestors were imprisoned after show trials, met with accidents, or simply vanished. Large portions of the HoloNet were reserved for the military, impeding the free flow of information. Slavery hadn't been abolished so much as it had been nationalized, with entire species deemed expendable. No organized opposition to the Empire existed, and yet Palpatine's war machine continued to grow, its capabilities swelled by clones, conscripts, and countless credits spent.

The Jedi Order had been reduced to a pitiful scattering of hermits and fugitives. But a few brave political leaders who believed in the ideals of the Republic united with a secret goal: overthrow Palpatine and restore the Republic.

THE FORMATION OF THE REBELLION

The origins of the Alliance to Restore the Republic date back to before the Empire, with clandestine meetings on Coruscant among Senators worried about how much power Supreme Chancellor Palpatine had claimed. Many of these Senators signed the Petition of 2,000, calling upon Palpatine to surrender his wartime emergency powers, open peace talks with the Separatists, and instruct his governors not to interfere with the Senate.

Around half of the petition's signees removed their signatures after the Declaration of the New Order. Of those who didn't, hundreds were questioned and dozens were arrested—with some never seen again. But three Core World Senators escaped prosecution (though not suspicion), and became the principal architects of the Rebellion. Alderaan's Bail Organa had witnessed the assault on the Jedi Temple, and learned the terrible secret of Palpatine's mysterious new servant Darth Vader. While speaking eloquently against Imperial policies in the Senate, Organa carefully couched his criticisms as those of a Loyalist. Chandrila's Mon Mothma walked the same line, though she was less restrained in her oratory. Corellia's Garm Bel Iblis was the Emperor's most outspoken critic, but protected by his system's importance and history of cranky independence.

Organa, Mothma, and Bel Iblis met many times at Organa's Cantham House residence on Coruscant, where they quietly arranged funding and protection for some of the groups staging raids against Imperial targets. After Imperial operatives killed his wife and children, Bel Iblis went into hiding, founding a resistance cell backed by Corellian credits. Mothma fled Coruscant before she could be arrested. That left Organa alone and isolated in the Senate, his every move watched by Imperial agents.

The three continued to meet secretly in bolt-holes across the galaxy and in 2 BBY they signed the Corellian Treaty, which established the Alliance's goals and structure. The Rebellion barely survived its own birth, as the three leaders needed help to escape an Imperial raid. Organa resigned from the Senate and returned to Alderaan, replaced by his daughter, Leia; Bel Iblis resumed command of his Corellian militia; and Mothma became the new Alliance's Chief of State, releasing a public Declaration of Rebellion.

Mothma's Declaration had been intended to give hope to resistance cells and inspire the Empire's enemies to secretly work together, but it backfired, as a few foolhardy systems immediately declared their allegiance to the Alliance. Branded the Secession Worlds, they were quickly crushed by the Imperial Starfleet. Other planetary leaders were more circumspect, quietly making contact with Rebel agents and pledging credits, ships, weapons, and soldiers. Mothma's eloquence and diplomacy united the galaxy's resistance groups, the discipline brought by Imperial defectors made them into a dangerous fighting force, and word of Imperial atrocities spread the fire of Rebellion to more and more worlds. At first Imperial officials dismissed Rebel raids and ambushes as the work of pirates and bandits. But soon the truth became apparent: The Empire was at war again.

ALLIANCE COMMAND

The top ranks of the Alliance were divided into a civil government and a military hierarchy, led by a Chief of State and a Commander in Chief, respectively. Yet the two positions were occupied by the same person: Chandrila's Mon Mothma.

The Alliance was effectively a dictatorship, as Imperial propagandists delighted in pointing out. The Chief of State had virtually unlimited power, and could only be deposed by a two-thirds vote of the Advisory Council. But it was a dictatorship with a built-in expiration date: The Corellian Treaty mandated that the position be abolished when the Emperor was deposed, died, or resigned, after which a Constitutional Convention would decide how to govern the restored Republic.

Mothma—the only Chief of State to serve—rejected the idea of establishing a Republic-in-exile that would claim to be the galaxy's rightful government. She noted that though few remembered it, the Confederacy of Independent Systems had had a representative government—one rendered all but superfluous by the Separatist hierarchy that prosecuted the war. A toothless shadow Republic would only remind the galaxy's citizens of the Confederacy—and a declaration of a separate government would acknowledge the Empire as a legitimate state, instead of treating it as an illegal and immoral perversion of the Republic.

Mothma was also Commander in Chief of the Alliance military, with the seven Supreme Allied Commanders of the High Command reporting to her. The Alliance's command structure was an odd amalgam reflecting its reliance on centralized military power (balanced uneasily between the capabilities of capital ships and starfighters), local military forces, and secretive resistance cells.

Sector Command oversaw the Alliance's thousands of Sector Forces while leaving them generally free to pursue their own missions, so long as they limited themselves to attacking Imperial facilities and abided by the rules of civilized warfare. The name Sector Forces reflected politics more than reality, though: Some sectors were home to dozens of different Rebel groups, while others heard barely a whisper of dissent against the Emperor's rule.

In principle, Sector Forces belonged to the local governments supporting the Alliance, known as Allied Commands, but the High Command claimed supreme military authority over them, and used its resources to create extra Sector Forces where no friendly government existed.

Sector Command sometimes asked individual Sector Forces to lend ships or starfighters to the main Alliance fleet for critical operations—requests that were a source of constant friction within the resource-strapped Rebel movement. The Alliance fleet took its orders from Fleet Command, formally led after 4 ABY by Admiral Ackbar. Starfighter wings, meanwhile, answered to Starfighter Command, which was subordinate to Fleet Command in rank though rarely in spirit. When attached to a subdivision of the fleet, starfighter pilots reported directly to ranking captains or admirals for the duration of an operation, as did special-forces personnel.

A meticulous, orderly thinker, Ackbar was exasperated by the ragtag navy he inherited and the difficulty of coordinating

action among its scattered assets. He reorganized the fleet and retrained many of its commanders—a new focus on discipline that attracted new pledges of support from star systems and an influx of Imperial defectors who no longer scorned the Rebellion as a disorganized rabble.

While hailed as the father of the Alliance fleet, Ackbar chafed at what he couldn't change. He loathed the Alliance's reliance on privateers and smugglers, whom he regarded as criminals, and disliked the practice of detaching subdivisions of the fleet on an ad hoc basis and handing command of them to an Allied government or Sector Force.

Throughout the Alliance's history the Empire sought to exploit dissension in its ranks, working to infiltrate Rebel cells and bringing overwhelming force to bear against sectors it learned had been stripped of Rebel units. But wise leadership and dedication to the restoration of the Republic kept the Alliance intact despite provocations, military defeats, and its own internal feuds.

The organization of the Alliance fleet was as follows:

- **Element:** A single starship, commanded by a captain.

- **Section:** A small number of starships, typically light capital ships working in conjunction and commanded by the senior captain in the section. The Alliance, adopting ancient seagoing tradition, referred to a section made up of capital ships and close support vessels as a flotilla.

- **Squadron:** A squadron—the most typical Alliance fleet detachment—consisted of three or four sections working in concert, such as a line of capital ships supported by a section of escort ships and a flotilla acting as a picket line. A senior captain, commodore, or line admiral would command a squadron.

- **Battle group:** Consisting of two to four squadrons, battle groups were mostly theoretical, as the Alliance could rarely spare so large a single detachment. In practice, a few Allied Commands maintained battle groups, which were commanded by line admirals.

- **Fleet:** Three to six battle groups would form a fleet, led by a fleet admiral.

WAR PORTRAIT: JUNO ECLIPSE

Message to Jesmin Ackbar from her uncle, Admiral Ackbar, in 6 ABY, as recorded in *Ackbar: Wartime Correspondence*, volume 8:

Jesmin,

Your question about allowing former Imperials into the New Republic ranks is heartfelt, and certainly one we wrestled with in the early days of the Alliance. If anything, I believe it struck us more deeply: The Emperor's spies were everywhere, and ultimately all we had was instinct in determining whether a new recruit's passion was genuine or the product of intelligence training. And how could we in good conscience treat those who had the blood of millions on their hands as colleagues? Should a late change of heart serve as a pardon for terrible crimes?

But Jesmin, the ranks of the Alliance were filled with men and women who could fairly have been called mass murderers in the service of the Empire. Crix Madine, for one, founded and trained the Emperor's Storm Commandos and was part of the operation that released the Candorian Plague on Dentaal—a shocking act of genocide. Yet where would the Alliance have been without his service?

And there are other stories, ones that are less well known. When this question comes up—by which I don't mean to dismiss it, Jesmin—I think back to Juno Eclipse, and the beginning of my own service to the Alliance.

In her youth, Juno was the very model of what the New Order hoped all its children would be. She was the youngest cadet ever accepted to Corulag, and became the commander of Darth Vader's Black Eight Squadron. Three years before the Battle of Yavin, Black Eight assaulted the planet Callos. Under Juno's command, Black Eight neutralized its military objectives—yet Vader told her to continue the bombardment. When she protested, Vader told her that disabling a planetary reactor would fulfill the mission without further harm to the Callosians. Juno carried out those orders, and the damaged reactor spewed poison into the atmosphere. Within a year Callos was a dead world.

Did that make Juno Eclipse a war criminal? I think we'd agree it did—at least then. Was she still a war criminal after her horror at what she'd done led Vader

to remove her from command? After she risked her life to rescue the Rebellion's leaders from Imperial custody and certain execution? After she defected to the Rebellion and became the captain of the frigate *Salvation*? After she confessed her past to her crew? After her first mission for the Alliance? Her third? Her tenth? When is absolution obtained, Jesmin?

Those were uneasy days—Bail Organa, Garm Bel Iblis, and Mon Mothma were united in their determination to overthrow Emperor Palpatine, but divided about how to pursue that goal. Mothma feared that the Alliance was too weak to risk its forces pursuing even symbolic victories, Bel Iblis feared that holding back would lead to frustrated Rebels following their own paths, and Organa was caught in the middle.

I am immensely proud to be able to say I helped bridge those divisions—at least as much as I could. But it was Juno who allowed me to serve that purpose, just as it was Juno who helped the Alliance find its way, through her bravery, determination, and a bit of subterfuge.

I had escaped from Grand Moff Tarkin's service and pledged myself to the Alliance cause, but Dac remained in Imperial hands. Together Juno, Bail, and I brought Dac into the Alliance fold—that's a story you may have heard before. But you may not have grasped how important a role Juno played. She fought alongside me at Heurkea and engineered the plan that sent the 181st TIE Fighter Squadron off on a bantha hunt, publicly embarrassed Tarkin, and gave our people and the Quarren the courage to rise up against the Empire. The campaign at Dac would become a template for our efforts—a small, strategic attack with enormous symbolic value.

And remember, Jesmin, that I wasn't alone in the Heurkea operation: The leader of the Quarren operation was Seggor Tels, who had disarmed our planetary shields and allowed the Imperials to occupy our planet. Seggor acted out of hatred—the hatred that has so scarred our world and our two species over the millennia. But he discovered a higher purpose, and sought forgiveness for his crimes. Some part of me wanted to see him dead or brought low, Jesmin—how could I not feel that way, after all he had done? But if I could trust Juno Eclipse, the destroyer of Callos, how could I deny Seggor Tels a chance to redeem himself?

And if I could allow Seggor that opportunity, how could I deny it to Crix Madine—or some former Imperial commander about whom I knew nothing? Be wary,

Jesmin, of deciding who is beyond repentance, lest you exclude someone who may help us lead the rest of the galaxy out of captivity.

/ message ends

SEPARATISTS, IMPERIAL DEFECTORS, AND OTHER REBELS

The various groups fighting the early Empire had little in common except their opposition to the New Order. Some considered themselves Republic Loyalists and sought to restore what had been, others were determined to resist any outside rule, and a few were simply opportunists looking to profit from disorder.

And then there were the former Separatists.

Mon Mothma, Bail Organa, and Garm Bel Iblis differed sharply about what role, if any, former Separatists should play in the Rebellion. Bel Iblis argued that Separatists who hadn't committed war crimes should be accepted, noting that the Alliance had found a place for groups that sought their own regions' independence, a goal that would have been called Separatism just a few years before. Organa disagreed, contending that all Alliance members must accept that the Rebels' first and foremost goal was the Republic's restoration. Mothma acknowledged Bel Iblis's point—after all, she'd joined Padmé Amidala's calls for peace talks with the Separatist leadership—but worried that accepting Separatists would play into the hands of Imperial propagandists, drying up sympathy and support for the Alliance.

A few Separatist holdouts did eventually join the Alliance after publicly disavowing their pasts: The CIS general Horn Ambigene became the leader of the Bryx Freedom Fighters, bringing his followers under the Alliance banner as the Bryx Sector Forces. (This did Bryx sector little good: It was brutally subjugated by the Empire.) Blox Hatha, a Neimoidian captain in the Trade Defense Force, was refused formal membership in the Alliance, but became a renowned privateer bearing a Rebel letter of marque.

Elsewhere, Rebel cells and Separatist true believers settled on a tacit policy of quiet mutual support or at least noninterference. But sometimes active hostilities broke out: Atravis sector was scarred by years of clashes among the Empire, pro-Republic resistance groups, and Separatist holdouts.

The Imperial ranks proved a far more fruitful source of

A Rebel Blockade Runner faces long odds in combat against an Imperial Star Destroyer (Dave Seeley)

Alliance recruits. While many Imperial officers were staunch believers in the ruthless, anti-alien tenets of the New Order, others began their Imperial service thinking of the Empire as a continuation of the Republic, one that would do a better job at keeping the galaxy peaceful and orderly. Those who held such sentiments—often found among the "generationals" in the navy—found their faith in the Empire tested by its rabid expansion, brutal subjugation of peaceful dissent, and arbitrary enforcement of the law. Many who held such doubts assisted the Rebel cause through a form of benign neglect: Supply caches were left lightly guarded, information security about anti-Rebel operations was lax, and reports of Rebel fleet movements were acted upon with a curious lack of haste.

But for others, such tacit support wasn't enough: They defected from Imperial service and took up arms against the government they had served.

The Alliance's top ranks were thick with former Imperial officers, including a number who had helped shape the forces and strategies of the Republic, Empire, or both. Jan Dodonna had been a hero of the Clone Wars and the Empire's early campaigns, and his gift for logistics stood the Alliance in good stead. Dodonna's friend Adar Tallon was similarly well known, an expert in starfighter tactics who'd faked his own death to escape Imperial service. Crix Madine had formed the Empire's feared Storm Commandos, but grew increasingly agitated about the brutal orders his men were given and defected, later to lead the Alliance's Special Forces.

And of course many rank-and-file Imperial crew members, pilots, and soldiers broke with the Empire or the Planetary Security Forces under its command. Many Rebel troopers had originally served with the Imperial Army, and Rebel pilots such as Biggs Darklighter, Hobbie Klivian, and Tycho Celchu began their careers flying TIE fighters in the Empire's service.

DEBRIEFING: REBEL TROOPERS

The soldiers fighting for the Alliance came from any number of worlds, species, and backgrounds, and weren't a conventional army like the Imperial Army, with its strict hierarchy, standard uniforms, and rank insignia. Imperial officials made much of the Rebels' ragtag appearance, using it to portray them as common criminals, not enemy soldiers.

Most Rebel troopers served in individual Sector Forces, which differed in everything from how they organized soldiers into units to what equipment might be available. A few Sector Forces had considerable military capabilities and organization, outfitting tens of thousands of troops and backing them up with ground vehicles and artillery. Many more had just a few thousand irregulars and whatever equipment could be stolen, scrounged, or captured.

The most capable Alliance soldiers were its special forces, veterans attached to Alliance High Command and given rigorous training. Permanent SpecForce detachments also defended the main Alliance fleet and High Command's critical bases. While SpecForces were organized in units mimicking the Republic Army, they generally operated as additions to regular forces, fighting side by side with troopers and guerrillas.

While the Alliance had no standard uniform for its troopers, it did manage to outfit many of them in helmets and uniforms reminiscent of those worn by Planetary Security Force ground troops in the final decades of the Republic. Imperial propaganda noted that these uniforms were the same as those worn by Alderaan's defense troops, and that was true—but such uniforms had been worn by better-funded Planetary Security Forces across the Core, Colonies, and Inner Rim. When the Empire took over the Planetary Security Forces, a glut of such uniforms and equipment became available, with DH-17 blaster pistols and A280 blaster rifles flooding the black market. The irony that the Empire had effectively outfitted many Rebel irregulars was something Imperial propaganda rarely saw fit to mention.

THE ALLIANCE STRIKES

14

> "Develop technology without wisdom or prudence and
> your servant shall become your executioner."
> —Walex Blissex, chief shipwright, Rendili Star Drive

THE AGE OF SUPERWEAPONS

From Xim the Despot to the mightiest Republic chancellor, every ruler of a sizable portion of the galaxy has faced the same problem: Space is immeasurably vast, too vast for any military force to control. A cunning enemy will always have the advantage of being able to disappear into the trackless void, and be able to keep a much more powerful opponent off balance by popping up where least expected to conduct raids or assault a target left briefly unguarded.

Over the millennia this problem has bred a predictable cycle of strategic thrust and parry. An enemy pursuing the "stateless" strategy of holding little or no territory and harassing a larger entity can prosper for a time, but inevitably battlefield successes lead to the stateless organization possessing territory and needing to defend it, upon which it is no longer stateless and itself becomes vulnerable to the stateless strategy. In theory, galactic civilizations should be able to shrug off stateless enemies as an annoyance whose greatest weapon is the fear they engender, but most fall prey to their own people's demands for safety, causing them to either embark upon a ruinous spree of military spending or retrench to defend fortress worlds. Either extreme gives stateless enemies even more freedom to maneuver.

The Death Star—the battle station imagined by Raith Sienar and brought to life by a hive of Geonosians and laboratories of Imperial scientists—was an attempt to break this ancient cycle and impose a new strategic reality upon the galaxy. The threat of planetary annihilation, Grand Moff Tarkin proposed, would undo the stateless strategy: No

world would dare to harbor insurgents if the cost of doing so was destruction.

The two Death Stars were the ultimate expression of this philosophy, and icons of the Empire's willingness to spend stunning amounts of credits in search of a military superiority that none would dare challenge. But the Death Stars were not the only superweapons of their time: the *Eye of Palpatine*, the *Tarkin*, the Darksaber, the Sun Crusher, the *Eclipse* warships, and the Galaxy Gun also haunted the galaxy during the age of superweapons.

THE DEATH STARS, THE *TARKIN*, AND OTHER SUPERLASERS

The Death Star began as one of Raith Sienar's many ideas: The Wizard of Coruscant imagined a one-hundred-kilometer sphere with a smaller sphere at each pole, and a huge turbolaser at its core. The sphere would require advances in hypermatter technology—an implosion core big enough to power something the size of a small moon. Sienar thought the design impractical, but Wilhuff Tarkin was impressed enough to champion the idea before Supreme Chancellor Palpatine.

Palpatine turned Sienar's idea over to Bevel Lemelisk, ordering him to pursue the needed advances in hypermatter science with Poggle the Lesser's Geonosian hives. Lemelisk did so with the help of the Twi'lek scientist Tol Sivron, only to have the plans fall into enemy hands when the Geonosians joined the Separatists. But like most in the galaxy, Lemelisk

had no idea that the Clone Wars were part of Darth Sidious's plot: As Republic warships strafed Geonosis, Poggle gave the plans to Count Dooku, who took them to Sidious. Sidious was pleased to see his world-destroying weapon taking shape, and silently amused to find plans set in motion by Palpatine returned to him by the Separatists' leader. By the end of the Clone Wars, the Death Star was taking shape in the outer reaches of the Geonosis system, with its construction overseen by Wilhuff Tarkin.

The Death Star posed a number of technological challenges, but none compared to the superlaser, which emerged from the long-running Hammertong Project. The massive prime weapon sat at the center of a circular cannon well, originally planned for the battle station's equator but later moved to the dorsal hemisphere. Eight amplification crystals positioned around the circumference of the well generated tributary beams, which were combined over the superlaser's central focus lens, creating a single energy beam capable of destroying a planet.

The tributary beams had to be perfectly calibrated and aligned, or the central beam would misfocus and dissipate in a flurry of backscatter that was more dangerous to the superlaser housing than it was to any target. The battle station's hypermatter reactor powered the superlaser, and early designs required so much energy that the station's other systems—including shields and life support—would be knocked offline. The firing process also generated magnetic fields and gravitational flux, which had to be dissipated for fear of tearing the station apart or misaligning the amplification crystals. (All these challenges were solved, but the first Death Star was still only capable of firing its superlaser at full power once every twenty-four hours.)

A proof of concept took shape at Tarkin's secret weapons laboratory inside the Maw Cluster. The Death Star itself moved multiple times during its construction, relocated from Geonosis to Seswenna to Patriim to Horuz. At Horuz, the battle station at last began to become a reality, as slave laborers mined metals that were fed into automated smelters and extruders, creating the components that slowly filled in the armillary sphere hanging in the blackness of space.

When complete, the Death Star was a weapon on a heretofore-unimaginable scale: 160 kilometers in diameter, with a crew of more than a million. Besides its superlaser, it boasted some fifteen thousand turbolasers, seven hundred tractor beam projectors, seven thousand TIE fighters, four strike cruisers, twenty-thousand-odd military and transport vessels, and more than eleven thousand combat vehicles. Ion engines propelled it at sublight velocities; for hyperspace jumps, it relied on a network of 123 hyperdrive field generators.

Much like the celestial bodies it was meant to imitate, the majority of the Death Star's habitable zones were close to the surface, within the battle station's "crust" and above kilometers of stacked decks, machinery, engines, and ventilation shafts, with the reactor core at the heart of the sphere. The battle station was divided into twenty-four zones, each subdivided into city sprawls with hangar bays, detention blocks, medical centers, armories, command centers, barracks, and even cantinas. Each zone had its own bridge, which reported to the Death Star's overbridge, located just above the superlaser well.

When the *Millennium Falcon* reached the Rebel base on Yavin 4, the Alliance finally had a full set of plans for the battle station, kicking off a frenzied search for a weakness in its defenses. The most obvious tactic for attacking the Death Star was to destroy or damage the amplification crystals producing the superlaser's tributary beams. But that would take capital ships that the Rebels didn't have, and the Death Star's defenses had been designed to repel exactly that kind of large-scale assault. Whatever plan the Rebels came up with would have to be carried out by Massassi base's squadrons of X-wings and Y-wings.

An alternative to attacking the superlaser was to disrupt or destroy the main reactor. With no time to organize an infiltration team, Massassi base's technicians pored over the schematics in a mounting panic—and finally found something. Right below the battle station's main exhaust port was a tiny auxiliary exhaust port used for venting waste heat. The port, which led directly to the main reactor, was protected by a ray shield but not by a particle shield, which would have prevented heat from escaping. A direct hit on the auxiliary exhaust port with proton torpedoes should start a chain reaction that would overload the reactor and destroy the station.

Massassi base's Rebel commanders decided to send Blue and Green squadrons on attack runs against the superlaser. They reasoned that sufficient damage might be done to render it inoperable—and if not, the strategy would draw attention away from Red and Gold squadrons' attack runs on the exhaust port. It was a desperate plan, based on the hope that a pilot could run the gauntlet of the Death Star's formidable cannon and TIE fighter defenses and somehow hit a two-meter target at attack speed. Somehow, a Tatooine farm boy who was a last-minute addition to the pilot roster made that seemingly impossible shot.

But before Luke Skywalker fired his torpedoes, Emperor

Palpatine had ordered the creation of new superlaser weapons. Hyperspace tugs and threadships were extending an obscure hyperspace route called the Silvestri Trace from its origin near Sullust all the way to Endor, on the galactic frontier. There, a second, more powerful Death Star was in the initial stages of construction.

The second Death Star was far larger than its predecessor—nine hundred kilometers in diameter—to allow for a graduated series of three massive reactors instead of the first battle station's single reactor. With two reactors reserved for its superlaser, the second Death Star could fire every three minutes, and Lemelisk overhauled the superlaser's network of targeting computers so it could fire accurately at capital ships. Lemelisk eliminated the small gaps in the shields that had allowed starfighters to penetrate the first Death Star's defenses, and protected the battle station's surface with additional banks of turbolasers that would be able to track fighters. Finally, the auxiliary exhaust port was eliminated in favor of millions of millimeter-wide channels to dissipate waste heat. Once its superstructure was in place, this second Death Star promised to be immune to external assaults—but the Rebel fleet destroyed it at Endor before it could be completed.

But the Emperor had imagined other uses for the superlaser. Above Kuat and Byss, the keels of two massive dreadnoughts hung in space. These were the first of the massive *Eclipse* class of warships, designed to mount a superlaser as an axial weapon. To test the ship-mounted superlaser and divert attention from the second Death Star, a prototype dreadnought—dubbed the *Tarkin* in honor of the martyred Grand Moff—took shape above Patriim. The *Tarkin* was never designed to be a proper warship—it was a test bed, with modules and systems assembled around the superlaser dish. Princess Leia Organa's Rebel strike team destroyed the *Tarkin* soon after the Battle of Hoth; its superlaser was only fired once, when Grand Admiral Martio Batch used the prototype to shatter Aeten II, freeing lodes of stygium crystals he needed for his TIE Phantom project.

The *Eclipse*-class dreadnoughts' superlasers were less powerful, though still capable of doing substantial damage to a planet. From bow to stern, *Eclipse* and *Eclipse II* measured 17.5 kilometers of jet-black durasteel and quadranium. But the ships were delayed for years as the Empire fragmented after Endor. *Eclipse* was destroyed at Da Soocha by Skywalker and Princess Leia in 10 ABY, while *Eclipse II* was destroyed at Byss in 11 ABY when R2-D2 sent it on a collision course with the Galaxy Gun. Skywalker, Organa, Lando Calrissian, and Wedge Antilles could all claim to have destroyed an Imperial superweapon, but the distinction of having destroyed two at once belonged to a humble astromech.

WAR PORTRAIT: GENERAL DODONNA

Jan Dodonna served the Republic, Empire, Rebel Alliance, and New Republic, and all four hailed him as a war hero.

Born on Commenor, Dodonna began his long military career with the Judicial Forces. But he first rose to prominence in the Clone Wars, commanding the Republic's Victory Fleet alongside Terrinald Screed. It was Captain Dodonna who finally cornered the Separatist admiral Dua Ningo at Anaxes, fighting furiously until Screed's forces could spring their ambush. Decorated at Anaxes, Dodonna would later see action at Rendili, Cato Neimoidia, and Mygeeto.

Dodonna then served the Empire, winning honors for his pursuit of the Separatist holdout Toonbuck Toora, destroyed by Dodonna and Admiral Adar Tallon at Trasemene. But Dodonna saw what the Empire was becoming, and decided he could no longer serve in good conscience. Despite that decision, he regarded the Rebellion as a foolish provocation, one that would only cause chaos and misery. Weary and unhappy, he retired from Imperial service to Commenor's moon, Brelor, where Mon Mothma's agents repeatedly tried to woo him to defect. He turned them all away, even after

(CONTINUED ON PAGE 157)

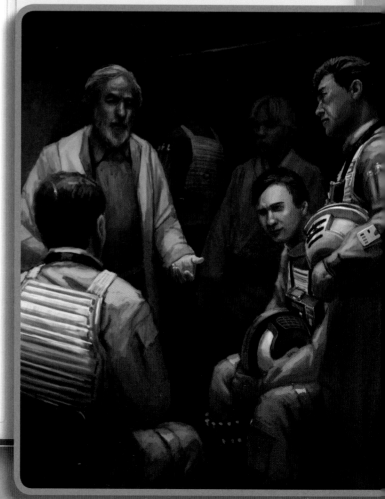

ARMORY AND SENSOR PROFILE

CORELLIAN CORVETTE

The Corellian Engineering Corporation's corvettes were mainstays of the space lanes a century before the Galactic Civil War began, and remained common sights a century after it ended. That's a testament to the adaptability and reliability of this 150-meter warship, a favorite of everyone from navy officers and corporate buyers to smugglers and pirates. Corellian corvettes saw service as troop carriers, escort vessels, blockade runners, cargo transports, and passenger liners, offering fast sublight engines, a speedy hyperdrive, and powerful turbolasers.

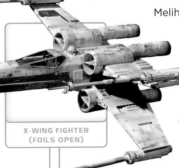

CORELLIAN CORVETTE

Corellian corvettes were easily recognized by their clustered engine block and CEC-trademark "hammerhead" bridge sections. They were easily modified, with a modular design that allowed them to be reconfigured for different purposes. Two of the most common models were the CR70 and the later CR90, but a corvette could be turned into almost anything its owner desired, thanks to mountings that allowed it to sport additional weaponry, expand its cargo capacity, or even carry starfighters.

The Judicials, Planetary Security Forces, and Republic Navy all made extensive use of the CR90 corvette, which saw service during the Clone Wars. The Empire used corvettes for anti-starfighter missions, as escort vessels, or as diplomatic boats. The Alliance, however, put them on the front lines, using their speed to run blockades and their weaponry to team up against larger Imperial warships. Princess Leia's *Tantive IV* was a Corellian corvette, and saw action at Ralltiir, Kattada, and Toprawa before Darth Vader's *Devastator* captured it over Tatooine. After the Alliance became the New Republic, Corellian corvettes remained a crucial part of the New Republic Defense Fleet until phased out in favor of more modern craft.

X-WING FIGHTER

The T-65B X-wing space superiority starfighter was the primary weapon of the Alliance. Measuring 12.5 meters from bow to stern, its fuselage consisted of a long nose packed with sensor equipment, a single-seat cockpit, and a hyperdrive block with integrated astromech socket. Four ion engines flanked the rear of the hull, their wide intakes allowing for extra atmospheric thrust, and long wings reached out on either side, scissoring open to become strike foils that acted as powerful heat radiators and provided optimum deployment for four wingtip KX laser cannons.

X-WING FIGHTER (FOILS LOCKED)

Two proton torpedo launchers beneath the fuselage gave the X-wing enough punch to challenge capital ships, while its hyperspace capabilities made it useful for hit-and-fade raids and asymmetrical warfare. The X-wing lacked the TIE fighter's extreme acceleration and maneuverability, but was more forgiving to fly and far more durable thanks to its sturdy spaceframe and generous deflector shielding powered by the hyperdrive core. The most underrated and important part of the fighter, however, was the sensor array in the nose—a suite of Fabritech scanners originally designed for larger ships, augmented by specialist packs from traditional Incom subcontractors Melihat and Tana Ire. These systems, which had no equal among Imperial fighters, gave the X-wing the ability to operate independently, without a capital ship to provide telemetry and flight control. They proved fundamental to the fighter's success.

X-WING FIGHTER (FOILS OPEN)

The X-wing was still a top-secret project within the Incom skunkworks when Incom's scientists received word that the Empire planned to nationalize the company. Key members of the design team defected, escaping with the plans and prototypes and wiping Incom's computer networks clean before they made their getaway. While the Empire struggled to reconstruct Incom's corporate records, Rebel raids emptied its facilities of virtually its entire stock of T-65s.

The Alliance now possessed the best starfighter in the galaxy, but it needed more of them. It shared the X-wing plans with the Verpine, Mon Calamari, and other sympathetic governments, which built X-wings in clandestine dry docks and secret hangars across the galaxy. But the T-65's systems were so complex that the Alliance had to endure agonizing waits for more fighters.

Already, though, the X-wing had earned its reputation. Even a few flights of fighters could make their presence felt, with repeated raids that embarrassed TIE units and Imperial commanders and turned high-profile New Order projects into rubble. Unsupported X-wings destroyed Star Destroyers, shipyards, and local fleets—not to mention the Death Star. But the Rebellion chose its battles carefully—70 percent of X-wing sorties were reconnaissance missions, and wing commanders were taught to attack in strength "only when the results will be spectacularly successful."

The T-65 was unquestionably a superlative fighter. In the first nine months of the Fei Hu campaign, the Lightspeed Panthers wing—famed for their fang-jawed nose art—destroyed at least 286 TIEs, losing only four T-65s. The Empire responded with the *Lancer* frigate and the TIE Interceptor, and later campaigns were less one-sided—but even if the margins of victory grew narrower, the Rebels retained their dominance in the air.

X-wing variants were produced throughout the Galactic Civil War and the history of the New Republic, continuing a line of development that reached back decades to the original Z-95 Mark I.

Y-WING FIGHTER

While X-wings were the main starfighters *built* by the Rebellion, Koensayr BTL Y-wings were far easier to *acquire*— thousands were brought by pilots defecting from Planetary Security Forces, liberated in raids on Imperial surplus depots and scrapyards, and bought from pirate gangs and corrupt governors.

The standard Y-wing was a sixteen-meter starfighter with a two-seat cockpit module, a surprisingly slender spar fuselage housing its hyperdrive and power systems, and two bulky R200 sublight engines extended on pylons at either

side. The earliest variant to see active service was the BTL-B fighter-bomber, which proved itself with the destruction of the Separatist dreadnaught *Malevolence* at Kaliida in 22 BBY. Pilots soon found that removing the plating from the BTL-B's elegant fuselage made the spaceframe lighter and kept its components cooler, noticeably boosting performance.

Even with these improvements, Y-wings were too sluggish to be effective space-superiority dogfighters—but they hadn't been built for that. When properly used by commanders such as General Grisserno and his protégé Horton Salm, Y-wings didn't *have* to dogfight. Instead, they accelerated toward bigger targets, relying on their gunners and wingmates to take care of the TIEs on their tail.

The armament for both the Clone Wars BTL-B and the Rebel BTL-S3 included a missile launcher, two IX4 blasters, and a twin ion cannon. The munitions bay beneath the cockpit carried a standard complement of eight torpedoes, but could be adapted for a wide range of ordnance, enabling Y-wings to attack ground targets and capital ships. The turreted ion cannon, originally designed to fight off vulture droids, could disable and capture freighters, making Y-wings excellent commerce raiders. Powerful shields completed the design, allowing Y-wings to absorb repeated hits from TIEs or even glancing blows from enemy cruisers.

The BTL-A4 variant had no gunner and reduced deflector strength to boost engine speed, a combination that proved lacking and gave the Y-wing a bad reputation among pilots. More successful was the S3B, which retained the gunner and shields, but swapped the ion cannon for twin blasters.

Y-WING FIGHTER

(CONTINUED FROM PAGE 154)

they warned him that the Empire regarded his loyalties as uncertain and had targeted him for assassination. Dodonna survived the assassination attempt, fleeing in his nightshirt, and was spirited off Brelor by an Alliance freighter commanded by General Roons Sewell.

Made a Rebel general, Dodonna took over much of the Rebellion's logistics and supply operations, as well as its starfighter corps, which he strengthened by working with Walex Blissex to modify the R-22 Spearhead into the speedy A-wing starfighter. He also commanded the Alliance's ground headquarters, moving the base across the galaxy in order to keep its location safe from the Empire. When the Imperials at last discovered Dodonna's cell at Yavin 4, he planned the successful assault on the Death Star, overseeing the battle from the Massassi war room.

Dodonna was thought killed in the frantic evacuation of Yavin 4, but he had survived. Captured by Imperial forces, he was taken to the secret Lusankya prison, where he remained for seven years until found by Rogue Squadron's Corran Horn. Freed, he became part of the New Republic's famed Gray Cadre until his retirement to New Alderaan. He died shortly before the Yuuzhan Vong invasion, and while his counsel was sorely missed, the New Republic leaders for whom he had been a mentor were relieved that the old warrior had passed away in a galaxy at peace.

MANUFACTURER: INCOM

The Torranix Inertial Compensator Corporation originally designed high-performance repulsorlift platforms. Its greatest project was Bespin's Cloud City, constructed around 400 BBY.

In 147 BBY it shifted its focus to atmospheric warplanes, joining forces with starfighter manufacturer Sublight Products. The Incom/Subpro collaboration produced many designs, but the best known was the Z-95 Headhunter, once the most popular fighter in known space.

When Palpatine took power, Incom was forced to dissolve its partnership with alien-owned Subpro, and ordered to shift most production from Z-95s to army landing barges. The design team defiantly began a skids-up redesign of the Z-95, producing a sleek long-range fighter with powerful combat capabilities and scissoring "strike foil" wings. It was officially called the T-65, but always known simply as the X-wing.

A year before the Battle of Yavin, the Empire nationalized Incom in an attempt to halt production of the T-65, but the Imperial officials arrived to find an empty factory. The prototypes, the design team, and the assembly line itself all ended up in Rebel hands, and the X-wing would become the icon of the Alliance's struggle for freedom.

The Rebel designers registered a new corporate identity under the name of FreiTek, but resumed control of Incom after Endor, with the FreiTek marque becoming the weapons-and-avionics division. One former subsidiary not reabsorbed was Longspur and Alloi, which had inherited Incom's old repulsor business. Sold off by the Empire and renamed Bespin Motors, it eventually became a part of the Tendrando Arms syndicate.

DUTY ROSTER: RED SQUADRON

Red Squadron's initial mission was the attack on the first Death Star. The unit began as an ad hoc starfighter squadron cobbled together from other Rebel cells. The core members of Red Squadron were holdovers from the Alliance's former Dantooine base, with their ranks swelled by arrivals from the Tierfon Yellow Aces and the Griffon Flight Wing.

Red Leader: *Garven "Dave" Dreis, Virujansi.* The former leader of Dantooine Squadron, Dreis had served the Rebels over many campaigns, flying everything from X-wings to Y-wings to R-22 Spearheads. While General Dodonna thought Gold Squadron's Y-wings might be able to batter their way through the Death Star's defenses and hit its vulnerable exhaust port, he pinned his hopes on Dreis—first flight's leader—to make a successful attack run. If anyone could keep his cool under heavy fire in the tight confines of the battle station's trenches, it was Dreis. ***Killed in action.***

Red Two: *Wedge Antilles, Corellia.* An orphan who saw his parents killed in a pirate attack, Antilles became a smuggler in Booster Terrik's organization, often running guns for the Alliance. The Rebels' bravery and dedication made an impression on the young Corellian, who answered their call for pilots, serving in the Tierfon Yellow Aces before his transfer to Yavin. Dodonna and Dreis admired Antilles's skill behind the stick and ability to improvise, but thought he needed further seasoning.

Red Three: *Biggs Darklighter, Tatooine.* An Imperial deserter who'd trained at Carida and Prefsbelt and served as a TIE pilot, Darklighter stood out as resourceful

and imaginative whether flying an X-wing or meeting underworld contacts on the Alliance's behalf. He arrived at Yavin alongside Derek Klivian, his fellow escapee from the *Rand Ecliptic*. Klivian invented a mock unit—the Ecliptic Evaders—for the two. ***Killed in action.***

Red Four: *John D. Branon, Dalandae*. A young pilot from the Tierfon Yellow Aces, Branon replaced Cesi "Doc" Eirriss after she was killed at Commenor. Porkins attested to Branon's bravery, while worrying that by speaking up for his friend, he was sending him to his death. ***Killed in action.***

Red Five: *Luke Skywalker, Tatooine*. A late replacement for the sidelined Derek "Hobbie" Klivian, Skywalker arrived aboard the *Millennium Falcon* having come into possession of the Death Star plans carried by R2-D2 and rescued Princess Leia from the battle station. Skywalker's heroism earned him a spot leading Red Squadron's second flight. Knowing that Darklighter would worry about his childhood friend, Dodonna put them together for the mission.

Red Six: *Jek "Tono" Porkins, Bestine*. A heavyset man drafted from the Tierfon Yellow Aces, Porkins honed his skills as a skyhopper pilot and free trader, but turned to the Rebel cause after the Empire took over his homeworld. He was supposed to remain at Tierfon when the call went out for pilots to protect the Yavin base, but replaced his friend Wes Janson. Porkins quickly became friends with Klivian, Darklighter, and Eirriss. ***Killed in action.***

Red Seven: *Elyhek Rue, Brentaal*. A veteran of Griffon Flight Wing, Rue took part in numerous raids at Ralltiir, distinguishing himself with his acrobatic ease at the controls of an X-wing and his cool in a firefight. He was given charge of fourth flight in the hope of keeping the talented but wayward Red Nine focused. ***Killed in action.***

Red Eight: *Bren Quersey, Lantilles*. An Imperial Academy washout, Quersey burned to take the lives of those who had failed to see his worth. After his arrival with Dantooine Squadron, General Dodonna paired him with Antilles on several missions in the hope that the Corellian's dedication to the Rebel cause might calm Quersey. He replaced the veteran Jal Te Gniev for the Death Star mission. ***Killed in action.***

Red Nine: *Nozzo Naytaan, Regellia*. A dazzlingly skilled pilot from the Minos Cluster, Naytaan deserted Imperial service in horror after his TIE squadron was ordered to bombard civilian targets on Pulassas Minor. Naytaan led the Tierfon Yellow Aces' relief effort at Clak'dor, becoming an ace in just two missions. Dodonna and Dreis considered him Red Squadron's most promising pilot, but feared his recklessness would cut his career tragically short. ***Killed in action.***

Red Ten: *Theron Nett, Ord Mantell*. A former smuggler who considered himself lucky to have survived his wild years, Nett found a purpose in the Rebel Alliance and a mentor in Dreis, serving as the older pilot's wingman on numerous Dantooine Squadron missions. Nett grew close to Naytaan after the formation of Red Squadron, and sought to curb the younger man's excesses. ***Killed in action.***

Red Eleven: *Wenton Chan, Corulag*. Leader of Red Squadron's third flight, Chan grew up amid wealth and privilege on Corulag, but rebelled against his family and their Imperial connections, fleeing for a life as a smuggler, gunrunner, and finally Rebel pilot. He came to Red Squadron from Griffon Flight Wing. ***Killed in action.***

Red Twelve: *Puck Naeco, Denon*. Red Squadron's pilots admired Naeco's accuracy as a gunner while tolerating his penchant for practical jokes. A transfer from the star cruiser *Independence,* Naeco served as a mentor for young pilots such as Keyan Farlander, Milar Travis, and Fin Danglot. ***Killed in action.***

Following the Battle of Yavin, Red Squadron continued to see service against the Empire and gave rise to the famous Rogue Squadron.

Garven Dreis poses with fellow pilots before the Battle of Yavin (Tommy Lee Edwards)

WAR PORTRAIT: GARVEN DREIS

Helmet tucked under one arm, Red Leader strode across the Massassi base hangar, now thrumming with activity. Yavin 4's collection of battered X-wings and Y-wings had sprouted fuel hoses and diagnostic monitors as orange-suited pilots, technicians, and droids all raced to get the fighters ready for takeoff. Red Leader's eyes flicked across the men and women preparing the birds for a hellish encounter with the battle station inexorably approaching the jungle moon. He saw anxiety and fear, but neither panic nor hopelessness. The Rebels had a job to do and they were doing it, despite knowing that job would likely be followed, in harrowingly short order, by their deaths.

But two young pilots beneath the wing of a T-65 weren't grim at all. They were downright giddy, talking excitedly over each other with dazed grins on their faces. The taller one was Biggs Darklighter, Red Three, and the other was the new kid, Luke Skywalker.

That name sent Red Leader's mind back two decades, to the borecrawler caves of Virujansi. He'd been just Garven Dreis then—a kid barely graduated from a T-16 to a Z-95 Headhunter, pressed into service with the Rarefied Air Cavalry to hunt the Seppie droids that had infiltrated the caverns. Instruments had been useless in there—it was stick-and-kick flying, blasting any tinnie that stuck its head up and trying not to become a smoking spot on a rock wall. Fortunately, he'd been flying those caverns his entire life, and knew every twist and turn as well as the rolling hills of his family farm.

"Dave" Dreis might have been a kid then, but he was also the hottest pilot Virujansi had ever seen—with one exception. That was Anakin Skywalker, the Hero With No Fear, who'd arrived with a Republic task force to kick the Seppies off the planet. Dreis had flown lead on Skywalker's first trip through the caverns, wondering how long the Jedi would be able to stay with him. Skywalker had sat a meter behind Dreis's left wing for two minutes, then snap-rolled his Delta-7 and taken lead. It had been Garven who'd struggled to keep up. Later, back at base, Skywalker had registered Dreis's astonishment and just grinned.

And now, here was another Skywalker. A farm boy from Tatooine, same as Darklighter. Interesting.

Red Leader had seen too much since Virujansi. He'd seen his village burning, the fields he'd tended reduced to ash by the Empire. He'd seen transports cracked open by TIE fighters on the slightest suspicion, their passengers spilling out with mouths gaping uselessly in space. He'd seen men and women who could no longer stand aside make the same decision he had, and take to the skies against the Empire's pilots. They'd died by the dozens, by the hundreds. He'd recruited many of them to do so, sent them to their deaths, sacrificed all they had been and all they would be in the hope of ever so slightly slowing the Imperial war machine. And now these boys would be next. In an hour, in all likelihood, they'd be particles of frozen meat orbiting the gas giant overhead.

It didn't seem like anything to laugh about.

"Are you Luke Skywalker?" he demanded. "Have you been checked out on the Incom T-65?"

Skywalker looked frightened, but Darklighter stepped in before he could respond: "Sir," he said grandly, "Luke is the best bush pilot in the Outer Rim Territories."

Dreis knew what his old friend Davish Krail would have done—he'd have fixed these two with a murderous look and then left tooth marks all over them, letting them know what they'd be facing up there, what the consequences of the slightest slip-up would be, and demanding to know why he shouldn't get two stick-jockeys who'd be double-checking preflight instead of giggling like a couple of addled cantina girls. But Pops was busy with his own Y-wing, and Dreis had never been one for chewing up his own pilots. What they'd meet up there would do that soon enough.

Besides, there was something to be said for being the best bush pilot around. Particularly with that name.

Skywalker. Red Five.

Maybe it was a good omen. They could sure use one.

"You'll do all right," he told the boy, forcing a smile onto his face, one that might even convince Luke he thought it was true.

WHEN THE EMPIRE STRUCK BACK

"The cruelty of war minimizes its terrible duration. If you would reform war, you must answer for extending that duration."
—Gar Stazi, admiral, Galactic Alliance

THE REBEL MILITARY

By one estimate, at the height of the Galactic Civil War the spacegoing forces of the Rebellion amounted to just 7 percent of the Imperial fleet's strength, while the total number of Alliance troops was just 3.5 percent of the New Order's military forces.

Those numbers didn't sound overwhelming, but they were the equivalent of Imperial occupation forces for fifteen sectors—and devoted almost entirely to offensive operations, not territorial control. Given that the Rebellion was in large part a clandestine insurgency, its strength was more impressive than a direct comparison with the Empire's suggested. This was made possible by a key decision at the Corellian System Meetings in 2 BBY—the Alliance was to be a genuine *alliance,* a coalition among disparate groups opposed to Palpatine's tyranny.

Each local component of the Rebellion was designated as a Sector Force, but in practice they had little in common. Some, such as the Airam Clans or the Karthakk resistance, were able to support respectable fleets and armies from their own resources. Others amounted to a few teams of saboteurs and agitators with some crates of blasters and detonators.

The Alliance's initial war plan, Operation Domino, called for the stronger Sector Forces to defeat local Imperial Army garrisons in showpiece battles, then dig in behind their planetary shields—proving that planets could free themselves, and inspiring revolution across the galaxy. But most of these uprisings led to crushing defeats. There was no revolution; dozens of Alliance armies were destroyed, and surviving units fled.

Operation Domino taught Mon Mothma a valuable lesson. A hundred Sector Forces had mustered infantry brigades, but this was only *part* of an army—some lacked bases, others lacked air support or spare parts, and most lacked training. A centralized corps answering to the High Command was necessary, if only to provide them with the training and equipment they lacked.

Moreover, the Rebellion's sacrifices provoked a surge of sympathy in the most unexpected place of all—the ranks of the Imperial Army. Top officers like General Kryll and Commander Harles defected mid-campaign and took command of battered Rebel brigades, reorganizing them into what became the Alliance Special Forces.

Optimized for commando warfare, and mustering barely one hundred thousand beings, the SpecForces became a flexible backbone for the entire Rebellion. Barracks regiments acted as specialist support echelons for other elements of the military, while the actual fighting was done by temporary task forces, with the size and mix of troops chosen for each individual mission. More often than not, both regiments and task forces were used to buttress Sector Forces' weaknesses.

As ground tactics shifted, Starfighter Command came to the fore. This happened largely by accident—the Alliance needed an overall military commander who was well respected and could broker the three-way tensions among Corellia, Alderaan, and Chandrila. It found it in Commenor's Jan Dodonna, who espoused the unfashionable view that starfighters should be a separate arm of the military.

Dodonna believed hyperspace-capable starfighters could

undermine the Empire's control of space, and demonstrate this to the galaxy by winning high-profile victories. Relying on hidden bases and converted cargo haulers for support, they could appear without warning and fight without the support of capital ships.

To prove his point, Dodonna's Y-wings defeated Star Destroyer fleets at Denab and Tarawa, and staged a series of successful raids against Imperial convoys and bases. Finding targets for starfighter raids became the top priority of Alliance Intelligence, while the Support and Supply commands focused on giving Dodonna the men and matériel he needed.

As the Rebellion grew, starfighters became its primary combat force—but there were soon too many squadrons to coordinate them all from one command. While Starfighter Command still oversaw pilot training, fighter maintenance, and squadron deployment, it only retained tactical control over a few "rogue" units on special assignment. The majority of fighters were attached to various Sector Forces—or to the increasingly powerful Fleet Command.

In the Rebellion's early years, the brunt of space combat had been borne by Sector Forces units—particularly the Corellians. Fleet Command was created to oversee a miscellany of cruisers that had escaped their home sectors—most notably the flagship *Independence,* which had escaped the occupation of Mon Calamari. Most of these old vessels were only suitable as depot ships and mobile headquarters, and the success of their own starfighter tactics led many Rebel commanders to distrust cruiser warfare. But Mothma insisted on building up a battle line, led by the ex-CIS battleships *Rebel One* and *Fortressa*.

A series of events in 0 ABY altered the character of the struggle—the withdrawal of the Corellian leadership, the loss of General Dodonna during the evacuation of Yavin 4, and the destruction of key parts of the Rebel fleet at Deepspace Besh.

The seeds for the disaster at Deepspace Besh were planted at Jabiim, where the Empire captured Jorin Sol, a mathematician who specialized in navicomputer encryption codes. Rebel agents led by Luke Skywalker rescued Sol from Kalist VI, but had no idea he had been reprogrammed as an Imperial agent. Cleared to return to duty, Sol gave the Empire the Rebel fleet's current coordinates—code-named Deepspace Besh—as well as the escape algorithms that determined where the fleet would jump next. After a task force commanded by Darth Vader arrived, Sol managed to fight off his programming long enough to beg Alliance personnel to order the decimated remnants of the fleet to scatter instead of jumping into another trap.

Deepspace Besh might have been a mortal blow, but the Rebellion was saved by the Mon Calamari, who had ejected the Empire from their world in one of Operation Domino's few victories.

After throwing off the Imperial yoke, the Mon Calamari had mined and disrupted existing routes into their sector while scouting new secret routes, ensuring that their territory couldn't be reclaimed without a brutal struggle. The Empire was hesitant to engage in such a campaign, fearful that anything other than a speedy victory would embolden other rebellious systems. (The Calamarian Council wisely exploited those fears by officially declaring itself neutral.) Despite this face-saving declaration, the Mon Calamari had become an essential source of ships and supplies for the Rebellion; after the disaster at Deepspace Besh, they donated their entire naval strength to the Alliance and became the backbone of its rebuilt fleet, led by Admiral Ackbar.

Ackbar had served aboard the *Independence* before Yavin, working closely with Mothma—and he shared the Chandrilan's unease about the increasing reliance on raids by SpecForces and StarCom. Under his leadership, the fleet grew into a disciplined collection of ships and commanders. Now Ackbar and Mothma devised a new fleet-first strategy for the Rebellion—issued in the name of the Chief of State as an executive order, but in fact drafted by the admiral himself.

Despite the failure of Operation Domino, traditionalists in the Alliance still advocated reclaiming and holding territory, beginning with a move from Mon Calamari Space into the Tion and proceeding from there down the Perlemian to claim restive systems such as Roche, Contruum, and Kashyyyk. Mothma's opposition to this plan was steadfast: It was a recipe for disaster, one that would end with another incarnation of the Outer Rim Sieges.

The traditionalists hailed Ackbar's reorganization of the fleet into a single armada powerful enough to challenge any Imperial battle squadron. But its role wasn't to fight campaigns. Rather, it would be a symbol of the Rebellion. By holding back from combat and building up its strength, the fleet became an ever-greater psychological threat, undermining the New Order's power by simply continuing to exist. The actual Alliance fighting force consisted of small raiding flotillas rotated out of the fleet, with never more than 25 percent detached at a time.

After Ackbar's reorganization of the fleet, the main subdivision for both fleet maneuvers and raids became the battle line—a group of two or more cruisers with a subordinate close support line of escorts and a picket line of starfighters.

Even in the early days, the main fleet battle line always had at least eight heavy cruisers, but in practice a typical roving line had only two cruisers, a frigate and a corvette.

Under Ackbar, the rest of the Alliance military was increasingly subordinated to the fleet—Starfighter Command's independence was diminished, while command of SpecForces was given to the Imperial defector Crix Madine, who preferred destroying targets to worrying about interservice politics.

But not all elements of the Rebellion fell into line so easily. The powerful Corellian and Bothan Sector Forces continued to launch high-profile raids, and the reputation of another Imperial defector, Admiral Adar Tallon, made it impossible politically to subordinate him to Ackbar. Meanwhile, the minister of supply, General Muvunc, created a powerful fleet of privateers, including several former Imperial frigates and light cruisers, with which he disrupted Imperial commerce.

DEATH SQUADRON AND THE NAVY RESURGENT

When the Death Star was destroyed at Yavin, more than a few Imperial naval officers allowed themselves a smile of satisfaction. Yes, the Alliance had struck the Empire a grievous blow. But those ragtag pilots in their snubfighters had also eliminated a searing threat to the navy's preeminence.

Men such as Grand Moff Tarkin and Admiral Motti had despised the navy's generationals for their belief in such ancient values as stability and order: Rather than establishing peace, they had sought to rule through fear. Now Tarkin and Motti were dead, atomized in the explosion of the technological terror they'd constructed, and the navy would succeed where they and it had failed. The Death Star project had diverted untold credits and talent from the Imperial Starfleet, which had backed the creation of a new class of Star Dreadnoughts that would be a new pinnacle of capital ship power. The project had been plagued by delays, but now took on newfound importance to the Empire.

After the Death Star's destruction, the Imperial Starfleet and the Rebels played a dangerous game, marked by symbolism and brinksmanship. The Empire expected the Rebels to flee Yavin 4, but that didn't happen: Some heavy equipment and critical supplies were removed, but General Jan Dodonna realized that most of the Massassi base's personnel and equipment could be hastily evacuated. He convinced Mon Mothma that keeping the base in place would be a powerful statement of defiance and a valuable recruiting tool.

To keep the Imperial Starfleet off balance, the Alliance launched large-scale raids on such targets as Reytha. That presented the navy with a dilemma. If they concentrated their forces on chasing the Rebels off Yavin, Mothma's forces might launch a devastating raid somewhere else, making the Empire look impotent. On the other hand, if the Empire brought insufficient forces to bear, Mothma might intervene in force, winning a second Battle of Yavin and inflicting a fresh humiliation on the navy. The sheer size of the Empire made it vulnerable; even scattered Rebel victories undermined the belief that it was all-powerful. And now, with the Senate dissolved and the Death Star destroyed, such doubts were dangerous to the New Order.

The new Star Dreadnoughts could change that calculus, but the first of the line—the *Executor*—was still in the final stages of fitting out at Fondor, supervised by Darth Vader, who had returned from the Outer Rim. Vader was determined to lead the assault on the Massassi base in his new flagship: Having destroyed one symbol of Imperial might at Yavin, the Alliance would be driven from the system by another.

But the *Executor* wasn't ready. Until she was, Yavin was blockaded by a task force assembled from capital ships earmarked for Vader's task force, supplied by the Tagge family, and requisitioned from Nox Vellam, the luckless Grand Moff of the Bright Jewel Oversector that contained Yavin. Riven by infighting, the Yavin blockade was largely ineffective, a problem Vader had little interest in putting right, lest he be cheated of his revenge.

When the *Executor* finally joined the fight, fear of Vader silenced the squabbling commanders. Vader dealt brutally with the ambitions of Baron Orman Tagge, coerced the support of his more pliable younger brother Ulric, and awaited the fleeing Rebels on the trade route known as the Tertiary Feswe. But Admiral Amise Griff—a Vellam loyalist—rushed to engage the Alliance ships, only to come out of hyperspace and crash into the *Executor*'s shields. The Massassi leadership escaped.

Thwarted, Vader disbanded the blockade and took command of his own task force, Death Squadron, whose mission was to hunt down Luke Skywalker and the rest of the Rebel leadership. The squadron formally consisted of the *Executor* and five Star Destroyers—the *Avenger, Conquest, Devastator, Stalker,* and *Tyrant*—but Vader had the authority to attach other warships if he deemed it necessary.

Death Squadron soon became the terror of the Outer Rim. It assembled at Centares, then traveled along the Triellus

Trade Route, joined by warships contributed by regional governors as it went. In every sector, Death Squadron left ruin behind it: Smugglers' hideouts were erased by orbital bombardments, pirates' bolt-holes torn apart by TIE squadrons, and shadowports destroyed by Imperial ground assaults. Those fleeing ahead of the campaign were snapped up by Interdictor cruisers and interrogated.

The plan, masterminded by Grand Admiral Thrawn, was to disrupt the Alliance's supply network by displacing or capturing the smugglers and shady free traders whose shipments wound up in Rebel hands. Tracking and interrogating smugglers would uncover Rebel cells and bases—including, it was hoped, the Rebel fleet.

Imperial slicers and strategists pored over transcripts of interrogations and the hints and rumors turned up by Death Squadron's operations, with Thrawn's uncanny ability to discern patterns proving vital in sorting through the evidence. An Imperial blitz in the Ulkantha asteroids tipped Death Squadron off to a Sakiyan smuggling ring operating out of the notorious shadowport of Syvris, near Hutt Space. Death Squadron all but obliterated Syvris, capturing key members of the Sakiyan ring, whose operations extended from Corellia to Terminus. While Death Squadron continued its deadly cruise along the Triellus,

Thrawn uncovered a Corellian operation running war matériel up the Hydian Way, and ordered the interception of a key Rebel convoy at Derra in the Expansion Region.

Between Vader's firepower and Thrawn's deductive skills, High Command sensed a noose was closing: Rebel forces in numerous Outer Rim sectors fled their bases, resistance cells dispersed for fear of being uncovered by Imperial agents, and Mothma and Ackbar moved the fleet repeatedly.

Vader finally discovered High Command's hideout through luck. The Derra convoy's supplies had been ticketed for Hoth's Echo Base, located on a little-traversed bypass of the Corellian Trade Spine. The Derra ambush didn't uncover Echo Base's location, but it gave Death Squadron enough of a lead to order patrol craft and probe droids to blanket the Outer Rim sectors of the Western Reaches. One of those thousands of probe droids landed on Hoth, from which it transmitted images of a shield generator and other fortifications to the *Executor* at Qeimet. Admiral Ozzel dismissed the report, weary of operations against smugglers' nests, but Vader's intuition told him the probe had found Skywalker's hideaway.

The Alliance began a hasty evacuation of Hoth, but Death Squadron arrived before it was complete, its already

(CONTINUED ON PAGE 168)

ARMORY AND SENSOR PROFILE

THE *EXECUTOR*

The *Executor* and the other ships of her class were the product of a long-running, fabulously expensive effort to create a massive capital ship so powerful that the mere threat of its vengeance would pacify multiple sectors.

The first warship accorded the Anaxes War College designation Dreadnought was the eight-kilometer-long *Mandator,* built by Kuat Drive Yards two decades before the Clone Wars as the centerpiece of its sector defense fleet. While Ruusan regulations limited the *Mandator*'s speed and armament, the humpbacked battleship was still a formidable vessel, and the galaxy's wealthiest sectors clamored for similar warships. By the Clone Wars, seven of what KDY called Star Dreadnoughts were in service: Three defended Kuat, while the Azure, Ixtlar, Alsaka, and Humbarine sectors had one each. During the Clone Wars, KDY unveiled the *Mandator II* class, offering heavier armor and weapons and better hyperdrive capabilities. Three new Mandator IIs were built, while three earlier Mandators were uparmored and refitted. All wound up in Republic service, defending the Core against Separatist incursions.

The Empire was just weeks old when it ordered Kuat Drive Yards to begin design work on an even larger dreadnought—one twelve kilometers in length. Lira Wessex designed the new warship, which took shape as Project Sarlacc, a secret effort pursued on Kuat, Coruscant, and ultimately Byss. Rebel agents destroyed the prototype before it left dry-dock. But that was time enough for the Empire to decide to build on Wessex's work, ordering the creation of four new dreadnoughts, each nineteen kilometers long.

Navy traditionalists were aghast, fearing that further efforts could bankrupt the Empire. Fleets of patrol boats, frigates, and cruisers struck the traditionalists as much more effective for policing the vastness of space. The Empire already had a vast collection of such warships inherited from the nationalized Planetary Security Forces; to those,

it could add the ever-growing numbers of Star Destroyers, which boasted firepower that few could match. To those who thought the Star Destroyer sufficient for policing the galaxy, battlecruisers and dreadnoughts—lumped together under the derisive tag "Super Star Destroyers"—seemed like sops to the bottomless egos and ambitions of Moffs and Imperial advisers, not pieces of any coherent military strategy.

But that was before the Death Star emerged as an even greater threat to the navy's prestige. Given that alternative, the navy reluctantly embraced the Super Star Destroyer as a lesser evil. The *Executor* was largely built in the Scarl system, then completed at the great starship yards of Fondor. The massive warship was the culmination of some two decades of astonishing expense—and nothing in the galaxy could hope to survive an encounter with her.

The *Executor* boasted more than five thousand turbolasers and ion cannons, and carried two full wings of TIE fighters and as many as two hundred small armed starships such as gunboats and attack shuttles. A full stormtrooper corps served on board, along with thirty-eight thousand other ground troops, ready to deploy with twenty-four AT-ATs, fifty AT-STs, and three prefabricated garrisons.

THE *EXECUTOR*

As Darth Vader christened the *Executor* with a devastating raid on the Rebel base at Laakteen Depot, three other ships of the same class were nearing completion. The second and third, the *Reaper* and the *Aggressor,* were taking shape at Kuat, while the secret construction facilities at Scarl were busy working on the *Brawl*.

The *Executor* served as Darth Vader's flagship, leading the attack on Hoth, but was overwhelmed by Rebel fire and collided with the second Death Star at Endor in 4 ABY.

The *Aggressor* saw extensive service in the Inner Rim before becoming the centerpiece of Grand Admiral Grunger's forces; she was destroyed at Corellia in 5 ABY.

The *Brawl* anchored the fleet units of the Quelii Oversector and was renamed *Iron Fist* by Zsinj, who emerged as one of the more formidable warlords of the Imperial Fragmentation. She tormented New Republic forces before being destroyed, along with her master, at Dathomir in 8 ABY.

The *Reaper* served as Ardus Kaine's flagship, becoming

a cornerstone of the Pentastar Alignment's military defenses and later those of the Imperial Remnant. She was destroyed at Celanon in 13 ABY.

But these four were not the only members of their class. It was thought that more than twenty were ultimately built, with an exact count proving fiendishly elusive for New Republic asset trackers. On the one hand, evidence suggested the Emperor and his top advisers had ordered the construction of a number of *Executor*-class ships off the books, holding them in reserve at secret Imperial bases, dispatching them into the Unknown Regions, or concealing them for Palpatine's own dark purposes. (Those arguing that more dreadnoughts were out there inevitably noted the concealment of the *Executor II*—later dubbed the *Lusankya*—beneath the Coruscant cityscape.) On the other hand, there was evidence of dreadnoughts budgeted but never built, phantoms to hide other plans of the Emperor's and keep his servants guessing at one another's resources. Moreover, several other classes of dreadnoughts were built, ranging from the *Mandator III* to the massive *Sovereign*, *Eclipse*, and *Vengeance* classes.

THE *HELMSMAN*

BATTLECRUISERS

Informally, *battle cruiser* has been used for eons to refer to massive, heavily armored battleships designed for a single purpose: the destruction of other capital ships. Formally, the designation was reserved for capital ships measuring between two thousand and five thousand meters and designed for long-range independent operations.

While some military historians insist that a few legendary ships of the ancient galaxy—such as Xim's *Eibon Scimitar* or the Alsakani *Bloodshield*—would qualify as battlecruisers under the Anaxes system, most agree that the first warship deserving formal recognition as such was the *Procurator*, constructed by Kuat Drive Yards two centuries before the fall of the Republic. Bristling with weapons, the twenty-five-hundred-meter *Procurator* was the template for a series of ever-larger KDY battleships, nominally built to protect Kuat sector but really aimed at attracting contracts from wealthy Core planets, sectors, and powerful mercantile fleets. By the time of the Clone Wars, dozens of battlecruisers

defended Core and Colonies sectors. The *Procurator*-class Star Battlecruiser was refined several times before being supplanted by a four-thousand-meter descendant, the *Praetor* class, though the Ruusan Reformations limited both classes' hyperdrive capabilities and armament.

The majority of these great ships found their way into Republic service during the Clone Wars. Most served as a line of defense against big Separatist warships such as the Bulwark Mark I and Mark II battleships (technically Star Destroyers according to the Anaxes system) and the massive flagships *Malevolence* and *Devastation*. Other battlecruisers were uparmored, fitted with powerful new hyperdrives, and became the spearpoints of task forces sent against key Confederate worlds. The *Quaestor*, a Republic *Praetor*-class battlecruiser, led a raid against the Separatist shipbuilding facilities at Pammant, where her hyperdrive was damaged by torpedo droids. The *Quaestor*'s hyperdrive engaged, rocketing the great ship into the planet. The impact scattered radioactive particles through Pammant's atmosphere and frac-tured its core.

After Palpatine became Emperor, KDY unveiled the Praetor Mark II, at forty-eight hundred meters the largest battlecruiser yet seen, but the Empire commissioned relatively few of these ships, seeing them as more expensive and less versatile than Star Destroyers while not instilling the same terror as dreadnoughts. (Smaller models within the Battlecruiser class were known as Star Cruisers, though few recognized this as a formal capital ship class.) The Empire primarily used battlecruisers to defend key areas in the Core, though some anchored armadas undertaking dangerous missions on the fringes of Imperial space. Admiral Mils Giel requisitioned the *Helmsman*, a Praetor Mark II, to transport the mysterious life-form known as the Teezl from the distant Valtha Divide to Coruscant.

(CONTINUED FROM PAGE 165)

formidable numbers strengthened by a quartet of Star Destroyers borrowed from Juris Sector Forces. The Rebellion was dealt a terrible blow: Of thirty transports fleeing Echo Base, seventeen were destroyed or captured. Death Squadron's Star Destroyers then pursued the *Millennium Falcon* into the Hoth system's tumbling asteroids. Han Solo eluded capture, attaching his ship to the *Avenger*—but the bounty hunter Boba Fett figured out what Solo had done, and calculated that the crippled Falcon was headed for Bespin. When the freighter arrived, the *Executor* and Death Squadron were hiding in the system—and Darth Vader awaited the *Falcon*'s passengers on Cloud City.

THE GRAND ADMIRALS

Two years before the Battle of Yavin, Emperor Palpatine's New Year's Fete-week appearance on Imperial Center included an unexpected announcement: The Emperor had elevated twelve military commanders to a new rank, making them Grand Admirals of the New Order and parading them in white dress uniforms decorated with gold epaulets. Palpatine's announcement surprised the navy's top brass, who immediately fell to guessing at his motives.

Four of the new Grand Admirals—Josef Grunger, Miltin Takel, Osvald Teshik, and Rufaan Tigellinus—were respected strategists with years of service as fleet admirals, and their appointments brooked little argument. But many an admiral in the starfleet's ranks could claim service records comparable with those of Nial Declann, Octavian Grant, Afsheen Makati, and Peccati Syn, making them odd candidates for such a lofty promotion. Two other new Grand Admirals—Mario Batch and Demetrius Zaarin—were better known for supervising military research than for battlefield successes. And Ishin-Il-Raz and Danetta Pitta were New Order zealots notable only for the ferocity of their politics. (The Empire did name a few Grand Generals, but the rank was largely honorary.)

One of the benefits of being Emperor is never having to explain yourself, and so the conspiracy theories flew whenever officers of the starfleet gathered—and intensified after the traitorous Zaarin was killed and replaced by the mysterious Chiss known as Thrawn. Curious officers noted that only Grant, Grunger, Syn, and Tigellinus continued their regular naval service, and of those four, only Tigellinus benefited substantially from his newfound rank, becoming a Core Worlds Grand Moff. The other Grand Admirals were tasked with special projects, or given missions outside the

naval ranks. Some of the Grand Admirals espoused the values of the navy's generationals—Teshik had dwelled in Anaxes's Sirpar Hills for centuries—while others were the worst sort of High Human Culture bigots. And yet the alien Thrawn had been elevated to their ranks, and rumors circulated freely about Pitta's bloodline.

When Palpatine died at Endor, the Grand Admirals became wild cards in the struggle that consumed the suddenly rudderless Empire. Declann had been killed at Endor; Teshik had been captured; Thrawn was thought dead; and Batch was in hiding after the failure of his TIE Phantom project. Makati, Syn, Takel, and Tigellinus continued to defend their areas of operations while waiting for guidance from Palpatine's successor; Grunger and Pitta set themselves up as warlords; Grant supported the breakaway Grand Moff Ardus Kaine; and Il-Raz went mad, attacking Outer Rim worlds seemingly at random.

As the New Republic exploited the Empire's fragmentation, it kept careful track of the Grand Admirals and their fates. But only three of the Grand Admirals would die at New Republic hands: Teshik was executed, Syn died in the liberation of Kashyyyk, and Makati was killed trying to keep the Corporate Sector an Imperial possession. The others died by other means: Batch's crew killed him and backed Warlord Harrsk;

Il-Raz plunged his Star Destroyer into the heart of the Denarii Nova; Grunger and Pitta killed each other fighting over the Corellian sector; and Takel and Tigellinus were killed by potential Emperors who doubted their loyalties. When Grant defected to the New Republic two years after Endor, he was allowed to retire to Rathalay as the "last Grand Admiral."

But one Grand Admiral remained alive: Thrawn had watched the Empire's disintegration from the Unknown Regions, disgusted at how the New Order had torn itself apart. He vowed that when he returned, things would be different.

DUTY ROSTER: ROGUE SQUADRON (AS OF THE BATTLE OF HOTH)

After the Battle of Yavin, Red Squadron was reconstituted as a pair of flights, dubbed Renegade and Rogue. Commander Arhul Narra tapped Luke Skywalker to lead Rogue Flight, with Wedge Antilles as a second in command. The Rogues' early missions included assisting with the evacuation of Yavin 4; fighting at Barkesh, Gerrard, Jabiim, and Vactooine; and aiding Crix Madine's defection on Corellia.

After Renegade Flight was destroyed at the Battle of Derra IV, Skywalker and Antilles decided to expand Rogue Flight into a full-fledged squadron serving High Command. Their plans hadn't progressed beyond poring over lists of pilots when Skywalker was injured and General Rieekan ordered the evacuation of Echo Base. Members of Rogue Flight and Blue and Green squadrons were pressed into service as Rogue Group, doubling up as pilots and gunners for the Alliance's T-47 airspeeders, which had been converted for the frigid conditions of Hoth just days before.

Rogue Leader: *Luke Skywalker, Tatooine (pilot), and Dak Ralter, Kalist (gunner).* Commander Skywalker had barely emerged from a bacta tank when he led Rogue Group against the AT-ATs of Blizzard Force. Ralter grew up in an Imperial penal colony, escaped and joined the Rebellion. He served with the Tierfon Yellow Aces before joining the Rogues. ***Shot down; Ralter killed in action.***

Rogue Two: *Zev Senesca, Bestine (pilot), and Kit Valent, Huulia (gunner).* Senesca grew up on Kestic Station, a depot on the outskirts of the Bestine system. His parents were free traders with Rebel sympathies who encouraged him to join the Alliance. After a year with the Rebellion, Senesca learned his parents had been killed in an Imperial raid. Blaming the Alliance, he abandoned the Rebel cause for life as a free trader—but learned the raid had originated with his own careless talk about his parents' activities. Senesca rejoined the Rebellion, vowing to atone for his terrible mistake. Valent grew up as a roughneck spaceport kid on Huulia, hiring on to freighters and transports in his teens to see the galaxy. What he saw convinced him that the Empire had to be overthrown, leading him to join the Rebels. ***Shot down; Senesca and Valent killed in action.***

Rogue Three: *Wedge Antilles, Corellia (pilot), and Wes Janson, Taanab (gunner).* Antilles and Janson became friends while serving with the Tierfon Yellow Aces. Antilles was transferred to Yavin Base, while Janson was placed on a list of pilots to be transferred in case of emergency. When the request came through, Janson was ill with Hesken Fever. His friend Jek Porkins went instead, and died above the Death Star—a substitution that haunted Janson for years. He joined the Rogues soon after Yavin, rekindling his friendship with Antilles, who was also haunted by what he thought of as his failure at Yavin. ***T-47 intact.***

Rogue Four: *Derek "Hobbie" Klivian, Ralltiir (pilot), and Kesin Ommis, Coruscant (gunner).* Klivian trained with Tycho Celchu and Biggs Darklighter at the Prefsbelt Naval Academy, and after receiving his commission led a mutiny aboard the frigate *Rand Ecliptic*, joining the Rebellion with his fellow mutineer Darklighter. He was too ill to fly in the Battle of Yavin, and his spot in Red Squadron went to Skywalker. Klivian survived a number of horrific crashes, resulting in bacta sessions and the replacement of parts of his body with cybernetic parts. Ommis joined the Rebellion soon after the Death Star's destruction; he and Klivian were pulled from starfighter duty to pilot snowspeeders shortly before the Imperial ground assault began. ***Shot down; both survived.***

Rogue Five: *Tycho Celchu, Alderaan (pilot), and Tarn Mison, Las Lagon (gunner).* Celchu graduated from Prefsbelt as one of Soontir Fel's more impressive cadets and distinguished himself as a TIE pilot aboard the Star Destroyer *Accuser*. On his twenty-first birthday, he was speaking to his family and fiancée via the HoloNet when the transmission cut off. When Celchu learned Alderaan had been destroyed by the Empire, he deserted and joined the Rebellion. Mison grew up as a superb bush pilot and became a smuggler working the Shipwrights'

Trace, with his interests revolving around credits, not politics. He took a job running supplies to a colony of conscientious objectors on Farbinda III and arrived to discover that an Imperial strike team had rounded up the colonists; though they offered no resistance, the Imperials killed them all. After several months of struggling with what he'd seen, Mison brought his skills to the Rebellion. *T-47 intact.*

Rogue Six: *Samoc Farr, Chandrila (pilot), and Vigrat Pomoner, Iotra (gunner).* Farr grew up in a family loyal to Mon Mothma and staunchly opposed to the Empire; with help from sympathetic Chandrilan authorities, the Farrs and several other families faked a transport crash in which a number of their children were reported killed, among them Samoc and her sister Toryn. Samoc and Toryn were spirited offworld and joined the Rebellion, with Samoc becoming a superb pilot. Both were assigned to Echo Base. Pomoner, a hulking Iotran, was the only nonhuman Rogue, and joined the Rebellion after an Imperial Army unit sent his Iotran Police Force into an ambush because nonhumans' lives were expendable. *Shot down; Pomoner killed in action.*

Rogue Seven: *Nala Hetsime, Pa Tho (pilot), and Cinda Tarheel, Socorro (gunner).* The dour, laconic Hetsime was a mystery to his fellow pilots, who failed to draw more than the most basic personal information out of him, but couldn't argue with his skill and bravery in the cockpit. Tarheel was the opposite, a fast-talking, quick-shooting former smuggler whose superb reflexes allowed her to escape her own rash combat decisions. *T-47 intact.*

Rogue Eight: *Zev Kabir, Ahakista (pilot), and Stax Mullawny, Corellia (gunner).* An older man, Kabir worked with resistance groups on his homeworld before concluding that the Empire could only be defeated by striking closer to the source of its power. The scarred, sardonic Mullawny was an inveterate tinkerer who knew a tremendous amount about the weak points of Imperial warships and garrisons. *Shot down; Kabir and Mullawny killed in action.*

Rogue Nine: *Stevan Makintay, Hargeeva (pilot), and Barlon Hightower, Lantillies (gunner).* Born into royalty on Hargeeva, "Mak" Makintay at first welcomed the Imperial annexation of his planet, as it allowed him

to trade expertise with a sword for pilot training. But his father used his new position as Imperial governor to oppress the Hargeevans and disinherited his son, shipping him off to a penal colony. Makintay escaped and returned to Hargeeva to lead a revolt, which was brutally suppressed. Hightower spent years as a transport pilot for various Lantillian guilds, during which he became convinced that there was no place for neutrality in the Galactic Civil War. After narrowly evading arrest, he joined the Rebellion. *T-47 intact.*

Rogue Ten: *Tarrin Datch, Duro (pilot), and Hosh Hune, Fondor (gunner).* Datch grew up on Pellezara Station, where he was piloting tugs and freighters before his teens and quickly demonstrated that he could fly anything spaceworthy and more than a few things that didn't quite meet the definition. While servicing a freighter, he discovered stolen fuel slugs and a wounded Rebel agent named Jan Ors. He helped her escape and joined the Rebellion, where his piloting abilities proved invaluable. The bald, grim Hosh Hune was a low-caste Fondorian given an apprenticeship in that planet's Guild of Starshipwrights as a reward for generations of his family's guild service. Hune soon discovered he was working on weapons systems for the *Executor;* after agonizing over wasting his family's efforts, he deserted his post and joined the Rebellion. ***Shot down; T-47 salvaged; Hune killed in action.***

Rogue Eleven: *Tenk Lenso, Glova (pilot), and Jek Pugilio, Glova (gunner).* An expert gunner, Lenso was the lone survivor of the Deretta Destroyers, a mixed squadron of X-wings and Y-wings ambushed at Tarabba. The experience haunted Lenso, who suffered flashbacks and found himself unable to serve as a gunner. Hoping to salvage Lenso's promising career, General Rieekan made him a pilot in Rogue Group and asked a fellow Glovan, the soft-spoken Jek Pugilio, to try to help him. Lenso and Datch brought Han Solo and Chewbacca to Echo Station 3-8 to investigate transmissions made in Imperial binary code. ***Shot down; Lenso and Pugilio killed in action.***

Rogue Twelve: *Dash Rendar, Corellia (pilot).* Rendar's parents owned a lucrative Corellian shipping company, and won Dash a commission to the Imperial Naval Academy. But a competitor sabotaged one of their freighters, which crashed into the Imperial Museum on Coruscant, killing Dash's brother. Furious over the loss

of valuable artifacts, the Empire seized the Rendars' company, exiled the family, and expelled Rendar from Carida. Dash became a pilot-for-hire, professing to care only about credits. His ship was on Hoth when the Empire attacked, and Han Solo convinced Luke Skywalker to give Rendar a temporary place in Rogue Group. Despite not having a gunner, he managed to down an AT-AT. *T-47 intact.*

WAR PORTRAIT: ADMIRAL PIETT

Born on Axxila in 39 BBY, the teenage Firmus Piett wanted nothing more than to go to war. After the corporate interests that controlled the Ciutric Hegemony supported the Separatists, Piett and his family relocated to Halmad, along with many other so-called Free Axxilans. He graduated from the Quelii Sector Academy, just days before the war came to an end.

A young man with few connections, Piett found himself patrolling the backworlds of the Ciutric Hegemony with veterans of the Ciutric Planetary Security Forces, now wearing the uniform of the Imperial Navy. For decades such patrols had made tidy sums by ignoring smugglers and pirates, but Piett refused to do so—and he had the good fortune to enter the service shortly after the reform-minded Moff Pensar Luc became the Hegemony's governor. Luc assigned Piett to a new task force staffed by officers he felt he could trust, and directed them to clean up the Ciutric space lanes.

Piett made many arrests and seizures and rose rapidly through the ranks, assuming the leadership of Axxila trade enforcement operations. He also carefully cultivated his contacts elsewhere in the navy, going as far as to reshape his Rimmer accent in favor of the clipped tones of the Core Worlds.

Piett's record and experience rooting out smugglers and pirates caught the eye of Darth Vader, who appointed him captain of the *Accuser,* one of Death Squadron's Star Destroyers. Piett's unflappable demeanor and no-nonsense approach won him a promotion to captain of the *Executor* shortly after the Rebels evacuated Yavin 4—an important post but one without real command duties, as the *Executor* was the flagship of Death Squadron's admiral, Kendal Ozzel.

Piett soon discovered that Ozzel was alternately impetuous and languorous, and automatically ridiculed underlings' ideas and findings to protect his position. Ridding the galaxy of Rebels—whom Piett saw as next-generation Separatists—was too important to be left to such a man, and

(CONTINUED ON PAGE 173)

Rogue Squadron prepares to defend Echo Base (Tommy Lee Edwards)

ARMORY AND SENSOR PROFILE

THE *MILLENNIUM FALCON*

Luke Skywalker called her a piece of junk. Lando Calrissian amended that slightly, saying she was the fastest hunk of junk in the galaxy. For years Han Solo and Chewbacca called her home.

The *Millennium Falcon* began life as a stock Corellian Engineering Corporation YT-1300 transport, one of millions sold over more than a century after the model's introduction in 72 BBY. The freighter's first owner was a shipping firm called Corell Industries Limited, which named her the *Corell's Pride;* she would bear many names and pass through many hands over her first several decades. She was given her permanent name in 10 BBY by a Rebel agent named Quip Fargil, and wound up in the possession of Lando Calrissian five years later. Calrissian's friend Han Solo took a liking to the battered freighter, and won her in a sabacc game on Cloud City in 2 BBY.

Solo loved to tinker almost as much as he loved to fly, and he outfitted the *Falcon* with whatever gear he could get his hands on, paying no mind to Imperial regulations. A customs official on Byblos once said the *Falcon* had so many illegal systems that it would have been easier to list the legal ones—a remark Solo took as a compliment once he and Chewbacca had escaped custody.

Calrissian replaced the *Falcon*'s mandible-mounted blasters with CEC AG-2G quad laser cannons, but Solo made further modifications. The cannons packed a greater punch after he increased the size of each barrel's energization crystal to allow for greater beam intensity, then supported those modifications with enhanced power cyclers, high-volume gas feeds, and custom laser actuators. Concussion missile launchers were hidden above and below the freight loading doors, and Han added a BlasTech Ax-108 "Ground Buzzer" repeating blaster that could drop from the ship's belly and be fired from the cockpit.

When Solo won her, the *Falcon* already had illegally augmented shields; Solo acquired shield generators from the Myomar shipyards that boosted her shielding to military grade. He also added an oversized rectenna sensor dish linked to high-grade sensor suites and powerful sensor jammers.

MILLENNIUM FALCON

Perhaps the *Falcon*'s most surprising system was her hyperdrive, which made her one of the fastest ships in the galaxy. Her customized Isu-Sim SSP05 hyperdrive was twice the size of a stock freighter's, giving her a 0.5 hyperdrive class—twice the speed of Imperial warships. Solo credited the outlaw tech Doc Vandangate for modifying the hyperdrive to streamline the *Falcon*'s mass profile in hyperspace, but Han himself had installed her Quadex power core and the jury-rigged components that cut her jump sequence to a baseline of three minutes. The *Falcon*'s Girodyne SRB42 sublight engines were nearly as impressive, allowing the freighter to maneuver like a starfighter—and at near-starfighter speed.

A ship cobbled together from so many systems was inevitably subject to malfunctions, burnouts, and other problems. Making all these systems work together was a job not just for the pilot, but for the *Falcon*'s rebuilt Hanx-Wargel SuperFlow IV computer and its three subsidiary droid brains, scavenged from a military-issue R3 astromech, a V-5 transport droid, and a corporate espionage droid of uncertain origin. R2-D2 found the *Falcon* a grouchy but intriguing conversationalist, and was amused by the droid brains' ceaseless arguments. But C-3PO found the freighter's peculiar dialect and foul language appalling.

Solo resisted the New Republic's entreaties that he retire the *Falcon* to a museum and choose a safer craft to fly, but never passed up a chance to add the kind of military components he'd dreamed of as a down-on-his-luck smuggler. After the Battle of Endor, he replaced the *Falcon*'s quad cannons with light turbolasers, upgraded the power generators to top-of-the-line military models, and overhauled her propulsion systems. But in 16 ABY, a well-meaning New Republic yard boss went too far for Han's liking; despite promising Solo that he'd touch nothing, his techs gave the *Falcon* a thorough overhaul. Nearly 15 percent of the ship's structural parts and the escape pods were replaced; the weapons, shields, and propulsion systems were upgraded and recalibrated; electronics were properly grounded and pulse-shielded; cables were bundled and tagged; the acceleration couches were recushioned and the crew quarters recarpeted.

Chewbacca liked the rebuilt *Falcon* better than ever, but Solo was horrified: Not that he minded the drive matrix's new Sienar Systems augmenter, but the *Falcon* now flew too smoothly for his taste, with nary a shudder or creak, and he vowed to take a hydrospanner and loosen every fastener he could find so he'd feel at home again.

Piett expected to die—but Darth Vader swept by him in silence and headed for his own quarters. By surviving, Piett became a navy legend—the man who had proven so valuable that he was above even Vader's wrath.

Piett sensed he had lived not because of his battlefield successes, but due to something at work in Vader's own dark mind. After Bespin he treated Vader with deference and respect, but never with fear, serving ably as Death Squadron's admiral until the Battle of Endor. After a barrage of Alliance fire damaged the *Executor*'s guidance systems and brought down her forward shields, a Rebel starfighter smashed through the command bridge's viewports, killing Piett instantly.

WAR PORTRAIT: GENERAL RIEEKAN

Many of the Rebels at Echo Base found Carlist Rieekan hard to love: The general seemed unrelentingly grim, a man who thought disaster was lurking everywhere and couldn't fathom why everyone wasn't preparing for it as meticulously as he was. Princess Leia didn't disagree that Rieekan was hard to understand, but when she overheard griping about him, she tried to explain what had made him that way.

Born in 47 BBY, Rieekan grew up on Alderaan and enlisted in the Republic's Judicial Forces at seventeen, fighting for the Republic Army during the Clone Wars. After the Declaration of the New Order he returned to Alderaan to serve House Organa, and soon became one of Bail Organa's inner circle, advising the viceroy on how best to give covert aid to Rebel freedom fighters.

Rieekan was inspecting a satellite transmission station orbiting Delaya, Alderaan's sister planet, when the Death Star arrived in the system. Rieekan knew what the massive battle station was and what it was capable of, but he ignored the frantic calls for advice and help from Alderaan. If transports began lifting en masse from the planet, he reasoned, Grand Moff Tarkin might think his station was being attacked—and at the very least, he would have proof that Organa had told others about the battle station. Besides, it seemed inconceivable that Tarkin would dare turn the Death Star's superlaser on one of the eldest of the Core Worlds—some ultimatum would be forthcoming.

Rieekan was still convincing himself that he'd made the right decision when the battle station fired on his home-world, destroying it in an eyeblink. Despite assurances from Alderaanian refugees that nothing could have been done, Rieekan would brood over his inaction for the rest of his life.

(CONTINUED FROM PAGE 171)

Piett began thinking about how to engineer Ozzel's downfall.

After a probe droid transmitted video of a suspiciously large shield generator on the ice plains of Hoth, Piett waited until Vader was on the *Executor*'s bridge to tell Ozzel. Ozzel dismissed the report, but Vader overheard, and overruled the admiral. When Ozzel then brought the *Executor* out of hyperspace too close to the Hoth system, alerting the Rebels to Death Squadron's imminent attack, Vader had had enough. As Piett watched with a queasy mix of satisfaction and horror, Vader strangled Ozzel with the Force and handed command of Death Squadron to Piett.

Death Squadron tracked the *Millennium Falcon* to Bespin, and Piett's men sabotaged the freighter's hyperdrive after Cloud City's mechanics repaired it. The *Falcon* rocketed away from Cloud City, but the *Executor* was waiting. As the great battleship closed on the doomed freighter and the boarding party prepared for action, Piett allowed himself a moment of satisfaction. His squadron had crippled Alliance High Command, and would now take custody of Leia Organa, Luke Skywalker, and Chewbacca—three of the Empire's most wanted war criminals. But then, somehow, the *Falcon* vanished into hyperspace.

Rieekan became a general in the Alliance, setting up bases for High Command and the Rebellion's most important cells. After Jan Dodonna was believed killed in the evacuation of Yavin 4, Rieekan was appointed commander of Alliance operations.

The general had his doubts about Echo Base from the start. Its location just off the Corellian Trade Spine was advantageous for operations, but the Ison Corridor was a decaying bypass that was difficult to navigate to Rimward and had only two exits, making it easy to trap Alliance forces within it. And Hoth itself troubled Rieekan: It was freezing, pelted by meteorites from the asteroid belt, and had no other sentients to mask the Rebels' presence from Imperial patrols.

Rieekan did everything he could. He restricted traffic in and out of Hoth to the bare minimum. He requisitioned and installed a planetary-class shield generator and an ion cannon capable of damaging orbiting capital ships, then ringed the base with trenches and laser turrets. Rebel scouts were constantly sent out on tauntaun patrol, and evacuation drills were routine. Rieekan insisted that Echo Base be ready to pack up and go with just minutes' notice, and have sufficient defenses to engineer a fighting retreat.

When Han Solo and Chewbacca destroyed an Imperial probe droid, Rieekan ordered an immediate evacuation, overruling objections that the Empire would merely conclude the probot had discovered a smugglers' nest, or send a patrol. Rieekan had paid the price for underestimating the Empire's murderousness once already. Despite the Rebels' best attempts, the Empire did indeed arrive before Hoth could be left behind. Playing for time, Rieekan sent snowspeeders and soldiers to defend against a ground assault while Echo Base's starfighters and ion cannon guarded transports running the gauntlet of Star Destroyers closing in on Hoth. Rieekan escaped on the last of the transports. Hoth had been a costly loss, but without Rieekan's careful preparations and quick action, things would have been much worse.

After the Battle of Endor, Rieekan helped plan the drive to Coruscant, and later served as the New Republic's minister of state and director of Intelligence. He retired in 17 ABY, but returned to active duty during the Yuuzhan Vong War, working to defend Coruscant against the extragalactic invaders.

> "A wise admiral is never surprised by a scenario, for he has run them all in his head during sleepless nights."
> —Gial Ackbar, admiral, Alliance to Restore the Republic

SHOWDOWN IN THE OUTER RIM

The destruction of the first Death Star had infuriated Emperor Palpatine. But despite such reversals, events in the galaxy still hewed closely to his visions—and the Dark Lord of the Sith was certain that his long struggle to bring peace to the galaxy would soon end.

For years the Rebels had actually been helpful to the Emperor—they offered a convenient focus for the galaxy's fears of chaos and disorder, much as the Separatists had a generation earlier, when he was consolidating his power and plotting the downfall of the Jedi Order. But now Darth Sidious no longer needed such distractions. A new Death Star was taking shape above the remote world of Endor, one shorn of its predecessor's vulnerabilities. And soon Sidious would have a new Sith apprentice—one who could tap the dark side's full potential.

The Rebels had won a substantial victory at Yavin, one that caused many more systems to reject the Empire's rule. But since then, the Galactic Civil War had been a disaster for Mon Mothma and her fellow conspirators. The Empire's ambush of the Rebel fleet at Deepspace Besh had deprived the Alliance of numerous capital ships; only the intercession of the Mon Calamari had kept the Rebellion alive. Daring raids on targets such as Gerrard, Milvayne, and Bannistar Station had kept the Empire off balance for a time, but the Battle of Hoth had been a disaster, decimating the Alliance's primary base.

With the Rebellion still trying to regroup, Palpatine knew it was time to draw Admiral Ackbar's fleet into a fatal showdown and force Luke Skywalker to confront his destiny. And so he quietly set his trap in motion.

The rumors seemed hardly credible at first: The Empire was building a second, more powerful Death Star somewhere on the fringes of the galaxy—one that would be invulnerable when construction was complete. But as more and more such reports reached Alliance High Command, Mothma began to believe them. Rebel agents destroyed the *Tarkin* and its turbolaser at Patriim, and learned of the construction of the Sanctuary Pipeline, a secret trade route driven at staggering expense from Sullust to the fringes of Wild Space. At Bothawui, Skywalker and Bothan agents intercepted the freighter *Suprosa,* whose computer core contained blueprints and construction schedules for the second Death Star. Then at Dennaskar they retrieved data tapes obtained by the Rebel agent Tay Vanis that confirmed the project's existence.

The effort to warn the Alliance cost the lives of Vanis and many Bothans. But the Rebels didn't realize they were walking into a trap. It was Palpatine who had arranged for the Bothans to discover the Death Star plans—just as it was Palpatine who made sure High Command learned he would be personally overseeing the new battle station's construction.

After sending a strike team to destroy the shield generator protecting the Death Star, the Alliance assembled the largest armada in its history and raced down the Sanctuary Pipeline to Endor. There, they had a horrible surprise. The Death Star's protective shield was still in place, and its superlaser was operational. Even incomplete, the Death Star's gravity well made it difficult to jump to hyperspace—and Palpatine had deployed Interdictor cruisers to make escape impossible. Ackbar and General Lando Calrissian found themselves

Carlist Rieekan with Leia Organa and Han Solo (Tommy Lee Edwards)

trapped—and from the far side of the Endor Moon came a task force of more than thirty Imperial Star Destroyers and support ships, led by the *Executor*.

Elsewhere in the galaxy, massive invasion fleets were moving into position, advancing on Mon Calamari Space and the rebellious world of Chandrila. The Alliance Fleet would be destroyed, and the Mon Calamari and Chandrilans pinned in place. They would have a few months to contemplate their mistakes before the new Death Star arrived to incinerate their worlds and end their insurrection.

A SOLDIER'S STORY: HOW I WON THE BATTLE OF TAANAB

In this excerpt from Voren Na'al's *Oral History of the New Republic*, Lando Calrissian looks back at one of his most famous exploits:

Taanab? Really, Voren—that tale's been told so many times. Maybe another day...wait, where are you going? Tell you what, kid—because I like you, and because I know you feel like getting me another glass of Corellian Reserve, I'll tell it just one more time. But only this once.

Taanab's not much—an ag world whose only redeeming feature is that it sits at the intersection of the Perlemian and the Hapan Spine. I was there not long after Yavin, nursing a warm Ebla in Pandath's least-worst casino, when the alert sirens started going off.

The Taanab defense fleet was a bunch of rustbuckets, gunships that were old when Hutts had a conscience. I didn't think they'd even get out of the atmosphere, and I said so. The sad-sack bartender told me it would be better if they didn't— the inbound ships were the Norulac pirates, arriving for their annual tribute. And the only question was if they'd feel like shooting this year.

I couldn't believe it—the Norries were low and mean, but they were also a bunch of amateurs and everybody knew it. There was no way the Taanabs should have let themselves be pushed around by such a sorry lot, but once you get used to being scared, you let a lot of things happen to you. I watched on the holovid as the Norries intercepted the week's rhuum convoy. There were about two

dozen of them up there, maneuvering like a herd of nerfs. They couldn't have flown worse if they'd already hit the rhuum, and I knew just one real pilot with a little courage could mop up the lot of them.

And then it hit me: There was a real pilot right there on Tanaab, one who just might be crazy enough to pull it off. I don't need to tell you who that pilot was, do I, Voren?

What's that? Uh, no. He wasn't there.

Stang, Voren, you know I meant me. I told everybody in that cantina as much, and this rich merchant—guy named Danager—laughed and said if I drove the Norries off, he'd give me the deed to one of his breweries on Clendor. That got everybody laughing at me—I think I also got offered the Imperial Palace and the Sceptre of Nopachi— but I didn't mind. I love a good Clendoran ale, and this was a chance at a lifetime supply.

So a few minutes later I fired up the Mama Tried, *stood her on her tail, and went topside. The Taanab boys were spread out in orbit around the Banthal docks, leaving a trail of bolts behind them. The Norries, meanwhile, were still trying not to fly into each other and whooping over the comm. They had two corvettes and a bunch of rusty gunships painted with badly drawn fangs and claws—typical tacky pirate stuff.*

So I headed for the Taanab moon's ice ring and waited.

See, I'd picked up several hundred Conner nets I'd promised to run out to Socorro for this guy I knew. When the Norries got close enough—which took the better part of forever—I shot out among them and let the Conners go right in the middle of their formation. Being vac-heads, about half of them immediately hit their jets, flying right into the nets and shorting out their systems. Three or four of the others flew straight into each other like spooked nuna.

Before they could get it sorted out, I fired up Mama's tractor beam and started slingshotting chunks of ice from the ring into them. The Norries might have been amateurs, but they were spitting mad now, and I didn't want them to open up on me or the Taanabs. Speaking of the Taanabs, that was about the time they arrived with guns blazing. I racked up nineteen kills in about as many minutes, and shot

up the corvettes' coolant pipes, taking their engines offline. I had a bunch of nets left, so I fired those into the escape pod bays. After that, nobody was getting off those corvettes. The Taanabs called in the Imps, who showed up a few days later and captured the corvettes with all hands. And that was the end of the annual tributes.

The Taanabs offered to make me marshal of their defense fleet, but I said no. You know what salary a planetary militiaman pulls down, Voren? Besides, nothing ruins the cut of a good suit quicker than epaulets. You remember that—they ever want to make you a general, you insist on braid. Epaulets are showy; braid's classy.

Besides, I had a new brewery to inspect. One that turned out to be run by a Zeltron who was pretty as a Tellanadan moonflower and mean as a Hismauli hawk-snake. But Voren, my friend, that's another story.

MANUFACTURER: MON CALAMARI

The Mon Calamari shipyards have been the pride of the Calamari sector since before 4000 BBY. Toward the end of the Republic, they became a key Rendili affiliate, producing Dreadnaught variants alongside their native vessels.

During the Clone Wars, Mon Calamari supported Palpatine, but the pro-Separatist opposition made several attempts to liberate the shipyards, while exiled shipwrights revised the Rendili Dreadnaught into the Confederacy's *Providence*-class battleship. Moff Tarkin later subjugated the system, hoping to retool the shipyards for Imperial use, but the navy quickly dismissed the Mon Cals' technology as too alien.

Nonetheless, Tarkin admired the elegant winged hullforms of the latest MC80 cruisers, so he allowed the shipyards to build variants as luxury starliners for Galaxy Tours and Kaliida & Rimward. The Mon Cal shipwrights repaid him by developing every component of these new liners as a prototype for future warships.

(CONTINUED ON PAGE 182)

ARMORY AND SENSOR PROFILE

A-WING

The fastest starfighter to see service during the Galactic Civil War, the RZ-1 A-wing was assembled by hand in secret Alliance factories and combined extremely powerful sublight engines with extraordinarily sensitive controls. Not since the Jedi starfighters of the Clone Wars had there been a starfighter so perfectly suited for an ace pilot—or so unforgiving of a lesser pilot's mistakes.

A-WING

While the A-wing resembled the ancient Aurek starfighter, its direct ancestor was the R-22 Spearhead, a speedy starfighter favored by pilots who liked to tinker, further increasing the Spearhead's speed and maneuverability by upgrading its flight systems and stripping it of any and all components that could be jettisoned. The Rebel pilot Jake Farrell was one such tinkerer, and brought a pair of R-22s to Yavin 4's Massassi base.

After the Battle of Yavin, General Jan Dodonna, Adar Tallon, and Walex Blissex decided the Alliance needed a new starfighter that was faster than the X-wing—particularly since the Empire was already beginning to deploy speedier TIE models. Working with Farrell, the team began drawing up designs.

The A-wing got its speed from two Novaldex J-77 Event Horizon engines; its maneuverability came from a combination of adjustable thrust-vector controls and thruster-control jets. The fighter needed every bit of its speed, as its armament was much lighter than that of an X-wing or Y-wing: two wing-mounted blaster cannons that could pivot sixty degrees up or down to cover a greater field of fire. To take on bigger targets, A-wings generally carried concussion missiles. The starfighter was lightly armored, carried a small shield generator, and had no astromech—though it did compensate for these weaknesses with powerful sensor jammers that could blind enemy pilots.

A-wings were prone to breakdowns and notoriously hard to keep flying; flight crews hated them, and officers planning offensives had to wonder if the fighters would be available. But they proved their value in raids, activating their sensor jammers, streaking in to hit blinded targets with concussion missiles, and then racing away before an effective defense could be mounted.

A-wings helped turn the tide at the Battle of Endor, as pilots from Green Squadron destroyed the *Pride of Tarlandia* and then the *Executor*. Gemmer Sojan—a Rogue Squadron veteran flying as Green Two—destroyed the *Tarlandia,* degrading the Imperial fleet's communications, and Farrell (flying as Green Four) and Green Leader Arvel Crynyd brought down the shields protecting the *Executor*'s command bridge. Struck by point-defense turbolasers, Crynyd guided his tumbling A-wing into the bridge, causing the dreadnought to collide with the Death Star.

The New Republic turned A-wing production over to Incom, whose standardized methods made for more reliable fighters. The Rebel leader Garm Bel Iblis developed the A-wing Slash, a tactic in which a group of X-wings would attack an Imperial convoy, with A-wings flying right behind them. The X-wings would pull away to draw enemy fire, and the A-wings would unleash their concussion missiles into the convoy's heart.

B-WING

The B-wing was created by the Alliance to be a ship like no other—a starfighter that could ignore opposing starfighters and attack capital ships head-on.

The B-wing boasted powerful shields energized by a Quadex power core, same as that used by the *Millennium Falcon*. The power core also drove fast sublight thrusters and a long-range hyperdrive. In place of the astromech and scanner array found on most other snubfighters, the B-wing carried a powerful navicomputer and sensor suite, both originally designed for small capital ships.

B-WING

It also boasted the most powerful armament seen on an Imperial-era fighter. A turbolaser cannon and two proton torpedo launchers delivered a devastating punch against armor and shields, while three ion cannons assisted in commerce raiding, and twin blasters defended against starfighters.

The B-wing's spaceframe was a complex blade-shaped

design, capable of flying either as a vertical keel or a horizontal wing. The cockpit rotated in a gyroscopic frame, remaining upright no matter what the hull was doing, with small strike foils folding out on either side of the the keel during combat. The fighter normally sat vertically in its launch rack—standing 16.9 meters tall—but the horizontal option enabled it to set down on landing pads, and also provided superior flight characteristics in atmosphere.

The B-wing was officially designed by the Verpine of the Slayn & Korpil construction hives, but a key role was also played by the Mon Calamari shipyards, where many B-wings were built. It was developed in secret among the Roche asteroids under the supervision of Admiral Ackbar, with the first squadron entering service in the months after Yavin.

The B-wing had its critics—it was expensive to build, difficult to fly, useless in a dogfight, and costly to maintain. Imperial captains learned to fight B-wings by sending out TIE bombers to launch salvos of unguided missiles into their attack flight paths. Nonetheless, the B-wing proved its worth many times. Unsupported B-wings destroyed two Star Destroyers at Endor, and after 10 ABY the design superseded the Y-wing as the New Republic's assault starfighter.

MON CAL STAR CRUISER

Some saw the Mon Calamari Star Cruisers as the soul of the Rebellion—elegant, streamlined ships, each a unique work of art, with bespoke sensors and a sculpted hullform. They were also large and heavily armed. A typical MC80 of the Civil War era measured around twelve hundred meters and was armed with forty-eight turbolasers, twenty ion cannons, and thirty-six starfighters.

Mon Cal cruisers were originally built as exploration vessels for deep voyages into Mon Calamari Space, but carried military shields and starfighter wings, and became the main defense force for a colonial empire spanning several hundred systems.

When the Empire conquered Dac, a handful of exploration cruisers escaped and joined the Alliance fleet—notably the *Independence,* which served as the Rebellion's spacegoing capital. Meanwhile, in the occupied shipyards, Mon Cal workers initiated a secret rearmament program, and

MC80 STAR CRUISER

when the Mon Cal resistance destroyed the Empire's garrison in 1 BBY, their plan swung into action.

Under Imperial rule, the shipyard had built luxury cruise liners, which were swiftly fitted out for war—as had always been the Mon Cal designers' plan. Viewports were plated over and turbolaser batteries added. While these Star Cruisers lacked the raw firepower of Imperial Star Destroyers, the strength of their shields and the accuracy of their targeting computers gave them the edge in long-range duels. The older command ships were given new weapons and deflector shields, and as soon as they were refitted construction began on a lean, combat-focused variant cruiser known as the MC80A.

After Endor Star Cruisers increased in size and numbers—the MC80B outgunned an Imperial Star Destroyer, while the MC90 was the most powerful warship built for the New Republic before the Yuuzhan Vong invasion, with seventy-five turbolaser batteries, thirty ion cannons, six heavy proton torpedo tubes, and two full wings of starfighters.

In 25 ABY, as the first alien scouts appeared in the Outer Rim, two even larger types entered service. *Mediator*-class battlecruisers were fast and powerful successors to the MC80, but proved poorly armored in close-range battles with the Yuuzhan Vong. The massive *Viscount*-class Star Defenders, meanwhile, represented the apogee of Star Cruiser design. As with all Mon Cal classes, no two Star Defenders were alike: The prototype *Viscount* was an impressive three-kilometer battlecruiser, but the mighty *Bounty* and *Krakana* that followed were seventeen-kilometer dreadnoughts, intended as the centerpiece of the Outer Rim defenses.

Even incomplete, *Bounty* deterred the Yuuzhan Vong from attacking Mon Calamari until the desperate last stage of the war. *Krakana* was ordered to Kuat in 27 ABY, where the Defense Force planned to use her as an orbital artillery battery, but the Vong destroyed her en route.

(CONTINUED FROM PAGE 178)

Pinpoint targeting computers were devised for sport lasers on the promenade deck of the *Kuari Princess,* while the RNS *Queen Amidala IV* boasted an innovative Class One hyperdrive. This was only part of a wider plan for liberation. The Imperial garrison was ejected in 1 BBY, and Mon Calamari committed fully to the Alliance two years later.

By the Battle of Endor, Mon Calamari had also produced eight new heavy cruisers based on the *Kuari Princess* design, and nearly fifty escorts—an even more impressive achievement considering that a good chunk of the shipyards' resources was given over to starfighter construction at the same time.

After Endor, the shipyards doubled their production every year, taking advantage of massive New Republic funding: In some years, as much as 5 percent of the entire government budget was assigned to Mon Cal-led shipbuilding efforts. In response, the designers created increasingly powerful battleships.

WAR PORTRAIT: ADMIRAL ACKBAR

The most famous leader in modern warfare, Ackbar was the victor of Endor and Bilbringi and twice liberator of Coruscant. While Luke Skywalker destroyed the Emperor, it was Ackbar who brought down the Empire. His stature is such that none need explain who he was or what he did.

Gial Ackbar was born into a prominent merchant clan in the city of Foamwander, served his planet's king during the Clone Wars, and held high military and political office in the early years of the Imperial era. At first, Ackbar saw the New Order as restoring Republic law and justice—but the Empire soon brought an invasion fleet to his homeworld. The peaceful cultural and technological achievements of Dac had to be suppressed to preserve the idea of human superiority.

Ackbar was taken prisoner, and after the pacification was assigned to the Conqueror of Calamari, Grand Moff Tarkin, as a valet—a slave in all but name.

Despite his situation, Ackbar managed to make contact with the Alliance. His position, while humiliating, made him an ideal spy, and after contributing valuable intelligence about the Death Star project for many months, Ackbar escaped and resumed his rightful place as a fleet commander.

Ackbar became the senior admiral of the small Rebel Navy, leading a battle line of exiled Mon Cal cruisers under the overall command of General Jan Dodonna. But when his people threw off their Imperial shackles, they invited him home to lead their rebuilt fleet.

Resigning from the Alliance, Ackbar worked to secure Mon Calamari's commitment to the Rebel cause while continuing to supervise Project Shantipole—a secret project to produce the B-wing starfighter. After Dac became a full partner in the Alliance, Ackbar returned his flag to the *Independence*. After that, he was the undisputed head of the navy and senior commander of the military. Over the years, his title changed—Supreme Commander, minister of defense, Commander in Chief, Admiral of the Fleet—but the rank hardly mattered. He was Ackbar.

Ackbar's military thinking was cautious, conservative, and ruthlessly effective. He was a fleet officer to the core of his being, and saw capital ships as the decisive force in warfare—like the mighty ocean predators of his homeworld, their role was to stay safe in the deep and then strike when their enemy showed weakness.

Ackbar's leadership enabled the Alliance Fleet to win at Endor, and allowed the New Republic Defense Force to triumph over repeated Imperial challenges in the years that followed. He was a master of administrative and technical details, serving as project lead on the B-wing, the MC90 battle cruiser, and the *Viscount*-class dreadnought. He also personally oversaw the basic structural and logistical aspects of the navy, guiding its development from a single squadron of aging cruisers to the powerful fleet of the dominant galactic hyperpower. Politically, he also served—somewhat against his will—as his people's chief representative in the government. As the onetime Rebels established themselves as galactic rulers, he ensured that both Dac and the Defense Force were unstinting supporters of the civilian democracy and the Jedi Knights.

If Ackbar had a weakness, it was that he was irreplaceable. He retired in 25 ABY following the liberation of the last Second Imperium fortress worlds, and his absence was keenly felt when the Yuuzhan Vong crossed the Rim. During the invasion, he took charge of the defense of his homeworld and its shipyards. When the Senate relocated to Dac in 27 ABY, the aged admiral returned to public duty, drafting the war plan that turned the tide against the Vong.

Ackbar refused a formal military title, but continued to guide the new Galactic Alliance until his death shortly before the liberation of Coruscant and the final victory over the Vong.

The Ewoks join the fight (Chris Scalf)

A SOLDIER'S STORY: DEATH IN THE WOODS

Excerpt from *Portraits of the Galactic Civil War*, by Cindel Towani, 41 ABY:

Hume Tarl. I served six years in Tempest Force, rising to sergeant. We were one of the finest legions in the New Order. Saw action at Kashyyyk, Marcelan Prime, Sarko, Aurimaus, and a lot of places you never heard of. We were on the Endor Moon for nine months—nine months at the back of beyond, with occasional liberty on Annaj. You've never been to Annaj, Miss Towani, but trust me—only someone doing time on the Endor Moon could find it interesting.

Our survey teams had discovered the indigenes, of course—you think we'd establish a shield generator protecting a project of this importance without a thorough survey? They were primitives—hairy dwarf bipeds with spears and slings, living in tree houses. We paid them no mind—they didn't seem inclined to cause problems begging or stealing things, which is what most abos like to do. That would have led to an excision within a defined perimeter. But like I said, they seemed afraid of us—they didn't like approaching the shield generator. And we didn't think we'd be staying long enough for them to get acclimated and become a problem.

We were all on edge. Emperor Palpatine was aboard the Death Star—we'd shined up the plastoid and deployed aboard the battle station a few days earlier for a big ceremony to mark his arrival. I only saw him across the hangar, but even from far away your eyes were drawn to him.

We were protecting our Emperor—and we also knew there were Rebel agents on the moon. We'd had a speeder bike patrol go missing and we were on high alert. Then the craziest thing happened: A Rebel surrendered himself to us and handed over an old Jedi laser sword. I didn't know it was Luke Skywalker—he seemed awfully short to be the most wanted Rebel in the galaxy. Skywalker claimed he was alone, but nobody believed that—I'd heard stories about the Jedi, but no way just one of them could take out an entire patrol. Lord Vader took him up the gravity well on a shuttle, and I assumed that would be the last the galaxy would ever hear of him.

The next day the Rebel fleet arrived, and we were attacked by Rebel guerrillas who'd been hiding in the woods. We captured them, and word was that the orbital battle was going the way the Emperor had planned. The officers were even talking about how we'd always remember the day we witnessed the end of the Rebellion.

And then it happened—the indigenes attacked.

I've seen the holo-thrillers, and those directors should admit they're paid to tell New Republic lies. They make those things—those Ewoks—look cute, like stuffed toys. I was there, Miss Towani. They weren't anything close to cute.

The first wave of troopers died with arrows through the gaps in their armor. The indigenes were primitive, but later I read about the bows they'd used, how they were engineered for immense leverage. I saw troopers falling with arrows that had gone completely through their throats. They were the lucky ones—some of our men took what looked like minor wounds, and minutes later they were clawing their helmets off and gasping for air. The abos had dipped their arrows in some kind of nerve toxin that paralyzed every muscle in the body. Troopers who got hit suffocated because their lungs wouldn't work. I saw dying men staring into the sun, trying to blink.

Some of our men chased the indigenes into the woods and fell into hidden pits lined with stakes fixed in the ground. Scout troopers flew into trip wires that broke their necks. Elsewhere the indigenes overpowered troopers through sheer numbers, holding them down until they got their helmets off and other abos could kill them with stone axes and knives made of volcanic glass.

And every time one of our men fell, the indigenes had another blaster. They knew every tree and rock, and they picked us off one by one.

You look like you don't believe me, but I was there. I saw what those Ewoks did. The historians love to talk about alleged Imperial atrocities, but what about what I saw on the Forest Moon? They slaughtered us like animals, Miss Towani. Shouldn't that count as an atrocity?

AN EMPIRE IN FRAGMENTS

> "The general who fights all the time is rash. The one who never fights is weak. The one who fights when it suits his purposes is victorious." —*Sayings of Uueg Tching*

IMPERIAL FRAGMENTATION

The death of Emperor Palpatine sparked celebrations, but the Empire remained largely intact, and the Rebels were in no position to capitalize on their victory, not with nearly three-quarters of the Rebel capital ships that saw action above the Forest Moon needing extensive repairs.

Captain Gilad Pellaeon of the Imperial Star Destroyer *Chimaera* knew the Rebel fleet had been battered, and guessed that the Alliance had thrown the bulk of its forces against the second Death Star. But he was unable to do anything about it.

With the destruction of the *Executor* and the *Pride of Tarlandia,* command of Death Squadron had fallen to the *Chimaera,* the next communications ship in line. The *Chimaera*'s commander, Admiral Horst Strage, had been killed when an ion blast overloaded his neural shunt, leaving command in Pellaeon's hands. With the Imperial forces in disarray, Pellaeon ordered a retreat to Annaj, the Moddell sector capital—a two-day journey that left him brooding over whether he'd done the right thing, and what he ought to do next.

Pellaeon wanted to fight. Death Squadron had sustained serious losses: the *Executor,* one of its two battlecruisers, a *Tector*-class Star Destroyer, and fifteen of its thirty-three Imperial Star Destroyers. But that still left a formidable force. At a council of war, Pellaeon urged a return to Endor, insisting that the Rebel military could be crushed before word of the Emperor's death spread.

But other officers had also been thinking during the two-day trip to Annaj. Speaking from his bacta tank, Admiral Blitzer Harrsk coldly informed Pellaeon that with the battle over, his command was nullified and belonged to Admiral Adye Prittick, the ranking admiral. That was fine with Pellaeon; he didn't care who commanded Death Squadron so long as it returned to Endor.

But Prittick couldn't make a decision. That touched off a quarrel among the flag officers; the council of war broke up acrimoniously when Harrsk declared he was taking the battlecruiser *Ilthmar's Fist,* the two remaining Tectors, and three Star Destroyers into the Deep Core until a clear chain of command was established. That prompted the two surviving captains from Elrood sector to return there for orders. Death Squadron was reduced to twelve Star Destroyers—a significant force, but one Prittick declared too small to guarantee victory. He ordered a withdrawal to Yag'Dhul, a missed opportunity that would torment Pellaeon.

Similar scenes unfolded all over the Empire. Palpatine had never provided a succession plan, leaving any number of Grand Moffs, advisers, and admirals to see themselves as able successors. The best claim belonged to Sate Pestage, Palpatine's Grand Vizier and head of the advisers' Ruling Council. But many dismissed Pestage as weak and made their own plans. Some officers, such as Harrsk and Admiral Gaen Drommel, declared themselves warlords. Others, such as Admirals Zsinj and Teradoc, fortified their holdings, claiming loyalty while quietly pursuing their own ambitions. Still others broke with the Empire without making a formal declaration: Grand Moff Ardus Kaine infuriated Pestage by abandoning much of Oversector Outer to defend a portion of the New Territories.

Pestage and his advisers sought to fortify their holdings. Convinced the Rebels would soon assault the Core, they defended the inner systems' key strategic and economic worlds, giving Admiral Ackbar, independence-minded planetary leaders, and warlords free reign.

With the Empire in disarray, the Rebels—now reconstituted as the Alliance of Free Planets—were able to fend off attacks from the Ssi-ruuk, Nagai, and Tofs. But those campaigns stretched the Alliance to the breaking point, and Mon Mothma decided not to press the attack on the Imperial successor states. Instead, she would use diplomatic levers to further dismantle the Empire.

The fledgling New Republic sent envoys to thousands of worlds. Many systems joined the new government, standing alongside the likes of Bothawui, Mon Calamari, Corellia, Duro, Kashyyyk, Sullust, and Elom. But many others declared themselves independent—which the New Republic respected. Mothma's government would not be the Empire, but a voluntary union for the common good.

Toward that end, Mothma made a fateful decision, one Ackbar later admitted delivered more worlds to the New Republic than any dozen campaigns could have. The Defense Declarations devolved control of Planetary Security Forces nationalized by the Empire to their sectors. New Republic member sectors would be expected to support the military's starfleet, but would retain command of their local forces.

Word of the Defense Declarations rippled through the galaxy. Sectors loyal to the Empire (or at least ruled by powerful Moffs) dismissed the measure as illegal, but for others it was the deciding factor that led them to break with the Empire or join the New Republic. And some sectors' loyalties proved sharply divided, leading to hundreds of battles between rival Imperial task forces that further diminished the Empire's ability to wage war.

INVADERS FROM BEYOND

A day after the Emperor's death, an Imperial drone ship arrived at Endor warning that the planet Bakura was under attack by unknown invaders. Mon Mothma sent a small task force to the planet's defense, and a brief-lived alliance between Rebel and Imperial forces drove the Ssi-ruuk back into the Unknown Regions. A Rebel task force made up of the captured Ssi-ruuvi *Shree*-class battle cruiser *Sibwarra* (technically a Star Destroyer) and a dozen Nebulon-B frigates

New Republic forces face Nagai invaders led by Lumiya (Bruno Werneck)

would later push their way into the Ssi-ruuvi Imperium—only to discover the battered remnants of a domain that had already been devastated by red-eyed, blue-skinned near-humans from elsewhere in the Unknown Regions.

Just days after the Ssi-ruuvi invasion, another previously unknown enemy attacked. The chalk-skinned, angular Nagai hailed from the satellite galaxy known as Companion Besh, and began by attacking the frontier worlds of the Western Reaches. Some observers found the Nagai's wirework ships—of which no two were the same—twisted and alien, while others found their apparent fragility beautiful. The bulk of the Nagai expeditionary ships were frigates and corvettes, backed up by a handful of *Yulari*-class cruisers, designed by a species from Companion Besh known as the Faruun. Nagai navicomputers were extraordinarily quick at calculating jumps, and relied upon tachyonic observational sensors to map realspace hazards and landmarks much more efficiently than Imperial technology. Nagai scouts used these sensors to chart courses through the galaxy's stellar halo, allowing them to bypass blockades and establish forward bases deep within the galaxy.

Aiding the Nagai were stormtroopers loyal to Lumiya, the cyborg and Force-wielding dark adept once known as Shira Brie. The invaders set up their primary forward base on Kinooine, where they were joined by their main invasion fleet. From there, they hopscotched among backworlds until they reached Terminus, gaining access to the Hydian Way and the Corellian Trade Spine.

Alliance forces learned the Nagai were refugees who'd had their own homeworld stolen by another species from Companion Besh—the massive, green-skinned Tofs. The Tofs had followed the Nagai, and pursued them to Trenwyth and then all the way to Zeltros in giant, eighteen-hundred-meter bulk cruisers whose durasteel hulls were crafted to look like huge sailing ships from some lost surface navy.

At Zeltros, Alliance troops joined with the Nagai, Mandalorian commandos, and elements of Lumiya's forces to defeat the Tofs. When it was learned that the Tof Prince Sereno had established his headquarters at Saijo, Luke Skywalker led a raid on the prince's quarters while the Alliance Star Destroyer *Emancipator*—known as the *Accuser* before its capture at Endor—moved to engage the Tof bulk cruiser *Merriweather*. The *Millennium Falcon* and Rebel pilots who'd scrambled from the *Emancipator* destroyed the *Merriweather*'s complement of starfighters, and Skywalker's task force captured Prince Sereno. The Tof invasion had failed, while the Nagai had gained new allies in their efforts to reclaim their home planet.

AGAINST THE WARLORDS

After surviving threats posed by the Ssi-ruuk, Nagai, and Tofs, the leaders of the newborn New Republic met on Mon Calamari to plan the assault on the inner systems.

Admiral Ackbar noted that a number of events had already proved favorable to the New Republic. Rather than attack Mon Calamari in force, Grand Moff Kaine had withdrawn to the other side of the galaxy. Moffs and admirals with Imperial ambitions of their own had begun battling over territory. Patient diplomacy and the Defense Declarations had divided the Imperial military, with many units deciding that their loyalties lay with their home sectors, not the vacillating Ruling Council. And the New Republic's swift victories over the Ssi-ruuk and Tofs had reassured citizens who'd doubted the former Rebels could defend the galaxy.

For all that, the task ahead would be tremendously difficult. The Empire still possessed a large advantage in terms of military power and economic resources—and lacked only a capable leader to emerge from the scramble for power. Palpatine had aided the New Republic cause by keeping his advisers, Moffs, and military leaders struggling for influence and prestige throughout his reign, ensuring that they would battle after his demise. In the decade after the Battle of Endor, New Republic agents worked in the shadows to exacerbate such tensions through a campaign of sabotage, disinformation, and occasional assassinations. Referred to as Shadow Operations, these operatives first reported to Airen Cracken and later became the heart of the secretive unit known as Alpha Blue.

While Shadow Operations waged war quietly, the New Republic fleet did so loudly—but even here, Ackbar and his cadre of military leaders moved carefully, working to keep the Empire divided. Over three years the fleet marginalized and eliminated warlords and slowly tightened a vise on the Core and Colonies, with several key battles shaping the borders between the New Republic and territory that would eventually become the Imperial Remnant.

After the initial period of chaos that followed the Battle of Endor, the portion of the Imperial Starfleet that proved loyal to Sate Pestage—led by officers such as Betl Oxtroe, Uther Kermen, and Gilad Pellaeon—defended fortress worlds in the Core and Colonies. Elsewhere, six major warlords emerged.

The most powerful of these warlords posed the least threat to the New Republic: Ardus Kaine defended a shrunken Oversector Outer in the New Territories and showed little interest in the rest of the galaxy's affairs.

leadership in Mon Calamari Space; Third Fleet operated out of Bothan Space and was assigned to the Slice; and Fourth Fleet also made Bothawui its headquarters and stood ready to reinforce either First or Third fleet.

First Fleet, commanded by Admiral Firmus Nantz, began its campaign at Saijo, site of the Tofs' defeat. The stooped, cadaverous Nantz raised eyebrows for his brutal candor—he once told a delegation of unaffiliated planetary leaders that "an admiral's business is to industrialize murder at a distance"—but was a superb tactician. Under his command, First Fleet smashed the Eiattu pirates at Abraxas and drove Delvardus's forces back from Glova, where General Tyr Taskeen led the New Republic ground attack with the help of Sullustan irregulars. The Glova campaign prevented Delvardus's Eriadu Authority from linking up with Imperial forces in the Elrood and Minos sectors, limiting his influence.

Nantz then won a skirmish with Prentioch's forces at Kriselist, bypassing him and seizing Moorja, where a fleet of Nebulon-B frigates backed by Y-wing bombers destroyed Delvardus's *Praetor Mark II*–class battlecruiser *Thalassa*. With Adar Tallon supervising starfighter operations, Nantz ordered a battle group to Bannistar Station, which he captured after heavy bombardment, and from there to Glom Tho, where Taskeen's forces seized several key foundries. The Hevvrol Sector Campaign ruined Moff Lankin's dreams of conquest, penning him within Lambda sector.

Ackbar himself took charge of Third Fleet, moving from Bothan Space to Kashyyyk, where his forces slugged it out with Moff Hindane Darcc and Grand Admiral Peccati Syn. Ackbar's *Home One* and Captain Verrack's *Maria* caught the Grand Admiral's Star Destroyer *Silooth* in a crossfire, with a volley of proton torpedoes vaporizing its bridge. Privately, Ackbar admitted Bothan agents had delivered the victory, sabotaging two of Syn's Interdictor cruisers and impersonating Teradoc's top aides to promise Syn that Greater Maldrood fleet units would come to his assistance.

Kashyyyk sat at a nexus of six hyperspace routes; from there, Ackbar and Rogue Squadron planned a daring raid on the Core world of Brentaal, defeating Admiral Lon Isoto and capturing the TIE ace Soontir Fel. Fourth Fleet, under the command of the Duros Admiral Voon Massa, moved from Bothan Space to Druckenwell, capturing a key industrial world on the Corellian Run and linking up with First Fleet.

Not everything went well for the New Republic in the first year of the campaign. Second Fleet's command officially belonged to Admiral Hiram Drayson, though operations were conducted by a trio of capable Mon Calamari admirals:

Kaine occasionally squabbled with the flamboyant Grand Moff Zsinj, who had turned the Quelii Oversector into a powerful military state on the Hydian Way. But Zsinj's wrath was primarily reserved for High Admiral Treuten Teradoc, who placed Grand Moff Ambris Selit under house arrest and took control of the Greater Maldrood, a large chunk of the Perlemian Trade Route, and a number of productive industrial worlds.

The most powerful warlord after Kaine, Zsinj, and Teradoc was Admiral Sander Delvardus, who refused to follow Kaine into the New Territories and fortified Eriadu, from which he controlled a chunk of the Hydian Way and the Rimma Trade Route. Delvardus's chief rival was Moff Utoxx Prentioch, who turned Sombure sector's large, capable fleet into a power base on the Corellian Trade Spine. Finally, there was Moff Par Lankin of Lambda Sector, who controlled a relatively small territory but was a respected strategist. (A seventh major warlord, Admiral Blitzer Harrsk, vanished into the Deep Core soon after Endor.)

In 4 ABY Admiral Ackbar organized the New Republic's forces into four fleets: First Fleet began operations in the Western Reaches; Second Fleet protected the New Republic

Kalback, Nammo, and Ragab. Second Fleet won early victories as Kalback and Nammo drove Imperial forces from Emmer with the help of Colonel Horton Salm's Y-wings. But Imperial agents discovered one of the Mon Cals' secret routes to the Hast system, where a number of Mon Cal warships and captured Imperial vessels were being repaired. Admiral Llon Banjeer, who'd allied himself with Zsinj, persuaded the D'Asta family to lend him several bulk cruisers, which he retrofitted as carriers for TIE fighters and TIE bombers. Banjeer's forces destroyed or damaged more than thirty New Republic capital ships, derailing the Second Fleet's planned assault on Zsinj and Teradoc.

The year 5 ABY saw Massa's Fourth Fleet push Coreward along the Corellian Run to Milagro, held by Admiral Uther Kermen. General Duron Veertag landed New Republic troops in the hope of taking Milagro's manufacturing facilities, enduring a three-month slog marked by open combat between Imperial AT-ATs and New Republic hovertanks and airspeeders, as well as subterranean struggles between both sides' sappers and miners. Knowing defeat was imminent, Kermen withdrew and bombarded the planet's surface, denying the Rebels its facilities. He fled to Spirana, but then launched a surprise attack that nearly caught Mon Mothma while the New Republic Chief of State was meeting the Fourth Fleet's commanders. Massa beat back the attack and lunged farther down the Corellian Run to take Spirana.

The First Fleet, meanwhile, had an easier time of it: Nantz won a relatively easy victory at Yag'Dhul and seized Thyferra before linking up with the rebellious worlds of Cilpar and Mrlsst (both sites of earlier actions by Rogue Squadron) and opening relations with the neutral forces of Herglic Space. Behind Nantz's front lines, Delvardus tried to retake Sullust and was badly defeated by First Fleet elements under the command of a bold Sullustan captain named Sien Sovv. Secure in his position, Nantz sent a task force up the Rimma to support the Sullustans. Delvardus lost a series of lightning-quick battles on the perimeter of his territory and fled into the Deep Core.

In the north Ackbar handed temporary command of the Third Fleet to Kalback and Willham Burke, who sought to sever Teradoc's forces from the Core. Leading from the Mon Cal Star Cruisers *Justice* and *Remember Alderaan,* they defeated Teradoc's task force at Togoria, then fought their way to Lantillies, where they linked up with Contruum's defense forces to establish a beachhead on the Perlemian. From there, Burke pushed Coreward to Chazwa, where his forces met those of Admiral Ledre Okins, based at Colla. The two admirals stalked each other through a lengthy series of

raids and feints before Burke tricked Okins into diverting key units of his fleet to Pindra, where he ensnared them in a grav trap laid among the system's tumbling asteroids. Burke then ran Okins down at Colla and destroyed him, opening the way to the New Republic enclave at Brentaal.

Kalback had less luck, however—at Corsin, his attempt to seize a beachhead on the Hydian Way failed, as Zsinj's Super Star Destroyer *Iron Fist* drove his forces out of the system. He retreated to Obroa-skai, where his warships were added to the New Republic's Rapid Response Task Force, commanded by Luke Skywalker. It fell to Kalback and Skywalker to eliminate the mysterious warlord known as Shadowspawn, whose TIE defenders had launched a series of vicious raids on New Republic worlds in the Inner Rim, Expansion Region, and Mid Rim. With the aid of Mandalorian Protectors led by Fenn Shysa, Shadowspawn was killed—as was Kalback.

In 6 ABY Nantz moved in force against the isolated Prentioch, who was taken prisoner after a siege at Bomis Koori. The Western Reaches were now firmly in New Republic hands, leaving Nantz free to plot the conquest of the Southern Core. The Fourth Fleet's Massa was killed in a savage battle with Kermen at Denon, but his successor, Admiral Chel Dorat, broke the Imperial lines, advancing the Corellian Run front to the edge of the Colonies.

The bulk of the fighting was undertaken by the Third Fleet, now reinforced by Ackbar and his cadre of Mon Cal officers. Burke and General Brenn Tantor took Reytha, Gyndine, and Commenor, placing the task forces of Burke, Dorat, and Nantz in position to advance into the Core. To the north, Ackbar hoped to push Zsinj up the Hydian and cut Coruscant off from the Loyalist systems of the New Territories and the Pentastar Alignment. The drive up the Hydian from Brentaal began well enough, with victories at Uviuy Exen and Drearia, but Zsinj's Raptors overwhelmed Ragab at Paqualis, further elevating the warlord's profile.

Checked, Ackbar ordered a move to Palanhi, setting up a push down the Namadii Corridor to Coruscant. Mindful of Imperial forces to Rimward, though, he sent Nammo and the *Defiance* to seize Bilbringi. There, Nammo was bested by Admiral Teren Rogriss, assisted by the 181st Imperial Fighter Wing under Turr Phennir. Zsinj remained a stubborn adversary, and Ysanne Isard still commanded numerous fortress worlds in the Core and Colonies. But years of constant pressure had brought the New Republic to Coruscant's doorstep.

WAR PORTRAIT: YSANNE ISARD

The head of the Senate Bureau of Intelligence, Armand Isard, believed that a strong and ruthless hand was needed to reform the Republic. He found that hand in Supreme Chancellor Palpatine, and raised his daughter Ysanne as an enthusiastic proponent of the New Order and its programs.

Ysanne spent much of her youth in her father's secret underground headquarters in Lusankya—a long-forgotten district of Galactic City buried beneath later developments and converted into a hidden SBI prison. Here, "defective citizens" were made more useful—the best Rebel spies were turned into brilliant double agents, and maverick Imperial personnel were retrained as obedient servants of the New Order.

By her twenties Ysanne Isard was one of Imperial Intelligence's best field agents, specializing in "dagger and fist" missions alongside her personal brute squad of ex-stormtrooper NCOs—men chosen for their physique rather than their intelligence, and widely believed to be Ysanne's lovers as well as her muscle. Agent Isard certainly had little time for a conventional social life, living entirely within the structure of the New Order.

The brute squad and her uses of them also marked a departure from her father's policy of subtle and civilized

ruthlessness. Ysanne appreciated new-generation Imperial projects such as the *Executor* and the Tarkin Doctrine in a way that her father never could, and when Armand Isard attempted to overthrow Palpatine, Ysanne unhesitatingly betrayed him, and was rewarded with his role as director of Imperial Intelligence.

Isard's power was officially circumscribed by a group of powerful advisers known as the Ubiqtorate. The young Isard made no argument about this arrangement, perhaps because she knew its real purpose was to allow her to monitor *their* behavior; those who attempted to use the Intelligence apparatus for their own ends were quickly reassigned to Lusankya. Isard rose steadily until she oversaw the entire Imperial security apparatus, suppressing elite intrigues and civic unrest alike.

Isard moved swiftly after Endor, declaring martial law on Imperial Center and using stormtroopers to suppress pro-Rebel agitation before it became a popular uprising. The fact that none of the other surviving Imperial leaders had even reacted to the protests convinced her they were incapable of leading the New Order, and she quickly engineered the fall of Sate Pestage, General Paltr Carvin, and Grand Moff Hissa.

By 5 ABY Isard was the effective ruler of the Empire. Although she allowed the toothless Ruling Council to remain as a notional legislature, it was the director of Intelligence who now boasted a permanent escort from the Imperial Royal Guard, a visible symbol of her acceptance as quasi-Empress by the remains of the New Order hierarchy.

But she was trapped within a shrinking territory—a trap she sought to escape. Her retreat from Coruscant in 7 ABY was a ploy to overextend the New Republic in the Core, one that nearly succeeded—as did her attempt to destabilize the New Republic and destroy Rogue Squadron during the so-called Bacta War. Even when defeated at Thyferra, she managed to disappear, assembling Loyalists and warlords who continued the military advance against the New Republic after Grand Admiral Thrawn's defeat.

At this point, however, she was contacted by agents of the clone Emperor, and sternly ordered to personally recapture her former command ship, the Super Star Destroyer *Executor II,* which had acquired the name of *Lusankya* after being buried at enormous cost and effort on the site of her father's old headquarters.

Isard must have known that stealing the galaxy's largest warship from a New Republic dockyard at Bilbringi was a suicide mission, but she never hesitated to obey. Just hours before her forces staged their successful attack on

Coruscant, she was killed in a chaotic firefight aboard her former flagship.

New Republic officials strenuously denied rumors that Isard had survived and was being held without trial in a secret facility. But privately, those same officials conceded that "the idea does offer a certain poetic justice."

THE PENTASTAR ALIGNMENT

Appointed Grand Moff of Oversector Outer after the death of Wilhuff Tarkin, Ardus Kaine believed that the destiny of humanity and the Empire lay among worlds unspoiled by the weak, pro-alien policies of the Republic. Toward that end, he moved the headquarters of his oversector—the largest in the Empire, though many of its trouble spots also belonged to overlapping oversectors—from Tarkin's homeworld of Eriadu to distant Entralla, in the New Territories. Kaine was loyal to Palpatine and proved one of the more effective Grand Moffs, even as he openly favored the New Territories in allocating military forces and economic benefits, citing security as justification for ordering lucrative tax breaks and deals to lure key Imperial corporations into opening subdivisions, joint ventures, and branch offices within the region.

When Palpatine died at Endor, Kaine ordered Scourge Squadron, the task force of Imperial Star Destroyers at the heart of Oversector Outer's defenses, to regroup at Entralla. Between Scourge's twenty-four Star Destroyers, led by the *Reaper*, and the hundreds of capital ships assigned to the New Territories' sectors, Kaine controlled one of the most powerful starfleets in the galaxy.

It took awhile for Sate Pestage to realize that Kaine's starfleet was no longer his to command. At first Kaine simply ignored the Imperial regent's inquiries; later, he dismissed them. With the Rebels triumphant and central authority crumbling, the totality of Oversector Outer was indefensible; under his guidance, the New Territories would flourish. Kaine warned that the Core Worlds would fall, and invited Imperial forces to join him in a new cradle of human civilization. He was unmoved by the Ruling Council's accusations that the Outer Rim was only indefensible because of his dereliction of duty; he was done defending decadent alien civilizations and foolish ideas about galactic unity.

Disputes with neighboring warlords and New Republic forces persuaded Kaine to consolidate his holdings further. In 4 ABY he met with the Moffs of fourteen New Territories sectors and a quintet of Imperial corporations at Muunilinst and signed a treaty creating the Pentastar Alignment. (Outside the Alignment's borders, Moffs continued to rule their sectors in the name of the Ruling Council.)

Kaine sought to eliminate some of the inefficiencies that had plagued the Empire. The Alignment was divided into two arms: Order and Enforcement. The heart of Enforcement was the Pentastar Patrol, made up of former Imperial Navy forces, supplemented by a fleet of six-hundred-meter *Enforcer*-class picket cruisers built by the Jaemus shipyards, home of the Pentastar subdivisions of Kuat Drive Yards and Sienar Fleet Systems. The Alignment was governed by the Chamber of Order, led by Kaine and consisting of the Moffs and key corporate officials.

The New Republic largely left the Alignment alone as it defeated warlords elsewhere in the galaxy, a drumbeat of victories that troubled many in the Alignment. Its former Imperials had seen Kaine as the Empire's brightest hope, and assumed one day his warships would return to the Core Worlds in force. But that hadn't happened, and every month the Empire's prospects dimmed further.

Pestage died, Imperial Center and the Core fell into New Republic hands, and Ysanne Isard was believed dead. In 8 ABY Zsinj was killed and High Admiral Teradoc fled the Greater Maldrood for the Deep Core. The new seat of Imperial power was Orinda, where Ars Dangor led a resurrected Ruling Council. But the Council's hold on power was tenuous, and a day of reckoning appeared imminent: Admiral Ackbar drove into the New Territories, seizing Ord Mantell, Ithor, and Agamar. New Republic forces now controlled territory perilously close to the Alignment. But still Kaine looked inward.

The Alignment was ripe for revolution—and it came in the person of Grand Admiral Thrawn, though he never claimed the title of Emperor. A series of victories over pirate bands and raids against Ackbar's forces rallied the Imperial military to his cause and won him the support of the D'Asta clan. Bitterly aware that the officers of the Pentastar Patrol saw Thrawn as the Empire's savior, Kaine agreed to give Thrawn control of the Alignment's forces, calling the arrangement a temporary military confederation. But he refused to hand over the *Reaper*, depriving Thrawn of a powerful flagship.

After Thrawn's death, Kaine sought to shore up his support, swearing before the Chamber of Order that he would continue the Grand Admiral's cause. A year later, he was forced to prove it: The reborn Emperor summoned Kaine to Byss, where the former Grand Moff acknowledged Palpatine's authority. Kaine died at Palanhi when his shuttle was ambushed, supposedly by New Republic E-wings.

The Alignment's architect was no more; in 12 ABY Gilad Pellaeon asked the Chamber of Order to accept annexation by his Empire—whose borders were largely the same as the chunk of the New Territories that Kaine initially decided to defend. Pellaeon defended this latest incarnation of the Empire valiantly, but could not hope to hold out against the swelling power of the New Republic. In 17 ABY New Republic forces seized the Empire's eastern holdings, pushing Pellaeon back into the eight sectors around Bastion that had been the heart of the Alignment. Those eight sectors would endure as the Imperial Remnant. Ardus Kaine had dismissed the Empire and seen the Alignment as its successor. But in the end, his efforts ensured the Empire's survival in the very sectors he had defended.

WAR PORTRAIT: ZSINJ

The son of a shipyard mechanic from Fondor, Zsinj was dismissed by his instructors and peers at Prefsbelt as a dull sort. His most notable trait was that he had no first name, following an ancient tradition from his Fondorian caste.

In fact, Zsinj was a gifted linguist, mathematician, and businessman, as well as a skilled tactician and engineer. Hyperintelligent, eccentric, and often bored, he adopted various unlikely personas over the course of his career—thus confusing potential rivals, and keeping himself entertained.

Claiming he wanted to become a great warrior, Zsinj accepted command of a Victory Star Destroyer in Quelii sector. Few other officers saw glory in helming an old cruiser on a mapping patrol, but Zsinj proved effective on mission after mission, rising to become Grand Moff of the Quelii Oversector, High Admiral of Crimson Command, and one of the select few officers to earn the ceremonial rank of Warlord of the Empire. When he was charged with controlling the Rimward stretch of the Hydian Way and conquering the Drackmarians, his Sector Group was reinforced with a hundred refitted *Victory*-class Star Destroyers and the Star Dreadnought *Brawl*—making it the largest fleet in the navy. Zsinj was now the very model of a modern Imperial governor.

After Endor, Zsinj refused to obey the Ruling Council, built up his forces, and sent out agents to recruit other Imperial officers—as well as pirates, mad scientists, and corrupt business partners. Now sporting a well-tended mustache and a theatrical uniform, Zsinj brought together unlikely allies including the buccaneering courtesan Leonia Tavira, the Dathomir-born Inquisitor Lanu Pasiq, and the Hutt economist Teubbo.

The key to Zsinj's power was the *Brawl*, now renamed the *Iron Fist* after the elderly Victory Star Destroyer that had been his first command. But Zsinj saw his domain as a successor to the Empire, not its continuation. He formed his own elite military, known as the Raptors, and outfitted them with armor, starfighters, and warships created in his shipyards. Zsinj's Raptors stopped the New Republic's initial probes of his territory, but his pride drew him into war with the former Rebels nonetheless.

After Coruscant fell, many former Imperials supported Zsinj—but he also attracted the full attention of the New Republic, which could no longer ignore the well-armed warlord of the Hydian Way. To defeat Zsinj, the New Republic turned to its own maverick geniuses, Han Solo and Wedge Antilles. In 7 ABY they almost destroyed the *Iron Fist* at Selaggis; then Solo stumbled on Dathomir, thanks to a subtle tip-off from the Drackmarians. With the support of a Hapan fleet, he destroyed both the *Iron Fist* and Rancor Base.

Without its ruling genius—and his Super Star Destroyer—Zsinj's revived Empire fell apart, ravaged by the Imperial Remnant and the New Republic.

Zsinj at the height of his glory (Chris Scalf)

FELINX-AND-RODUS AT BRENTAAL

For the New Republic, the Battle of Brentaal was the most important fight between Endor and the Liberation of Coruscant. Brentaal was the greatest hyperlane crossroads in the Core; a victory there would place Rebel units within striking distance of the capital and limit the Empire's access to the eastern and southern quadrants.

Ysanne Isard, the director of Imperial Intelligence, saw it rather differently. If she could engineer a Rebel victory at Brentaal, she could overthrow the regency of Sate Pestage, weaken the Ruling Council, and position herself to seize the throne. By allowing the enemy to take and hold a key Core world, she would also draw the New Republic's leaders and soldiers into exposed positions, where they would be vulnerable to her planned campaign of military and political subversion.

Isard called her plan Project Ambition.

The New Republic committed their very best to the liberation of Brentaal. The X-wings of Rogue Squadron spearheaded the campaign, followed by the assault starfighters of General Horton Salm's Aggressor Wing and the infiltrators of Kapp Dendo's Commando Team One—all backed up by an invasion fleet led by the Star Cruiser *Independence,* with Admiral Ackbar himself in command.

The Imperials defended Brentaal with a trio of Star Destroyers and a fortified moon base, but Isard's plan depended on less conventional assets: an inept and indecisive admiral named Lon Isoto, the TIE interceptors of the legendary 181st Fighter Group, and the pride of Baron Soontir Fel.

The essence of Isard's scheme was simple—Isoto would lose the battle, but Fel, the 181st's renowned commander, would win several tactical victories along the way, making the Imperial defeat appear convincing. The details, of course, were far more complex.

Isoto obligingly bungled the initial phase of the defense. He would have bungled the next phase, too, but Fel's fighters won the second round, almost preventing the Rebels from landing on the surface—almost, but not quite. Isoto ordered them to pull back too soon—and as Isard had predicted, Fel was too honorable to disobey a personal order from a fleet admiral, no matter how inept.

Isoto, predictably, hailed Fel as a hero.

Next morning, Rogue Squadron moved on the capital. Once again, Isoto bungled the defense; once again, the 181st fought well and nearly won the battle—and once again, Isoto

threw away their gains. This time, he had been duped by Isard into ordering the entire Imperial force into a full retreat.

Fel had had enough. He ordered his TIEs to pull out as commanded, but remained behind at Vuultin and defected to the New Republic.

That seemed like a disaster for the Empire, but Isard was pleased. She had suspected that a conspiracy of military commanders was about to offer Fel the throne, which he very well might have claimed. And even had he refused, Fel's vision of what the Empire should be would have eventually led him to oppose her manipulation of what it was. Now he had effectively taken himself out of her way; the military's plans to seize power were thrown into confusion; Isoto was dead, shot on Isard's orders; and Pestage knew he could no longer retain control of the Ruling Council.

There was no one in a position to stop Isard from taking power, and from implementing her plan to save the Empire. All in all, she reflected, it had been well worth a planet and a few days' work.

BACTA

A salve that could heal a startling number of species, bacta revolutionized medicine and, inevitably, became a precious commodity that many galactic powers sought to control.

Bacta wasn't a single substance, but a compound. Its basis was a lotion used by the Vratix species of Thyferra to heal wounds. Bacterial particles of alazhi and kavam were spun into this lotion, which was then mixed with a colorless liquid called ambori. Bacta, it was believed, mimicked the body's vital fluids; when patients were suspended in tanks of it, the alazhi and kavam particles coated wounds and caused rapid tissue regrowth. Days in a bacta tank could heal wounds that might otherwise have been fatal, with the only side effects a sickly-sweet smell that lingered in the mouth and nasal passages. In situations where a rejuvenation tank wasn't practical, bacta could be applied through patches, though its effectiveness was reduced.

Bacta's properties became general knowledge around 4100 BBY, and vaulted the insectoid Vratix to galactic prominence. Vratix excreted a curious chemical called denin, which altered their coloration to reflect their moods, and were known for being slightly telepathic. Scientists argued for eons about the possibility of a connection between these characteristics and the nature of bacta.

The Empire carefully controlled the production of bacta, ensuring that it stayed limited to two bacta producers, the Zaltin and Xucphra. Ysanne Isard released the Krytos virus on Coruscant in 7 ABY and then gained control of the Xucphra Corporation and Thyferra, giving herself control of the bacta supply when it was desperately needed. The Thyferran government refused to move against Isard, and the New Republic felt it couldn't depose an elected planetary leader, even if she were a psychotic Imperial with her own Super Star Destroyer. That task fell to Rogue Squadron, whose pilots resigned their New Republic commissions to pursue an ostensibly private war against Isard. The Rogues allied themselves with a Vratix resistance group, disabled the *Lusankya,* and reclaimed control of the bacta supply for Zaltin.

Many a soldier had the disorienting experience of waking up suspended in bacta, wearing a breath mask and trying to reconstruct what had happened. Luke Skywalker recuperated in bacta after his mauling by a wampa and near-fatal exposure to Hoth's icy night, and veteran Rogue pilot Hobbie Klivian suffered so many injuries and spent so much time in a bacta tank that his fellow Rogues jokingly accused him of loving the stuff.

WAR PORTRAIT: WEDGE ANTILLES

Wedge Antilles was synonymous with Rogue Squadron and often acclaimed as the best starfighter pilot in the galaxy. The Corellian tried to deflect such honors, insisting that he'd flown with better pilots in Luke Skywalker and Soontir Fel, but it was hard to argue: No one else had the silhouettes of two Death Stars among his fuselage's kill markers.

Orphaned at seventeen, Antilles joined the Rebellion after an Imperial bombardment killed his girlfriend Mala Tinero. He survived the Death Star run at Yavin and formed Rogue Squadron with Skywalker, taking over its leadership after Luke turned to his Jedi studies. He stole the shuttle *Tydirium* used to infiltrate the Imperial lines at Endor and flew as Red Leader in the showdown with Emperor Palpatine, helping Lando Calrissian destroy the second Death Star. He then led Rogue Squadron on dozens of missions as the New Republic eliminated the warlords, took Coruscant, and then held it against repeated threats.

Though Antilles had never wanted anything except to fly a starfighter, he eventually bowed to the inevitable and took a role in fleet operations, commanding Rogue Squadron from the bridge of the Super Star Destroyer *Lusankya*. He retired after a stint as chief of staff of Starfighter Command,

hoping to spend the rest of his years with his wife, Iella Wessiri, and daughters.

It wasn't to be: The Yuuzhan Vong invaded the galaxy, forcing Antilles to come out of retirement. A second retirement was also short-lived: He was imprisoned by the Galactic Alliance as tensions between Coruscant and Corellia exploded into war. Wedge escaped and found himself commanding the Corellian Defense Force against his best friend Tycho Celchu and his daughter Syal, who were flying for the Galactic Alliance. Increasingly disgusted with the Corellian leadership, Antilles resigned and offered his assistance to the Jedi Order instead.

Though Antilles could be chilly in the cockpit, the Rogues found him an approachable, affable commander outside of it, one who tried to shrug off his fame and accomplishments. Still, many observed that there was a sadness about him that never quite seemed to lift.

Only Wedge's few close friends understood where that shadow came from: Antilles had started killing men when he was in his teens, and never stopped. Countless Imperial pilots—many of them young, scared, or both—died under his guns, as did pirates, Yuuzhan Vong, and others. Innocents died, too, when the Rogues fought above cities or had to hit military targets in civilian areas. And as a squadron commander, Antilles was forced to send inexperienced pilots into combat against long odds. Their deaths, too, were on his head.

Antilles accepted that this was his job—he was a killer who trained others to become killers, and he never lost his belief that eliminating those who would harm innocents made the galaxy a better place. But every time he turned an enemy fighter into a ball of flame, sent a torpedo winging across a cityscape, or ordered a green pilot to engage a hostile formation, he prayed that it would be the last time.

THE TAKING OF KUAT

Kuat was one of the Empire's crown jewels—the home system of Kuat Drive Yards, chief supplier of the Empire's warships, and one of the galaxy's most efficient shipyards. Capturing Kuat—preferably with its shipyards and orbital manufacturing facilities intact—would be a giant step forward in the effort to defeat the Empire.

The New Republic tried to take over the system in 4 ABY and again in 7 ABY, only to be foiled by such adversaries as Boba Fett, Tyber Zann, and Zsinj. It wasn't until Zsinj's death

in 8 ABY that the New Republic was finally able to seize the system.

After Zsinj died, Kuat was one of a handful of Imperial fortress worlds remaining in the Core, along with the likes of Corellia, Chasin, and Rendili. Yet most of the Imperial warships guarding Kuat had departed for the New Territories, leaving Kuat to rely on its own defenses.

Those defenses were formidable, however: The Kuati Sector Forces had been among the strongest in the galaxy for centuries, and KDY had always employed its latest designs for self-defense. More than a dozen Star Destroyers defended Kuat, as did the Star Dreadnought *Aurora* and a trio of battlecruisers—the *Event Horizon, Stellar Halo,* and *Luminous.* And one of the Empire's best commanders, Admiral Teren Rogriss, had been sent from Orinda to take the *Aurora*'s helm.

Wedge Antilles, Airen Cracken, and Ral'Rai Muvunc, the Twi'lek minister of commerce, engineered the plan that finally captured Kuat. The New Republic directed an impressive array of Mon Cal Star Cruisers to Horthav, a staging system just minutes away from the system, where they waited for the rest of the plan to come to fruition.

Under Cracken's supervision, New Republic slicers had worked painstakingly for months to insert astromechs into the KDY droid pool and get them aboard key Kuati warships. Those droids had loaded an ingenious coded virus into the computer networks of five warships, then erased all trace of their malignant programming. When the virus was ready to activate, a transmission went out from the *Event Horizon*—not to Horthav but to another nearby staging system, Venir.

There a squadron of A-wings commanded by Tycho Celchu jumped into the Kuat system. Surprise Squadron, as Celchu called it, had been fitted with experimental ion torpedoes that packed a ferocious punch. Within minutes the *Luminous* and three Star Destroyers were struggling to get their systems back online—only to find that the *Event Horizon* and four other Star Destroyers had locked down their flight hangars and turned their weapons on the other Kuati ships.

Now it was Muvunc's turn. He hailed the KDY directors with a curious demand: an emergency shareholder meeting. Muvunc asked the puzzled directors to review a series of financial transactions that had been made over the last eight months. KDY stock had been essentially valueless for years given the Empire's stranglehold on the megacorp's affairs, but a number of private trusts and investment companies had bought up small collections of shares from discouraged KDY investors, after which they were acquired in turn by a holding company. Muvunc explained that he was the chief executive of that company, and now controlled 34 percent of KDY.

When the flummoxed directors objected that control of KDY was currently a military matter, Muvunc invited them to consider the situation: In just minutes, the New Republic had taken nine warships out of the fight. The Empire might control KDY, but Orinda was tens of thousands of light-years away, while the Mon Cal Star Cruisers could be in-system in minutes. Kateel of Kuhlvult, KDY's chairman, dismissed Muvunc haughtily—but three other board members promptly voted their 18 percent of KDY shares in favor of surrender to the New Republic.

Rogriss and his command crew were permitted to withdraw and allowed safe passage back to Orinda. It looked like the New Republic had won an enormous victory without a single pilot being killed. But other forces were at work within KDY, too. Within hours of Kuat's surrender, Imperial agents activated from deep cover: The *Aurora* and the *Stellar Halo* engaged their hyperdrives and streaked into Kuat's sun. More agents triggered explosions that ripped through the yards, then abducted KDY's key designers and fled for the Deep Core aboard the partially completed *Eclipse*.

"The best way to have many opportunities is to seize a few."
—Traditional Corellian proverb

NEW REPUBLIC FLEET ORGANIZATION

The Imperial Navy's primary missions had been invasion and occupation, but the New Republic Fleet would concentrate on peacekeeping, patrols, and defense against external attacks, while complementing Planetary Security Forces that answered to sector authorities. That meant the New Republic Fleet would be smaller than the Imperial Starfleet, with a focus on rapid response rather than overall firepower. It would be built around starfighters, with capital ships playing two principal roles: providing support for fighter squadrons, and engaging enemies at long range while fighters sped in for strikes.

In practice, the early organization of the New Republic Navy emphasized flexibility, with preexisting squadrons and flotillas remaining intact and local loyalties taken into account. Battle groups were designed so they could be shifted within the four major fleets and area commands as required or sometimes deployed independently—the Solo Command that fought Warlord Zsinj was perhaps the most famous example of this.

Planetary assault became the most common mission profile, with Special Forces repurposed as bridgehead commandos, while a larger New Republic Army was created for occupation and peacekeeping duties.

The biggest challenge was creating a truly unified navy out of disparate units with contrasting regulations, tactics, and traditions. To achieve this, the squadrons that had not been part of Alliance Fleet Command were largely broken up, with ships and crews sent to different units. This provoked some opposition—the Bothan Combined Clans and the Corellian government-in-exile responded by withdrawing most of their units from the navy, but Admiral Ackbar was content to let them go. Fleet integration would now proceed even faster.

By 8 ABY the First Fleet guarded reconquered Coruscant, while the other three fleets had become permanent regional commands based at Elom, Kashyyyk, and Bothawui, fully integrated into the federal military. This arrangement served the New Republic valiantly against Thrawn, the Dark Empire, and the continuing threat of the warlords. By 12 ABY the battle group and squadron forces met Ackbar's exacting standards for strength, unity, and discipline, and a more serious military reorganization could begin.

The army—which had suffered badly in Operation Shadow Hand—was abolished. Many of its responsibilities and resources were reallocated to local defense forces, and all federal military forces were placed under the four fleet commands as part of a fully integrated Defense Force. The battle groups became subcommands with defined sectors, with large forces blockading the main Imperial holdouts and smaller squadrons assigned to peacekeeping patrols inside New Republic territory.

One battle group in each fleet served as a mobile reserve, but temporary reinforcements could turn each of these into a powerful fighting fleet, thanks to a new system of multi-role task forces.

These were standardized squadrons containing a mix of vessels with complementary capabilities, designed to perform equally well at different mission profiles. The standard

Kuat Drive Yards (Darren Tan)

deployment was three Star Destroyers or heavy cruisers, two light carriers, four escorts, and five attack ships, plus a line of seven scout and support vessels. Broad terms such as *cruiser* or *scout* could denote ships of varying capabilities, but standing orders mandated that the balance of ships in each task force should be kept roughly equal, rather than allowing the bias to slip too far toward battleships or pickets—it was the number of task forces in a battle group that defined its role, rather than the internal balance of ships.

After the reorganization led to the four fleets becoming increasingly tied down as territorial deployments, a separate rapid-reaction command was activated in 16 ABY, initially consisting of five task forces and numbered as the Fifth Roving Battle Group, but commanded by a flag officer with equal status to the fleet admirals. The "Fighting Fifth" was rapidly assigned full fleet status and by 19 ABY had been enlarged to full strength, with five hundred capital ships in five battle groups and many thousands of starfighters.

When he stepped down as Supreme Commander in 25 ABY, Ackbar called the Defense Force "the best navy I can imagine. It is modern, streamlined, and high-tech, unbeaten in any conflict since Endor. It has liberated the galaxy from the worst tyranny in known history, and is capable of handling any threat that the New Republic could imagine."

THRAWN'S STRATEGY

After the death of Warlord Zsinj at Dathomir and the dismantling of High Admiral Teradoc's Greater Maldrood, the sectors beyond the Hydian Way and the Inner Rim still swore loyalty to the Ruling Council, as did scattered systems in the so-called Borderlands between the Perlemian and the Hydian and a few lonely fortress worlds in the Core. But the New Republic had seized Ord Mantell and a corridor around the Celanon Spur, knifing into Imperial territory. Ardus Kaine's Pentastar Alignment was a strong state, but Kaine remained stubbornly isolationist, and the Imperial Moffs squabbled endlessly, paying the Ruling Council little mind.

The Empire's days seemed numbered. But a visionary leader was about to appear, one who would rekindle the memory of Imperial might during a glorious but all-too-brief campaign.

Thrawn, the last of Emperor Palpatine's Grand Admirals, returned from the Unknown Regions in 9 ABY and swiftly rallied the Empire's Moffs by promising to solve "the only puzzle worth solving—the complete, total and utter destruction of the Rebellion."

Though Thrawn was given nominal control of military forces by Ars Dangor's Ruling Council, the Pentastar Alignment's Kaine, and the Ciutric Hegemony's Prince-Admiral Krennel, in reality he was starved of assets: The Moffs lived in perpetual fear of not just the New Republic but also one another. Thrawn made little protest; his reorganization of the Empire's forces left the Moffs with adequate defenses and reinforced Orinda as the seat of Imperial power, while giving the Chiss Grand Admiral himself a decidedly modest complement. He took command of the fleet defeated at Endor, now reduced to just a dozen Imperial Star Destroyers, of which only six ships were judged fully loyal to Bastion (the *Chimaera, Death's Head, Judicator, Inexorable, Nemesis,* and *Stormhawk*), while the remainder formed a second force under the ambitious Captain Dorja of the *Relentless*. Thrawn accepted this state of affairs with equanimity, assuring Captain Gilad Pellaeon of the *Chimaera* that the opening stages of his campaign would require relatively few warships. If anything, he seemed to relish the challenge.

The first inkling the New Republic had that something was afoot came with raids against systems in the Borderlands: Individual Star Destroyers hit such systems as Saarn and Draukyze. After studying the New Republic's response to border incidents, Thrawn struck Obroa-skai, where he routed an Elomin-led task force that intercepted his ships, destroying four Assault Frigate Mark I's and three wings of X-wings. The brief battle helped cement Thrawn's legend as a cunning tactician, but the Grand Admiral was far more interested in the information his slicers had extracted from Obroa-skai's archives: the location of Palpatine's secret storehouse of artifacts.

After a side trip to Myrkr, Thrawn journeyed to the Mount Tantiss installation on Wayland, where he retrieved Spaarti cylinders, a prototype cloaking device, and an insane clone of the Jedi Jorus C'baoth, whom Thrawn had confronted in his younger days. Thrawn directed Imperial engineers to begin testing twenty-three cloaking devices big enough to hide a small capital ship and establish cloning facilities using the Spaarti cylinders. Used in conjunction with Force-blocking ysalamiri from Myrkr, they would allow him to grow clones to maturity in just weeks. Thrawn also made use of C'baoth's Force abilities—they allowed his warships to coordinate attacks with incredible precision.

The Grand Admiral stepped up his raids, hitting a trio of systems in Sluis sector and assaulting Nkllon, where he stole fifty-one mole miners from Lando Calrissian's mining operation. Now that he had all the pieces of his initial plan in place, Thrawn turned to the Moffs for additional assistance.

He augmented his armada with additional *Strike*-class cruisers, *Carrack*-class light cruisers, and TIE squadrons. His target was the New Republic shipyards at Sluis Van, where more than a hundred warships were being refitted as cargo haulers for a relief effort in Sluis sector.

A cloaked A-class bulk freighter delivered the TIE fighters and mole miners to Sluis Van. As the TIEs swarmed over the yards, the mole miners attached themselves to Mon Calamari Star Cruisers, Nebulon-B escort frigates, *Dreadnaught*-class heavy cruisers, Corellian corvettes, and other warships, inserting spacetroopers and army units into the empty ships. Overcoming minimal resistance, the saboteurs began steaming away from the Sluis Van docks in their stolen capital ships—which Thrawn's clones would crew.

The plan would have worked flawlessly if not for Calrissian's quick thinking. The mole miners' command codes had been hardwired, and Lando remembered them from tedious troubleshooting on Nkllon. He activated them remotely and watched as they burned through the stolen ships. Thwarted, Thrawn withdrew his forces. But he wasn't dissatisfied—the warships weren't his, true, but they'd been badly damaged.

Thrawn continued his raids, materializing in New Republic systems to assault planets and convoys before slipping away again. His was a classic variation on the ancient "stateless" strategy practiced by insurgents for millennia: The New Republic military had to keep every one of its systems safe or seem weak to panicked citizens; to look strong, Thrawn had only to stage high-profile raids and evade capture. The Rebels had once used the same strategy to erode the perception of Imperial power; now a rogue Imperial was using it against former Rebels.

But Thrawn wasn't content with playing pirate. He had another source of ships for his clones—the *Katana* fleet, a task force of two hundred Dreadnaughts lost before the Clone Wars when a hive virus drove its crews insane and the task force's captain jumped the ships blindly into hyperspace. The New Republic learned of Thrawn's target and the race for the lost fleet was on—a race Thrawn won, making off with 178 warships.

Now that Thrawn had his capital ships, his tactics changed. He began reclaiming territory, yet sleight of hand and misinformation remained his greatest weapons. He turned his attention to the Rimward precincts of the Corellian Run, where New Republic paranoia was running high. Feints at Ando, Filve,

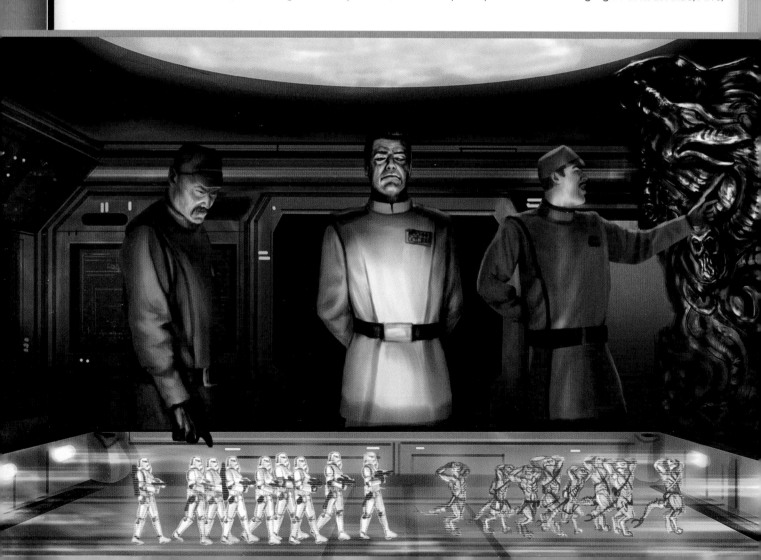

and Condre brought the warships of the New Republic out of their base at Ord Pardron, which Thrawn promptly leveled.

That same day he seized the agricultural world of Ukio with a cunning trick: Thrawn slipped cloaked heavy cruisers beneath the planet's shields, then fired his Star Destroyers' turbolasers at the shields in the exact spot beneath which the cruisers waited. C'baoth's Force abilities allowed the cloaked cruisers to open fire at the proper second, giving the illusion that the Star Destroyers' turbolaser blasts had passed right through the shield. Ukio promptly surrendered. Over the following days, Thrawn would use the trick against other worlds, but by then it was hardly needed: Word of his coming caused New Republic and neutral systems to hastily swear allegiance to the Empire.

Thrawn roared through the Outer Rim and sent his task forces down the Rimma Trade Route and the Namadii Corridor, the beginnings of a pincer movement on the Core. He then upped the stakes, raiding Coruscant itself. The raid did little damage, but Thrawn seeded the capital's orbit with twenty-two cloaked asteroids while dry-firing his tractor beams to make it seem as if 265 more had been deployed. Coruscant was trapped behind its planetary shields, which it dared not deactivate for fear that cloaked asteroids in decaying orbits would impact the planet. Until the New Republic could figure out just how many asteroids Thrawn had launched and ensure they'd all been destroyed, the capital was effectively besieged.

Thrawn's triumph was in sight. The Imperial forces in the New Territories awaited orders to move on the Core, while the inner systems' fortress worlds readied their forces to join his invasion fleets. In the Deep Core, the surviving warlords had heard of his campaign and began to stir. The New Republic's rapid-reaction fleets deployed to defend Coruscant, Mon Calamari, Kashyyyk, and Bothawui, as if a holo-documentary of their post-Endor gains were running in reverse.

Admiral Ackbar knew the New Republic desperately needed a victory, one that would reverse Thrawn's gains and prove to frightened citizens that he had no superweapons at his disposal, just trickery involving cloaked ships and asteroids. Ackbar focused on Bilbringi, a key Imperial shipyard that possessed one of the galaxy's few crystal gravfield traps. (A CGT was a sensor suite that could detect cloaked ships—Bilbringi's had been used on secret expeditions into the Unknown Regions ordered by Palpatine.)

The New Republic feinted at Tangrene in the hope of drawing Thrawn's forces away from Bilbringi, but the Grand Admiral wasn't fooled, and awaited Ackbar in force: Some two dozen Star Destroyers were deployed, as were eight Interdictors, thirty Katana Dreadnaughts, numerous Strike and Carrack cruisers, and TIE fighters including the 181st. Against them, Ackbar had eleven Mon Cal Star Cruisers, two assault frigates, the Star Destroyer *Freedom,* various escort ships, and squadrons of X-wings, Y-wing bombers, A-wings, and B-wings.

Thrawn arranged several of his Interdictors to bring the New Republic forces out of hyperspace short of the shipyards, with additional Interdictors deployed to prevent them from escaping. That left Ackbar's task force struggling to re-form its lines under murderous fire. The New Republic received a badly needed break when a band of smugglers attacked the shipyards, forcing Thrawn to redeploy some of his Star Destroyers and starfighters to protect them, but by then Ackbar's forces were in disarray.

It was at that moment that disaster struck for the Empire. Thrawn had long relied upon his Noghri bodyguards, who had served Darth Vader and then the Empire in return for assistance saving their poisoned homeworld of Honoghr. But Leia Organa Solo had shown the Noghri they'd been duped—the Empire's efforts were actually continuing to poison Honoghr. Thrawn's Noghri bodyguards had waited for the right moment to betray him; at Bilbringi, one stabbed him through the heart.

Captain Pellaeon briefly continued to give orders to the fleet, but word spread that Thrawn had been killed, and the Imperials began to panic—a New Republic victory at Bilbringi could mean the end of the Empire. With requests for new orders pouring in, Pellaeon ordered a retreat. Thrawn's campaign was over, and the New Republic had been spared.

Arguments raged for decades among galactic historians about what would have happened had Thrawn lived. Ackbar insisted until his death that his forces had recovered from the initial attacks, and the best Thrawn could have managed was a draw—which considering the mismatch between the two powers would have been as good as a defeat. But many military historians maintained that Ackbar had stood on the edge of ruin. Pellaeon remembered that he and Thrawn had been close to summoning reinforcements from neighboring Imperial sectors to destroy both Ackbar and Rogue Squadron, and the Pentastar Alignment's Grand Moff Kaine insisted he had decided to commit his warships (including the Super Star Destroyer *Reaper*) when word came of Thrawn's death.

WAR PORTRAIT:
GRAND ADMIRAL THRAWN

From *Mitth'raw'nuruodo Reconsidered: A Patriot's Perspective*, by Lenang O'Pali, 55 ABY:

Thanks to decades of contact with the Chiss, we now understand much more than our predecessors did about Mitth'raw'nuruodo. To them, he was a red-eyed alien from a mysterious species from the Unknown Regions, known by the truncated name Thrawn. But these days we know the Chiss Ascendancy as a real place, not a name slapped on a blank spot on a map. And as we have come to better understand the Chiss, so we have come to better understand Mitth'raw'nuruodo.

He struck his contemporaries as noble, a being who spoke carefully and precisely in any of the many languages he knew. Yet we know he was a commoner who achieved adoption into one of the Chiss ruling families through his illustrious military service—then gave all of that up because of his beliefs and what he learned about the galaxy.

Since we obtained access to the records of the Empire of the Hand, we have known the basics of Mitth'raw'nuruodo's fateful encounter with Outbound Flight, the expedition into the Unknown Regions led by the Jedi Jorus C'baoth in the final days of the Republic. We know that Darth Sidious sent a Trade Federation task force commanded by Kinman Doriana to destroy Outbound Flight, but that Doriana ran afoul of Mitth'raw'nuruodo's forces and was defeated. We know that Doriana told him of the peril posed by the Far Outsiders—beings we now know all too well as the Yuuzhan Vong. We know that Mitth'raw'nuruodo heard of this peril from Darth Sidious himself. And we now know why Mitth'raw'nuruodo believed Sidious—because the Chiss had already encountered the Vong at Vun'Hanna and the Twilight Void.

Given what we now know, let me speak plainly: Mitth'raw'nuruodo was one of our greatest heroes, a brave and principled being who devoted his life to preparing for the Vong.

He broke with his own people—at considerable cost to his own reputation and standing—to accept service in the military of the Empire, whose leaders often treated him with prejudice and disdain. We know he spent much of that service beyond the galactic frontier, becoming a bulwark against the invasion that only he and a very few knew was coming. He created the Empire of the Hand. He crushed the Ssi-ruuvi Imperium before it could attack our civilization in force. And I have no doubt that he encountered and destroyed enemies whose secrets he took to his grave.

But if so, my critics ask, why was Mitth'raw'nuruodo's first act upon returning to wage war against the New Republic?

Consider: When Mitth'raw'nuruodo returned, the New Republic was clearly the dominant power of the galaxy, with the Empire in sharp decline. Mitth'raw'nuruodo sought to overturn that order. He plunged the galaxy into chaos. Why? If our civilization needed to be prepared, why not serve the New Republic? Why not awaken its leaders to the peril drawing ever closer to the galactic edge? Why further weaken the galaxy through the loss of so many lives and the destruction of so many military assets?

The answer is that Mitth'raw'nuruodo took Mon Mothma and the rest of her cadre at their word. He believed they were creating another Republic, and this new government would be much the same as the last one to bear that name. It, too, would babble about democracy and diversity while doing nothing to combat dissent, inefficiency, and corruption. Such failings might be tolerable in a civilization with centuries to engage in self-improvement, but there has never been such a civilization—and anyway, the Vong were coming.

Which brings us to Emperor Palpatine.

During Mitth'raw'nuruodo's campaign, the galaxy thought Palpatine dead. We now know he was not—he had returned to a clone body and was plotting his return on Byss. But did Mitth'raw'nuruodo know that? I firmly believe that he did—and that it was Palpatine who called him back.

I am baffled by critics who accept Mitth'raw'nuruodo's account of his discussion with Palpatine about the Far Outsiders, yet refuse to revise their opinions about either man. They ignore what Mitth'raw'nuruodo reported Palpatine believed: that the weak Republic would be destroyed by the Vong, and had to be reforged into an orderly, militarized society able to resist them. They refuse to consider the possibility that the Empire's apparent brutality and ruthlessness were necessary parts of preparing for that terrible war. Why do they refuse to do so? Because that would lead them to the only logical conclusion: that Palpatine was right.

Recent galactic history is not the struggle for freedom our children are force-fed—or should I style it Force-fed—on HoloNet channels controlled by Mothmatist news agencies. Rather, it is a succession of unlucky events that left our civilization defenseless against the Vong. The second Death Star promised to eliminate the sedition and separatism of the Rebellion, but it was destroyed and the Emperor was betrayed and slain, forced into an agonizing convalescence on Byss. During his long absence, a continuation of the destructive conflict between the Empire and the Rebellion battered down the galaxy's defenses.

Mitth'raw'nuruodo responded to his Emperor's call and tried to rebuild the tattered Empire.

Amazingly, against all odds, he nearly did so. But for the treachery of a Noghri, he would have prepared the galaxy for Palpatine's return and then helped restore the defenses they had worked so hard to build.

Even so, there was another chance. Palpatine had another clone body—and so did Mitth'raw'nuruodo. But both were lost—Palpatine was gunned down by the Corellian gangster Han Solo, of all people, and Luke Skywalker and Mara Jade destroyed Mitth'raw'nuruodo's defenseless clone at Nirauan, a decade after his defeat at Bilbringi.

The Mothmatists see these events as victories. But if they were honest, they would see them for what they really were: missed chances to prevent the ruin of so much that we held dear. Our Emperor and our Grand Admiral were taken from us before their plans could be brought to fruition, and as a result we stood naked before the Yuuzhan Vong and the bleak destiny they sought for us.

THE DARK EMPIRE

Airen Cracken famously remarked that the secret of being a successful intelligence analyst is being able to discern patterns that are there without imagining ones that aren't. Striking the right balance was rarely as challenging as it was in the months before Grand Admiral Thrawn's rampage through the galaxy, when New Republic Intelligence had to consider many strange reports.

The most worrisome report was that Admiral Feyet Kiez and his command crew had absconded from Anaxes with the Star Dreadnought *Whelm*. When Osted Wermis surrendered Anaxes to the New Republic soon thereafter, he admitted he was as baffled about Kiez's destination as anyone else. And there were other incidents to ponder. The warlord-turned-pirate Inos Fonada abandoned his bases in the Vatha sector and disappeared down the Corellian Trade Spine with his armada of scavenged Imperial warships. The top designers of an Imperial skunkworks on the fortress world of Kelada vanished, along with hundreds of schematics for experimental weapons. From the Pentastar Alignment to isolated Imperial satrapies, there were reports of Moffs, warlords, and fleet commanders gone missing, often with their warships.

New Republic Intelligence's initial thought was that one of the warlords hidden away within the Deep Core had gained

(CONTINUED ON PAGE 209)

ARMORY AND SENSOR PROFILE

CLOAKING DEVICES

Traditional cloaking devices used stygium gems from the Dreighton Nebula—a form of lightsaber crystal with the ability to warp perceptions around them. Known since at least 4000 BBY, stygium gems powered the cloaking technology used on Sith Infiltrator starships such as Darth Maul's *Scimitar* and the *Rogue Shadow*. However, declining stocks made their use increasingly limited, while sensors became more capable of detecting them. The last significant use of stygium cloaks was in the modified V38 starfighters of the TIE Phantom project. In 3 ABY the Empire's entire reserve of the crystals was destroyed with the Super Star Destroyer *Terror*.

An alternative to stygium was hibridium from Garos, employed in the research projects of Grand Admiral Demetrius Zaarin. Such efforts gained additional impetus after the destruction of the *Terror*, but hibridium cloaks proved to have prohibitive power and technology constraints, and were never truly practical.

The first commander to really use cloaking devices as more than a parlor trick was Grand Admiral Thrawn. It was long believed that his design was a perfection of the hibridium system, but while Thrawn initially pursued this angle, he acquired an alternative technology in 9 ABY, one believed to have been seized by the Empire from the Xi Char aesthete-corsairs. These cloaking devices required no special materials or large generators, and were undetectable by anything except a crystal grav trap sensor array—or a Jedi Master. The only downside was that the cloaking field was double-blind—what was inside could not see out.

With the assistance of the Jedi clone Joruus C'baoth, Thrawn used cloaked Star Destroyers and TIE fighters to devastating effect in his campaigns against the New Republic. Cloaking devices remained standard on Imperial warships for the next decade, but the technology was banned under the Bastion Accords in 19 ABY.

THE WORLD DEVASTATORS

Palpatine's grand vision for the Imperial military involved three basic elements: terror weapons to make the rabble cower in fearful obedience; capital ships and starfighter swarms to destroy any who chose armed resistance; and shipyards, factories, and raw material facilities to fuel this war machine. After his rebirth on Byss, the Emperor activated projects to integrate the three concepts into a single fearsome design.

The new Master of Imperial Projects was Umak Leth, who adapted factory ship designs to house molecular furnaces, a new technology from the Maw Installation. Inspired by hyperspace vortices, molecular furnaces consumed raw material and converted it to energy, which could then be reconstituted into whatever pattern was needed. The furnaces' vast energies also powered impregnable shields and powerful turbolasers, making Star Destroyer–sized factory ships into unstoppable battle stations called World Devastators.

The World Devastators were designed to operate in fleets, and capable of enlarging themselves by constructing extra hull sections in their onboard factories.

WORLD DEVASTATOR

The largest of them, General Titus Klev's command ship *Silencer-7*, grew to be thirty-two hundred meters long with a towering hull that stood fifteen hundred meters high, giving it the tonnage of a dreadnought. It boasted an armament of 125 heavy turbolasers and eighty proton torpedo launchers, plus two hundred anti-starfighter blasters and fifteen ion cannons.

There was no need now for mining shuttles, or for an assault fleet to pacify the target before the factory ship arrived. A Devastator simply powered across a battlefield, using its guns and shields to destroy enemy ships and vehicles and its tractor beams to grab the shattered vessels and feed them to the molecular furnaces. The onboard factories were modular, capable of being reconfigured in moments to produce anything the Empire might want—from probe droids to AT-ATs.

As the first stage of Operation Shadow Hand, the Devastators were unleashed against Mon Calamari. The civilization that had inflicted the most damage on the Empire would be obliterated, its curved artifacts remade into sharp-edged Imperial weapons.

But Palpatine knew that an ambitious commander with a

single Devastator could rapidly produce a battle fleet of his own. To guard against that, the entire fleet was governed by a single series of automated control codes. That proved the Devastators' undoing—the command codes were stolen by R2-D2, and the Rebels were able to deactivate the entire dark fleet.

Most of the Devastators were eliminated on Mon Calamari, but a small number were pressed into service by the Alliance, used for fleet support and reconstruction projects in the months that followed. Amid outcries about their continued use, they were scrapped by the New Republic around 12 ABY.

THE DEFENDER AND THE NEW CLASS PROGRAMS

The early New Republic military was a hodgepodge of the old Alliance fleet, Imperial warships captured or donated by sectors declaring themselves New Republic members, and ships produced by Allied Commands, most notably the Mon Calamari.

The first significant new capital ships designed for the New Republic appeared before Coruscant was retaken. The 1,250-meter *Republic*-class Star Destroyer's systems were designed by Walex Blissex, and far more cost-effective than those of its Imperial counterpart. The ship was billed as a Rendili StarDrive design—a bit of political theater intended to woo Rendili away from the Empire, as its bulbous, organic lines were a tip-off that it had been inspired and built by the Mon Calamari. Meanwhile, the 2,500-meter Bulwark Mark III battlecruiser was built for the New Republic by TransGalMeg using the old Techno Union design as a starting point.

Shortly after the fall of Coruscant, the New Republic unveiled the Defender program for new warship classes, a combination of smaller-platform capital ships and starfighters in keeping with New Republic military principles. The Defender ships would be built by individual shipbuilders under the aegis of Republic Engineering Corporation, a shipbuilders' consortium working in conjunction with the military.

The Defender starfighter (already in service) was a souped-up version of an old Incom design used for short-

NEBULA-CLASS STAR DESTROYER

ENDURANCE-CLASS FLEET CARRIER

range planetary defense. The *Defender*-class assault carrier was designed to house three wings of fighters. And the *Nebula*-class Star Destroyer (formally renamed the Defender once it was made part of the program) refined the core of Blissex's *Republic* design in a new angular hull, augmenting the earlier craft's firepower while shrinking its dimensions further to 1,040 meters, which earned the Nebula the tag "pocket Star Destroyer."

Later, a pair of new ship classes were added to the program, allowing two liberated shipbuilding worlds to contribute: Loronar designed and built the 400-meter *Belarus*-class cruiser, a rethinking of the versatile Strike class, while Kuat Drive Yards built the 275-meter *Corona*-class frigate, modeled after the Nebulon-B. (A contemporary of these new classes was the MC90 Star Cruiser, the first Mon Calamari design intended for other species.)

The Defender program was delayed by political distractions and the campaigns of Thrawn and the Dark Empire. When it resumed, it was as part of the New Class modernization effort. The New Class program extended the Defender principles: The *Nebula*-class Star Destroyer's basic design and hull were reused for the *Endurance*-class fleet carrier, while the *Defender*-class assault carrier was the basis of the new *Majestic*-class heavy cruiser. A quartet of new ships filled out the program: One basic 375-meter hull design was shared by the *Sacheen*-class escort cruiser and the *Hajen*-class fleet tender, while a 190-meter design gave rise to the *Agave*-class picket and *Warrior*-class gunship.

Neither program included battlecruisers or dreadnoughts, which the New Republic's military strategists saw as obsolete. But the lessons of the Dark Empire, the Battle of Orinda, and the Black Fleet Crisis forced a change in philosophy, leading to the Mon Calamari creating the *Mediator*-class battlecruiser and then the massive *Viscount*-class Star Defender.

(CONTINUED FROM PAGE 205)

the upper hand over his fellows. But New Republic Intelligence received regular reports about the likes of Harrsk, Delvardus, Teradoc, and the former Moff Foga Brill—and there was no indication they'd abandoned their scheming and skirmishing. And few of the former Imperials who'd disappeared had ties to those petty tyrants. Nor was Thrawn the hidden attractor—neither the *Whelm* nor any of the missing former Imperials played a role in his campaign.

The flurry of strange reports was largely forgotten in the chaotic months after Thrawn's death, as the New Republic sent its fleets back to the Outer Rim, eliminating the Ciutric Hegemony's Prince-Admiral Delak Krennel and seeking to take other chunks out of the rump Empire before the Ruling Council could reestablish control of its forces. That left the Core Worlds lightly guarded—and set the stage for disaster.

Out of the Deep Core came a trio of massive task forces of Star Destroyers, anchored by massive dreadnoughts the New Republic had thought destroyed or lost: four *Executor*-classes (including the missing *Whelm*), five Mandator IIIs and three *Vengeance*-classes. The New Republic mustered what forces it could in the Core, moving to check the incursion at Metellos—only to be surprised by a fleet of raiders sent to Coruscant by the Ruling Council, which also sent task forces across the Borderlands to Contruum and Columex. Beaten at Metellos and its capital, the New Republic fell back from the Core, and ground forces led by General Alix Balan marched triumphantly through the grandest boulevards of Coruscant.

But the Imperial forces then turned on one another in an orgy of senseless destruction. Imperial commanders who survived the Imperial Mutiny remembered that it began with the Ruling Council and the Moffs squabbling over the selection of a new Emperor, a disagreement that became a bloody free-for-all between those two groups, naval commanders, the Inquisitorius, COMPNOR, and the Imperial Security Bureau. But these facts seemed a poor summation: All agreed that a madness seemed to consume men who had worked patiently for years to restore the Empire. The *Whelm* and the Mandator III *Panthac* destroyed each other above Alsakan; the captain of the *Vengeance*-class dreadnought *Javelin* piloted his massive ship into the torpedo sphere guarding Chasin; and squadrons of robotic TIEs tore apart the Mandator III *Aculeus* at Drearia.

The New Republic struck back with raids into the Core, including ravaged Coruscant. There the architect of the horror and misery was revealed: Darth Sidious had somehow returned from death.

After becoming the Sith Lord's apprentice, Luke Skywalker

learned the truth: Sidious had found a way to preserve his spirit after the loss of his physical body. After dying at Endor, he had taken possession of one of many clone bodies kept in his secret citadel on Byss, at the heart of the Deep Core. It had taken Sidious years to rebuild his strength. Once he succeeded, he began to summon his faithful servants and activate long-dormant weaponries and shipyards secretly constructed in the Deep Core a generation earlier, assembling a massive fleet.

Sidious did nothing to stop the Imperial Mutiny, perhaps because he had weapons of his own: two massive *Eclipse*-class dreadnoughts and a new superweapon, the dreaded Galaxy Gun. He also unleashed his World Devastators upon the galaxy, doing terrible damage to the homeworld of the Mon Calamari, whose ruin he had sought for so long.

The Emperor died aboard the *Eclipse* at Da Soocha, but returned again in a deteriorating clone body during Operation Shadow Hand, a second wave of destruction overseen by his dark side servants. Sidious's final death came at Onderon, where the Jedi Empatojayos Brand sacrificed himself to drag the Sith Lord's struggling spirit into the Force, never to return.

The Dark Empire dissipated like a fever dream, with the New Republic returning to the Core and rebuilding Coruscant. But though the New Republic leadership mourned a year of terrors, the effect on the Empire was worse. The Imperial Mutiny shredded the Empire's fleets and killed many capable officers. The Empire would limp along under a succession of leaders, but its dreams of reconquering the galaxy were dead.

WAR PORTRAIT: GARM BEL IBLIS

Tough-minded and ferociously independent even by Corellian standards, Garm Bel Iblis was one of the architects of the Rebel Alliance, though political disagreements and his own pride caused him to turn his back on it for years.

In 35 BBY Bel Iblis became Corellia's Senator, and emerged as one of Palpatine's leading critics during the Separatist Crisis and the Clone Wars, openly questioning whether the repeated grants of emergency powers to the Supreme Chancellor were necessary and whether he could be trusted to relinquish them once the Separatist threat was extinguished.

Amid the bitter debate over the Military Creation Act, Bel Iblis and Corellia's ruling Diktat invoked *Contemplanys Hermi,* an obscure proviso in the Galactic Constitution that

The World Devastators ravage Mon Calamari (Stephan Martiniere)

dated back to the First Alsakan Conflict. *Contemplanys Hermi* allowed Corellia and its dependencies to withdraw from the Senate without relinquishing their status within the Republic—a measure that had historically caused the rest of the Senate to reconsider actions that Corellians thought perilous. But Bel Iblis's gamble didn't work: The Military Creation Act passed, and the galaxy was torn apart by war.

Corellia did its part for the Republic, sending task forces from its powerful sector fleet to beat back Separatist advances and aid the Jedi. But Bel Iblis no longer had any illusions about Palpatine. In secret meetings with Senators such as Bail Organa, Mon Mothma, and Padmé Amidala, he spoke openly and urgently about the need to oppose Palpatine's rule.

After the Republic became the New Order, Palpatine struck *Contemplanys Hermi* from the Constitution as an ancient relic, compelling Bel Iblis to return to the Senate. Bel Iblis soon became one of the Emperor's most dogged foes, speaking publicly about subjects that were forbidden in ways that had caused less powerful worlds' leaders to disappear.

When Mothma fled Coruscant and went into hiding, Bel Iblis knew his time was short. At Anchoron his wife and children were killed in an explosion engineered to eliminate him. Bel Iblis fled and was believed dead, though Organa

and Mothma knew he had survived, and continued to meet secretly with him to plan the resistance against the Empire.

Bel Iblis's Corellian Resistance became one of the most successful Rebel groups, and he was instrumental in the drafting and signing of the Corellian Treaty formally declaring the Alliance to Restore the Republic. But there were tensions between Bel Iblis and Mothma from the beginning: He suspected she was more interested in accumulating power than military victories, just as Palpatine had been in his time. A sharp disagreement over an Alliance attack at Milvayne led to a break between them, with Bel Iblis leaving to wage his own private war against the Empire. After the Battle of Endor, he warned his lieutenants to prepare for Mothma's declaration of herself as Empress. But Mothma did nothing of the sort, and soon Bel Iblis had to accept what his aides had known long ago: He had been mistaken about his former friend's motives.

For the proud Bel Iblis, knowing this was one thing—admitting it was something else entirely.

The way back came through a chance meeting with Han Solo and Lando Calrissian. Bel Iblis's own lieutenant urged Solo and Calrissian to persuade Mothma to ask Bel Iblis to come back—for the Corellian would never do so on his own.

Bel Iblis returned without the issue being settled, assisting the New Republic in its fight with Thrawn over the

Katana fleet. Mothma welcomed Bel Iblis back and made him a general, but the Chief of State had her own pride to overcome, and denied him a place on the Provisional Council. The breach wasn't repaired until Thrawn's assault on Coruscant, when Mothma herself asked Bel Iblis to take command of the planet's defenses from the overmatched Admiral Drayson. The proud Corellian had finally come home, and an old wound in the heart of the New Republic was healed.

THE BATTLE OF ORINDA AND THE IMPERIAL REMNANT

After the collapse of Operation Shadow Hand, Gilad Pellaeon was appalled by the state of the Empire. The Pentastar Alignment's Ardus Kaine was dead, the Moffs were divided, and the Ruling Council was a collection of petty would-be tyrants. The Empire had enough military strength to ensure its own security, but lacked a leader to use that strength wisely. The Dark Empire was succeeded by the Crimson Empire, led by the former Royal Guardsman Carnor Jax. But Jax's realm quickly fell apart, leaving the Moffs even weaker and more divided.

Pellaeon watched Jax's rise and fall from afar—despairing, he'd taken his own task force into the Deep Core and joined the service of High Admiral Teradoc, who commanded the largest fleet. But Teradoc and his rival warlords were even worse than the men Pellaeon had left behind, wasting their soldiers' lives on ludicrous quarrels among the densely packed stars at the heart of the galaxy. Eventually Pellaeon did find a potential leader to follow: Admiral Natasi Daala. Daala, too, was tired of useless squabbling—and with Pellaeon's help, she ended the infighting with vicious efficiency, luring the majority of the Deep Core warlords to a meeting and poisoning the lot.

Daala unified the Deep Core, but despite Pellaeon's warnings, she squandered her forces with a doomed campaign against the New Republic in 12 ABY, one that led to the loss of her Super Star Destroyer *Knight Hammer*. Humiliated, she handed authority over to Pellaeon and went into seclusion with a handful of ships and adherents. The Deep Core, Pellaeon decided, could never support a functioning society—at best it could be a refuge for Imperial ideals. It had to be abandoned.

But first, Pellaeon swore he would gather whatever hadn't been destroyed. First he sifted through the records of the warlords who'd served the reborn Emperor. Then, taking Daala's fleet, he surveyed the abandoned Imperial armories that hadn't been left unreachable by the shifting hyperspace lanes of the Deep Core, retrieving squadrons of robotic TIEs, caches of arms, and mines. In doing so, he made a breathtaking discovery: The Star Dreadnoughts *Megador* and *Dominion* had survived the war and been abandoned, empty but spaceworthy, at Harrsk's shipyard Deep 3.

Pellaeon decided to approach the Imperial Rim factions, confident that three dreadnoughts—the *Megador, Dominion,* and Kaine's *Reaper*—would be enough to defend the Empire against the New Republic. The Moffs agreed, making Pellaeon the Imperial military's Supreme Commander—and he immediately decided to put his forces to good use. The campaigns around Orinda would prove critical not only to the later history of the Empire but also to the development of dreadnoughts under the New Republic.

A graceful trade world, Orinda had emerged as one of the Empire's proudest holdings, serving as the headquarters of the Ruling Council until the New Republic reclaimed the planet after Thrawn's death.

Pellaeon saw Orinda as the ideal place to demonstrate to the New Republic that the Empire wouldn't simply vanish. Reclaiming Orinda and holding it, he felt, would prove an effective demonstration of Imperial power without being provocation enough to demand an overwhelming response.

Leaving the *Megador* at Agamar to defend against a New Republic attack from Celanon or Ithor, Pellaeon took the *Reaper* to Borosk, where he picked up a complement of fighters from the 181st Fighter Group, commanded by Turr Phennir, the Empire's greatest starfighter ace.

Pellaeon and Phennir swiftly took Orinda and six systems Coreward of it along the Entralla Route, holding the line at Lonnaw. Entrenched there, Pellaeon immediately dispatched emissaries to Ord Mantell, informing New Republic officials that he had secured the Empire's borders and retaken a world of great cultural importance to it; if the Empire's claim were respected, no further offensives would be launched.

Pellaeon was sincere, but the New Republic leadership feared yet another assault on the Core and responded forcefully, sending Wedge Antilles to the front aboard the Star Dreadnought *Lusankya*, accompanied by Rogue Squadron.

It was a controversial choice. The New Republic's military strategists had seen dreadnoughts as a relic of the Imperial past, preferring a combination of smaller-platform capital ships and starfighters—a philosophy that informed the Defender program. After her capture from Ysanne Isard, the *Lusankya* had been all but abandoned in the Scarl military shipyard, used as a medical research facility.

But nothing in the New Republic arsenal had been a match

THE ORINDA CAMPAIGN
AND THE IMPERIAL REMNANT

PELLAEON'S REORGANIZED
IMPERIAL REMNANT

Reaper
181st F. G. **1**

Dominion
6 Interdictors **11**

Reaper
181st F. G. **10**
vs.
Lusankya
Rogue Squadron
Endurance†
E-wings†

181st F. G.
vs
Rogue Squadron **7**

Reaper **5**

181st F. G. **8**
vs
Lusankya

Reaper
181st F. G. **6**
vs.
Lusankya
Rogue Squadron

Reaper **3**

181st F. G. **4**
ISD complement

Endurance **9**
E-Wings

Lusankya
Rogue Squadron **2**

BORDERS OF THE
NEW REPUBLIC
CONTROLLED SPACE

	New Republic Victory
	Imperial Victory
→	Imperial 12–13 ABY
	New Republic 12–13 ABY
	Imperial 17 ABY
	New Republic 17 ABY

OVERVIEW MAP OF THE IMPERIAL REMNANT

THE 8 REMAINING
SECTORS AFTER 17 ABY

PELLAEON'S REORGANIZED
IMPERIAL REMNANT AFTER 12 ABY

Sartinaynian
(Bastion)

Dominion
Megador †
EX-F †

Capturing of the
Guardian (16 ABY)

Guardian
3rd & 5th Fleets

Reaper †

Imperial
occupation
(12 ABY)

Almanian
Uprising
(17 ABY)

Jedi Academy

Reaper
181st Fighter Group
Dominion

Lusankya
Rogue Squadron
Endurance †

Guardian
3rd, 4th and
5th Fleets

BORDERS OF THE
NEW REPUBLIC
CONTROLLED SPACE

for the horde of battleships unleashed by the Dark Empire. With New Republic Intelligence unable to swear that other Super Star Destroyers, World Devastators, or worse weren't still to be encountered, the *Lusankya* was hastily refitted for active duty, seeing action against the Crimson Empire at Phaeda in 11 ABY.

Now, a year later, the *Lusankya* and *Reaper* stalked each other through the Mid Rim, as Phennir's 181st and Antilles's Rogues clashed in a series of strikes and parries. Reports of the great capital ships' duel enthralled citizens in the New Republic and the Empire alike. The New Republic military found the spectacle less captivating, and hastily dispatched the fleet carrier *Endurance*—commanded by Admiral Areta Bell and loaded with squadrons of new E-wings—to join Antilles.

Pellaeon carefully monitored this complex interplay of New Republic military politics, alert for any hint that Coruscant knew of the existence of the *Megador* and the *Dominion*. He concluded their survival had remained a secret—and therein rested the Empire's best hope.

Pellaeon gradually fell back, with Antilles and Bell following. Antilles cared nothing for the military debate playing out on Coruscant, and merely hoped for a decisive battle that would destroy the Empire's last Super Star Destroyer. Bell, however, was under tremendous pressure to prove the superiority of starfighters in general and her E-wing squadrons in particular. And serving alongside a legendary X-wing pilot didn't help relieve that pressure.

Fittingly enough, the showdown came at Orinda: The *Lusankya* and the *Reaper* squared off, trading broadsides like seagoing battleships of old, while Antilles exhorted Bell to launch her fighters. But Bell waited—her E-wings had suffered from malfunctions and were designed for pinpoint attacks, not sorties against a huge capital ship. When the *Reaper*'s defenses had been reduced further, she promised, she would strike.

That was when Pellaeon sprang his trap: A sextet of Interdictors decanted in the system, and were followed by the *Dominion*, commanded by Admiral Teren Rogriss. Antilles and Bell were caught between two massive capital ships. Antilles fell back, with the *Lusankya*'s shields a sheet of flame. The *Endurance* was swiftly destroyed, her squadrons still in their hangars.

Antilles was preparing to abandon ship when the Rogues punched a hole in the Interdictor screen, allowing the *Lusankya* to flee under heavy fire. The Super Star Destroyer was saved, but the battle had been lost.

Orinda secured the Empire's southern borders, though skirmishes were routine and the two sides constantly maneuvered for advantage in systems such as Adumar. The battle also reshaped the New Republic's military philosophy: The age of the dreadnought wasn't over after all.

But Orinda would come to be seen as a lost opportunity for the Empire. Pellaeon had succeeded too well. A month later, the New Republic pushed through the Borderlands after defeating Getelles, the warlord of the Antemeridian sector. The Moffs, emboldened by Pellaeon's recent victory, ordered him to go on the offensive.

Pellaeon reluctantly agreed, and was soundly defeated, losing the *Reaper* to the Dornean admiral Etahn A'baht at Celanon. Hoping the Moffs had learned their lesson, he sought to build up the Empire's defenses and turn it into a functioning state, one with the strength to defend its own traditions while coexisting with the New Republic.

But the Moffs would once again fall prey to old hatreds. In 17 ABY, the New Republic Senate lifted its ban on former Imperial officials holding elective office. The move was intended as a peace offering, but the Moffs saw it as prelude to an invasion. They contacted Daala and convinced her to fight, and ordered Pellaeon into battle. Pellaeon followed their orders, launching what would prove a disastrous campaign: Daala was routed at Columus, after which Garm Bel Iblis's Fourth Fleet and Admiral Ackbar's Third and Fifth fleets pummeled Pellaeon's forces at Champala, Ketaris, and Tangrene.

At Anx Minor, Pellaeon deployed both of his surviving dreadnoughts and the *Sorannan*-class Star Destroyer *Rakehell*, known as the *EX-F* when salvaged by survivors of the Empire's Black Fleet. Pellaeon hoped for a repeat of Orinda, but New Republic Intelligence knew something about the *Rakehell* that he didn't: There was a weak point in the armor protecting its antimatter reservoir. From the bridge of the Star Dreadnought *Guardian*, Ackbar ordered repeated strikes against the *Rakehell*'s weak spot; the explosion of its antimatter reservoir destroyed several of Pellaeon's warships and damaged the *Megador*.

Pellaeon ordered an immediate retreat to Bastion, where he convened the eight Moffs whose forces still held their sectors. There, he told them he was done with obeying their orders: Their delusions had undone five years of work in mere weeks, and brought the New Republic to their very door. The chastened Moffs accepted this declaration. Pellaeon had at last found the Empire's leader—and he was it. Two years later he signed a peace accord with the New Republic, formally ending the Galactic Civil War that had consumed so much of his life.

THE NEW JEDI ORDER

**"Many men will volunteer to die,
but few will be patient in the face of pain."**
—Attributed to Canderous Ordo, Mandalorian Neo-Crusader

Yavin 4, 27 ABY. Partial audio reconstruction begins.

The . . . to understand about . . . Vong isn't that they invaded the galaxy from . . . Rim. It isn't that they . . . based on pain, or a broken connection with the Force, or a caste . . . collar around your throat—or even that they shun machinery, and use biotechnology that scurries and bites.

The most important . . . Vong is this: They don't believe in death.

Some of their sects say the Changing is . . . of reincarnation, while others speak of a greater world beyond this reality. Some . . . mystical explanations, while others are poetic descriptions . . . But they all agree that life—each individual, precious, sentient life—continues after death.

That is why . . . so freely in battle—and that is the terrible logic . . . mass sacrifice of slaves and prisoners. What better fate . . . exalted through a noble, agonizing death—to win them a better . . . next life? What better offering to the skies than purified living souls . . . exposed to truth?

None of that, however, really explains why they invaded the galaxy. If you want . . . listen to me.

The woman . . . eyes is Master Shaper Mezhan Kwaad . . . striking cheekbones is Priestess Ngaaluh of the Deception Sect.

And my name, little Jedi, is Vergere.

We represent a secret society . . . overthrow of the Yuuzhan Vong religion—along with the . . . and torture, the petty caste system, and the calcified rituals and superstition that keep these people in self-inflicted torment.

Sounds noble, doesn't it?

Unfortunately—Tahiri, I believe your name used to be? We're not here to rescue you.

The only way to sever the Yuuzhan Vong . . . by destroying their entire society . . . The dominant elite will helpfully get themselves killed . . . lumpen masses will be enlightened by the horrors of the battlefield . . . defeat. We've been working on this for fifty years, and . . . can't allow one blond Jedi apprentice—or her blue-eyed boyfriend—to stop us.

Why have I told you all our darkest secrets, little Jedi? Because you won't remember any of this—not even meeting me.

That collar around your neck—horrible, isn't it?—is a mind-control creature called a provoker spineray. You're docile . . . already programmed you . . . We're about to do a thousand horrible things to your mind . . . a slavish disciple of everything I told you about at the start.

Why? To give the galaxy another agonizing symbol of all the inherent wrong of Yuuzhan Vong society. To mobilize the military potential . . . such as Anakin Solo to help us . . . tear down the rotting walls, and . . . out of their dead-end culture and into a better, brighter future.

So . . . for a good cause, you see.

Now, Ngaaluh and I . . . Mezhan can get back to her work, burning away your human soul.

And, like they used to say in the spy holos, we never had this conversation.

Partial audio reconstruction ends.

ORGANIC WEAPONS

Fifteen-year-old Jedi apprentice Tahiri Veila, victim of a half-successful Yuuzhan Vong braintwisting, gave this "know-your-enemy" briefing to Corellian Security personnel in 27 ABY, at the request of retired CorSec director Rostek Horn. She was accompanied by Anakin Solo and his sister, Jaina.

Yuuzhan Vong weaponry is, in a word, weird. We use sharp-edged eels that serve as whips or edged weapons, blobs of jelly to tie up people's limbs, and flying bugs in place of detonators. But it's perfect for melee fighters and silent infiltrators. No noise, no telltale energy discharge, no circuits or power cells for sensors to detect. Vonduun armor is the living ebony shell of a man-sized crustacean, reworked to fit around a humanoid body. It may look weird—especially when they leave the limbs on—but it's tough enough to stop blaster bolts.

Imagine being on perimeter patrol, or crouched waiting in trench positions. At night. In a rainstorm. Now imagine exploding bugs and venom-spitting whips and monsters in spiked armor—suddenly right on top of you, coming out of the dark from the wrong direction, with no warning. That is how we fight.

Our slave infantry don't try to hide—they're designed for wave assaults, but they aren't expected to do much fighting until they get into a melee, either. They're just expendable. So you gun most of them down with auto blasters, and the ones who are left claw their way into your position, and start biting you. We're not a nice people, as I've repeatedly tried to explain to Anakin.

Where necessary, we've proved entirely capable of turning our biotechnology into guns—volcano cannons, your pilots call them. Our primary weapon for armored vehicles and warships is the yaret kor, or plasma mortar, which works just like a turbolaser, while most of our big ships fire magma missiles, flying spikes of rock that work just like proton torpedoes. Jaina says they have a better maneuver pattern than anything from Incom.

Of course, it all probably still looks weird to you, just like it looks weird to the part of me that's

still human. Take the Rakamat, the big warkeeper that Master Skywalker killed at Dantooine. It's a six-legged armored monster the size of a krayt dragon, with plating a foot thick, and plasma cannons and dovin basals implanted along its spine. Those massive projecting plates along its back act as cooling vanes for its overheated biology. And it has a control room and troop compartment in its belly, which somehow doesn't seem gross to me anymore.

And I think that's enough explaining for today, if you don't mind.

YUUZHAN VONG WARRIOR CASTES

Yuuzhan Vong society is divided into castes. Some are skilled and privileged, including administrators, scientists, and hierophants. Others—the laborers, the unclean, and the slaves—simply live to serve the elite. Every caste is subdivided into domains, political factions who claim shared descent from ancestral heroes.

The domains of the warrior caste form the backbone of the Yuuzhan Vong military, but vary widely in size and organization. Smaller septs supply a few infantry companies, along with recruits for the fighter squadrons and warship armada. Although the largest domains maintain powerful fleets, most warships—especially fighters and pickets—are part of an armada that belongs to no domain, and which recruits personnel from the other castes. Cadres of intendants serve as tacticians and villip handlers, while shapers act in place of engineers and science officers, all fully integrated into the military chain of command.

Most of the other castes also have their own troops, primarily as a counterweight against warrior dominance. The most notable are the Praetorite Vong, a subdivision of the intendant caste—their role includes military logistics, reconnaissance, and bridgehead assaults, as well as providing the personal bodyguard of the warmaster. Suicide missions are entrusted to expendable cadres of Shamed Ones, unclean ex-warriors expelled from their caste due to dishonor.

Slaves—a mixture of ancient servant species and prisoners of war—are also used in large numbers as expendable assault troops. The bravest of these can earn promotion into the warrior caste, but a typical slave soldier is no more than a living battle droid, fitted with yorik coral implants that work like restraining bolts and commanded by a combination of braintwisting and mind control.

In the final stage of the war, the false Shimrra created an elite order known as the Slayers. Combining the attributes of priest and warrior, and commanded by female shaper-intendants, they were placed outside the caste system, and designed as the advance guard of a new religious and social system. Compact and heavily muscled, they had dark, scarless skin that was impervious to lightsabers and blaster bolts, and were gifted with fighting reflexes faster than the greatest warrior champions. While most Yuuzhan Vong recognized that they were abominations born in a shaper's lab, with sculpted bodies that were little more than living suits of armor, few dared to guess they had originated as Force-sensitive human slaves bioengineered from Jedi tissue samples.

THE YUUZHAN VONG INVASION

This scandoc circulated widely in Confederation holofeeds in 40–43 ABY. It was variously claimed to be an Imperial Naval Academy lecture, an address to the Council of Moffs, or part of a memoir by Jacen Solo or Natasi Daala. Its true authorship has never been established.

In 25 ABY, alien invasion fleets attacked several remote systems in the northern quadrant of the Outer Rim. At Artorias and Vonak, they enslaved whole civilizations.

In response, the New Republic Defense Force let them advance unopposed, allowing them to conquer countless unprotected worlds and enslave as many beings as they wanted.

Seen from the clean decks of the Admiralty, the doctrine made sense—don't waste troops and ships in pointless battles; hold back your forces, build up your power, lead the enemy to a battleground of your own choosing; then fight a decisive battle from a position of strength, and destroy your enemy. That was how the Rebel fleet destroyed the Empire, and variations on the same theme had served the New Republic well.

The top flag officers seemed to know what they were talking about. The new Supreme Commander was Admiral Sien Sovv, a Sullustan with a tenacious reputation as a task-force commander. His chief of staff was a dashing cruiser captain, Commodore Turk Brand.

(CONTINUED ON PAGE 219)

Yuuzhan Vong warriors (Chris Scalf)

ARMORY AND SENSOR PROFILE

CORALSKIPPER

The coralskipper was the standard starfighter of the Yuuzhan Vong, known in their own language as a *yorik-et*. It was a short-range fighter, comparable in role to the TIE fighter, but like all Vong vessels it was a biotechnological creature, organically grown in petrochemical paddies on plantation worlds. The living spaceframe was a slim delta wing of black yorik coral, typically around thirteen meters long, with a cluster of brightly colored nodes around the bow and a cockpit canopy perched toward the rear.

Like most Vong craft, a coralskipper was controlled by a cognition hood, a telepathic cowl that enabled symbiosis with the ship's sensors and systems. The nodes at the bow included as many as three *yaret-kor* plasma cannons—even one of which boasted greater firepower than an X-wing's quartet of lasers—plus a dovin basal that provided propulsion, inertial compensation, and shielding capacity. The coralskipper's acceleration and maneuverability rivaled the best New Republic and Imperial Remnant starfighters, but the alien ships' shielding capabilities were inconsistent, and opposing pilots developed several ways to penetrate them.

The Vong also used heavy starfighters, comparable in firepower and capabilities to Skipray blastboats. The *yorik-akaga* was a dedicated fleet escort, while the mandible-bowed *yorik-vec* was a long-range infiltrator that could fill a variety of roles, from escort patrol to commando insertions. A larger coralskipper variant with a hyperdrive was assigned to the elite Slayers in the final weeks of the conflict. Rumor had it these starfighters were created in part with voxyn genes in an attempt to give them rudimentary Force sensitivity.

CORALSKIPPER

KOR CHOKK GRAND CRUISER

YUUZHAN VONG CAPITAL SHIPS

At first sight, Yuuzhan Vong warships seemed as alien as the rest of their biotechnology. There were vessels resembling dark spires of basalt, spiky seedpods, and faceted crystal vertices. A closer look, however, revealed familiar principles of design and classification.

Small warships, corresponding to corvettes and frigates, made up around 90 percent of the Vong capital ships. Most were between one hundred and two hundred meters in length, crewed by just three or four pilots and a squad of gunners—but like all Yuuzhan Vong creations, these warships were living things, and veteran escort vessels could grow to the size of a light cruiser or larger. Regardless of size, these ships were more heavily armed than typical New Republic escorts, with plasma cannons and magma missile launchers on their bows and flanks. Their lean, narrow hulls tapered into points, designed to focus all weapons in a devastating forward salvo—but their ability to defend themselves and other ships was inferior to New Republic ships. This lack of protective escorts was one of the Vong's major weaknesses.

The larger warships were more heterogeneous, but divided into two general classes, corresponding to the New Republic's traditional heavy cruisers and Star Destroyers. The *matalok* was slow and defense-oriented, while the *Miid Ro'ik* was a faster type with armament meant for attack. Although hullforms varied widely, most Vong capital ship analogues had multicolored spars protruding at bow and stern that acted as docking racks for fighter squadrons. Many housed their weapons emplacements in recessed trenches cut across the width of the ship, so that the alternating pattern of rocky armor and dark shadow gave a banded appearance to their hulls. More distinctive vessels included bulbous-hulled *yammosk* carriers and twin-dagger *Vua'spar* interdictors, but these were classed as variants of the *mataloks* or *ro'iks*.

MIID RO'IK

The largest Vong ships corresponded to dreadnoughts, and again fell into two classifications. Grand Cruisers were monster vessels with hunched, lopsided silhouettes, created by armoring victorious flagships with the bulging carapaces of broken escorts and defeated opponents. They were popular flagships for aggressive warrior domains, decked with trailing battle flags and decorated with bold heraldic glyphs. The greatest domains, however, had ancestral worldships—massive brethren to the transports that housed most Vong civilians. The ebony hulls of these warrior worldships were pitted with weapons and encircled by rings of huge claw-shaped docking pylons. The largest worldship of all, Domain Lah's *Baanu Rass,* was the size of a Death Star. Parked in orbit at Myrkr, it housed the premier Vong military academy, and was the headquarters of the invaders' project to hunt down and enslave the Jedi Knights.

WORLDSHIP

(CONTINUED FROM PAGE 217)

But neither of them knew how to fight a war. They had no experience in large-scale fleet command, and their campaign thinking was learned from scandocs. Their key aides were specialists in tactical analysis and logistics rather than actual combat veterans, and many of them fetishized military discipline and pride to the point of obedient conformity.

Etahn A'baht, the only fighting admiral to retain a senior role, repeatedly called for a change of plan, but he was marginalized by Sovv and Brand, and resigned his commission less than a year into the war. He went off to take charge of the Dornean Navy in his home sector, and fought the local Vong to a standstill.

Sovv and his team were honest by their own standards, and took no pleasure in the duty of sending troops to fight and die. Necessary was a word they used a lot. Heroism, they said, usually cost more lives than it saved. At least that was what their books had told them.

In practice, though, their war plan made the Defense Force seem weak, and made the enemy seem unstoppable. And on a level that really mattered, this weakened the New Republic's fighting ability. Among civilians and low-level military personnel, panic spread without restraint. Most front-line troops went into battle expecting to take a beating from the galaxy's new apex predators.

Thus, the war assumed a grim, depressing pattern—a series of attempts by the military to lure the invaders into a decisive battle, which looked to everyone else like retreats and botched holding actions.

It didn't have to be that way. At Ithor, the Imperial Navy stood and fought, with Bothan and Jedi support. They didn't wait for Sovv's permission before they forced the battle, and they destroyed the Domain Shai warfleet with minimal casualties. Perhaps if Sovv had given them more support, fixed defenses would have been in place, and the Vong wouldn't have burned the jungle as they went down. But it was the Jedi and the Imperials whose reputations were tarnished, leaving Sovv in firmer control of the war.

By now, the admiral and his aides had a good picture of enemy strength and intentions, and believed they could lure a major part of the Vong

fleet into a decisive battle. They put their plan into action—and their opponents manipulated them every step of the way.

The New Republic laid their trap at Corellia—and the Vong fell on the undefended Fondor shipyards. Only the desperate firing of Centerpoint prevented the complete annihilation of the New Republic Defense Force. This time, the Corellians took the flak because half the Hapan fleet was caught in the Centerpoint backblast, but the shock of what Centerpoint did overshadowed the fact that the Defense Force had caused itself even more damage that day, and in a straight fight. The First Fleet was obliterated, the Third and Fifth mauled by enemy minefields, and the New Republic's second-largest shipyard was out of the war.

Now the Vong warmaster took personal command of the invasion armada—Tsavong Lah, 150 kilos of armored muscle, a grinning face all slashed up with scars, and a military brain as sharp as a lightsaber. In three months, he conquered the Hutts and advanced to Duro, on the edge of the Core.

Then he stopped, and offered Sovv a cease-fire.

Sovv accepted. He reckoned that the Vong decision to take the longer southern route through Duro meant the New Republic defenses around the northern Core were impregnable, and he calculated that a pause in hostilities would favor his shipbuilding and recruitment statistics more than the Vong's.

The Jedi Knights—seen by the military as undisciplined amateurs—were allowed to be hunted like animals.

And the Jedi weren't the only people the High Command sacrificed to the enemy that year. The Vong had spent decades infiltrating the Empire and New Republic, laying the seeds of a thousand brushfire conflicts—resentments that festered like infected wounds, ready to flare when they were scratched. Combined with the biggest refugee crisis in years and the looming presence of insane alien conquerors, civilian confidence in the ability of the New Republic to maintain peace and justice collapsed. Hundreds of undefended local governments surrendered to the Vong.

The Defense Force ignored it all. They prioritized shipbuilding, munitions factories, and recruitment.

They told themselves it was necessary, and that giving in to emotions was a dangerous weakness.

But they were already losing the war. In the northern and eastern quadrants, the Yuuzhan Vong now ruled.

No one knows if the skirmish at Yavin 4 was a deliberate provocation, Tsavong Lah's way of finding an excuse to restart the war. It doesn't matter. A group of smugglers and rogue Jedi apprentices liberated one of the invaders' largest slave plantations.

There's a holo of Han and Leia's three kids standing on the dirt strip with lightsabers drawn, and Talon Karrde's ships coming in to land behind them to free the slaves. That marked the resumption of the war—but perhaps more important, it served as an example of what the Defense Force was failing to do.

The Vong now showed their hand, using their Duro base to move west through undefended space lanes to Yag'Dhul, then bringing up new fleets to smash the Core defenses on the other side, Sovv's impregnable Northern Line—thrusting through Bilbringi and Borleias, until they were standing right on top of Coruscant.

By now the Jedi were gearing up to fight their own war on their flank—starfighter raids, refugee support, all the stuff the New Republic wasn't doing. To draw them off, the Vong feinted at their own private psychological flank—with a project to create Force-hunting monsters at Myrkr.

The Jedi fell for it, sending off their best young Jedi Knights on a pointless suicide mission.

Sovv, meanwhile, concentrated his three fleet groups at the capital, anticipating the decisive clash, or planning to destroy the enemy units before they could combine. It almost worked—with a little help from Han Solo, he caught the second-largest Vong fleet near the Black Bantha protostar and won a crushing victory—but their main force converged too quickly, and Sovv was forced to fight in the sky above Galactic City, with his back to the planetary shield.

The Battle of Coruscant was the blackest day in New Republic history, and the nadir of Sien Sovv's career. At the start of the main battle, Chief Fey'lya tried to fire him, so he surrendered the

Luke Skywalker meets Shimrra Jamaane in battle (Bruno Werneck)

tactical initiative to ensure the support of influential Senators and evacuated the Admiralty and NRI halfway across the galaxy to Mon Calamari.

After Coruscant, the Vong ruled the capital, and had consolidated their grip on the Core and most of the Inner Rim, taking tribute from systems that surrendered, and conquering the remaining New Republic bases.

Relatively quickly, however, the Defense Force put forward a new analysis: The Vong had suffered massively from their loss of ships and troops above Coruscant, and were now committed to fortify exposed positions in the Core. This received more emphasis than the enslavement of a trillion beings and the New Republic's obliteration as a functioning state.

Sovv spent the next few months calmly reorganizing the military, training recruits and building new ships, regrouping battle groups that had escaped intact from the rout, and sending them out on meaningless skirmishes to temper them for battle—a tactic the Vong had employed early in the

war. Their first offensive move was an Intelligence-led raid to assassinate the Vong monarch at Obroa-skai. It was the sort of offer you couldn't really pass up, and perhaps the first smart move they'd made in the whole war—but it was deemed a failure. The Alliance had been fed false intelligence, and the Yuuzhan Vong had sacrificed a spare worldship to sneak the real Supreme Overlord through to Coruscant.

Then, a few weeks later, Sovv managed to force another decisive battle. With Imperial help, he finally lured the enemy fleet into a trap at Ebaq 9 in the Deep Core, and threw everything he had at them—smugglers, mutineers, conscripts, even Jedi.

And won.

Tsavong Lah's ships were surrounded and besieged, trapped in low orbit under New Republic guns. The warmaster was killed in a brutal lightsaber duel with Jaina Solo. Sovv, at last, had his decisive victory.

Decisive victory, however, proved to have no major effect on the wider flow of the war. The defenses of the Vong occupation zone proved

The Hutts defend their ancient holdings (Drew Baker)

rather more resilient than the Northern Line had been—or else Sovv was content to allow half the galaxy to remain enslaved while he played with his statistics. Kashyyyk, halfway to the void, was now the First Fleet's forward base—supported by a chain of systems stretching back toward Mon Calamari, rather than a linear frontier. The rest was given to the Vong.

The leading Jedi Masters were still regarded with polite disdain because they wouldn't join the Defense Force and had blocked the use of genocide weapons. So they were allowed to launch a mystic quest into the Unknown Regions in pursuit of Zonama Sekot, a legendary living world that figured in the Yuuzhan Vong mythology.

Meanwhile, attempts were made to acquire expendable troops from neutral powers—the entries of the Hapans, Imperial, and some Chiss elements into the war were hailed as a series of diplomatic triumphs for the Galactic Alliance, the powerless new government-in-exile that had come into being alongside the High Command.

Finally, after another year of preparation, the Alliance fleets began to lumber into action. Sovv and his aides devised a complex series of feints and strikes, designed to conquer staging systems for an assault on Coruscant. This Trinity plan proved a disaster. It reminded the Vong that the Alliance systems were more than a series of game preserves for hunting wild infidels. In response, they went on the offensive against New Republic shipyards, overrunning Kuat and Hakassi before moving on to Mon Calamari.

Mon Calamari was barely saved when Zonama Sekot came out of hyperspace near Coruscant—the mythical world turned out to be a living battle station, a forest-covered Death Star that could summon Force lightning superlasers from its treetops to destroy Vong dreadnoughts. This made the Vong panic. They recalled their entire fleet to face their crazy mythological enemy.

The Defense Force had avoided another pointless mauling at Dac, and now the Vong simply gave them the opportunity that years of campaigns had failed to create. Thanks to Sekot, the enemy's military strength was concentrated in one place—Coruscant—and Sovv had another chance to win a decisive battle.

The battle didn't happen the way Sovv planned. Instead, it split into multiple distinct engagements in different parts of the system. Hapan Battle Dragons defended Sekot against one Vong force, while Imperial Star Destroyers and TIEs established local air and space superiority above Galactic City to support the ground assault, and in a third battle, the Galactic Alliance was thrashed by the new warmaster, Nas Choka. It was all rendered irrelevant by an uprising, secured by oppressed heretics, antiwar factions in the Vong elite, and a few veteran Rebel operatives who'd wound up in the undercity by accident.

The destruction of the Supreme Overlord's flagship by Jedi Knight Jacen Solo provoked the enemy's surrender, but in retrospect, that may have been less significant than it seemed—the Vong had lost Coruscant, and the fleet battle was basically a brutal draw already. They didn't have the strength or will left to fight anymore.

Under Jedi pressure, the surviving Vong were resettled in the Unknown Regions without further punishment, prompting Sovv to haul down his flag in protest; but the civilian government proved unable to function without him, and he was soon reappointed as Supreme Commander.

In hindsight, it seems clear that the Vong's success owed a great deal to New Republic and Galactic Alliance failings. The Defense Force commanders surrendered territory and worlds to chase the mirage of a decisive fleet battle.

They also neglected commerce raiding, pinpoint attacks, and local defense—tactics that had been instrumental for the Rebellion. Above all, they didn't allow local commanders much freedom to maneuver. Tsavong Lah was more than half monster, but at least he rewarded initiative, whereas Sovv sidelined and court-martialed people for it.

That's not the whole story, though.

It's all very well to say that Sien Sovv and Turk Brand sacrificed unnecessary lives to the dark gods of logistical discipline. It's probably true.

But no one stopped them, either. A lot of ordinary people saw what they were doing—and let them do it.

And that, I suppose, is what's really meant by the banality of evil.

THE NEW GALACTIC CIVIL WAR 2

"Violence is the irreducible essence of war, and only fools are moderate in its application."
—Firmus Nantz, admiral, New Republic

AFTER THE VONG

With the Yuuzhan Vong defeated, the Galactic Alliance sought to rebuild worlds devastated by their invasion, resettling populations and working to reverse the effects of Vongforming. At first, the galaxy seemed united in this effort, with rich worlds helping poorer ones and populations that had escaped harm pledging to assist those that had not.

But this spirit of cooperation didn't last. The galactic economy had been badly damaged, and many systems found once-profitable trade links broken or industries disrupted, leading to poverty and unrest. Galactic Alliance rebuilding efforts were hamstrung by inefficiency and corruption, which led to angry talk that worlds were being favored or ignored. Some systems, megacorps, and other organizations benefited from government reconstruction credits and the reshaping of the galaxy's economic and political map, but their gains were mirrored by other worlds' losses, breeding resentment.

The Galactic Alliance Defense Force weathered the Swarm War of 35 ABY between the Killiks and the Chiss, but the conflict revealed that the Defense Force was ill prepared for a major war. After the Swarm War, the Senate passed measures requiring more reconstruction taxes and military resources from its member states, causing some systems and sectors to balk at the idea of surrendering more credits and crews to Coruscant.

The decision to weaken the centralized military in favor of local authorities had worked to the New Republic's advantage in defeating the remnants of the Empire and establishing itself. But now, local control of military forces was becoming a source of concern for the Galactic Alliance. Systems and sectors were seeking more powerful defense forces, citing the familiar threats of pirates, incursions from the Unknown Regions, or conflicts with destabilized neighbors.

In 37 ABY the Galactic Alliance passed the Sector Defense Limits, putting ceilings on military forces and their capabilities in an echo of the Ruusan Reformations. But enforcing the limits was a challenge, and investigations and political pressure could only do so much to prevent determined sectors from arming themselves.

The chief antagonists as tensions mounted were the Galactic Alliance and Corellia, whose prickly independence had posed a challenge for Coruscant throughout galactic history. Corellia's government delayed its military and economic contributions and consistently opposed greater control over systems and sectors. Worse, there was growing evidence that the Corellians were covertly building warships with fast-strike capabilities and long-range weapons. Corellians countered that the Sector Defense Limits prevented member states from adequately defending themselves in a dangerous age, noting that they had always willingly borne a heavy burden in galactic conflicts, and that their planet was being taken advantage of by worlds to which it had made reconstruction loans and with which it had struck favorable trade deals.

As the crisis intensified, other independent-minded worlds such as Commenor and Fondor backed the Corellians. And the Galactic Alliance received unsettling news that the Corellian government had managed to reactivate Centerpoint Station, the ancient Celestial artifact capable of destroying worlds. Soon everything from fleet movements to stock-

market gyrations pointed to the same grim conclusion: The galaxy was once again on the brink of civil war.

THE NEW CIVIL WAR

From *Portraits in Late Galactic History*, by Thull Kabanard, 81 ABY:

Depending on whose interpretation you believe, the Second Galactic Civil War was fought because the Galactic Alliance Defense Force wanted to take control of all military assets in the galaxy, or because the Corellian government was trying to reactivate the Centerpoint superweapon.

The conflict began with an Alliance attempt to impose regime change on Corellia through force of arms, and ended as a civil war between factions of the Alliance itself, each backed by a section of the Imperial Navy and the Jedi Order. The original fight against Corellia and her Confederation allies had become a stalemate several months earlier.

Most histories of the conflict construct their narrative out of the fleet battles and planetary assaults of the naval war. The Galactic Alliance's initial plan was based on the calculation that the Second Fleet would be able to maintain unopposed orbital supremacy above Corellia, but they were driven back from there to an ill-advised occupation of nearby Tralus, and then successfully expelled from there, too.

The Alliance still enjoyed massive superiority, and warships returned in greater numbers in an attempt to blockade Corellia into surrender; but as the Defense Force's agenda of centralizing all military resources became clear, systems with important shipyards, munitions factories, and defense fleets formed a breakaway military coalition. Led by Bothawui and Commenor, this Confederation liberated Corellia, and waged war against the Alliance.

Months of desultory skirmishing followed, punctuated when both sides attempted to force a battle at Gilatter VIII, and each refused the other's offer. The Alliance's civilian government was ousted by a military coup, while the Confederation went on the offensive, thrusting into the Core until their fleets were stopped at Kuat and Balmorra.

At this point, the Jedi left the Alliance, followed by Kashyyyk and Hapes—though officially neutral, they were now effectively at war with extremist elements on both sides. A Corellian ambush wiped out the Alliance's Second Fleet in deep space, prompting retaliatory assaults in which the Jedi destroyed the Centerpoint superweapon, but the Defense Force proved once again unable to sustain an occupation.

The finale began when the Imperial Remnant entered the war to support the Alliance's occupation of Fondor, the Confederation's largest shipyard. This attack ended with Defense Force elements shooting at each other, and the Alliance split into two factions, each claiming political legitimacy. The key clashes of this phase of the war were at Roche, where an unauthorized Imperial offensive precipitated several confused battles for control of the system, but the final clash took place at Shedu Maad, where a primarily Imperial fleet broke the line of a primarily Hapan one, then pulled back and offered a cease-fire.

Military strategists of later years found no satisfactory pattern in this sequence of clashes. As in the Yuuzhan Vong War, the repeated attempts to force a decisive naval battle were essays in futility, and even the greatest defeats did not make the losing side surrender.

Nor was there a real narrative in the clash among the various leaders who tried to impose direction on the war—Cha Niathal, Gilad Pellaeon, Thrackan Sal-Solo, Sadras Koyan, but above all Jacen Solo. All pursued the same barren search for a decisive fleet victory, underpinned by the same political ambitions, and as such failed to effectively take control of the conflict.

Solo has been particularly vilified. His fall to the dark side as Darth Caedus dominates most narratives of the Second Civil War, but his career as a leader was as predictable as everyone else's. He had the same motives and pursued the same tactics. If he was wrong, so were they.

Perhaps the truth was seen best by Jacen Solo—but at a younger age, when he was a teenage Jedi grappling with the Yuuzhan Vong invasion: "The galaxy is broken, and this cease-fire will not heal it. There is a fracture between what our minds

have been trained to understand, and what our souls truly know—that is the true meaning of the dark side, and we went to war because we did not want to admit that we had fallen."

DEBRIEFING: THE GALACTIC ALLIANCE GUARD

The Galactic Alliance Guard was created to combat security threats from "non-military groups opposed to the Alliance." Intended to be a force of anti-terrorist commandos, under Colonel Jacen Solo their role was quickly widened to justify the mistreatment of minority species and the transfer of millions to concentration camps.

Colonel Solo quickly expanded the Guard's remit further, to include police-state control of civilian systems, direct command of the military, and the usurpation of executive power from the Senate. By the end of the war, the Guard had replaced the state, and Colonel Solo was Emperor in all but name; but the upper command structure remained at infantry battle group level, leading to the collapse of effective government—every major decision had to be approved by the Commandant, and Colonel Solo was too busy to even glance at the files crossing his datapad.

The Guard's standard mission profile was despicably crude. Drop ships off-loaded ground troops with a mix of riot and combat weaponry, with orders to pacify a target zone and then arrest and detain all survivors—a tactic used with little modification whether the people on the ground were enemy paramilitaries, peaceful protest marchers, unaligned civilians, or kidnappers and their hostages.

An equally serious flaw was the Guard's reliance on droid technology. Droid brains were ideal for monitoring seditious chatter on the HoloNet, while combat drones were useful for suppressing primitive insurgents, but when faced with skilled military or criminal opponents, GAG quickly found their equipment rendered useless by ion weaponry and signal jammers. Confederation combat and sabotage tactics often turned the Alliance's technological superiority into a fatal weakness.

These basic tactical and technological prejudices were inherited from the Defense Force, GA Intelligence, and Coruscant Security, who had spent three decades fighting tin-pot warlords

Hutt warships returning to the galactic stage (Darren Tan)

and aliens who never developed anti-sensor weapons. The Guard simply diverted excessive funding and training to perpetuate the basic mistakes of the system it sought to replace.

THE NEW HUTTS

The Yuuzhan Vong treated Hutt Space with particular brutality, ravaging its worlds and making them canvases for their alien biotechnology. The Hutts seemed finished as masters of the galactic underworld—but in the years after the Vong defeat, spacers brought strange tidings back from Hutt Space. On many Hutt worlds the organisms spawned by Vongforming were sickly or dead. As Galactic Alliance scientists negotiated for access to worlds displaying this resistance, the Hutt clans slowly but surely worked to regain their former influence.

But the Hutts had learned a terrible lesson, one that drove them to alter the fundamental tenets of their philosophy. To the astonishment of the galaxy, in the years after the Vong invasion armed starships of Hutt design began to reappear on the space lanes. Cantina talk had long told of strange, bulbous Hutt ships that plied routes among the central Hutt worlds, following an ancient network of jump beacons. But most had

dismissed such reports as legends. Sightings of them indicated that something had profoundly changed within Hutt Space.

Ever since the ancient civil war known as the Hutt Cataclysms, the Hutts had rejected war and territorial expansion in favor of economic dominance—a philosophy known as *kajidic*. That philosophy had made the Hutts immensely rich, and let them endure the tides of war that swept over the galaxy through the millennia. But it hadn't saved them from the Vong, and it might not save them from the next adversary, either.

In the Second Galactic Civil War, Hutt *batils* and *tarradas*—the equivalent of gunships and frigates—supported Confederation actions at Balmorra and Kuat, joined by gleaming, chrome-clad eight-hundred-meter warships the Hutt servants called *chelandions*. The Hutt warships proved capable in battle, with powerful turbolasers and braces of missiles. Galactic Alliance analyses indicated that the *chelandions*' shielding was weaker than expected for a cruiser analogue, but their armor was surprisingly strong. Efforts to analyze wreckage of Hutt warships largely failed; the ships appeared to have built-in self-destruct sequences.

After the Second Galactic Civil War ended, Commenori and Corellian naval officers could offer little insight into their

former allies' technology or military hierarchy: They had dealt exclusively with intermediaries from the Hutts' many slave species. For the galaxy, the possibility of renewed Hutt militarism was a disquieting prospect.

THE BURNING OF KASHYYYK

Transcript of TriNebulon News feature "Wookiee World Horror Witness!" released to HoloNet channels, 41 ABY:

My name is Lieutenant Tirs Maladane. I was a gunner on the Anakin Solo, *Jacen Solo's Impstar Deuce. We called her the* Black Annie. *I fought at Hapes, and Kuat, and then Kashyyyk. Yeah, Kashyyyk. I was a turbolaser gunner—not the long-range guns, but the starboard lateral quad. And I was never GAG. To tell the truth, those guys scared me.*

I knew Kashyyyk was going to be bad the second we decanted. It wasn't the opposition—the Wooks didn't have much arrayed against us. It was that the Fifth Fleet was behind us, stacked up halfway to Zeltros. Solo meant business, and when he did, things got hot fast.

But I never expected the order I got. Fire into the forests? I had to ask my CO to repeat that. But that's what Solo wanted. And so every battery on the Black Annie *that had a firing arc opened up. Through my long-range scope I could see the smoke rising. And then the flames.*

I'm from Tatooine—Little Mochot. When I was fifteen my aunt sent me offworld during high summer to earn some credits logging greel wood on Pii III. I'd never seen anything like it. First day, it rained hard and I stood out in it laughing and cheering. The other timber rats thought I was crazy. When I got back to Little Mochot I used to dream of rain every night. And I'd read about trees.

So I'd heard about the Wookiee trees. I'd seen them on holos. How scientists thought they might be one big collective organism, the Wookiee planet's brain and heart and lungs and everything else. I thought that was pretty amazing.

I fired my turbos. I had to. Operations would have seen if I hadn't, and I'd have been in a brig with someone else in the hot seat. And firing at the surface, it wasn't like I could aim high to miss the shot. I couldn't do anything else, so I did what they told me to do and fired my turbos. If I could have done something else, I would have.

Some of those Wookiee trees were fifty thousand years old—they were a kilometer high before the Republic existed. You shouldn't be able to kill something that's fifty thousand years old by just squeezing a trigger. But that's what I was doing. The whole time, the tears were running down my face. And when bogeys started coming in, I was relieved. It's crazy to be glad you're under fire, but I was. At least now I was shooting at something that could shoot back.

WAR PORTRAIT: NATASI DAALA

Natasi Daala was born on Irmenu and raised in a COMPNOR orphanage run by Renatasian nuns on Botajef. She was drafted into the Academy of Carida in 3 BBY, based on her aptitude for competitive sports and unarmed combat.

Daala's training at the Academy was the formative period of her life, forging her strengths and crystallizing her vulnerabilities. She was initially selected for the stormtrooper program—her violent will to win on the shock-ball pitch, which often left her opponents in bacta, was seen as a trait that could be channeled into close combat training. Instructor Visk believed that if he could break her will with Imperial discipline, she would be an ideal clone template.

But simulator tests during basic training revealed that her ruthless approach to contact sports also translated well to capital ship combat sims. Chief Instructor Massimo Tagge followed up the anomaly, and was surprised to find that the unexpectedly gifted stormtrooper was a tall, attractive redhead. He promptly transferred her from Visk to his own navy officer-cadet course.

Daala thrived under Tagge's guidance, heading the fleet sim rankings for her year and producing a number of admired tactical analysis papers on the Tarkin Doctrine. Nonetheless, other instructors raised complaints—not all of them friends of the thwarted Visk. They warned that her simulator victories were always achieved with brute force and heavy losses, and that they depended too heavily on logistical superiority. In her final semester, Tagge's attempt to place her in the command class was overruled.

Instead of commanding a picket ship in the Academy flotilla, Daala was reassigned as a datapad assistant and then

as a galley yeoman. She became convinced that she would be denied an officer's commission, held permanently as a junior NCO in a dirtside assignment. Bitterness about the faculty, and about the aristocratic cadets who had usurped her place in the command class, would haunt her for decades.

But Tagge had forwarded her analysis of the Tarkin Doctrine to his cousin Cassio, who passed it to the Grand Moff himself. Tarkin came to Carida unannounced to find his brilliant disciple . . . and found her washing topatoes.

Before they left Carida, Instructor Visk had been reassigned to Sirpar, and Tarkin and Daala had become lovers. The initiative is normally attributed to Tarkin, but his own fragmentary memoirs suggest the teenage cadet took the lead.

Daala progressed rapidly from aide to adjutant, and from adjutant to admiral. When Tarkin departed with the Death Star to destroy Alderaan, she was assigned to guard the battle station's home base, the Maw Installation, and to await new orders.

She waited for more than a decade.

Daala suppressed whatever she felt, and continued to obey her orders until 11 ABY, when she emerged to find Tarkin long dead, the Empire almost destroyed, and the Rebellion in control of the galaxy.

In response, she embarked on the first in a long series of campaigns, all of which followed the same pattern—a series of brutal frontal attacks that destabilized her enemy but also devastated her own troops and ships, followed by a retreat into hiding to rebuild her forces, recruiting and rearming for her next attempt.

In short, she was replaying Academy simulator tactics, but the Empire no longer had the unlimited resources to make them work.

In the New Republic, her repeated attacks and defeats provoked fear and then mockery, but in the remnants of the Empire she became a hero. In a period of defeat and retreat, when Moffs and warlords who claimed to lead the Empire cowered behind their fortress-world defenses, Admiral Daala continued to strike back.

This lower-deck popularity accounts for the repeated willingness of Imperial factions to accept her leadership— the United Warlord Fleets, the Independent Company of Settlers, the Imperial Core, the Second Imperium, and the Maw Command.

"Daala has two types of troops," Admiral Ackbar once remarked. "The ones she's training now, and the ones she's killed already." However, while her major clashes with the New Republic all ended in defeat, Daala won victories against Imperial rivals and the Yuuzhan Vong. In 41 ABY Grand Admiral Gilad Pellaeon recalled her to his side, and after his death, she emerged as the new leader of the Galactic Alliance— the only candidate acceptable to the Empire, Alliance, and Confederation.

Daala quickly moved to consolidate her power, installing ex-Imperial allies in several key commands. She soon led the most powerful military and economic power in the galaxy— as a military dictator in all but name, controlling a state with all the resources she needed to make her tactics work.

WAR PORTRAIT: GILAD PELLAEON

Prepared remarks by Chief of State Natasi Daala, on the dedication of the Pellaeon Gardens, Bastion, 42 ABY:

> Today is Gilad Pellaeon's ninety-third birthday. If he were still here with us he would probably ask for all of us to stop talking about him, so he could tend his garden in peace and quiet. One reason Gilad loved gardens was because they were a place where he could get away from politicians and generals and admirals and aides and journalists. So

Gilad, on behalf of myself and all the politicians and generals and admirals and aides and journalists, I'm sorry. We'll say our few words and leave this beautiful spot in peace.

Peace. That was something Gilad often sought, but that never seemed to find him. Most of his life was spent at war. He applied to Raithal Academy when he was fifteen—too young to enter—and they never discovered he'd convinced a slicer to alter his records. (By the way, Gilad, Commandant Richeu assured me he won't place a posthumous demerit in your file. Just in case, I'll be watching him.) He served in the Judicial Forces, then the Republic Navy, fighting bravely against the Separatists and their mechanized warships. When the Republic became the Empire he served it, too. His first command was the Chimaera, and for years she was his garden. I once asked him if it bothered him that a Star Destroyer was the closest thing he'd had to a home, and he just smiled. "Natasi," he said, "if your heart feels at home, it doesn't matter what your eyes see."

Gilad served Grand Admiral Thrawn, and the Ruling Council, and for a brief time he served me. He

always did so with merit and with honor. He gave his superiors neither flattery nor scorn, but information and support—and counsel, if they were wise enough to ask for it. He demanded much of his subordinates, above all else that they served the Empire with the same professionalism and pride he brought to everything he did. And by doing so, he gave much to them, too. Many of them became honorable men and women because of his teachings.

And of course for many years he served these proud sectors and these bright stars. Gilad Pellaeon preserved the Empire. More than that, he saved it. He saved it from the territorial lusts of the New Republic and the murderous nihilism of the Yuuzhan Vong, leading from the bridge of Star Destroyers and once from inside a bacta tank. He saved the Empire from the abuses and prejudice with which an unprincipled few had blackened its name. And he restored the honor and order too many had forgotten the Empire once stood for. Right here, in these gardens, he nurtured what was good and weeded out what was not, until the ideals of the Empire flourished once again.

I said he once served me, and that was a great honor. But I am more honored to say that I once served him. The legends of my homeworld of Irmenu speak of the great mariner Darakaer, who sleeps until the faithful summon him by drumming out their call for help. When Gilad and I parted long ago, we reminded each other of that story, and we pledged that each of us would answer Darakaer's rhythm if the other should be in need.

As you know, Gilad served the Galactic Alliance as faithfully as he had served every other government—until he could no longer countenance the actions taken by Jacen Solo, lost in the madness to which Jedi seem so susceptible. He retired here for a brief time—but as always, war found him again. He agreed to assist the Galactic Alliance in the hope that it would end a terrible war more quickly and restore peace to the galaxy. But he had terrible doubts, doubts he shared with me. For he had drummed out the Darakaer, and I had answered.

The next time I heard those rhythms, he was dying—mortally wounded by a Jedi assassin. His final act was a signal to me that he and the ideals of the Empire had been betrayed. And so I answered.

As Gilad would have done, had our situations been reversed.

But let us not dwell on that terrible day. For with patience and care and constant effort we are healing this galaxy. It is the task before me every day, and when I falter, I think of Gilad. I ask myself what he would have done, and hope that some of his wisdom may be granted to me. I know leaders who arise after I am gone will do the same. They will not have been lucky enough to know Gilad, as I was, but in this quiet place they will know of him, and find inspiration in his example. Here, amid the beauty of the Pellaeon Gardens, let them nurture, and let them weed. And if they hold true to Gilad Pellaeon's example, they, too, will hear the Darakaer, and know what honor asks of them.

A NEW DEFENSE FORCE

After the war between the Galactic Alliance and the Confederation, the Alliance began to buy more warships for its centralized military, reducing its reliance on member worlds' military units for defense. This centralized military was built up through increased taxation and contributions from member worlds; in return, restrictions on those member worlds' own military forces were loosened.

This new bargain, made in an effort to ease the tensions that had led to the Second Galactic Civil War, largely kept the peace. The numbered fleets, comprising warships supplied by member worlds and allied autonomous states, gave way to named fleets assigned to regions of the galaxy. But military philosophy would continue to evolve; in the years leading up to the Sith-Imperial War, the Alliance worked to reestablish sector fleets, keeping member worlds' warships close to their homeworlds.

END OF A JEDI ERA

From the Holocron of Luke Skywalker:

There are some wars that only the Jedi can fight. After Darth Caedus's defeat, we mediated the appointment of Natasi Daala as Chief of State of the Galactic Alliance, and Jagged Fel as regent of the Imperial Remnant. Whatever their flaws—and

Daala had many—they were the right leaders to oversee the long process of reuniting the galaxy.

Two years later, I chose to respect Daala's commitment to peace and justice, and exile myself. I thought the Force wanted me to discover Jacen Solo's fate and to show the Jedi they could act without my leadership. Instead, I discovered threats that only the Jedi could oppose.

The first threat was a lost tribe of Sith from the forgotten world of Kesh. They were building a powerful war fleet, one made more powerful by the dark strength of every warrior serving their armada. Yet there was an even greater opponent—the mysterious entity known as Abeloth.

Such enemies are the Jedi's business. I have seen what happens when beings attempt to fight them without the Force as their ally. Only the Jedi, answering as always to the will of the Force, were able to pierce the shroud of Abeloth's will and push back that darkness.

Wynn Dorvan, the new Chief of State, has much to contend with. But for me, the lessons of the struggles on Coruscant and in the Maw are clear. The challenges we face and the mysteries we must explore are bound up with the Force, not Mandalorians or Moffs.

Abeloth is an entity from a much older order than the Sith. We must understand her origins and the nature of the Ones my father encountered years ago. By doing so perhaps we will find a way to destroy her. Or perhaps we will learn that the will of the Force calls for us to keep her at bay, or to acknowledge her role in the galaxy and forge a new order.

And we must learn the truth about this latest incarnation of the Sith. Who is the Dark Man who came to my aid against Abeloth? What has become of Vestara Khai and Ship? And what is the meaning of Jacen's vision?

The answers will not to be found on Coruscant, or emerge from service to the Galactic Alliance. To find them, we must withdraw from Coruscant and distance ourselves from the tumult of the galaxy. I said at the beginning of this entry that there are some wars only the Jedi can fight, and that is true. But it's also true that only the Jedi can restore Balance to the Force. And to do so, we must dedicate ourselves completely to the Light.

> "War will teach your soldiers to be sensible
> and your generals to be fools."
> —Balmorran proverb

THE ONE SITH

Darth Bane's Rule of Two decreed that there would only be two true Sith at a time—a master and an apprentice. This practice allowed the Sith Order to survive during the Republic's final millennium, with Darth Sidious eventually engineering the downfall of the Jedi Order and reestablishing Sith rule of the galaxy.

Sidious trained and created a number of Dark Side Adepts, but did not overturn the Rule of Two—his dark side hopefuls were denied the status of Sith or access to the Order's secrets, leaving Sidious and Darth Vader as the galaxy's only Sith Lords. Lumiya, who claimed the Sith mantle after Sidious and Vader died at Endor, also obeyed the Rule of Two, as did Jacen Solo when he became Darth Caedus. When Caedus died and his apprentice Tahiri Veila turned back to the light, the succession of Sith was believed broken, and the Order thought finally extinct.

But the Sith would be reconstituted from a surprising source. In 5000 BBY, a Sith starship in service to Naga Sadow crashed on the hidden world of Kesh. The survivors became the Lost Tribe of the Sith—an Order that grew and flourished on Kesh even as the Sith were forced into hiding in the larger galaxy. In 41 ABY, a Sith meditation sphere ended the Lost Tribe's millennia of isolation, informing them of the ancient Sith Empire's destruction at the hands of the Jedi, and preparing them to take their revenge.

The Lost Tribe ultimately failed to overthrow the Jedi, but the Sith survived their downfall, too, and their glory would be rekindled by one who had watched their triumph and ruin.

Darth Krayt had begun his life as A'sharad Hett, a human from Tatooine raised as a Tusken Raider and trained as a Jedi. Hett survived Order 66 and abandoned the Jedi, becoming a bounty hunter and wanderer in a war-torn galaxy. But though he thought himself done with the Force, it wasn't done with him. In the Unknown Regions, he was captured by the Yuuzhan Vong and tutored by the mysterious Fosh named Vergere, who remade his body through Vong experiments and taught him to open himself to the dark side. Taking the name Darth Krayt, he hid away on the Sith tombworld of Korriban. There he would draw lessons from the extinction of the old Sith Order under Darth Caedus and the Lost Tribe's defeat.

Rather than the Rule of Two, Krayt decreed that the Sith would obey the Rule of One, following the dictates of the Dark Lord who stood atop the Sith hierarchy. No longer would the Sith seek power as its own reward; now they would work to use that power toward a greater goal. His life span extended by the Vong experiments, Krayt secretly rebuilt the Order's numbers, and waited for a chance to cast down the Jedi and reclaim power. He found it, ironically, in a Jedi attempt to heal the wounds of the Yuuzhan Vong War.

SEEDS OF THE VONG

After invading the galaxy, most of the Yuuzhan Vong settled on the living world of Zonama Sekot. But a few chose to dwell elsewhere. Decades later, the descendants of these Vong often found themselves mistreated and reviled—vengeful Bothans hunted them, while other species refused to deal with them.

Darth Krayt and his revived Sith Order (Jason Palmer)

This troubled Kol Skywalker, leader of the Jedi Council—it was the Jedi's responsibility to seek justice for all members of galactic society, even the very least. *Particularly* the very least, Skywalker thought. After meditating on the problem for many months, Skywalker had an idea.

In 122 ABY Skywalker and the Vong master shaper Nei Rin tested using Vongforming techniques to terraform a desolate section of the planet Ossus. When Ossus became a lush green world once again, Skywalker and Rin persuaded the Galactic Alliance to let Vong shapers heal a hundred of the worlds devastated by the Vong invasion. This promising undertaking was called the Ossus Project.

But something disastrous happened—at first the worlds healed, but then plants and animals began sprouting hideous bony spurs akin to those that erupted from Vong captives in the original invasion.

The Jedi defended the Vong, swearing that the project had been sabotaged, and convinced the Galactic Alliance to protect them. That led to a succession movement—and hard-line Moffs in the Empire (now led by Roan Fel) saw a chance for the Empire to reclaim its supremacy. Over Fel's objections, in 127 ABY they left the Alliance, recruited disaffected worlds to their cause, and declared war.

A year into the war, the Sith—the Ossus Project's saboteurs—approached the Moffs and offered an alliance, which was accepted. Over the next two years, the Sith and Fel's Empire won victory after victory. At the Battle of Caamas, Grand Admiral Morlish Veed and his Imperial fleet crushed the Alliance's forces. They surrendered, with the exception of the Duros admiral Gar Stazi, who mustered what ships he could and fled. The Alliance surrendered days later, as did some members of the Jedi Order, who joined Fel's Imperial Knights. The other Jedi withdrew to Ossus, where they were massacred by the Sith and Imperial forces. Soon after that, the Sith led a coup against Emperor Fel. The Sith Lord Darth Krayt took the throne on Coruscant as head of a new Sith Empire that once more ruled the galaxy.

Fel and his Imperial Knights retook Bastion, and defended a portion of the New Territories against the ruthless Sith Empire, beginning a new galactic civil war. Admiral Stazi's forces, meanwhile, began a guerrilla campaign against the Sith. And the scattered Jedi Knights sought to rebuild their Order in secret.

ARMORY AND SENSOR PROFILE

PREDATOR FIGHTER

The TIE Predator was a deadly new version of the Imperial Navy's standard starfighter, designed to ensure space superiority in a new era.

The Predator retained the iconic TIE cockpit design and four L-s9.3 laser cannons, but combined them with new "mynock wing" arrays based on Chiss technology. These integrated the roles of solar panels and ion-accelerator pylons, and also acted as field generators for hyperdrive and deflector systems.

Although the Predator was faster and more maneuverable than any Alliance fighter, the complex technologies packed inside the slender wing arrays were a maintenance nightmare. Moreover, the redesigned forward viewport offered poor visibility, with narrow horizontal panes separated by thick struts.

Navy lobbying has forced Sienar to revive the circular viewport design found on older TIEs, but at first these modified fighters were only assigned to flight leaders.

PREDATOR FIGHTER

SCYTHE BATTLE CRUISER

The MC140 Scythe main battle cruiser was the Galactic Alliance Defense Force's greatest warship. The compact main hull was simply an armored nacelle for its mighty engines, with its weapons systems mounted in a huge vertical hammerhead bow. Forty proton torpedo tubes provided devastating firepower, supported by nine turbolaser batteries and two ion cannon mountings, plus three squadrons of CF9 starfighters carried within the lower section of the hammerhead.

This ship was built for a single role—defeating enemy warships in a head-on attack. With all its weaponry concentrated in the forward fire arc, the *Scythe*-class cruiser would make repeated attack runs on opponents, unloading

MC140 SCYTHE BATTLE CRUISER

devastating salvos against their shields and armor. Its debut in 92 ABY represented a decisive rejection of large fleet carriers and all-purpose battleships in favor of smaller warships focused on specific roles—but this specialization wasn't without its drawbacks. The cruiser's flanks and rear were defended only by shields, and it depended on starfighters and frigates for protection against Imperial TIEs and fast attack ships.

CROSSFIRE FIGHTER

The Incom CF9 "Crossfire" was the favored starfighter of the Galactic Alliance during the Sith–Imperial War, a multi-role successor to the Rebel starfighters of earlier generations.

Designed to complement the *Scythe*-class cruiser, the diminutive CF9 was essentially a flying engine, with the cockpit perched above the thrusters and the main weapons carried on a wide horizontal wing across the bow. This contained a powerful brace of six proton torpedoes, while its trailing edge pivoted into a vertical strike foil to deploy the starfighter's full attack armament of four IX9 wingtip cannons.

Due to its attack-oriented design, the Crossfire wasn't as maneuverable as traditional escort starfighters or the Empire's new TIE Predator. Instead, it relied on a pair of aft-facing twin blasters operated by a rear gunner, who defended the starfighter—and any capital ships it was escorting—against attacks from astern.

Some aspects of the design proved problematic. The vertical wing interrupted the pilot's field of view, and holographic attempts to erase it proved more distracting than the wing itself. The cramped rear gunner's seat also proved superfluous in dogfights. Nonetheless, pilots loved the Crossfire due to the durability of its shields and armor—and because the sturdy cockpit doubled as an escape pod. While the single-pilot CF9B was never put into production, the gunner's position was often modified for other purposes, especially by squadrons that remained loyal to Admiral Gar Stazi during the Second Rebellion.

CF9 CROSSFIRE FIGHTER

WAR PORTRAIT: GAR STAZI

Holomessage sent by Admiral Gar Stazi to Rogue Leader Jhoram Bey, 137 ABY:

War.

I think about it a lot, Jhoram. And when I do, I always come back to the same day.

Two years out of Anaxes, I was sent on a peacekeeping mission to the Sepan sector. It was the Dimoks and the Ripoblus, as it has been for centuries. We separated their ships, patrolled the trade routes, and did all the things you'd expect. The army had it worse—they were down on Kuthard, with its mixed population, sitting in walkers and wheelies, keeping Dims and Rips apart. I was sent down there as an observer, one of those boots-on-the-ground look-and-listens higher-ups periodically insist we navy guys do. I'm sure you did a few yourself, before Caamas.

I'm wandering through this half-bombed village in the Kuthard backcountry with a pack of Coruscant News Net journalists and a world-weary Tynnan diplomat. The newsies find this old Dimok matriarch and start asking her about the war. With the holocams rolling, she tells them, "All my life I've seen war. It is too late for my children. But I would do anything for my grandchildren to live in a world at peace."

Beautiful stuff, right? I confess my eyes were a little moist too, Jhoram—I was young then, not the cynical old greenskin you now know too well. So the newsies turn off their holocams and scamper off to their next shoot, and it's just the old Dimok and the Tynnan diplomat and me. I'm thinking about peace, the old Dimok is waiting to see if we're done with her, and the Tynnan's just standing there with this funny little smile on his face.

He catches my eye and starts asking the matriarch questions about her family, where their compound is, how long they've been in the village. He knows the whole sad history of the place—property claims, past atrocities, peace proposals, the lot. And so he asks the old matriarch—who was just talking about doing anything to ensure peace for her grandchildren, remember—if she'd give a certain small parcel of her family's land to the Ripoblus to settle an outstanding claim.

"Those rodders?" she asks, the spit flying from her mouth. "Thieves and killers, every one of them! I'll die before I see them take a millimeter of Dimok land!"

We—by which I mean hot-shot Weequay fighter jockeys, old Duros bridge lice, Dimok crones, gray-whiskered Tynnan diplos, and everybody else—were bred to compete. To struggle and succeed, or fail and die trying. And often that means we want or even need what someone else has, and isn't inclined to give to us.

And so we fight.

Everything about us is geared for it. Our eyes locate enemies, our hands strike and rip, and our brains think of ways to make the eyes and hands better at their jobs. And our anger keeps this whole fighting system fueled. Except once our anger only had nails and teeth and rocks at its disposal. Now it has weapons that can destroy entire worlds. But the system is the same as it was a hundred thousand years ago—eyes, hands, brains, anger.

Sometimes we think of ourselves as the brains, or the eyes, or at least the hands. But we're not, Jhoram. We're the nails and teeth and rocks. We are the ones called upon when the talking stops—when the anger can't be satisfied with loud words. You and I are killers. And the galaxy will always call upon us—that old Dimok crone talked of peace, but what she wanted was war.

If we defeat Darth Krayt, the galaxy will be at peace. For a while, anyway—maybe long enough for us to get old and sit on a porch somewhere and convince ourselves we were heroes. But then there will be war again. And new killers will be called.

I think that day on Kuthard was the last day I believed in peace, Jhoram. But it was the first day I started to believe in something else.

We are part of a brotherhood and sisterhood of killers—me, you, the rest of my crew, the rest of your Rogues, Fel's starfighter pilots, the fugitive Jedi, the Sith fleet commanders, everybody. There is no heroism in ending lives the way we do, Jhoram. But there must be rules for how it is done. There must be a code that we in this fraternity of killers understand and respect—not because it will save our lives, but because it is the best chance for giving our lives meaning and value.

War will always be with us, Jhoram. But we must always strive to be its masters, and resist becoming its servants. If we come to the end of our lives having made that our daily task—our hourly command—then we will look back and be able to say we were beings of honor.

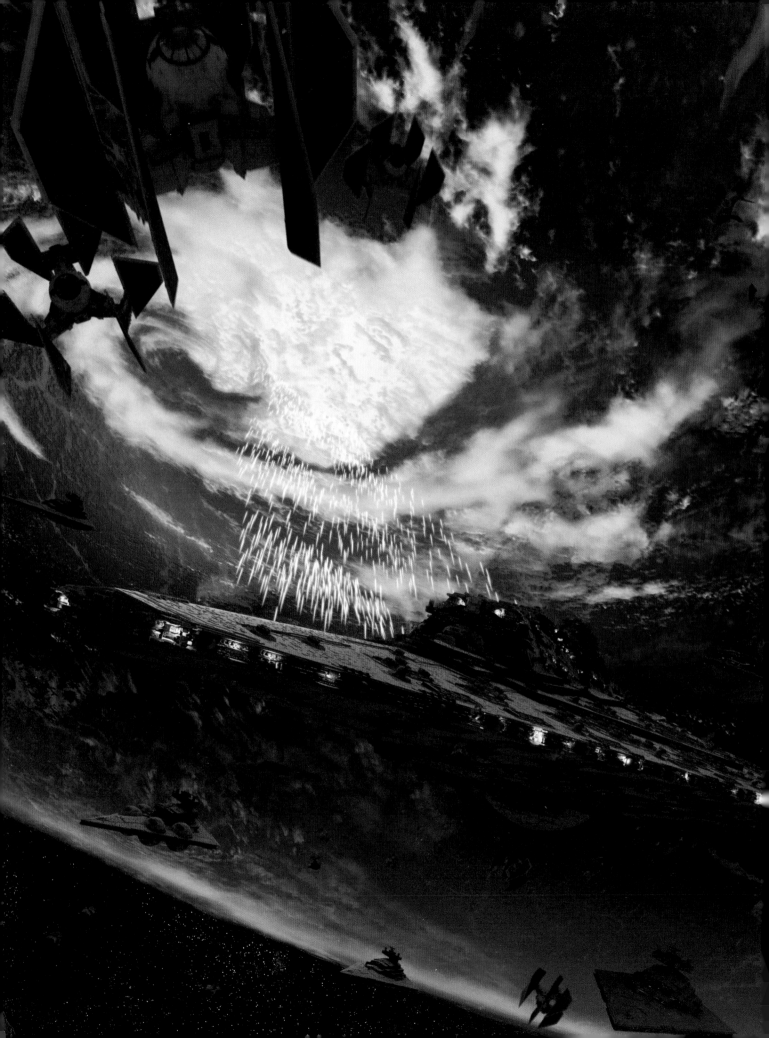

Star Wars: The Essential Guide to Warfare was in every way a collaboration—one involving not just the two of us but also our friends at Lucasfilm and Del Rey and authors, illustrators, researchers, and fans.

Art makes a book come alive, and it was a thrill to see each new marvelous illustration arrive from Drew Baker, Tommy Lee Edwards, Ian Fullwood, Ansel Hsiao, Stephan Martiniere, Modi, Jason Palmer, Chris Scalf, Dave Seeley, Darren Tan, John VanFleet, Bruno Werneck, and Paul Youll.

It was a great pleasure to work once again with Modi, the mapmaking wizard of *Star Wars: The Essential Atlas*.

Our thanks to Brad Foltz, who never bats an eye when presented with ten pounds of information to be crammed into a five-pound book, and somehow makes it work.

At Del Rey, Erich Schoeneweiss saw the book through from beginning to end, offering encouragement, humor, patience, clarifying advice, corrective action, congratulations, and firm refusals in the right proportions. Nancy Delia kept us out of trouble with her usual grace. And it's always a delight to compare notes with Keith Clayton, Shelly Shapiro, Frank Parisi, and Joe Scalora.

At Lucasfilm, our thanks to Leland Chee, Pablo Hidalgo, Tony Rowe, Robert Clarke, Sue Rostoni, Jonathan Rinzler, Troy Alders. and Dave Filoni for their wise counsel, intriguing backstories, cheerful fellowship, and steering through storms.

Thanks to Nathan O'Keefe for invaluable help shaping the story of Contispex's Crusades, Michael Kogge for more evocative Xim lore, Dan Wallace for intriguing tales of Waymancy and the Republic rocket-jumpers, Troy Denning for brainstorming about the Celestials and Rakata, James McFadden for help with Rebel pilots, and to Paul Kemp, John Jackson Miller, and Karen Miller for conversations and collaborations. And if you were part of the ad hoc group at the Hoth Bar at Celebration V when we decided to settle how exactly you fight with the blast shield down, beers are on Jace next time. (Particularly if you were the guy who walked by wearing that exact helmet when a close-up look was desperately needed. That was awesome.)

Thanks to everyone in the 501st Northeast Remnant Garrison and the 501st Legion's Empire City Garrison, with a special salute to Steve Iervolino, Bob Olszewski, and Dave Braun. And our heartfelt thanks to the worldwide membership ranks of the 501st and the Rebel Legion. *Star Wars* couldn't ask for better ambassadors, and authors couldn't ask for better friends.

Many previous *Star Wars* authors have tackled the subject of warfare in the galaxy far, far away, giving us a wealth of information to build upon. Our thanks to a very long list headed by Curtis Saxton, Haden Blackman, David West Reynolds, James Luceno, Bill Slavicsek, Curtis Smith, Michael Allen Horne, Greg Gorden, Paul Sudlow, Paul Murphy, Drew Campbell, Matt Hong, Timothy S. O'Brien, Jen Seiden, Eric S. Trautmann, Craig Carey, Ryder Windham, Ryan Kaufman, Karen Traviss, Steve L. Kent, Brian Daley, Sterling Hershey, Owen K. C. Stephens, Rodney Thompson, Gary Astleford, Patrick Stutzman, JD Wiker, Eric Cagle, and Abel Peña.

Finally, this book would not exist without the questions, advice, theorizing, debates and occasional insane digressions of the passionate fans and experts who have contributed so much to TheForce.net, Wookieepedia, RASSM, and other online communities. First, heartfelt thanks to our mini focus group: Tzizvvt78, AdmiralNick22, and blackmyron spotted errors, proposed new ideas and were superb sounding boards. The Warfare thread on TFN was the spot for posing questions, finding answers, soaking up knowledge, and recharging batteries. Thanks to all the posters there, on the apparently immortal Fleet Junkies thread and at other helpful online outposts, a roster whose ranks include AdmiralWesJanson, FTeik, Armchair_Admiral, MercenaryAce, Matthew Trias, CeiranHarmony, Taral-DLOS, TheRedBlade, Plaristes, Lord_Hydronium, dewback_rancher, Barriss_Coffee, Rogue_Follower, Cronal, RC-1991, SheaHublin, Sinrebirth, Ris_jSarek, Dark_Guardian, Havac, Robimus, The2ndQuest, KansasNavy, LordDarthPaxis, Vialco, Ketan-Shej, and VT-16.

And George Lucas, thank you for letting us dig in such a marvelous sandbox.

The *Assertor*-class Star Dreadnought *Wrath* leads a Base Delta Zero bombardment (Ansel Hsiao)

AUTHORS

JASON FRY is the *New York Times* bestselling author of *The Clone Wars Visual Guide* and co-author of *Star Wars: The Essential Atlas*. He has written more than a dozen other books exploring the *Star Wars* universe. He is also the co-author of the Transformers Classified series. On more mundane days, he writes about journalism, baseball, music, travel, and anything else that catches his eye. He lives in Brooklyn, New York, with his wife, son, and about a metric ton of *Star Wars* stuff. www.jasonfry.net

PAUL URQUHART is a pseudonym. He was born in Scotland between *A New Hope* and *The Empire Strikes Back,* and has been a *Star Wars* fan since he bought his first toy X-wing at the age of three. Although occasionally mistaken for a larger-than-life Ewok, he is in fact a historian, specializing in medieval society.

ILLUSTRATORS

At a crucial juncture during his formative years, **DREW BAKER** decided physics had gotten too weird, and he would go to art school instead. By night, he bends pencil, pixel, and paint to his art directors' wills. By day, he and his family feed their curiosity about life, the universe, and everything.

TOMMY LEE EDWARDS studied film and illustration at the Art Center College of Design and is now one of the most respected and versatile artists working today. He has designed videogames, created licensing style guides for films, and illustrated numerous comic books for DC and Marvel Comics. Edwards perhaps feels most at home putting his imagination and storytelling flare to the test while working as a conceptual and storyboard artist on such films as *The Book of Eli.* Fresh off the release of the graphic novel *Turf* from Image Comics, Edwards is hard at work on *Golden Age,* his next creator-owned comic with Jonathan Ross.

IAN FULLWOOD lives and works in Herefordshire, England, and has clients both at home and in the United States. Ian has more than twenty years' experience in technical illustration and commercial art, working with a range of clients, from publishers to engineering companies. Traditional drawing skills are the backbone of Ian's work, having progressed from the "old school" of pen, ink, and airbrushing. He now utilizes all that prior knowledge within Lightwave 3D to produce technically demanding pieces of work. www.if3d.com

ANSEL HSIAO has a PhD in cell and molecular biology from the University of Pennsylvania, and does postdoctoral research in microbial metagenomics and biology at Washington University. He has been an avid fan of the ships and worlds seen in the original *Star Wars* trilogy from an early age, and has been making 3D models and renders of *Star Wars* vehicles since 2001. Ansel lives in St. Louis, Missouri, with his wife, Esther, son, Ian, and cat.

STEPHAN MARTINIERE is an internationally acclaimed artist known for his talent, versatility, and imagination in entertainment fields, including feature films, animation, videogames, theme parks, editorial, and book covers. As the director of the five animated musical adaptation specials for *Madeline,* Stephan received the A.C.T Award, the Parent's Choice Award, and the Humanitas Award, and was nominated for an Emmy. He is the recipient of numerous artistic awards, and in 2006 Stephan received the Grand Master Expose Award for artistic achievement. Stephan was also the art director for the recently released videogame Rage for id Software. Stephan has done lectures and workshops in the United States and abroad and is also an advisory board member of the CG Society.

MODI lives in the central European country of Hungary. He is an autodidactic digital artist. A longtime fan of the *Star Wars* expanded universe, Modi fosters a strange obsession with drawing maps of that galaxy far, far away.

For any artist working in the field, a *Star Wars* assignment is a big deal. **JASON PALMER**'s first official *Star Wars* assignment came in 1992, painting a Rancor for Topps's first *Star Wars Galaxy* set. Since then, he's had the privilege to paint many more pieces for *Star Wars,* as well as for properties such as *Indiana Jones, Star Trek, Harry Potter,* and *A Game of Thrones.* Jason has recently developed a popular series of *Firefly* and *Serenity* art prints with Universal Studios. http://www.jasonpalmer.net/ and http://jasonpal.deviantart.com/

CHRIS SCALF grew up in Michigan, the middle child of a single mother. He didn't have much so he thrived on his imagination. He began drawing his favorite moments from the science fiction and monster shows he loved watching on TV. Eventually a high school crush led to marriage and Chris's desire to provide for his new family by making a living as an artist. In 2006 Chris was hired to paint his first *Star Wars* project, the R2-D2 mailboxes for the USPS. Today, Chris spreads his work between commercial art and advertising and the genre art he loved so much as a kid. He still lives in Michigan with his wife and daughter.

DAVE SEELEY is far more influenced by sci-fi film than by the legacy of science fiction illustrations. He was sitting in a theater as a teenager in 1977 when the first Star Destroyer rolled onto the screen and changed sci-fi forever. That indelible mark fuels his passion for creating *Star Wars* images. After earning degrees in architecture and fine art, Dave was seduced by the glamour of illustration. He derailed his career as an award-winning architect for the far more immediate gratification of image making. Though Dave no longer designs buildings, a materials fetishism and a love of spatial atmospherics are evidence that the inner architect is flourishing. www.daveseeley.com

Born and raised in Malaysia, **DARREN TAN** grew up drawing spaceships, dinosaurs, and the stuff of his imagination, which was fueled by movies and computer games. Inspired by these he went on to study animation and later graduated as a computer animator from Sheridan College, Canada. After a brief stint in 3D animation, he decided to trade in polygons for a Wacom tablet. Now he works as a digital concept artist at Imaginary Friends Studios and is enjoying getting paid for his hobby. Apart from his passion for art and *Star Wars,* he is also a big fan of The Lord of the Rings and enjoys delving into medieval and church history. He now lives with his beautiful wife in sunny Singapore.

JON VANFLEET was born into captivity and raised on Space Food Sticks and Bazooka gum. After graduating from Pratt Institute in Brooklyn, New York, John found instant success as a waiter. Unsatisfied with the food industry, John decided he would make some art. His work can be found throughout the comic book industry in the form of graphic novels and painted covers. John's client list goes beyond comics to include book publishers, videogame makers, film studios, and toy companies. When John's not working for the man, he creates 3D models. He says, "It's just like when I was a kid working on Aurora monster models. Minus the effects of the glue." johnvanfleet.com

Born and raised in Rio de Janeiro, Brazil, **BRUNO WERNECK** has been playing with markers and crayons since he was little. He was given a scholarship in 1997 to study at the School of the Art Institute of Chicago. While originally a graphic design major, he ultimately gravitated toward traditional animation, receiving his degree from Columbia College Chicago in 2002. Professionally, Bruno has done everything from print design to book illustration to visual concepts for films and games. Currently, he owns a boutique company in Los Angeles, Filmpaint, Inc., entrusted with the foremost task of bringing visions to life.

PAUL YOULL was born in Hartlepool, England, on June 8, 1965. He's the youngest of a set of identical twins. When asked, "Why become an artist?" Paul always says, "It's the love of science fiction that created the artist not the artist creating science fiction." Paul considers *Star Wars* the ultimate horizon in science fiction. www.paulyoull.com

*An **Altor**-class replenishment ship refueling an Imperial dreadnought and battlecruiser (Ansel Hsiao)*

THE STAR WARS LIBRARY
PUBLISHED BY DEL REY BOOKS

STAR WARS: THE ESSENTIAL READER'S COMPANION

STAR WARS: THE ESSENTIAL ATLAS

STAR WARS: JEDI VS. SITH: THE ESSENTIAL GUIDE TO THE FORCE

STAR WARS: THE NEW ESSENTIAL CHRONOLOGY

STAR WARS: THE NEW ESSENTIAL GUIDE TO ALIEN SPECIES

STAR WARS: THE NEW ESSENTIAL GUIDE TO CHARACTERS

STAR WARS: THE NEW ESSENTIAL GUIDE TO DROIDS

STAR WARS: THE NEW ESSENTIAL GUIDE TO VEHICLES AND VESSELS

STAR WARS: THE NEW ESSENTIAL GUIDE TO WEAPONS AND TECHNOLOGY

THE STAR WARS CRAFT BOOK

THE COMPLETE STAR WARS ENCYCLOPEDIA

A GUIDE TO THE STAR WARS UNIVERSE

STAR WARS: DIPLOMATIC CORPS ENTRANCE EXAM

STAR WARS: GALACTIC PHRASE BOOK AND TRAVEL GUIDE

I'D JUST AS SOON KISS A WOOKIEE: THE QUOTABLE STAR WARS

THE SECRETS OF STAR WARS: SHADOWS OF THE EMPIRE

THE ART OF STAR WARS: A NEW HOPE

THE ART OF STAR WARS: THE EMPIRE STRIKES BACK

THE ART OF STAR WARS: RETURN OF THE JEDI

THE ART OF STAR WARS: EPISODE I THE PHANTOM MENACE

THE ART OF STAR WARS: EPISODE II ATTACK OF THE CLONES

THE ART OF STAR WARS: EPISODE III REVENGE OF THE SITH

SCRIPT FACSIMILE: STAR WARS: A NEW HOPE

SCRIPT FACSIMILE: STAR WARS: THE EMPIRE STRIKES BACK

SCRIPT FACSIMILE: STAR WARS: RETURN OF THE JEDI

SCRIPT FACSIMILE: STAR WARS: EPISODE I THE PHANTOM MENACE

STAR WARS: THE ANNOTATED SCREENPLAYS

ILLUSTRATED SCREENPLAY: STAR WARS: A NEW HOPE

ILLUSTRATED SCREENPLAY: STAR WARS: THE EMPIRE STRIKES BACK

ILLUSTRATED SCREENPLAY: STAR WARS: RETURN OF THE JEDI

ILLUSTRATED SCREENPLAY: STAR WARS: EPISODE I THE PHANTOM MENACE

THE MAKING OF STAR WARS: EPISODE I THE PHANTOM MENACE

MYTHMAKING: BEHIND THE SCENES OF STAR WARS: EPISODE II ATTACK OF THE CLONES

THE MAKING OF STAR WARS: EPISODE III REVENGE OF THE SITH

THE MAKING OF STAR WARS

THE MAKING OF STAR WARS: THE EMPIRE STRIKES BACK